## DESIRE FLAMED IN HIS EYES...

And his mouth came down then, molding his soft lips against her own, and an uncontrollable shudder ran up her spine. She had no artillery for combatting this siege. Slowly he pulled back, his mouth releasing its tender prisoner, and he penetrated her with his gaze. She felt smothered in the furnace of his searing embrace.

What is happening to me? she wondered frantically. His lips traveled to her throat, seeking out the delicate pulse, and her whole body shuddered. Saura fought against the deliciousness that excited her. But he is a Tory! she thought, as he drew her mouth to his again. Then, as the sensation of his lips on hers flooded her senses: Ah, but he is a man...

# DARK SOLDIER

## KATHERINE MYERS

AVON
PUBLISHERS OF BARD, CAMELOT, DISCUS AND FLARE BOOKS

DARK SOLDIER is an original publication of Avon Books.
This work has never before appeared in book form.


AVON BOOKS
A division of
The Hearst Corporation
959 Eighth Avenue
New York, New York 10019

Copyright © 1983 by Katherine Myers
Published by arrangement with the author
Library of Congress Catalog Card Number: 82-90517
ISBN: 0-380-82214-8

First Avon Printing, February, 1983

AVON TRADEMARK REG. U. S. PAT. OFF. AND
IN OTHER COUNTRIES, MARCA REGISTRADA, HECHO EN
U. S. A.

Printed in the U. S. A.

WFH 10  9  8  7  6  5  4  3  2  1

## *Touch of the Tory*

What ill-bent
Autumn wind hast
Caught up the threads of
Our lives: mine,
Bright daughter of the Cause,
And thine, Sir rogue redcoat,
To entwine in such a
Knotted snarl?

The tallow of my
Patriot's pride
Stood strong against all Cause,
And still would light the way!
But lo!
Now lies melted at
Thy heated touch.

Alas!
Let me shout,
Or curse and call unfair
The twisting of our story.
Only let me shed no single tear
For thee,
Dark soldier Tory.

# DARK SOLDIER

# PROLOGUE:

## *The Exchange*

### January, 1759

THE MISTY FOG enshrouded London in mysterious shadows. Like a cat on silent paws, it crept about the city, muffling sounds upon the cobbled roads. Its swirling fingers reached out to engulf the buildings in its path.

The sound of hollow footsteps paused as a man stepped from beneath the arched overpass that led into the newer part of the city. He was tall, yet to an observer little else was discernible. Wrapped about him was a heavy black cape beneath which was a bulky bundle. He moved cautiously, stepping quickly from shadow to shadow, avoiding the bright pools of lamplight. A tricorn dipped low upon his forehead; his profile showed a straight nose and a mouth set with grim determination. He wove among the familiar, narrow streets, crossing paths trod many times before. He knew full well this was his last mission, and his most difficult. He reached the small brownstone house and discreetly knocked on the door, shifting his burden's weight from his right arm to his left. The portal was flung wide as he strode into the room.

"Thomas," he greeted the man with a quick nod of his head, his eyes fixed on the small woman seated in a chair across the room. She set down her tatting and stared intently at the visitor. Silence permeated the air until at last she spoke.

"Is there no other way, Peter?"

"If there were, Elizabeth, I'd have thought of it!"

She heaved a deep sigh and nodded. As she stood, she smoothed the wrinkles from her apron, then clasped her hands in silent prayer. Her apprehension was apparent as she left the room.

"This is hard on her, you must know," Thomas said quietly. "He has always been such a good boy and so long we waited for him." He spoke more to himself than to the visitor.

"It is hard on us both. I am still plagued with doubts, yet I see no other way to safety."

"I know. Though we have thought of a hundred answers, this is the only one that is truly safe. Who would have thought that such a simple mission would turn out to be so hazardous?"

"I will never forgive myself for your involvement— and the boy's."

Thomas shook his head. "Do not blame yourself. It was our desire to help, as it will always be."

Elizabeth returned to the parlor, her hand resting on the shoulder of a boy no more than ten years old. He stood tall for his age; his brown eyes were alert with suppressed excitement. Pulling on his coat, he fastened it up to the collar and donned his cap. "I am ready, sir."

"'Tis best you call me 'Father' from now on. Agreed?"

The boy nodded and turned to hug his mother farewell. They lingered for a while before he faced his father. Thomas motioned the boy nearer and took him into his arms. "I need not tell you to be a good lad for you've been nothing but. Take care of yourself."

"I will, Papa."

Elizabeth dried her eyes on the corner of her apron. "You'd best give her to me now."

2

Peter pulled back his cape to reveal a sleeping child of about a year in age. The slow breath of slumber issued from her parted lips; her cheeks were rosy from the warmth of her father's arms. He handed her to Elizabeth and upon the exchange, the infant's eyes opened. Brown shoe-button eyes, he was fond of calling them. Damp locks curled about her temples, baby curls moist from sleep. She rubbed her eyes and looked at her father.

"I've not the strength to leave her!" he said suddenly. "Give her back and let me be on my way!"

Elizabeth held the baby close. "It was you who said there is no other way. You know that I will love her as dearly as I loved the one I lost."

"Yes, I know that."

"Then be off with you, Peter. Be strong now to get us through. It is what Eleana would have wanted."

After a painfully quiet moment he turned and strode through the door, the lad in his wake. The swirling city mists engulfed them as they vanished from sight. Elizabeth stilled the ache within her, looking down at the little girl she clasped. This baby would be a soothing balm to the hurting. The child squirmed her way from Elizabeth's arms and to the floor, where she toddled off to examine her new surroundings. The sound of a door clicking open drew Elizabeth's attention and she looked up to see her sleepy little boy.

"Water?" he asked.

"Come here, dear," she said. "This is your new little sister; her name is Saura." The little toddler came over, planting her sturdy legs before the older child, looking up at him. "Do you like her?" Elizabeth asked, her arms around both of the children.

"No," the little boy answered firmly. "I don't need a sister."

"But she needs a family and we'll have fun. Wait here while I get your drink." As she went to the pitcher, the two children continued to study each other until the boy reached out a hand, placed it squarely on the toddler's head and shoved her down. She let out a squeal of indignation and a tear coursed down one chubby cheek.

"Lawrence!" his father exclaimed. "No, no. You must be nice to little Saura."

Lawrence took his drink and gulped it down, turned and went back into his bedroom, closing the door with a thump. His mother shook her head in bewilderment. Then she picked up the little girl, carried her to the high-backed cradle and rocked the child until she fell asleep. Thomas came over and stood by his wife. "The French-Indian War will be coming to an end in a while and, luck permitting, we'll see our son again, and the colonies too."

"Unless there is more trouble in the Americas," she said, distress coloring her words.

"You worry too much." He bent and kissed her hair. "All will go well, you'll see. And you have Saura to help you pass the time. You'll be busy with the two little ones."

"Yes, busy. And that will be all to the good. She's a pretty child, isn't she?"

"Pretty indeed. Makes up a little for the loss of our Bess."

Elizabeth nodded, too full of emotion to speak further. The flickering lamplight cast a warm glow as they sat in the small room, the three forming new bonds of family.

A new bond too was being forged between a man and a boy who boarded a ship in the cold fog off the Thames. They stood on deck, the elder's hand clasped reassuringly on the lad's shoulder. Tomorrow they would sail.

Happy the man whose wish and care
A few paternal acres bound,
Content to breathe his native air,
In his own ground.

—ALEXANDER POPE
*Ode on Solitude*

# Chapter I

SAURA AINSLEY stood on the rough planking of the pier,
the sea wind whipping her skirt about her legs. The
same wind lifted her dark brown tresses off her shoulders since she had no benefit of bonnet or cap. Her eyes
shone with excitement as she viewed the noisy activity
of the wharf. Although she was not yet fifteen, her
willowy frame and charming face caught the attention
of the sailors and workmen. Her oval face was graced
by large, almond-shaped eyes of deep brown fringed
with thick lashes. Across her nose a smattering of freckles danced, acquired from many days spent on deck
where she had watched the sailors, studying their activities and learning of the workings of the *Kingfisher*.
Her poor cousins, Nancy and Beatrice, had not been so
fortunate, the difficulties of sea travel having taken
their toll.

Behind her rested the ship she had just left, the familiar sounds of creaking ropes and canvas crackling
in the wind reaching her ears. She was waiting with

her cousins and their brother Timothy, for their trunks to be hauled up from below, much as she had waited for them to be put aboard the *Kingfisher* in England. She vividly remembered the day of her departure for the American colonies—it marked the first time that she had left her parents for a goodly stay. Her mother, Elizabeth, had smiled a bit worriedly but then she had brightened up. She was a strong woman and had borne a great deal. Saura's father, Thomas, although now nearly an invalid, still held fast his dream of coming to the colonies. Maybe they would be able to join their daughter in the next year. Her father had been too ill to see her off; he had had a relapse and Lawrence had come in his stead. Saura scowled a little as she thought of her brother. He had stood on the pier obviously thinking himself quite resplendent in his red military jacket, white breeches and black boots. Saura had thought that he looked as silly as a peacock and twice as vain but she had resisted saying so.

There was not a great deal of love between sister and brother, the fault, she felt, lying with Lawrence. His temper, his often smug attitude—and, most of all, his political opinions—left little for them to see eye to eye on. The lure of the colonies had appealed to her adventurous nature from the beginning and she had listened carefully as her father spoke about the opportunities in America. Lawrence, on the opposite, had detested his parents' views ever since he had gone away to school and gained friends of a military persuasion. These friends had convinced him to strive for a career as a king's soldier and made him blind to his parents' concern and their efforts to dissuade him. He felt himself a man now at eighteen and would listen to no one. Saura had smiled to herself when she had discovered that the rigors of his training were tougher and less romantic than he had originally imagined they would be.

He had been angry that day on the dock, striding up and down before her. "You cannot really be planning to go through with this voyage, silly twit!" he said for the third time.

6

"Stop repeating yourself, Lawrence!" she snapped, her patience coming to an end. "And if you call me a silly twit one more time, you're likely to find my foot at your shin."

He scowled angrily at her but knew that her word was good and the thought of an embarrassing scene prevented any action. When he felt himself unnoticed, he would put the girl in her place with a severe pinch, he decided.

"You should stop being so stuffy over the matter," Timothy had put in. "She's not stabbing George in the back but only coming with us for the summer."

"You should not speak so of the king," Lawrence scowled. "There is no reason for her to go traveling off to those infernal Americas at her age, especially with all the unrest there."

Indeed there is, with you in the house once more, Timothy had thought but instead he had said, "Those colonies you curse are the bread and butter that have put you through the academy. Just because your father can stay here to handle the book work for Ainsley and Comstock and mine must live part-time in the colonies to handle the trade and selling of the goods does not mean that we are less loyal. If you came to the Americas, you might even find that you liked it better there than here. But then, perhaps not, since it is less stuffy there."

Saura had not missed the teasing twinkle in his eye and she had laughed. Lawrence had turned on her, taken her elbow in a viselike grip and led her from their cousins. She pulled her arm away, rubbing it where he had pinched her, as he stood blocking her view of Timothy. "Let me give you some brotherly advice," he began.

"Brotherly?" She raised a mocking eyebrow in surprise with a sophistication disconcerting in a mere girl of fourteen.

"If you are fool enough to go on this voyage," he continued, ignoring her remark, "then watch your actions. Pay attention to your betters and try not to be so impertinent." While his lecture had droned on, she had studied his cravat, too tight about his thick neck. She took in his round face and full mouth and the heavy-lidded eyes that Beatrice declared gave him a romantic look. She could not see it but mused that perhaps it was because he was her brother; sisters did not often view their siblings as romantic. It had occurred to her that she would like his friendship if only he would be kinder and less prone to lecture her. She sighed, shifting her weight from one foot to another.

"Saura, have you heard one word I have spoken?"

"Indeed, too many of them. Are you done upbraiding me?"

"It is that kind of impertinence that makes one want to box your ears! Very well. You go on the voyage and I will see you at Christmastime when I come home from the drilling." He had lifted her face, peering at the pretty oval framed by brown wisps of hair and the white lace ruchings of her hat. In an action that appeared most brotherly, he bent down and kissed her brow; the moistness of his lips left a lingering brand that she had had to resist wiping from her forehead.

Timothy had come then to urge her aboard and she was was relieved to be freed from the imposing presence of her brother. Her mother had returned with Aunt Jane and Uncle Edward, finished with the final arrangements. Elizabeth hugged her daughter and Saura had lingered a bit in her mother's warm embrace. "I know I told Papa, but will you give him my love again?" she asked.

"It is only for this summer, dear," Elizabeth had said, her words of encouragement denying the concern she felt at sending off her young daughter. "You do want to go, don't you? If you have any hesitations, it isn't too late, you know. You can wait until we all go together."

"No, I do want to go and I have looked forward to it for two months now. It's just that I worry about leaving you alone with Papa so ill."

"The doctor assures us the lapse is only temporary and that Thomas will be on his feet in no time. And besides, I have Lawrence home for a while."

Saura nodded and then was rushed on board as the

*Kingfisher* lifted anchor, the wind filling the crisp sails as screaming sea gulls dipped and whirled overhead. The deck rolled beneath her feet and the ship moved out to sea. The churning green waves put a separation between the vessel and the docks. She had stood at the railing and watched her mother and the petulant Lawrence become specks of blurred color in the distance.

Saura's thoughts snapped back to the present, forgetting all about the docks of Bristol as her trunk was slammed down behind her before being put aboard the coach. So here she was—in the colonies she had heard so much about; excitedly she stood on the dock's edge. Sweating workmen lifted barrels to their shoulders, straining under the weight, thankful for the sea breeze that cooled the summer heat. Colonials in fine dress with lace cuffs and powdered wigs wove past the laborers; and the noisy clamor of the docks was not much different from that in Bristol. But the city's outskirts were somehow different here in Boston. They were fresher, with raw pine planking going up in many new buildings. There were also older buildings, brick or brownstone, but the green ivy growing on their walls was not as thick or as ancient. She watched all the passersby with curiosity. These colonials were not the barbarians that Lawrence had portrayed; if anything, they dressed in a more refined way than many in England. As she watched the crowds, a particular movement suddenly caught her eye.

A young man, tall and lithe, moved through the throng purposefully. There was no dandified wig covering up his thick brown tresses; they were instead caught back with the common black ribbon. Nor was his shirt of anything finer than white linen, wide-sleeved, its tails tucked in the waist of black breeches. Even with the knapsack under one arm and a rough brown coat cast over his shoulder, he did not seem to be a common worker. She thought as she studied him that were he a sample of colonial men, she would indeed like America. Pausing to get his bearings, he felt her eyes and glanced up. His black-brown eyes caught hers,

9

holding them in a moment of stilled time as she studied his handsome features.

"Time to go to the Boston Grande, Saura," Timothy said, coming up behind her and breaking the frozen moment. The man turned, apparently seeking one of the ships soon to sail for England, and lost himself in the crowd.

Saura climbed into the coach with Beatrice, who bubbled with excitement, and even the usually quiet Nancy caught the air of it all. Timothy thought that his cousin was rather subdued for one who had so eagerly anticipated their arrival. The coach lurched forward, taking them into the heart of the city.

The hard-packed earth road wove past rolling hills where maple, birch, oak and aspen trees showed their bright green leaves to the hot August sky. As Saura looked out the coach window at the lush hillsides, she reflected that the area through which she and Timothy traveled was certainly different from the teeming Boston town where she had spent most of the summer. Boston itself, a city of new building and hustling excitement, had been a contrast to her home in England but still, it was a city. Here, however, as they passed through villages and townships, she began to gain a new picture of this young country and to understand the look of dreams in her father's eyes when he spoke of the vast opportunities in the colonies.

At the thought of her father, she felt a wash of renewed sorrow as she looked down at the black crepe of her mourning dress. One minute she had been filled with anticipation as she waited for her parents' ship to arrive; the next she had stood on the pier with letters in hand, tears falling onto the heavy parchment of the one addressed to her from her mother, informing her of Thomas's sudden passing. Since that time she had been in a state of confusion, and uncertainty had etched itself into her future.

Her summer had been spent in Boston with the Comstocks for it was in the busy seaport that they contracted out for the furs the traders brought in from the hills. The furrier industry was full of lucrative opportunities; England had an insatiable desire for the lush pelts that trimmed garments or lined cloaks and hats. The Comstocks often spent their summers in Boston while Edward and Timothy purchased, graded and contracted for pelts. It had been Thomas's desire to come to the colonies and move the bookkeeping end of Ainsley and Comstock to Boston, leaving behind a single agent to handle the business trade in the mother country. Since Timothy was now old enough to remain in Boston as an agent, Edward Comstock was free to keep his family in England. Thus the elder Comstocks had set out for home, believing that they would cross paths with the Ainsleys en route.

So it was that Saura had awaited her parents' coming and this cruel turn of events had left her alone in Boston under the care of her young cousin, Tim. She had received three letters: one from her mother, sadly explaining the death of her father; the other two, written on the same heavy parchment and sealed with wax and the Ainsley stamp, addressed to Peter Blake, a name with which she was barely familiar. One of them bore her mother's handwriting; the other, her father's. She was instructed to take the letters to Greenhollow in Massachusetts, not far from Boston, to be delivered by her hand to Mister Blake. She had heard her father speak of him as a friend, closer than a brother, a colonist with dreams for America, but that was all she knew of the man. Once she gave him his two letters, what she was to do thereafter, where she was to go, she was quite unsure of. Elizabeth would come when she could, her letter stated. Saura was to wait. But how and where was not exactly clear, she could only hope that Mister Blake would advise her.

She looked out again at the beautiful, timbered landscape that her father had dreamed of seeing. How he would have loved this virgin countryside, she reflected. She thought again, as often she had before, that her father had passed on months before she even knew of it. His death had been mourned, his body buried and his passing noted while she had shopped at the milliner's or the dressmaker's, attended a play or a tea, and been unaware. It was this thought more than any other that threatened to bring the sting of tears. She blinked hard, trying to concentrate on the conversation between Timothy and an elderly clergy as the coach neared Greenhollow, heading into the valley and toward the village.

To one accustomed to the streets of Boston, the township was not very large but it was a clean little shire nestled among the hillocks and built along the banks of a twisting, lazy river of sky-reflected azure. Well-kept homes of brick or whitewashed wood were neatly placed along wide lanes, their lawns running down to the river's edge. The village square was spacious, and enclosed shops lined every side; they passed all these before the coach stopped in front of the Hollow's single inn. It was double-storied with tall, narrow windows whose panes were pushed open against the humid, late-August day. A large carved sign naming this the "Crooked Horne" swung from two thick chains above the double doors. These were pushed open by a tawny-headed youth as the coach lurched to a standstill.

Tim opened the carriage door, jumped down and turned to help Saura alight. She felt stiff from the long three-day ride with its too few stops and was glad that her journey was at an end, if only temporarily. She brushed away the dust that had turned her black dress gray, watching it puff off in clouds. She anticipated washing the road dust from her face and taking a moment's rest.

She and Timothy walked inside. The inn was not nearly as refined as was the Boston Grande where she and the Comstocks had stayed for the summer but it was neat and clean. While there was no ornately carved Chippendale furniture in this simple country inn, its open atmosphere had a certain rustic appeal. Timothy registered their rooms as Saura freshened up after finding a bowl of cool water in the women's parlor. She brushed her brown locks into place as best she could without the use of a mirror; despite all she had recently been through, she felt terribly young and inexperienced.

She returned to the common room, where Tim had ordered two cooling lemonades. The serving maid who brought them out was beautiful and caught Timothy's eye. Her burnished red curls against fair skin, her blue eyes, pale as an icy lake, and her figure, well-shaped in a blue muslin dress, were all very pleasing to the eye. She dried her hands on the hem of her white apron, then smoothed its folds, lingering a bit longer than necessary. Her departing smile and demure lowering of lashes were a bit obvious and a flush of red crept up Tim's neck, making Saura suppress a smile. She watched her cousin stare after the girl in obvious appreciation and she felt even more immature as she contemplated the older girl's womanly figure.

As they sipped their drinks, Saura studied the interior of the peculiar little inn. The long oak tables, sturdy but not ornate, the wall hooks that held hats and cloaks, and the blunderbusses above the huge brick hearth made this country inn a complete opposite to the inn where she had spent the summer. But the difference was not unpleasant, she decided, looking up at a pair of large pointed antlers that would have horrified Timothy's mother. The truth was, however, that her stay in Boston had finally become tedious and oftentimes boring. There were many teas, a play to see now and then, trips to the furriers of Ainsley and Comstock (but not to the back rooms where the tanning, sorting and stocking went on ) and fittings at the dressmaker's. Although she enjoyed buying a new dress or fine silk hosiery and shoes, she would have much preferred to explore the teeming marketplace and streets, where all the real excitement took place. This, of course, was not considered ladylike and so she found herself confined to the small social circles deemed proper. On a few occasions Tim had come to her rescue, sneaking her away for an hour or so to view the churning activity of the colonial city.

Greenhollow, however, was not like any place she had ever seen before. Although her home had been in

Bristol, they had often visited the English countryside for her father's health. But, she thought, that countryside was much different from this. What was considered country there was really a rambling town of manors and large estates. Here, far from Boston, people were still struggling to tame the beautiful wilderness into farmland and village. It was the vastness of the continent that so appealed to her.

Tim stated that he thought the inn drab—with the exception of the serving maid. And although Saura had to agree with him that the Boston Grande was the epitome of social refinement, she felt that the inn held a certain rough appeal of its own. The muskets and deer antlers spoke of the hunt and the freedom of rural life, and they held an excitement for her.

"I think we must be half mad to come running clear out here in answer to that letter," Tim said suddenly, putting down his glass. "Certainly I cannot leave you in this forsaken little township."

"We will know better when we talk to Mister Blake."

He smiled at the worldly calm displayed by a girl he considered not more than a few years out of the nursery. "If only your mother had been more specific, I would not be so worried. But we do not even know this man. Maybe it would be best if you came back to Boston and stayed with me."

"Convention would hardly allow that, Tim."

"Pah! You are not much more than a child. Convention could see no harm in your becoming my ward."

She shook her head and smiled fondly at her cousin. He was more a brother to her than Lawrence had ever been.

"You are far too busy now that you have been made agent-in-charge at the furriers'. Besides, I am anxious to meet Mister Blake. Papa spoke fondly of him, and Mama also. If he can shed more light on my situation and give me direction, I shall be better off. But I should hate to race back to Bristol only to miss Mother on a packet coming across."

The serving girl came up to collect the glasses and Tim put down more coin for payment than necessary.

She curtsied and gave him a dimpled smile, deftly pocketing the money in her apron. "Could you give us direction to a man said to reside here in Greenhollow, miss?" Timothy questioned. "Are you familiar with the townfolk?"

"Aye, sir, most everyone. Who might you be looking for?"

"A Mister Peter Blake."

"Oh, Peter! I know him well. Did you wish to see him?"

"Yes," Saura replied a bit anxiously. "Does he dwell far from here?"

She ignored Saura, piercing Tim with her wide blue eyes. "He is the local blacksmith and well liked about the Hollow. Would you like Willy to show you the way? I'd take you myself but this is our busy hour with the coach in and all, and the innkeeper would be angry."

"Willy will do the job. And thank you, miss." The girl coyly lowered her lashes and smiled before moving away and Saura rolled her eyes heavenward. How could Tim be so bright with the company books and so blind about life? Finally he tore his gaze away from the departing swish of skirt. "A blacksmith! Your mother has sent you to the care of a blacksmith!"

"It happens to be a most-needed profession even if not as grand as furrier or banker, Tim Comstock."

He sighed, "I suppose so. It's just that this is all so unconventional."

Saura laughed. "What has convention to do outside of Bristol or Boston? These colonists may rival the king's court in finery and powered wigs but at heart they are farmers and landowners and I think that makes me like it better here. Maybe I can be free of convention also if this is where I am to stay."

The sound of a throat clearing caught their attention and they turned to see the lad who had opened the inn doors when the coach had arrived. Perhaps only a year or two Saura's junior, he was shorter than she and spry, with an infectious grin and unruly hair. Just a few minutes earlier he had hauled their trunks up to their rooms.

"Molly says that there's a coin in it for me to show you the way to Peter's."

"Indeed!" Tim stated sternly. But Saura liked the youth and returned his grin.

"Can't stand here the whole day long," the lad stated. "Want my assistance or not?"

"We want it," Saura spoke up. "Give him a tuppence or two."

Tim dug into his waistcoat pocket and tossed the lad a coin. They followed him out the door as he snatched his rumpled hat off a hook. "No need for the carriage. 'Taint far." He led them down the lane in a northerly direction. "Molly said you have business with our blacksmith. Strange, though, since you've got no horse or carriage."

"Molly worked at the inn long?" Tim asked casually.

Willy smiled and glanced up at the young gentleman. "She came to the Crooked Horne about two years ago and my father hired her on to wait the tables. She's the oldest of eight and when her father fell to hard times, she came to work at the inn. Pa says she's good for business 'cause of her looks—and we get lots of lovey-eyed gentlemen at the inn," Willy added slyly.

Saura suppressed a giggle while Tim glared angrily at the back of Willy's head. They had passed the livery by this time and next to it stood the smithy's, a shop set well back off the lane.

"Why didn't you tell us that the blacksmith's was just two doors down?" Tim asked coldly.

"'Cause you didn't ask. Peter!" the lad called, leading them into the heat and darkness of the place, passing under a sign that announced: "Blacksmith and Wheelwright." Once their eyes adjusted to the darkness, Saura's glance took in the large wall hooks holding leather harnesses for horse or ox and the yokes and brass fittings. Large black barrels filled with equally black water stood against the wall, their tarnished bands catching a dull glint from the fire in the stone oven. A horse stood tethered inside and a man clothed only in leather breeches and apron brought the hammer down with a steady crack on red metal that rested in pincers on a large iron anvil. His back was to them but she could see that he was tall; his muscles were sinewy with effort and glistening with sweat. Willy shouted again over the ring of hammer to metal but he was not heard until the smithy thrust the horseshoe back into the hot coals. Then, startled by Willy's voice, the man turned and looked at the three visitors, wiping his black palms against his apron.

"These two have come to see you, Peter," Willy said as he turned and walked away, tossing his coin high in the air.

"How can I help you?" Peter asked.

Saura looked at his rugged features, handsomely outlined in the dark light. She judged his age to be about forty.

"Mister Blake, I am Saura Ainsley, Thomas's and Elizabeth's daughter, and this is my cousin, Timothy Comstock. I am here at my mother's request." She reached into her reticule and pulled forth her letters, holding them out to him. A peculiar expression crossed his face and abruptly he turned his back on them.

"Let me finish this last shoe," he cast over his shoulder as he brought out the red-hot metal and began hammering it fiercely. Saura was puzzled but stood patiently as the smithy completed his task. Holding up the shoe, he gave a nod of approval and plunged it into one of the barrels of black water, hiss and steam rising up.

Saura watched with interest as next he soothed the skittish mare, stroking her neck and settling her down before lifting her left hind leg and hammering on the shoe. He checked the fit, then scrubbed his hands in a large clay basin with strong lye soap, wiped them on a clean but stained towel and turned to her. He studied the girl briefly as he walked near, noting the dark brown tresses and amber eyes that graced a young face, fair in every detail. She held herself well for a girl of only fourteen. He knew her age exactly. Fifteen this Christmas.

"Sorry to keep you waiting. So you are Saura. The last time I saw you, you were no bigger than a mite. How are your parents?"

She cast her eyes down to the hard-packed earth. "Papa died only a few months ago, not long after I left Bristol." She looked up to see sadness wash over his features. "He had hoped to join me later, he and Mother, that is. Mother's letter came on the ship on which I had expected them to arrive."

"My condolences to you, child. I will miss your father greatly even though I have not had the chance of seeing him for a number of long years. Still, we kept in touch. We were great friends."

"He spoke of you highly, sir."

"Your mother is no doubt in grief," he said, almost as though to himself.

Timothy nodded. "Perhaps that is what accounts for the unusual turn of events. The letter Saura received instructed her to come to Greenhollow, to you. We are quite puzzled."

"Where else should she go except ... to me?" he asked, catching their puzzled glances. "Elizabeth did say that you were to come here, to live with me?"

"Yes, in a way. She did not say that I was to live with you but that I was to come to you and that you would tell me what to do until she could arrive. That is why Tim and I have been so confused. The letter I received was not long, no doubt written in a state of mourning for Father. She said that you would explain matters for me, so I have brought you these letters. One is from her and the other from Father, no doubt written not long before. ..." She paused, holding out the parchment envelopes sealed with the Ainsley stamp.

Peter took them, breaking open the seal of her mother's letter first, reading the delicate script. He nodded, folded it along its creases and put it back in the envelope. He did not open her father's letter. Both young people were most curious as to the contents of Elizabeth's letter since it pertained to Saura's future but Peter did not go into great detail.

"It is as I have assumed. Elizabeth has asked that you stay in my care until the time she can come, whenever that may be. It will perhaps not be as soon as you might hope. But I will do everything possible to make life for you here in the Hollow pleasant and comfortable."

"I had hoped that Saura would come back under my care," Tim said. "After all, she is familiar with me. I am her cousin. And Boston certainly has more to offer than this remote village."

Peter looked steadily at the youth until the latter became a bit warm. "Her mother has asked that she stay here, under my watch. I am her...godfather. Her best concerns are my desire."

Saura smiled. This was no gruff blacksmith of common stock, she noted. His strength was more than muscle. She knew now why her parents had spoken so highly of him.

"Don't you think Saura should decide what is best for herself, what she wants?"

"Of a certainty. What do you want, Saura?" His dark eyes held hers.

"I will be happy to stay with you, sir," she said.

Tim stared at her in surprise. "Are you sure?"

"I am always sure when I make a decision. I want to remain here in the Hollow with Mister Blake."

A smile touched the smithy's eyes. "You're everything your mother was."

"You knew Mama when she was young?" Saura asked.

He paused for a moment. "Knew her very well. And I must add that Elizabeth wrote to tell me of your family, and of you. You have grown more lovely than I had expected." He shook his head as though from a reverie. "Now, where are your things?"

"We've procured rooms at the Crooked Horne," Tim said.

"Then tell Wilfred to cancel them and have him bring your trunks around. My house is just next door."

"But I've paid for them and besides, we could not impose."

"'Tis a waste of good coin to reject my hospitality. And Wilfred will return your payment with no trouble."

Tim could see no way out of it and grudgingly he turned back in the direction of the inn. Peter led Saura

toward his house. It was a pleasant two-storied brown
brick structure set back on a carpet of green grass. They
went through an opening in the hedge and past a row
of trees to a stone path that led to the entrance. Tall
shrubbery grew around the base of the house, nearly
obscuring the bottom windows where lush green ivy
reached fingers upward. The tall, narrow windows with
their diamond-shaped panes caught the gleam of late-
afternoon sunshine. The shingled roof slanted upward
steeply and two brick chimneys could be seen, one in
the center and the other along the gabled end.

"It isn't as grand as the Boston homes or those in
Bristol, but it is comfortable."

"I like it," she said as he led her to the entrance
under the roofing, from which pots of geraniums hung,
and then through the solid oak doors.

Timothy came lumbering back to the smithy's home
loaded down with their baggage. "That no-good little
weasel! First he charges me a good coin to direct me
down the street only two houses and then when I really
need him, he's off on an errand. I feel like a drayhorse,"
he muttered grudgingly as he hauled the last of his
burden onto the porch and stopped to get his breath.
"Good-for-nothing bird, he is!"

"What are you grumbling about, Tim?" Saura stood
in the doorway, appearing cool despite the heat. The
apprehensive and sad expression that Tim had so recently seen upon her brow was gone. She looked relieved and fresh, again the confident Saura. And pretty!
Oh, but that girl could turn heads! America must agree
with her, he thought, for the summer had transformed
her from a somewhat skinny child into a gently rounded
young woman. Her cheeks were blushed pink with
health, her eyes bright. Her own natural color van-
quished the black mourning of her dress. It struck Tim
then that he would sorely miss her should she decide
to stay here. Perhaps that explained his own foul mood
of late. The very idea that she might remain was an
arrow piercing through him. He had always loved the
child but now he was falling in love with the budding

of the woman that would soon blossom. He choked back a knot in his throat and wiped his sweaty palms on his trousers. As Peter Blake stepped behind Saura, the spell was broken.

"Mister Blake, if you'll be so kind as to help with these, we'll see them well put into their respective places."

"Certainly, son. I have a room in the loft for you, and Saura can sleep in the room next to mine. Come this way and I'll show you."

Blake easily swung the baggage under his arms and strategically positioned it for the trip up the stairwell. As the two men climbed the stairs, Saura heard their voices fade away into the upper part of the house.

It was a uniquely lovely home and she was intrigued by it almost as much as by its occupant. The sparsely decorated walls of the hall and main room were paneled in light wood. It was not an ornately furnished dwelling such as that in which she had spent these last months but neither was it meagerly furnished. The wooden floors were covered by thick, soft-colored carpets. The large stone fireplace was cold in the summer heat; its broad mantel held an Eddystone Lighthouse clock encased in a glass dome. There was a turned sofa upholstered in dark blue turkey-work tapestry, and two Spanish leather chairs, stark without arms, stood on either side of a candle-stand table. On the wall above this there hung an oval looking glass with a miniature painting in the top of its carved frame. The picture was that of a young woman, fair and with a capricious smile. Saura examined it for a moment before glancing through the archway that led into the dining chamber. This room was dominated by a large, wainscoted table of carved oak. A maple Bible box sat in its center, the dark, leather-bound family Bible and quill inside. There was a sideboard that held the eating utensils; atop it were pewter mugs, and candlesticks with tall, white tapers.

Double doors opposite the fireplace led into the back garden. To keep out the fierce heat, draperies were drawn over the windows; the interior was cool and dark. Saura looked around, noting the spiral stairwell that led to the second floor. There were no vases with flowers, no needlework pieces, and few tatted seat and arm covers; it was obvious that no woman had decorated these rooms. But that was the only evidence that Peter was not married for the house was clean and well-kept, even if the furniture did lack an extra coat of beeswax. She heard a sound from the kitchen, then believed herself mistaken until a tall black man stepped through the doorway. He stopped when he caught sight of her. Although he said nothing in response to her unusual presence, she thought a glimmer of recognition crossed his brow. He nodded at her.

"I'm Saura Ainsley, come to visit Mister Blake," she said, wondering how a blacksmith could afford to keep a house slave. She had seen few blackamoors and noted that he was not dressed like a house servant despite the towel and breadloaf in his hands.

"Ah, there you are, Erastus!" Blake's voice carried before him as he marched down the stairs, Tim in his wake. "Fine servant you are, leaving me to haul the trunks up." Saura was pleased to note his happy manner.

"If you'd have a loyal servant, serve yourself," Erastus retorted.

"Ha-ha!" Mister Blake laughed. His lack of rebuke surprised Saura and she tried to puzzle out who Erastus might be. Tall, large of frame, with strong, broad features, his tightly curled black hair had gained a light tinge of silver at the temples. Yet she was sure that he was not old but close in age to Mister Blake. "Erastus was just fixing us a bit of lunch. No doubt you have had no refreshment since the coach just arrived. Erastus, this is Miss Ainsley and Mister Comstock, come to visit us. They will be staying."

Erastus seemed not in the least surprised; he nodded politely and retreated to the kitchen.

"Your home is lovely," Saura remarked—and Tim stared at her in wonderment. She had been in some of the most beautiful homes in Boston and hardly commented on their splendor, yet she spoke in favor of this one. Would he ever understand her?

"'Tis home," Mister Blake said. "Not fancy but Erastus keeps it well."

"Perhaps it's not my place to say..." Tim started, then paused to reflect that another's affairs were not his concern.

"Go on," Mister Blake prodded.

"Is it wise to let your servant rebuke you?"

"Erastus?" Mister Blake looked at Tim in surprise before chuckling softly. "He's no servant of mine. He is here only because he wants to be. He helps me at the anvil and in the house. But nobody owns him, you see. Though I doubt he'd leave me to my own, out of pity. I've a talent with the horses but no sense to housekeeping."

"Are you one of the league of bachelors, sir?" Saura asked.

"No, miss. Widower."

She kept herself from looking back to the miniature over the looking glass. A sound from the dining area drew their attention and they turned to see the table already set, dishes of food being placed on the sideboard. Mister Blake turned to them. "Let us take the repast since I must soon return to my trade." As they were walking in, Saura taking the lead, he put a restraining hand on Timothy's coat sleeve. His voice was low. "We've not your fancy Boston ways here in the Hollow, sir."

Saura filled her plate with cold roast beef, bread slices, beets and a few dollops of horseradish and mustard. Timothy held her chair and then took the seat next to her. He suppressed his dismay as Erastus took the seat across the table. He felt a nagging worry about the prospect of his cousin's staying in this less-than-genteel environment.

As Saura ate the late-day meal, she looked through the double doors that led into the garden. A wall of stone not more than three feet in height surrounded it, overgrown by wild, thorny rose bushes. The garden was not in very good repair and a small mill wheel turned sluggishly in the stream, clogged with weeds. Flowers bloomed despite the neglect and she thought that once the garden might have been tended by gentle hands.

23

She had meant what she said about liking this comfortable house. She felt that she belonged in an ornate Boston home as much as a fancy Chippendale table belonged in this country place. Despite its simple furnishings, she sensed an intrigue. She wished it were as easy to see the inside of the owner's mind as it was to view the house. But that could not be so. Her knowledge of him was limited, amounting to the few pieces of information she had learned from her parents. A good friend, a man of valor, educated and from the mother country. She did know too that Elizabeth had sent letters often and that they had been answered. But what did that have to do with her, Saura? Peter was no relative. Why would her mother have her come here, especially when she would normally stay with her cousin in Boston? The puzzle was missing some pieces. She would find them, she mused. She was about to ask Mister Blake some straightforward questions when he excused himself, saying that he still had much to do in the livery and that they were to enjoy their leisure.

Saura was shown to her room by Erastus. It was large, the white wooden fireplace guarded by a wicker screen. A tall candlestick graced either end of the mantel and a looking glass with a painted border was placed between. A tripod table with a round pie-crust top stood to one side holding a glass lamp; a corner washstand held a white bowl and pitcher. A high scroll-topped chest of drawers made of cherry stood on bowed legs. It matched the kneehole dressing table that was topped with a beveled mirror. A three-legged boffet chair was pulled up to it. The dark mahogany bedstead had a scrollwork headboard and tall, narrowly tapered posts. A large comfortable of blue and white homespun covered the old bed. Above the headboard there hung on the wall a sampler of advanced cross-stitch depicting three variations of the alphabet, intricate borders, flowers in pink and blue with green stems, and two birds in the lower corners. Saura admired the fine stitchery, regretting that she had never been handy with a needle and floss. There was one window in the room, a high arch with a tightly gathered white lace covering that fit the frame. The window opened to the side of the house, overlooking a clipped lawn. The front street could be seen to the side, a few distant shops visible. An enormous oak tree grew there, shading the house, its leafy green arms reaching out as though to enfold the building in its grasp. Two willows graced the lawn also.

There was a window seat upholstered in faded blue velvet. In a house so plainly masculine, this room was definitely feminine—as though waiting for the proper occupant. Saura shrugged and stretched, slipping off the dusty traveling dress and rinsing her hands and face in water from the pitcher. She pulled dark velvet drapes over the window and lay down on the bed, savoring the room's cool darkness. The muffled street sounds and the distant ringing of the smithy's hammer soon lulled her to sleep, the exhaustion of the journey easing from her small frame.

Timothy, on the other hand, cleaned himself up and on pretense of checking out Greenhollow, made his way swiftly back to the inn. Perhaps he could catch the serving girl in a bit of conversation.

Saura awakened from a dreamless slumber. The room was dark and warm. She rose and walked to the window, pulling back the heavy drapes to let in a stirring of cool twilight air. She quenched the dryness of her mouth with water from the pitcher, grown warm, and then shook the dust and wrinkles from her black traveling gown as best she could. She dressed, regarding herself in the mantel looking glass as she smoothed down her wayward tresses.

She made her way downstairs to find Erastus setting out dishes on the long dining table. He looked up as she entered but continued the chore. "Is Mister Blake still working?" she asked.

"He's about finished up. No point in working after the light's gone."

She nodded, watching with interest as the man brought out covered dishes to set on the sideboard and poured cool drinks into the pewter mugs. "The room I am staying in is very nice. Feminine, though, for the

25

home of a widower. I know little of Mister Blake's past except what my parents spoke of. Does he have a daughter?" There, she had started down the path of prying.

She thought that Erastus looked bemused as he pulled out the silver and the linen napkins. "He does."

"And she does not reside in Greenhollow?"

"She hasn't."

The man's obvious unwillingness to continue the conversation left the discussion at an end; she felt it would be rude to push for further information. She was distracted by Tim's return and chatted with him for a few minutes. Just as Erastus was setting out the mutton and fried potatoes, Mister Blake came in. His hands had been well-scrubbed with lye soap and he had doffed his smithy's apron and put on a fresh shirt. They sat down, enjoying the heavy evening meal and light conversation.

"Have you lived in Greenhollow for very long?" Tim asked.

"Only six months. The Hollow had need of a blacksmith. The former blacksmith had died in a sudden accident, kicked in the head by a bad-tempered horse. His wife went to live with her son in Virginia and so I bought the livery and smith along with this house. When I knew that I would be coming here, I wrote to Saura's family of it."

"Where did you live before?" Saura asked.

"Here, there. Concord last."

"Is that where your daughter is?" she queried. At his look of surprise, she hastily added, "Erastus said that you have a daughter. I inquired because of the room I am staying in. It is decorated to be a woman's dwelling, I am sure."

Tim caught the glance exchanged by Mister Blake and his servant as the former answered, "Many of the furnishings I bought with the house. But you are right, I have set the room up for my daughter."

"She must think it lovely."

"Actually," he said, wiping up the last of the gravy from his plate with a piece of bread, "she has not seen it before. Saura, it is time we talk." He arose, retrieved

26

the Bible box and opened it. He pulled out the letter sent him by her mother, handing it to her. "As you can see, your mother requests in her own hand that you stay here under my care until such a time as she can come."

While Saura read the letter, Timothy studied the man across the table. "Propriety bids me question such action," he said, going to the point. "I realize that you are a close friend of the family's, well-trusted and highly thought of. But I think of Saura's welfare. It is best that she stay with family until the time she can be turned over to her mother."

"Exactly," Mister Blake nodded his agreement. His statement took Tim by surprise but before he could speak again, Saura waved him to silence.

"I do not understand this line written by Mother. It says that the time has come for you to tell me everything. What does that mean?"

"You have heard of long stories but this is an unusual tale as well. Before I begin it, I must tell you that you cannot pass it to others since the lives of men will hang by it. Agreed?" His expression pierced Tim especially; the gravity of his tone made the younger man nod mutely. Mister Blake continued. "It is a story that will be missing certain details—those you will have to wait for. But the facts you need to know I can tell you. Nearly thirteen years ago circumstances made it impossible for me to stay in England. I had recently lost my wife, Eleana, and I struggled to take care of our infant daughter. When it became imperative that I come to the colonies, I feared for her safety during the long ocean voyage, especially without a mother's loving care. I will not go into detail but out of desperation I turned my tiny daughter over to my friend, who was dearer than a brother, and to his wife. They were grieving the loss of their own infant daughter and my child filled their need. There was no way that I could give her the love and care that Elizabeth could. But it was a terrible sacrifice."

"Do you mean to say that Saura is that little daughter?" Timothy cried.

"The same. And here are the letters sent as often as possible to tell me all about you." He pulled out a tall stack of yellowed letters tied with a black ribbon. "You can read them." He handed the packet to Saura along with a miniature portrait of herself.

"That is the miniature that...that Mama had done of me," she stammered.

"She had two and sent me one."

"This is incredible!" Tim said, his voice a whisper.

Mister Blake sighed and shook his head, resting his arms on the table. Saura turned to him. "I am sorry, sir, but it is just all so surprising. There are things from my childhood...things Lawrence said. Mama talked of losing little Bess but then she would always say that after that, God had sent her me. It is so hard to think of anyone else in Papa's stead."

Peter Blake fought the emotion in his voice. "Thomas *was* your father. He raised you and loved you as his daughter. I would not want to replace him. I would not ask you to call me 'Papa.' 'Peter' will do fine until you are used to this new notion."

"This is all quite extraordinary," Tim stated, still at a loss.

"The doors of wisdom are never shut," Erastus mocked.

Mister Blake ignored both of them. "What do you say, Saura?" he asked softly.

"I am quite set back. Give me a moment, if you will."

Timothy looked at her. "Even if this tale is true, you are not obliged to stay here. As I have said, my home is open to you."

"I do not push you to stay here," Peter countered. "But I would like to have you live here with us in Greenhollow. There is a span of over a decade in which I have longed to know my daughter through more than just letters."

Saura stared at the letters and then began reading through the chronicles of her life. Elizabeth spoke with love of the child for whom she cared, calming Peter's concerns and earlier worries. As the girl read through letter after letter, the three men watched her intently.

After a quarter of an hour, Erastus leaned over to his friend. "If you did ill to tell, the joy will fade. But if you did well, the pain will fade."

"There are no fools so troublesome as those that have wit," Peter hissed and Erastus suppressed a smile.

Finally Saura folded and put away the last letter, carefully tying the packet with the black ribbon. "'Tis a most remarkable thing," she breathed. "I've lost one father to death's hand only to be given another." She smiled at Peter Blake.

"Will you be staying then?" Erastus asked for his friend.

"Is that what you want, Saura?" Tim asked.

She looked at them. "Yes. That is what I want."

Blake rubbed his eyes, pretending they were tired, and then looked at his daughter. "Welcome home, girl."

"Thank you, Father." The title came easy for he did look like a father. But she would never call him "Papa." That title would always belong to Thomas.

They passed the evening in looking at the family Bible, examining the miniature portrait above the mirror of Saura's real mother and listening to her father tell stories of the past. Tim was confused by it all, feeling that little of it made sense. But if Mister Blake was her father, he decided, the best place for her was with him. He gained the courage to admit to himself that as long as Saura was with her family, it did ease his responsibilities. But he would miss her.

Saura herself was bemused, happy, wondering. She was amazed at all this—the totally unexpected solution to the puzzle left her astounded. It told her things about herself that she had never believed possible; she felt as though she were reading a novel. For a moment, however, her problem of what to do and where to go was solved. This was her home until her mother arrived. And Peter was a kind man, despite his muscle and rugged features. She had liked him from the beginning. The turmoil she felt, the trembling surprise of newly discovered emotions, left her exhausted. It was as though she were starting over, beginning a new life in the Massachusetts colony.

The candles had burned low into hollowed scoops of tallow when they retired. Peter saw her to her door, cautioning her and Timothy in what they did and said hereafter and neither questioned his reasons. His honest sincerity was enough of a voucher for them.

As Saura finished pulling on her nightgown and tying the sleeves, the candle flickered out. After the immediate blackness diminished a little, she looked out the window at the bright diamonds of starlight against the ebony of the sky. The evening air was cool and sweet, kissing her face. Her veins stirred with the excitement of new discovery, her life clothed in past intrigue. She lay down on the comfort of her bedstead, sleep coming slowly. Tomorrow she would start her existence afresh as a citizen of Greenhollow.

Mine eye hath play'd the painter,
and hath still'd
Thy beauty's form in table of my
heart;
My body is the frame wherein 'tis
held,
And perspective, it's best painter's art.

—SHAKESPEARE

## Chapter II

LATE AFTERNOON SUNLIGHT slanted across the ground,
turning cornstalks and sunflowers golden. The autumn
day retained the last heat of summer and it was hot in
the kitchen as Saura lifted the heavy copper kettle to
the stove top and poured the water in. The kitchen was
one of her favorite rooms with its brick floor worn
smooth; its hanging copper pots, wooden spoons, black
stove and brick oven were well-used. A large wooden
block for chopping was in the center of the kitchen while
a door to the east led into the well-stocked larder. It
was a familiar room to her and a much cleaner one
since her arrival three years earlier. Although Erastus
was a passable cook, the kitchen had been quite hap-
hazard; now, however, the cookery was neatly orga-
nized with a place for everything.

Its Dutch door, the upper half ajar to admit any breeze
that might stir, led into the garden. This, too, had

31

changed considerably since Saura's arrival. The rows of corn, late peas, squash, melons and turnips were straight and well-weeded. The mounds of golden pumpkins with their curling emerald leaves and the tall stalks of reddish rhubarb gave her a stab of pride as she glanced out the door. She smiled as she thought of Timothy's horror when he arrived for a visit and found her out digging in the fertile soil. Life was very different in the Hollow.

She reached for her basket, sorting through the small, hard bayberries that she would use to make candle wax. She pulled off the twigs or leaves before plopping the berries into the water that was heating; as she did the chore, her mind wandered over the last three years. Somehow she had not thought she would be staying so long. But letters had arrived explaining the difficulties and changes that had postponed Elizabeth's plans for coming to the colonies. Saura had not been too disappointed. She had come to love Peter and to call him "Father" with ease. He was kind, knowing and well-humored, and he did not restrict her life with the tidy rules of young womanhood to which she had been subjected in both Bristol and Boston. She did not mind working in the kitchen or garden or learning to make a batch of bread. Miss Bathsheba Brightwater helped with some of the house chores, baking bread and cooking. She was an elderly lady, never married, who provided a living for herself and an invalid brother by doing small services from baking to mending. Bathsheba had shown Saura how to make the bayberry candles. Clothed in a white starched apron and a billowing cap, under which sprouted yellowed curls and a rice-pudding face, the Miss Brightwater was a library of knowledge. Even though determination and primness were the lady's most prominent qualities, Saura liked her enormously.

She had also come to know and respect Erastus. As Peter had said, Erastus was his own man. She had learned to enjoy the two men's debates and discussions, witty remarks and discourses. Most of these were about the state of the colonies and the British discriminations.

Saura had come to gain wide political knowledge and a strong allegiance to America.

She brought down a long-handled wooden spoon and began stirring the boiling kettle, watching the hard berries swirl about. Her first year had been unsettled and she had had a bit of homesickness but gradually it had dissipated. There had been many things to do in the Hollow. It was surrounded by wild countryside that she had come to know well. Peter had let her learn to ride since she had continual access to the livery and Erastus had taken her fowl-hunting on a few occasions. For the first time in her life she was free of the restrictions that had always held her bound. She would not have left the Hollow for all the tea in Boston harbor.

She brushed aside a moist tendril of hair, shoving it back under her cap, letting the fire die down as the wax rose to the top of the kettle. She called into the dining area, "Erastus, can you carry it for me?"

He put down his almanac, lumbered into the kitchen and heaved the big kettle, setting it down in the cooler; then he returned to his reading. She reflected that through his friend Peter, Erastus had a considerable voice in the community, especially since the establishment of the Committee of Correspondence. This had been formed in Boston not long after her arrival as a means to exchange information with groups in other areas about the resistance to British measures. Peter Blake and Wilfred Wyte, the innkeeper, headed the branch in Greenhollow. Meetings were often held at Wilfred's inn and sometimes in Peter's library. When the latter occurred, Saura would bring in cakes and ale, listening quietly to the heated discussions. The incident two years ago in which several youths and adults, throwing snowballs and stones at British troops, had been shot down was still remembered bitterly as the Boston Massacre.

She realized that increasingly she had become the colonist, taking sides against King George. The opinions of her two fathers would always bear the strongest influence in the forming of her judgments. Lawrence would be horrified if he knew. After picking the last of the raspberries for dinner's tarts, she returned to the kitchen, going into the cooler. She skimmed the bayberry wax off the kettle and placed it in a pan, remembering the last two summers as she worked. Just as she had experienced growing pains, so had America. The previous summer the Tea Act had been passed, enabling the British East India Company to sell tea cheaper than the smuggled brew, thus paying the Townshend duty. Enraged, the colonists had filled the harbor with that tea.

During this time Tim's visits had become less frequent and she had seen him only once or twice a year. Satisfied that she was well, if not ladylike, he let his worries of business take over. Although she missed Tim, she was somewhat relieved since she was ill at ease when she had to play the proper lady for his benefit. Not only that, he had become enamored of the barmaid, Molly Yates. An obvious flirt, Molly had tried to befriend the younger girl, hoping to thus gain an in with her handsome cousin. Saura had seen through her as though she were the thin cheesecloth that Saura now unfolded. She strained the hot wax through it—a tedious job, especially in hot weather, and her brow beaded with perspiration. Finished, she began to pour the wax into the candle molds, carefully wiping up the drippings. Just this year the Intolerable Acts had been passed by the British and things had come to a boil. The Acts closed the port of Boston, thereby depriving Massachusetts of self-government, and provided for the compulsory quartering of British troops by the colonists. The First Continental Congress met in Philadelphia and demanded a repeal of the Coercive Acts and made plans to boycott British goods.

The colonies were in turmoil. Saura reflected that some colonists were loyal to King George, some were striving for independence and some were like the proverbial fence-sitters, wanting neither war nor oppression. She carefully put the molds aside; they would need to set for six hours. Tomorrow she could light the candles after dusk, letting their aroma fill the house, the scent wafting upward from their flickering flames.

Saura wiped her hands on her apron and untied it. She smoothed her dress—it had become too short and was too tight across the bosom. Slender still, she was now more the young woman. She did not see the change in herself as clearly as Peter, Bathsheba and those around her did. The freckles had gone from her nose and cheeks, her skin was smooth and golden. Long dark lashes were lacy above her brown eyes, her hair was thick and as brown as the back of a meadowlark's wing. She was unaware of her beauty that seemed to blossom more with each passing day. Puzzled by the recent attentions paid her by the local youths at church meetings or in the market, she had asked Peter what their trouble might be. When he explained that several had asked his permission to call she had laughed in surprise.

"They cannot mean to court!"

"They do," he assured her. "And they are quite serious about it."

"How can any youth who looks after this skirt or that at church, and talks about war in the next minute, be serious? Those are the same that would not let me join in the horse race last summer even though I could have won!" she said.

"A horse race is no place for a lady," he said sternly as before, inwardly proud of the fact that she was an accomplished horsewoman. "Perhaps it is time that you start thinking of marriage," he mused.

"Marriage? To whom, might I ask? You couldn't mean to one of that pack of baying pups!"

He smiled to himself, thinking that Elizabeth would be surprised if she could observe the change in her child. "'Twas only a thought," he said, raising his hands in pretended defense.

The truth was that her fate had repeatedly crossed her mind of late. Although Willy was a great friend at hunting and finding secret places in the surrounding forest (she did not know of his proud reputation among his friends for being with her), he and her father and Erastus were no longer enough. She was aware of her womanhood, if only recently gained, and she felt something lacking. More and more she had put away her childish whims and play. Beatrice and Nancy wrote of coming out into society and although that was not what she herself wanted, she was aware of new desires. Bathsheba was making her some new dresses in exchange for coin, candles, garden produce and several batches of pies and tarts. Although Saura had accumulated a number of bolts of fabric from Peter's coin, she had not had the courage to start sewing since she had almost no skill with thread and needle. Of late she had had the desire to look more the part of a woman, although not for the sake of the local swains.

If there was something lacking in her life, she was not sure of what it was. She loved the peace and beauty of Greenhollow and her home with Peter. Although she lacked formal education, she enjoyed Peter's library and currently she was reading Shakespeare's "A Midsummer Night's Dream." Peter had most of the old master's works as well as other writings, many of them political. The latter were what really fired her imagination for her mind was as sharp as that of any young man's and her sense of debate was keen. It was through the fiery writings of men like Samuel Adams that she found herself caught up in the bright cause of revolution. And this, she thought, was more pertinent to life than any myths or tales. The smell of war hung over the country, upsetting to everyone. With increasing frequency, redcoats—or lobsterbacks, as Willy called them—were seen around Greenhollow, as they were in many neighboring towns. Here more so than in other places though, for they camped along the Posthaste Road to Boston.

Saura retreated to the coolness of her room, pulling off the wilted cap and brushing out her locks until they resembled heavy silk. She lay down on her bed, Peter's words coming back to her. If she were to marry, if there were someone for her, he was not to be found in the Hollow. But it was not something to think about now. Marriage need not come for another year or two, she decided.

One day the following week she was up early, packing a large basket with two fresh pies and just-picked grapes, purple jewels with their dusting of white. She was taking them to Bathsheba, who was going to fit her with the new dresses. There was a rap at the door and it opened; Willy stepped in. He had grown several inches taller since she had known him but he was just as mischievous as ever. His eyes were bright with excitement and she anticipated gossip.

"Morning, Will. What is happening this day?"

"Where's Peter?"

"He and Erastus are shoeing. Didn't you see them?"

"I came the back way. Pa's mad as a soaked hornet!"

She raised her eyebrows in pretended surprise, noting that he seemed about to burst. "At you?" she teased.

He shook his head. "At the lobsterbacks! They're in town. Is that fresh pie?"

Now she did look at him in surprise. "In town? Here, in the Hollow?"

He nodded. "They came in last night. Staying on, they will be. They are quartering the king's troops right here. Pa is being forced to put up five of them at the Crooked Horne. He had a run-in with their snooty captain but there isn't much he can do about it now. It may be treason to refuse. They could take away the inn, or so that Major Putnam said. I think we ought to band together and whup their hides!"

"Talk like that before the redcoats and they are likely to whup yours."

Will shrugged, watching her load the basket. "Want to go fishing this afternoon? I have fresh worms."

"Thank you, no. I've a fitting with Bathsheba for some new dresses," she said, putting in a jar of apple butter.

Saura was not the same young girl who had come to Greenhollow two years earlier and who had gone hunting or fishing with him in the forested hills. She was growing up, and away. They had struck off a rather odd relationship from the beginning; their bond was one of honest friendship. More and more of recent the local youths were hanging about her, lovesick. Willy found it disgusting. They had not treated her with friendship—or even politeness—when she had wanted

37

to race against them or when she was caught with himself down at the fishing stream. Now those same foolish bucks were following her about, trying to talk to her and even coming to him for advice. He could not help but be a bit proud of the respectful teasing he had received. The appleheads did not understand that their relationship was one of friends. A year her junior, he did not yet comprehend the plague of longing youth and thought the whole situation a puzzling jest. He leaned over the basket, peering in. "Is that pumpkin pie?"

"Squash. The other one is rhubarb. I'm taking them to Bathsheba's." She tucked a linen around the basket top and strode out the door. Since it was warm enough to do without a shawl, she cast her apron across the closed lower portion of the door. "There's some pie in the cooler," she called over her shoulder. "You can have one piece but leave the rest for Peter and Erastus."

Willy looked through the cooler, finding the pie and cutting a sizeable chunk. He took a bite as he went through the door to find the smithy.

Saura walked down the street toward Bathsheba's, noting the tingle of excitement in the town. The pleasant air was alive with distant, raucous sounds. It was a beautiful day, still warm and breezy, with a pale blue sky. Too bad it had to be ruined by the British. She walked along, enjoying the freshness of the air on her face and thinking of the previous Sunday. Peter had indeed given permission to the local swains to call. She grimaced as she remembered the arrival of two within the same hour. There she had sat for the most uncomfortable part of an afternoon listening to the two braggarts. In time they were hardly speaking to her, so engrossed was each in proving superior to the other. She had excused herself for a moment, slipping out the kitchen door and into the forest behind the house. She had gone for a walk that had lasted late into the day, leaving Peter to make her apologies. He was there to confront her with it when she returned.

"'Twas a rude thing to do, girl," he said, hands on hips.

She raised her eyebrows in surprise. "I was not the

rude one. They are the ones who ignored me, speaking as though I were not there at all!"

"Why should they do that?"

"They thought to battle out for my benefit which one was the better suitor, one displaying brawn, the other showing off his brains, or what little there were. And what was expected of me but to fawn and smile and listen with bated breath? I have better things to do on a Sunday afternoon than be subjected to such buffoonery!"

Erastus burst out laughing and could not be silenced by Peter's stern frown. "The girl is right. When knaves betray each other, one can scarcely be blamed or the other pitied."

"I have no pity for them but she that sows thorns should never go barefoot and it is best she learns it now."

Saura had shrugged and turned away, thinking that if this was the best that courtship had to offer, she was better without. She knew that Peter was only concerned for her but she would not put up with such foolishness from others for his comfort of mind.

By now she had reached Bathsheba's house, a little one-story with a wooden fence and brick front. She strolled up the walk, greeted by the woman's small dog, and rapped on the door. After a few minutes it was pulled open cautiously by Miss Brightwater, her curls bouncing from beneath the white cap, her mouth in a silent *O* of recognition. "Come in, dear. It is such a relief to see that it is only you! I had quite forgotten that you were coming and, why, with those dreadful troops quartering in town, I have just been a knot of nerves." She ushered Saura in, shutting the door and guiding her into the tidy little parlor. "Just imagine! Housing soldiers right in your own home. The Blackwells and Crombys have been forced to take them in, and even poor Mistress Shoburry, despite her being a widow-lady. What is this world coming to?"

"They are forcing Wilfred to put them up at the inn," Saura said, watching Bathsheba flutter about in dismay.

"I hope they do not come here. We simply do not have the room. I will just have to explain that to them. Poor Alfred could not stand all the upset."

"How is your brother?" Saura asked politely.

"Same as always. Doctor Barton says he's finally over the ague. But I hate to think of how this will upset him. Even the news of those Intolerable Acts sent him off into a spell. Heaven knows I have always been opposed to war, having been loyal to King George and our mother country, but one simply cannot put up with such indignities. Imagine, a common soldier, a stranger, right in your own home!"

"Perhaps they will stay for only a few days," Saura said comfortingly.

Miss Brightwater eased a bit at the thought, pulling out her sewing basket and unfolding the dress she had made for the girl. Saura took in a breath. "Oh, 'tis lovely!" And it was. Anxiously she threw off her old dress and pulled on the quilted petticoat of blue poplin and Bathsheba tied the gathering strings. Then she put on the outer skirt and top. They were of a lighter blue, with a square neck and quarter-length sleeves, the skirt cut away in front to reveal the quilted petticoat. It fit most becomingly. The sleeves and bodice were trimmed with white silk ruching, thriftily obtained from the scraps in Bathsheba's remnant bag.

Saura turned to examine herself in the mirror and was amazed. In this simple but elegant gown she looked quite womanly.

"Don't you look just lovely! I have quite outdone my stitching this time. One other thing..." Bathsheba began rummaging through her sewing goods. She found what she was looking for, pulling out a white silk flower and a length of blue silk ribbon. She tied the latter skillfully around Saura's throat, cutting off the excess and attaching the flower. "There. You are pretty as a portrait, my dear."

"I am most grateful," Saura said, tearing her gaze from the looking glass. She went into the dining room and took from the basket the grapes, apple butter, pies and a small purse of coins. Miss Brightwater smiled in expectation.

"Two pies! What a lovely treat. Alfred will be quite pleased, I am sure." She said nothing about the anticipation she felt at spending the coins. "Now you enjoy your new dress and I will have the others done in a week or two."

"Do not rush," Saura said, catching up her empty basket. "I know that you are busy. And I must be off to the market."

"And most fetching to go shopping," Bathsheba called after her, thinking to herself that indeed Peter's girl was thoughtful and pleasant. She was also an excellent cook, she thought, slicing into the rhubarb pie.

Saura strolled down the street toward the blacksmith's. Greenhollow had not yet had a first frost and the day was still pleasant, with a mild breeze. The clouds floated thick across a pale sky and she took in a deep breath, sensing the day to be peculiar in a special and unknown way. Perhaps it was just that she felt very pretty in her new poplin dress. She reached the open portal of the smithy's and watched as Erastus and Peter calmed the skitterish nerves of a young stallion. Silently she admired their control over harness and horseflesh as they worked in rhythm together. Once shoed and stalled in the livery, the animal settled and she caught their attention.

"Who might this young woman be?" Peter asked in surprise. "This cannot be the same girl who donned boys' breeches to race a horse!"

"I believe it is. But I wonder, what has happened to force her into lace and poplin?" Erastus mused.

She turned about, letting her skirt swirl a bit for their admiration. "It is only the fact that I am growing out of hem and bodice in my other dresses! Discomfort does a good deal of urging." As the two men laughed, she smiled down at the pretty dress. "Bathsheba is good with the needle. I think her work is lovely."

"Pretty, true," Peter said. "But not as lovely as she it dresses. You are not the child that came to me three

*41*

years hence, girl. If those two ardent swains fought over you last Sabbath, they're like to club each other now at the sight of you."

A frown caught between her eyes. "I can think of better use for their time. If they were loyal to the cause, they would fight for our homeland instead."

"That is dangerous talk, lassie," Peter cautioned. "The Hollow is alive with redcoats."

"You've heard then?"

Peter nodded. "They came last night."

"I do not understand why we sit mealy-mouthed when war can only be months away! How can the British take our cause seriously when we cower in fear?"

"Because they think of the colonies as just a group of misguided children in revolutionary play. But remember that our chances to win our right are improved if this is what they believe. And for all our sakes, you had best not be spouting things you've picked up at the meetings."

She nodded. "You are right of course. I will hold my tongue and be as prim as the Cummin sisters. Now I am going to market. Is there anything you want?"

"Some of Uriah's hand balm. And you can tell him that there will be the meeting in my house tonight, but do it quietly."

"And watch out for the lobsterbacks," Erastus threw in between the ring of hammer on anvil.

"Are there many?"

"They spot the fair face of Greenhollow like a pox," he replied.

She smiled at this and went on down the street and past the Crooked Horne, its sign creaking in the breeze. The road leading into the marketplace was made of hard-packed earth and had banks of green on each side. Trees dappled her path with shade as she walked down the hill, catching a glimpse of the azure river, its diamond-sprinkled back snaking through the Hollow. She passed beneath a spreading maple tree with leaves like layer upon layer of tattered green silk. She stopped first at the open vegetable shop, greeting its keeper and selecting eight red apples. She deposited them in her basket and moved on. In time she came to the glassware shop and peered through the window. The shop was new, a novelty in the town. The Hollow was hardly big enough to gain substantial trade in glasswares but the young couple who had opened the shop also did a little silversmithing, and enough trade came in to keep the business alive. She watched Jonas dip into the melted glass in the white-hot heat of the brick kiln as his young apprentice moved the bellows up and down, fanning the heat. The long pipe held a small bit of molten glass as Jonas swirled it, the other end to his lips. By blowing, he was shaping the glass into the bowl of a goblet, later to be given a stem or a handle.

Her hands had been cupped against the window so that she might see in and as she turned to leave, she came face to face with one of the king's soldiers. She looked at him in surprise. His three-cornered hat was trimmed in braid, his coat red with big cuffs and buttons on the sleeves. His breeches ended below the knee, much in fashion, and his white hose were stained green from a recent skirmish in the grass. Red was a popular color with the citizenry in Bristol, and even in Boston, so the redcoats were not very conspicuous there. But here in Greenhollow the color was not one often seen.

"Miss," he said, raising his tricorn from a sandy brow. His plain features, set upon by a biscuit nose, smiled their admiration. Only a few years her senior, he was one of the many foot soldiers sent over by the king to help squelch the tempest of rebellion.

She nodded curtly before turning and finishing her walk to the shop of common goods. Now she began to notice many of the soldiers, apparently on a noon-hour cease. Some lolled against trees or buildings, others stood in clusters, talking boisterously. Erastus had been right. What a pox, she thought. She stepped into Uriah's store and looked around. He was busy helping Mistress Finchley choose a powder from England. Saura passed by the pungent barrel of apple vinegar, its cork tightly in place. There was flour, freshly ground from the mill house, cornmeal bins and a yeast barrel. The common store was always full of mingled smells. She liked the place—displaying as it did everything from pudding tins to the china dolls that Mistress Cronwiller dressed and displayed. Standing before the bolts of fabrics just in from the Boston docks, their price risen since the Intolerable Acts, she looked through the satin ribbons, holding them up to her hair before the looking glass, trying to select a few.

"Why, Miss Saura, what a pleasure! That is what it is, a pleasure!" She groaned inwardly, recognizing the voice of Harley Chase, Uriah's son and one of her ardent Sunday suitors.

She forced a smile to her lips before turning around. "Hello, Harley."

"What has brought you to our store?" He rubbed his hands together, looking down at her. Tall, skinny, he was a young study of his father, his beaked nose shooting out from under spectacles. In all fairness, he did have nice eyes and thick hair, red as a berry though it was, she mused.

"Hand balm."

"Pardon?" he asked.

"Hand balm for Mister Blake," she repeated.

"Oh! Certainly. Isn't that a new dress? If you wouldn't mind my saying so, it is most becoming. You look pretty as a portrait, the prettiest maid in the entire Hollow!"

"Thank you, Mister Chase," she said, fingering the ribbons.

"Would you mind if I ask permission of your father to call this Sunday afternoon about three o'clock?" he breathed, leaning close to her.

She found herself in the difficulty of trying to avoid such a commitment without being unkind. A Sabbath-afternoon caller was the last thing she wanted. She was spared the trial by Uriah's sudden appearance. "Good day, Saura. What can we help you with?"

"Hand balm for your local smithy."

"Harley, get that, will you?"

Saura was relieved when the son reluctantly went to do his father's fetching. She turned to the store-keeper. "Father said to tell you that meeting is in our library this evening."

"Thank you," he said, looking around nervously as though one of the king's men might be hiding behind the cider barrels.

"It has been several months since we have seen even half this many of George's men," she said.

"Indeed. They are as thick as clotted cream."

The bell over the door rang and Mistress Webster entered with her son. Uriah nodded at his new customer. "Will that be everything, Saura, or would you like some of these ribbons for your hair?"

She picked out several lengths. He cut off a yard of each and she folded them into her basket. "I'll just put this on your father's bill," he said. Harley brought up the hand balm but was sent to fetch a tea strainer for Mistress Webster; Saura quickly made her escape lest he return to resume their discussion.

Once outside the shop, she was confronted by a group of British soldiers who leaned against the support rails along the wooden walk. The soldier she had earlier run into was among them and he doffed his hat once more. "Hello again, miss."

"Do you know this young lady?" one of the others asked in surprised admiration. She moved to continue her walk when he blocked her way. "Introduce us, Rogers."

She leveled her eyes at him, no flutter in the thick cloaking of lash. "Out of my way, sir. You block my path."

The soldier, handsome in a common way, yet thinking himself much more, smiled at her jauntily. "'Tis a public path."

Now her way was blocked by other soldiers or she would have veered down into the street and passed him by. He leaned one arm against the brick of the common store, further blocking her path, and she looked harshly at him. "If it is a public path, then step aside and let the public pass."

He raised his eyebrows in mock surprise, taking in the soft curve of mouth well-set with determination. "Gentlemen," he said, motioning to the other young cocky soldiers, "it seems that this bit of Yankee poplin would be a better soldier than the cowards we've seen in Massachusetts drill."

A flush of pink tinged her cheeks as she felt her anger rise. When the admiring laughter of his companions faded, she raised her chin and leveled a burning stare at the flippant foot soldier. "You have seen battle?"

He swaggered a bit for her benefit. "Indeed I have! And much of it."

"I see. The king's army must be in dire need to send boys into battle," she mused innocently as a few older soldiers snickered their approval at his comeuppance.

"I am two and twenty!" he said hotly, red spreading up the back of his neck.

"Oh. I thought you much younger. My mistake, sir." Her feigned apology further angered him but she continued as though blind to his embarrassment. "If such a brave soldier will now let me pass, I will be on my way."

He stood his ground solidly, afraid to lose face with the other men, yet not knowing quite how to restore their admiration or attain hers. They stood face to face, neither moving.

Harley was looking through the panes of the store window, wringing his hands. What had Saura gotten herself into? She obviously needed rescuing but he had no idea how or by whom. Across the street the door to the *Publick Recorder* opened and out stepped Major Putnam and a British captain.

Major Putnam straightened his cutback jacket and leveled his tricorn as he moved out onto the street. He was a solid man, both in frame and mind. He looked at the tall young captain at his side who had just joined his ranks last night and concurred with his first opinion of the fellow. Seldom did he like the new breed of young soldier coming up in the ranks, holding frivolous ideas of battle, but Captain Adams was different. Young for his rank, true, yet he was quick to listen and slow to give comment or idea. That was the kind of man he needed. Perhaps his line of command would run smoother now. He reflected that even a mule would be improvement on Withers, his last captain, who had taken a bullet in the arm from rebel gunfire and was out of commission. That had been one of his own luckier days, he reflected. He whipped out his snuffbox, flipped the lid open and took a pinch. Inhaling deeply, he sneezed three times, recalling that he had snuffed long before it was popular with the Macaroni Club. He offered some to Adams, who shook his head, then snapped the box closed and put it away.

Catching sight of the troops across the street, he ceased to look for his horse. "What ruckus is that?" He nodded in the direction of the foot soldiers gathered in front of the common store.

Seth Adams followed the major's stubby finger as they stood viewing the incident, seemingly a confrontation between a soldier and a maid. As the crowd milled about he caught a glimpse of a young girl, clothed in a pretty dress of blue. She stood as straight as a rod, a white ribbon catching the dark locks that tumbled down her back. He caught only a glimpse of silken cheek and could not hear her words but he saw that her fists were tight against her hips. He noted the strain of laughter from the men, and the meaning of it. Striding across the width of the road, leaving the major gaping after him, he parted his way through the growing crowd of redcoats, pushing the soldiers aside.

"It is a sorry thing when a wayward girl is not taught proper respect for the king's army," he heard a soldier's voice, pitched high in anger.

"'Tis not the army I lack respect for," a honeyed voice said, "but one soldier in particular."

This evoked another rumble of laughter and Captain Adams caught sight of a face prettily flushed. The girl was young, yet well-gifted to hold her own. Her pink mouth, no doubt more sweetly soft at other times, made a tight line of determination; her brows, gently arched over deep brown eyes, were drawn into a scowl.

"Attention!" he barked, the soldiers snapping into line like stiff reeds. Saura's was the only form not to become a battering ram in taut salute. Walking between the men she saw a captain—British, or so the braid on his tricorn said. Older than the youth who had been verbally assaulting her, he was tall, with hair as brown as her own and dark eyes. As he came nearer, his straight, clean-shaven features caught her attention as did the neatness of his uniform. A long row of buttons ran up his sleeves and a short frill of lace graced the edges of his narrow cuffs. His neckcloth and breeches were white and there was a strict handsomeness about the man. His dress was simple and he did not wear the white wig so popular among the higher ranks, his hair being caught back instead by a common black ribbon. Yes, there was something about him that intrigued her as her anger ebbed away.

Captain Adams confronted the young soldier, who now stood as stiffly as though his wilted uniform were freshly starched. "Has the British army acquired the new skill of engaging the colonists in verbal battle, soldier?"

"Sir?" the soldier croaked, moisture beading his brow.

"Is there some reason why you harass this young woman?" Adams asked in a voice quiet, yet chilling.

"No, sir. Just engaging the young lady in a bit of discussion."

The captain made no reply to this but stood before the youth, looking him over for apparent flaws, the silence growing until it was all the lad could do to keep from squirming under the harsh stare. Saura suppressed a smile. Finally he spoke. "Where is your lieutenant?"

"Sir! He is at the inn, sir!"

"Since you have little better things to do with your time, I noticed that the horses' harnesses could use polishing. Get to it."

"Yes, sir." He turned on his heels and escaped to the line of tethered horses. The captain's stare dispersed the others without a word of dismissal and they hurried off to find things to do.

"My apologies, miss," he said, looking down at the young woman. "They sometimes forget themselves."

"I did not expect courtesy from the king's men and I was not disappointed." The barb was well-placed and he pierced her with his dark eyes. She did not flinch under that masterful stare as the soldiers had.

"No doubt your opinion of soldiers is not high after such an unfortunate incident. Let me prove the foolhardy soldier wrong. I will escort you home."

She looked at the British soldier in surprise. "There is no need, Captain."

"I insist on righting the wrong. Which way?"

A "Harumph" interrupted them and they turned to find Major Putnam standing at the edge of the walk, his hands clasped behind his back. "Sir," the captain said, "I wish to escort this young lady safely home without any further incident so that the good people in this town might know that we have their best interests in mind."

Saura refrained from snorting in derision only because it would really be unladylike as the major muttered, "Best interests...very well. I am quartered at the inn. We will supper there with the lieutenant and you can discuss the matter with him."

The major went in the direction of the ale shop as Captain Adams led Saura away. "I really need no escort, sir," she said sharply, the earlier events having singed her nerves.

"I did not want such a pretty maid going away thinking that all soldiers in the British army are rogues."

"How can I not assume what is already common knowledge?" she asked, strolling beneath the overhang of willows. She glanced up at him to see whether he were angry but his features remained calm. He appeared to ignore her barb.

"I have not introduced myself yet," he said politely. "I am Seth Adams, captain in His Majesty's command."

"Adams," she repeated.

"No relation," he said. When she looked at him questioningly, he added, "I mean, no relation to your revered troublemaker, Samuel, or his kin, John."

She was silent, feeling awkward with this handsome man by her side. He seemed to be waiting, until he prodded, "And you are?"

"Saura Ainsley," she said, distracted by the sudden

flight of a finch from a nearby bush. She looked up just in time to catch a glimpse of something in his face that she could not discern—but then it vanished as quickly as it had come.

"I am glad to make your acquaintance, Miss Ainsley. It is seldom that a soldier is fortunate enough to enjoy the company of such a lovely young woman."

She was surprised by this, and a bit embarrassed, and they walked on in silence until they came to the blacksmith's. "Here you are," he said and she looked at him inquiringly.

"How did you know this is where I live?" she asked suspiciously.

He looked down into the mahogany of her eyes. "My horse threw a shoe last eve on my way to Greenhollow. I stopped to have it fixed. The smithy spoke of his daughter, Saura. That is not you?"

She mulled this over for a minute and then, satisfied, responded, "It is."

Peter glanced up to see his daughter in the company of a familiar-looking British captain. He put down his hammer, looking at the two questioningly. "Saura?"

"This is Captain Adams. He said that you fixed his horse's shoe last night."

"That is right," Peter concurred. "Good day again, sir."

"I escorted your daughter home. She ran into a bit of trouble with one of the foot soldiers."

By this time Erastus had stopped work too and was raising a questioning brow.

"Trouble, my dear?" Peter asked.

"'Twas nothing. A soldier would not let me pass and we had words."

"I see." Did Peter frown at her? 'Twas hardly her fault, she thought. He rubbed his hands on his leather apron. "Thank you for rescuing my quick-tongued daughter."

The captain smiled and doffed his tricorn. "It was my pleasure. And as to the rescuing, I did more for my soldier than for your daughter, since she had him at a disadvantage."

Saura glared at him and his smile faded. Then her thoughts were interrupted by the call of a female's voice. They turned to see Molly Yates approach. "Why, Captain Adams, did your horse throw a shoe again?" She smiled her brightest and Saura reflected that in three years Molly had become more the woman than ever before, her flaming red locks and pouty mouth as attractive to men as ever.

"No, actually I was escorting Miss Ainsley home."

Molly turned to look at the younger girl, taking in the flushed cheeks and pretty new dress. Her eyes narrowed a bit. "Why, Saura, you look sweet in that new dress. It seems like just last week you were still in pinafore! I was just bringing over some custard for your dinner," she said, thrusting the dish into Saura's hands. Saura wondered what Molly was up to now, suspecting that it had something to do with Captain Adams since Molly had surely seen them pass the inn. Her gifts of food were common tactics whenever Tim visited.

Saura smiled at the captain before turning to take the custard inside. "Thank you for your escort, sir," she said, her civility surprising Peter and Erastus. Captain Adams watched her walk toward the gate in the wall. A breeze stirred the dark locks that hung down her back and her walk was pert and quick. There was something about the young girl that intrigued his taste. He tore his gaze away as Molly asked him a question for the second time and he mumbled an answer.

As Saura reached the gate in the low wall and pushed with her hip to open it, balancing the bowl of custard in both hands, it suddenly swung open before her and she looked up to see Captain Adams holding it wide.

"Your father said that you could give me a drink of water," he smiled. "Cooler than what's in the livery."

"In the kitchen," she motioned with a nod, stepping through the gate and walking along the worn path to the back door. She was well aware of the captain's eyes on her and aware too of her new weapon called womanhood. They stepped into the kitchen and she went to the counter where the bucket of water sat, putting down the custard bowl. She filled a tin cup and turned to hand it to him.

He was standing very close to her, looking down at her, and she felt disconcerted. But she would not weaken nor coyly turn away. Instead she stared back at him openly. She could not help but notice the line of his jaw and his cleanly chiseled features. She had to admit that he was handsome, with his straight nose, well-defined mouth and brown hair, a shade darker than her own and swept back under the tricorn. Yet it was to the mahogany of his eyes that she felt her gaze drawn, something in their depths speaking to her. They did not waver but stood her steady challenge. This was no cocky youth whom she could slice down with the sharpness of her tongue, she realized. As she caught a whiff of saddle leather, mingled with something else more earthy, she recognized him as a man who could meet her on her own terms. She handed him the cup and the warmth of his fingers brushed her hand as he took it. He drank and she looked away, angered at the blush she felt creeping into her cheeks.

Finished with the draught, he held the cup out to her but she would not take it, as though to put him in his place by making him set it on the counter. He seemed to pick up on the wordless challenge and he reached for her hand, catching it in his own and wrapping her fingers around the cup. His hand lingered on hers. "Thank you for the water," he said softly. "Perhaps we'll meet again, Miss Ainsley."

He released her fingers then and turned, striding through the door. She watched his back disappear through the portal. She lingered for a few seconds, then angrily threw the cup into the wooden sink. She went through the house and hurried up the stairs. Once in her room, she unbuttoned her dress and carefully hung it in the wardrobe before putting on the simple muslin in which she would prepare dinner. A cool breeze stirred the curtains and she sat down on the window seat, resting her elbows on the window's ledge. She could still see the front corner of the smithy's shop, where Captain Adams now stood talking to Peter. Molly had managed to stay around, she noted. Finally the captain turned to walk away and she caught the touch of a slight frown on his brow as Molly linked her arm through his and walked with him toward the inn. The girl chattered away happily as though she had snatched a prize.

Piper, Saura's gray and white cat, jumped up onto the seat, rubbing the arch of his back beneath her hand. She stroked his fur and sighed. Piper, so named for his role in catching mice like the piper of Hamelin, purred beneath the attention.

"That was Captain Adams, Piper. He saw me home from town." She shook her head in bewilderment. "A British soldier, and more than that! The man is a rogue, a redcoat who challenged me in some way I cannot name. And yet there were no words about it. But certainly it is the last we will be seeing of him, if Providence will but allow."

She sighed, tickling the cat under his chin. When she thought of the king's captain, she felt uneasy, the memory of him causing a foreign flush of warmth. Certainly she had met few like him.

That night Saura served pound cake and cider to the meeting in her father's library. The shutters were tightly closed and the bayberry candles scented the air as shallow flames lit the dim room. The meeting was not large. About two-thirds of the members had not been able to attend on one excuse or another. Instead of Uriah's loud complaint: "First they undermine our independence by encouraging frivolous imports and then they enslave us with heavy taxes!" or Peter's loud jest that bears and kings worry their keepers, the tone was tense and low. The drinks did not flow as freely as before and the meeting was over early. Saura speculated that when the British forces had left, the meeting would be restored to its former robust health.

She was right. The next day the British pulled out of Greenhollow and traveled along the Posthaste Road. It was the only thoroughfare of communication between Boston and New York. Winding out of the hill-nestled valley like a brown ribbon, the Greenhollow road merged with the Post, which disappeared into the thick forests of golden aspen and maple. And along this trekked the redcoats, Captain Adams among them.

By uniting we stand, by dividing we fall.

—JOHN DICKINSON

## Chapter III

THE HILLSIDES were amethyst. In daylight they were red and brown and gold but under the cloaking of twilight, they were purple. Saura closed all the windows against the new bite of autumn cold. Then she went into the kitchen, stirring the pot of pumpkin soup and slicing the rye bread. She set some of the bread and a slice of butter on a tray, then returned to the soup pot and filled a bowl. Adding a mug of warm spiced rum for medicinal purposes, she took the dinner up to Peter. He was ailing with a fever and aching ears and she had confined him to bed. He had protested at first but as the illness increased, he had given in to her pampering. With a hot, towel-wrapped brick at his feet and camphor smoking in the room, he was resigned to his sickbed. She knocked at the door before entering, then propped him against fluffed-up pillows so he could eat comfortably. She kept him company and then watched him settle down for his evening's nap before she dowsed the light and went downstairs.

The velvet of darkness had settled around the Hollow and she pulled the draperies. She sat down to a bowl of soup, thoughtfully reading one of William Byrd's discourses. She was alone tonight. Erastus had gone to Concord for three days, for what reasons she was not sure. He traveled there with his papers of freedom securely pocketed lest someone try to resell him as a slave. His size, however, would disperse most threats. Also, he was one of the few black men around who could read, having been a schoolmaster's servant in his youth before being freed upon his master's deathbed. He had hired out as a bond servant for seven years so that he could come to America, his passage paid by the bond. Then he had come to know Peter.

They had met at an inn in Providence where Peter had spoken too freely amid too many Loyalists. When a fight ensued, Erastus managed to save him from the brunt of the free-for-all. After that they had traveled together to Virginia and Massachusetts; Peter was one of the few men who treated him as an equal and appreciated his education. Then they had worked together and had lived in various towns in the colonies, Peter teaching his friend the smithing trade and Erastus caring for house and livery. Theirs was an unusual friendship and Saura knew little about the man's personal life. His trips occurred three, sometimes four, times a year.

She was only halfway through her meal when there was a sudden rap at the kitchen door. It startled her, for almost everyone came to the front. Thinking it was Willy, she went to it, throwing the bolt back and opening it. A gust of cool air swept in through the room as a man stepped in, a travel cloak about him and a tricorn pulled low. He looked at her in surprise for a moment before shutting the door behind him. He was of medium height, reddish brown hair and a square face his basic features. She had seen him several times before. Although a foreigner to the Hollow, he had made many visits to the smithy's.

"Pardon for this late hour, miss. Might I inquire if the smith is home?" His smile was swift, as were his actions.

"He is, but ill and in bed."

"And his blackamoor?"

"Erastus is out of town. If it is a problem with your horse, I'm afraid there's not much help at present."

"No, nothing like that." His eyes darted about the kitchen. "I must see Mister Blake."

She looked at him with growing suspicion. "As I've said, he is ill. I would be most reluctant to disturb him."

He looked at her with irritation, disliking being put off by a mere young woman. Testily he said, "I've a message to give into his hands only. Tell him Lewis wishes to see him."

She looked at him for a long time before ushering him into the library to wait. Then she went upstairs and awoke Peter. "There is a man here, a strange one with reddish hair and a ruddy complexion. He's come before. He says his name is Lewis. Last or first, I know not."

Peter struggled to a sitting position, resting his palm against his head. "Yes, go on."

"He says he has a message for you. He came to the back door. It is most peculiar, do you not think? When told that you were ill, he asked for Erastus."

Peter nodded. "Tell him I'll be down in a moment. Offer him some drink."

"You are not well enough," she protested.

"Go."

She left the room, hurrying downstairs and taking a pitcher of applejack and two glasses into the library. The man turned from the fireplace as she entered, his hands behind his back. "Mister Blake will be down presently."

Without so much as a nod, he turned back to the fire. Soon Peter came down, his hair mussed and his face bright with fever but his dressing robe securely tied. "Lewis," he said, stepping forward to shake the man's hand before shutting the door between himself and Saura.

She did not move but stood near the door. She could not help it if words spilled over the threshold. Sadly, the voice inflections and tones were all that carried. There was Peter's low rumble and the higher sounds of protest from the other. Presently the man left and Peter trudged upstairs. She followed him. "Who was he?"

"A man wanting his horse shod."

She snorted indignantly. "You take your daughter for a fool? He told me he had no need of shoeing. And he has been here before. He and a few others, night visitors coming to the back door. Rather strange, I think. What are you doing?" she exclaimed as he struggled halfway into a boot.

She watched in dismay as he tried to pull it on and, the effort proving too much for him, he sank back onto the bed. His face was flushed and the heaviness in his chest made him cough. When the seizure stopped, he sat up, attempting again to pull the boot on.

"What are you trying to get dressed for when you are fevered and ill? It has to do with that man Lewis and his message, hasn't it?"

Peter paused for a moment to catch his breath. "Yes. It is very important, Saura. Something has to be delivered tonight."

"Erastus will be back tomorrow and then he can take it."

"It cannot wait," he said, trying to work the buttons on his nightshirt, having given up for the moment on his stubborn boot.

"Then why didn't that Mister Lewis deliver it himself?"

"He ran a risk of bringing it this far. He could not take it farther. I cannot blame the man."

"How can you sit on a horse when you cannot even pull on a shoe?"

"But it has to be delivered!"

"Is it that important?"

"Yes."

58

"I know it has to do with the effort against the British."

Peter looked at her sharply. "How do you know that? The meeting?"

"Yes, partly. But I also know that we are frequented by visits from Lewis and other men, usually late at night. And then either you or Erastus mounts up and is gone. Sometimes for a few hours, sometimes for as much as a day or two. You could not expect me not to notice?"

He sighed. "No, I guess not. You have a keen eye." He reached into his nightshirt, pulling up a long chain and holding out the coin at its end. It glinted dull gold against the white of his garment. Finely etched on it was a spreading tree and beneath that, in tiny print, were the words: "In Liberty."

Saura gazed at it for a moment and then took in a deep breath. "That is the Liberty Medal! I've heard of it but never seen one before. You are one of the Sons of Liberty," she said, awe in her voice. "I knew where you stood but I did not realize that it was in such important circles. This is a wonderful secret indeed!"

Peter nodded, slipping the coin back to the security of his nightshirt. "Messages come here to the Hollow because it is a stopping point that can turn east to Boston or south along the Posthaste Road to New York. Who would suspect a blacksmith of passing a message along with a coachman or rider? But in this case it is most urgent that word reach Braintree. And secrecy is all-important."

She nodded gravely. "I understand. But just this once isn't there someone else who can take it? You would hardly be a good messenger, swaying ill on the back of your horse." She put a cool hand against his brow. "You are still hot with fever. What about Wilfred's taking it?"

"Yes. Yes, that is an idea. He could take it just this once. He did so one time before." Peter reached into his nightshirt and extracted a small envelope of heavy parchment sealed with wax. He held it out to her, pushing off his boot and lying back in the comfort of his bed to still the ringing in his head. "You must tell him to take it to the Musket Inn at Braintree. The proprietor there is named Stackpole. Wilfred is to give it into his hands alone and to no other, saying—and this is very important—saying that it is a letter of essay. Do you have that?"

Saura nodded, repeating the words back to him. "That is a good girl. Now hurry along." She pulled his comfortable over him and dowsed the light. Then hurrying downstairs, she snatched up a shawl and went out into the cool darkness toward the inn. The message was held tight in her folded arms. She scurried in through the inn doors only to be halted in her stride. There at three tables sat several men. The bright red of uniform declared them English soldiers. Knapsacks, Brown Bess rifles, cartridge cannisters and swords were strewn about as the men relaxed with mead and rye whiskey. She passed among them, catching their appreciative stares, and went on into the kitchen, where Molly filled a pitcher from the whiskey barrel. "Saura! What are you doing here?"

"I want to talk to Mister Wyte for a minute."

"He's busy with a Captain Cooke right now," Molly said over her shoulder as she carried a brimming tray out to the friendly soldiers.

Willy came into the kitchen then, dropping a load of firewood in the box. "Hi! What ya doing?"

"I need to see your father for a minute. Can you get him?"

"He's forced to entertain this uppity captain—white wig and all!—in the sitting room. I'll see if I can get him away for a bit if you want."

She nodded and he left. She sat down on a stool in a far corner and after a bit, a harried Wilfred emerged, wiping his hands on his apron. "What do you need, Saura?"

"Father is ill with a fever and confined to his bed. He sent this to you to deliver." She produced the envelope and he stared at it in horror.

"Put that away!" he whispered harshly. "Can you not see that the house is full of redcoats? Captain Cooke is expecting my conversation and I must return. Tell Peter I am very sorry but I can do nothing to help him— although I can send you home with some fresh pie for him." Willy returned and his father said, "Cut her a piece of pie, son."

Little consolation! she thought. Pie instead of patriotism. She watched Wilfred's back as he hurriedly left the kitchen, a sinking sense of worry filling her. Willy unwrapped the cloth from the apple pie and cut a generous slice, which he wound up in a napkin. What to do? She could not possibly go back home and tell Peter that Wilfred had turned coward. Peter would insist upon going himself then and would greatly endanger his health. She mulled the situation over, her lower lip caught between her teeth as Willy handed her the pie.

The words Peter had said rang through her mind. The Musket Inn at Braintree; she knew of it! The letter was to go to Stackpole, the proprietor there. Her mind worked the matter over until it all fell into place like a difficult arithmetic sum.

"What's the matter?"

She stared off into space a minute before her eyes focused on Willy. Suddenly she snatched the wool cap from his head and took his work coat from the back of a stool. "Let me borrow these, all right, Willy?"

"Sure, but what for?"

"Oh...just for fun." She hurried out the door with them before he could question more. Running home, she was breathless as she went in the kitchen door. Although she mounted the stairs to her room as quietly as possible, Peter heard her tread and called out to her. She opened his door a crack and peered in.

"Did you talk to Wilfred?" he croaked.

"Yes, I did. And everything is all taken care of so don't you worry. Go to sleep." She shut the door and he settled back into slumber, unaware of the full import of her words.

Saura hurried into her room, pulling off her dress and slip and casting them carelessly on the bed. Rummaging through the bottom of her wardrobe, she laid hand on what she was searching for. She pulled the rumpled clothes out and gave them a critical eye. Perfect. Haste made her yank on the old white hose, gray with stain, and the breeches from last summer's riding. Big then, they now fit; she fastened the pants up the front and at the knee. Fortunately her hips were still very slender. But her chest was another problem. She tucked in the chemise and then went into the laundry, rummaging through the soiled clothing until she found one of Peter's shirts. She took it back to her room, pulling it on and fastening it down the front. Her fingers quickly tucked it in and rolled up the sleeves. Then, pulling on a tight vest, she buttoned it down the front. This succeeded in flattening her bosom, giving her the look of a youth. Uncomfortable, but it achieved its purpose. She put on the boots kept at the back of her shoe drawer, fastening them with the buttonhook. Scuffed, worn down in the heel, she used them for racing or hunting when she wanted to protect her good shoes. They would serve.

Grabbing her hairbrush, she went to work on her tresses. They presented the biggest problem for they most eloquently bespoke her gender. If she were a true patriot, she told herself, she would not hesitate to cut them off. But even though she picked up the shears, she did not have the heart to use them. Besides, she rationalized, when she returned home, it would be impossible to hide her tracks if she had short hair. She twisted up the tresses, pulling on Willy's cap and tucking in the stray wisps. A bit too large for her head, the cap succeeded in hiding her hair. Then she pulled on Willy's work coat, the heavy cuffs and thick lapels adding further to her disguise.

She turned to the looking glass with a critical eye, the transformation complete. She stood before the glass—a scruffy youth, surprisingly small in oversized clothes. She grinned and the imp grinned back. What an amazing change! She peered close, then frowned. That face would never do! Even a drunken lobsterback would not be fooled by that sweetly curved mouth and those wide, dark eyes fringed in thick lashes. She was disgusted that such pretty features might be her undoing. Then she had an idea and reached for the chimney lamp, burning dimly. She ran her finger along the sooty rim until it came away black, then applied it to nose and cheek. This seemed to do the trick and so she took more until her face was smudged and all detail of prettiness hidden. She rubbed the remainder of the soot on her hands and then took a new appraisal in the glass. A lad, complete. She smiled. Not even Peter could see through this disguise unless he looked close.

She blew out the light, grabbed the envelope, stuffing it securely under her vest, and hurried down to the kitchen. There she filled a sack with a hunk of bread, some cheese, a small skin of cider and the pie that Willy had given her. She added a small knife and then scampered out the door and down to the livery.

She led a stallion out of the stall; he snorted at the late disturbance. Large, of mixed breed, he would be slower but not as noticeable as one of Peter's thoroughbred mares. She threw on the blanket and flat saddle, cinching the latter tight and shortening the stirrups. After checking the bridle and putting her food in a saddlebag, along with a narrow bedroll, she mounted up. The stallion turned his head to look at her as though in disbelief that so small a person should command him—until she snapped the reins and kicked him hard in the sides. Her mastery was quickly affirmed. His hoofs stretched out before him; they galloped along the ribbon of dusty road that crossed the rush of river and wound out of the Hollow.

Excitement coursed Saura's veins. Above her the sky was black except where the lopsided moon turned thick clouds gray. Although ringed and streaked by those clouds, its rays still sheathed the road sufficient to light the way. The autumn wind moved restlessly through the trees, turning up the undersides of leaves to shine silver under the moon. The night air smelled wonderful. Protected as she was by the heavy coat and cap, the chill freshness was brisk against her face and she bent low over the horse's back, breathing in the thrill of freedom as the ground sped away beneath them. For a time they traveled so, the only sound a medley of rushing wind, the horse's heaving breath and thudding hoofs. Once out of the valley and into the hills, she slowed the animal's pace a little, traveling on in a direct route along the road to Braintree. It was not too far from Greenhollow and had Lewis been of braver stock, he could have readily continued his journey for another day before returning to New York. She hoped to make it to the inn before daybreak. She continued on for some time, watching the scenery glide by, until the horse slowed his gait to a pace, both of them winded. Her traveling continued in spurts of galloping and then dropping down to slower paces.

After a while Saura's back began to ache and her fingers were raw from their tight grip on the reins and the cold air. She scolded herself for having forgotten her riding gloves. Her hands would show blisters on the morrow. She continued the pace for a few more miles and then finally brought the horse to a stop. He stood still gratefully, his sides heaving. She glanced around, having no idea of how far she had come, since there were no signposts. Hearing the sound of a running brook, she led the stallion off to the side of the road. The horse led her to the stream and they both drank. Saura suddenly felt bone-weary. She had had a long day even before starting out on her night travel. She tethered the horse, took out the bedroll and lay down on it. Her bones ached and she chastised herself for being so soft. She had grown too accustomed to short rides and eiderdown comfortables. She closed her eyes for a moment, deciding to give the horse and herself a moment's rest before traveling on to Braintree.

A horse's neigh and snort roused Saura and her eyes opened to stare up at the soft sunlight that filtered through pine needles and pierced the ground. The maple leaves were golden against the blue sky in the early fall. Morning! She pulled to a sitting position, stifling a cry as sore muscles were put to use. She felt inside her vest for the envelope, relieved that it was still there. Cautiously she stood, the cold ground not lending itself to comfort either. She hit her fists against her arms to bring life back into them. How could she have slept the night away, she worried. The fate of the Sons of Liberty was resting in her careless hands. So far she was certainly not doing well as a soldier.

The sudden sound of galloping hoofs caught her ear and she fell flat against the embankment, peering up at the lane. None too soon for several British soldiers raced past, ignorant of her presence. They were going in the same direction as she and Saura wondered if they were coming from the Crooked Horne. If so, she had been lucky lest they had caught up with her. Now she would have to wait for a while so that she did not catch up with them. She let the horse graze as she did a quick toilette as best she could with the aid of the stream. But the water was icy and she dared not wash off the carefully placed soot. She rolled and tied the bedroll and then delved into the saddlebag. She was grateful that she had remembered food and hastily did away with the cheese and bread and half of the cider. She decided to save the pie lest she got no midday meal. Deeming that enough time had passed, she mounted the horse, grimacing at the discomfort of the saddle on yesterday's chaffings. She spurred him onto the road and they traveled ahead, their speed more cautious than before as she watched for redcoats.

The morning was cold, the air bracing, and she decided that it had been light for only a short while. Sooner than she had expected, she reached the outskirts of Braintree and she let the horse stroll slowly into town. Haste would never do on a normally lazy morning. She slouched in the saddle so that any who saw her might think her a lad sent on some early chore. Since she had been here on several trips with Peter she was acquainted with the town's layout, somewhat larger than Greenhollow's. She led the horse to the Musket Inn, tethering him outside. Larger in size than Wilfred's inn, it was not as tidy nor as well-kept. Still, the smell of hot foods escaped the door, beckoning her to enter. She stepped through the portal—and stared about in disbelief!

A score of redcoats sat breakfasting at the long tables, heaping plates of hot ham and beer bread before them. Haversacks were cast about carelessly as well as wooden canteens, muskets and a variety of sabres and broadswords. She sucked in her breath as the envelope in her shirt seemed a sudden burning presence. A fear that would not have been otherwise present made her feel as though she had stepped into a swarm of hornets. They paid her no attention, however, since she appeared to them a mere errand boy. As slow as fear would allow, she turned around and was out the door again. A nest of redcoats! How was she to deliver a message to the proprietor of this place?

Saura felt desolate and loaded down with the weight of her duty. Why had she entered upon this wild scheme instead of leaving intrigue in the hands of men? She had been foolhardy. She forced herself to calm a bit, untying the horse and leading him off. There was no place else to take him and so she led him into a back stall of the livery, confiscating a bag of oats for the poor animal. He could stay here, unnoticed among all the cavalry horses. But what of herself? She knew no one in Braintree and had no coin. She must find a place in which to hide out until the soldiers took their leave, which certainly must be soon. She pulled off the horse's saddle and took her sack from the saddlebag. Then she went out the back way and into a small shed behind the inn. Here she leaned against the sacks of grain and rested for a while, worn by the night's travel. She slept for perhaps half an hour and awakened stiffer and thirstier than ever. Drinking the last of the cider, she ate the now-mashed pie. Cold, it was still delicious.

She was worried about Peter. She had hoped to be back by this time and had not planned on such delays. But maybe he could fend well enough for himself and would not be too concerned about her. Perhaps Erastus would be back by now. She was startled from her thoughts by the sound of voices and peeked through a crack in the wall of the shed. Soldiers grouped in back of the inn and she caught wisps of conversation before they went off. Then she heard the sound of drilling far off in the distance and several times soldiers passed by in the lane. This would never do. How could she explain her peculiar presence here were she discovered? She must do something else. When the last of the soldiers had passed by, she escaped the shed and went around the side of the inn. She would return to the livery, get her horse and ride him out of Braintree. It would be safer to watch the town from the woods.

Saura strolled casually down the length of the livery and neared the corner. As she was about to turn in toward the large doors, she froze. There, leaning against the front of the stable, were several soldiers talking lazily and chewing idly on straws. But the soldier that caught her attention was the cocky private who had bandied angry words with her in front of Uriah's store. She had felt confident in her disguise in the security of her bedchamber but here in this swarm of king's men, she was ill at ease. What if an escaping lock or feminine stride gave her away? And if anyone were to be ill-mannered enough as to pick on a young lad, it would be that cawing jack-a-dandy!

She made a quick turnaround and was about to go to the other side of the livery when the sound of approaching voices caught her ear. She glanced about worriedly, taking notice for the first time of a large, canvas-covered wagon pulled up against the side of the structure. She scrambled inside just in time for voices and the sound of boots hard on the ground were passing by; she pressed down against the bare slats of the floor. She noted the contents of the large wagon. There were several stacked crates the length of rifles, two pine packing cases, crates of powder horns, bullet molds and large powder barrels. Each of these was branded with the crest of King George's regiments.

She said a quick oath under her breath; out of the cooking pot and into the coals! This was the worst place to be found. She must get out as soon as the situation allowed, she decided, peeking over the wagon's back drop-rail, barely parting the canvas flap.

"She was a pretty wench all right," a voice was saying. "And the right amount of spirit too. Put you in your place, and quick, Bickers."

There was muffled laughter and the voices neared her. "She only played the game of teasing, I'll let you know," said a voice that she remembered as belonging to the soldier with whom she had argued. "I had chance to see her later and she came around nicely. Flowers and a smile won a kiss from that pretty maid."

"Go on!" said a doubting voice. The men drew nearer, some of them actually leaning against the wagon. Saura could see their shadows, silhouetted against the canvas by the bright sunlight. She pressed herself down farther, not daring to move. She could hear their every word now.

"True," Bickers said with bravado.

"Swear it," another said.

She heard him spit into the dust. "There. I swear it."

"She gave you a kiss, for real?" a younger voice asked in awe.

"Indeed she did. Just one though," he said, reluctant to press his luck at pulling the sheep's fleece over his companions' eyes. "Sweet lips she had," he confided. "And if ever we march through Greenhollow again, you can bet a sovereign that I'll stop at the blacksmith's shop." His companions were silent as they ruminated over this.

Saura nearly choked. It was she herself of whom they spoke. The knave discussed her! She bit her lip to keep her hot temper in check; how she would like to let her boot find the seat of his fine red breeches. And—worse— the other fools were believing the buffoon! How she thirsted for the chance of denial. She grit her teeth. Just let him pass through the Hollow. She hoped he might seek her out so that she could find the side of his head with a horseshoe! She would teach that braying army mule to sully her reputation.

Her anger was cut short by the bark of a curt command that dispersed the soldiers and she strained her ears to the new sound of approaching boots.

"Help me out with these bullet molds and we can end your laziness! You privates can pour bullets so we have an extra supply on hand," a surly voice ordered.

The full impact of the command struck her as she realized just where the bullet molds were stored.

Sergeant Gorely scowled at the shiftless soldiers who had lazed against the wagon, determined that since they had escaped the drilling, they could well put in double time with the bullet molds. A large man with unruly hair and a thick nose, he was older than many of the officers in higher rank. His uniform, never quite free from wrinkles, and his boots, seldom shiny, had long kept him from the post of an officer. But he paid that no mind. His gun was always clean, his aim unfailingly straight and his common sense well-placed. He was a commissioned soldier for His Majesty's army and he had been so for twenty-three years. He was a soldier throughout.

He grabbed the canvas flap, flipping it out of the way, only to find himself staring into enormous eyes centered in a small, filthy face. He started back in surprise. "What in the name of the king's fleet?" he cried. "What are you doing in the supply wagon?"

Saura felt herself grabbed ahold of and jerked out of the wagon. She was set so roughly on the ground that her teeth jarred together and she looked at the sergeant with surprise and anger. She had never been handled like that in her life! But anger turned to fear as the large soldier stood towering above her and glared down at her as others began to gather around.

"So! You must be the culprit who watered_down two barrels of powder the other night. You rascal! This is the traitor that you soldiers didn't manage to guard against! Why he's barely weaned!"

Raucous laughter rose up and Saura flushed beneath the dirt on her face. Traitor, yes—but not in a way they dreamed of! She cautioned herself lest she give away her feminine gender and she thought of Willy. She must act every inch the boy.

"I ain't done no such thing!" she bawled out, screwing up her face in denial lest the softness of her lips give away her disgust. "I don't know what you're talking about!"

The sergeant jabbed her with a thick finger. "Then what were you doing, hiding in that wagon?"

"I weren't hiding." She stared down at her boots. "I was sleeping." They looked at her with disbelief but she hurried on. "When I got here last night, I found that I was missing the coin I was to use for lodging. So I just looked around and saw this big wagon. I didn't think no one would mind if I used it for a bed. When I woke up, there were soldiers all around and I was ascared to get out, seeing where I was. I didn't know what I was in last night 'cuz it was so dark."

The soldiers mulled this over, the sergeant having lost his fervor at perhaps having caught a spy. He was still suspicious, however. "We'll just see what the captain says!" he declared, grabbing Saura by the scruff of her coat collar and leading her into the inn. She pulled away.

"I can walk by myself!"

He let go, but kept a tight lead lest she bolt. He needn't have worried. Saura knew that such a move would only sentence her as guilty; her best chance was to play the innocent. She shuffled through the large common room to the stairwell. He led her up and onto the second floor. They went down the hallway and stopped before a closed door. The sergeant knocked. Bade to enter by a voice on the other side, he pushed the door open and they stepped in.

Saura's heart leaped into her throat. Captain Seth Adams, his dark head bent over a ledger of neat rows as he quilled in bold script the accounts of horses, men and supplies, sat before her at a large mahogany secretary. He looked up, his deep, rust-colored eyes slowly drenching her with his cool stare.

These are the times that try men's souls.

—THOMAS PAINE
*The American Crisis*

# Chapter IV

SERGEANT GORELY poured out an edited version of the story and the lad's lame excuse while Saura stared at Captain Adams, her heart thudding. She knew that at any moment he would leap forward and pull off her cap, so closely did he scrutinize her. But as he leaned back in his chair, his hands clasped behind his head, she knew she had not had enough faith in her disguise. He did not recognize her. Not yet! As soon as she spoke, she might betray herself.

Captain Adams nodded. "Sounds plausible enough."

"But what about the gunpowder that was watered down last week? It would be just the likes of a lad like this to do such sabotage. You know how these colonists feel," Sergeant Gorely said.

Captain Adams nodded, thinking this over.

71

"I ain't done nothing to no gunpowder," Saura said as gruffly as she could. "And what I said was the truth. I'll swear it." She remembered Private Bickers's oath and raised her hand. "Want me to spit?"

"Not on the floor!" the captain exclaimed, looking at the ragamuffin with disdain. "I said I believe you. Now, where are your parents?"

The question caught her but she lied smoothly. "Ain't got none."

"Then where's your guardian?"

She had to be careful here lest she make a slip. "That's my grandma."

"And where is she?" he questioned a bit testily.

"Well...that's why I'm here. I was to come to Braintree from Boston an' wait here for her. She was to come from New York and get me and she'll be here in a day or two. But then I lost my coin for lodging...an' you know the rest." She was beginning to enjoy her first experience at bald-faced lying but it was cut short.

"Very well, we'll put you up here until she arrives."

"But I ain't got no coin!"

"I'll take care of that," the captain said.

"I don't take no charity."

"Then you can work."

"I'll just stay out in the woods."

The captain leaned forward, piercing her with his stare. "I'll brook no quarrel. It is too damp and cold in the forest and anyway we can't risk turning you loose. Since you might well be the troublemaker who watered down the barrels, we can keep an eye on you. When your grandmother comes, we will know the truth of your story." He dismissed the subject and turned to the sergeant. "Give the lad quarters."

"I'm afraid we're full up. There's three men in every room and I heard the quartermaster say that this inn couldn't squeeze in an earwig."

The captain thought for a moment. "Very well, bring a cot to my room and leave it there."

"I ain't sharing a room with no lobsterback!" Saura cried out and the two soldiers looked at her. When would she learn to think first?

72

"You got something against the king's army?" Sergeant Gorely asked, his suspicion flaring up again.

The silence grew thick. "And what if I do? Ain't a person entitled to an opinion? Or does your army prohibit against that too?"

"You really want to quarter this colonist?" Gorely asked.

The look the captain gave the two left no doubt that the discussion was at an end. "Have the lad bring up his bags. You do have luggage," the man asked her on second thought.

She gave him a hard stare. "And what if I don't? Have you got something to say about that?"

He shook his head, feeling sorry for this brave little lad, orphaned and penniless, who showed a thin facade of bravery under which lay fright and embarrassment. "Do you have a name?"

A name! "Willy," she said. It was the first to come to her mind and she supposed that her friend wouldn't mind if she borrowed it.

"All right, Willy. And have you eaten?"

"Had some bread and cheese," she answered, omitting the apple pie.

"You can join the midday meal after you've polished some boots. Show him the rags and boots," Captain Adams said, turning back to his ledgers in dismissal.

Saura sat in the corner of the large main hall, scraping mud off of heels and shining the leather boot tops. Sergeant Gorely had instructed her to give them a topnotch spit shine. However, spitting was foreign to Saura. It was not something that her ladylike training had included—but she did her best. The boots fairly gleamed after she had also applied mink-oil coatings. She had worked at the chore for two hours when Gorely came for her and sat her down at the long table with the men. She had grown hungry and the beef-and-beer stew and rye bread tasted good. As she sat there, dressed like a poor lad, she was afforded an entirely different view of her situation in life. Here she was ignored or rudely

73

pushed out of the way, while dressed in muslin, she was treated courteously and paid genteel attention.

Eventually she began to feel at ease. Apparently her disguise was as good as she had at first hoped and as long as she kept her cap pulled down around her ears, she felt safe enough. Perhaps this was for the best, after all. Soon the soldiers would leave and in the meanwhile the lie of her grandmother's coming made a perfect ruse. There was also the chance that she could slip the message to Stackpole and then escape before having to spend the night in the captain's room. That way no one would be the wiser. Her biggest problem and constant worry was that Peter would be concerned about her, and himself ill! But there was nothing that she could do about that now. Her current problem was to slip the precious envelope to the proprietor.

Stackpole fit his name perfectly, she thought. Tall as a corn stalk and nearly as slender, his clothes hung loosely on his angular limbs. A large nose in a long face ringed with straight brown hair added to his look of height. He served out ale and food with no comment, sure in the fact that the quartermaster would give him the right amount of coins for the services if not for the lodging. But bulk made up for smaller payment. And it also afforded him the chance to glean conversation for useful information.

There were three separate times when Saura seriously considered taking out the message and giving it to him. But each time the risk was too high and she dared not be foolhardy. She remembered Wilfred's horror at the sight of the letter in the presence of nearby soldiers; she was sure that Stackpole's reaction would be no different.

After the meal was over, she went back to the boots that had been thrown carelessly into a pile. Most of the soldiers departed, Captain Adams with them. There were still too many men about, she decided. She must wait until evening. Her chances might be better then; Gorely was still suspicious and kept a close eye on her. It took her the rest of the afternoon to finish the boots and she was nearly through when there was a commotion at the entrance of the inn. Several soldiers surged in, Captain Adams in their midst. His jacket was off and his usually immaculate appearance wrinkled and soiled. His white breeches were filthy with blood and dirt and his jaw was set in anger.

"I need no help! Take your hands off and I'll walk by myself." He limped in and struggled his way up the stairs, leaving the soldiers to stare after him. Gorely approached a private.

"Go to the local doctor and have him come. The captain would best be looked at."

"What happened?" Saura asked, her curiosity getting the better of her.

The sergeant barely glanced the way of the lad, answering instead the questioning looks of the proprietor and the others. "Kicked by an ornery supply mule."

Saura grimaced, thinking the situation painfully tinged with humor. No brave battle, this. She jumped as the sergeant barked at his men.

"No more lolling about in here! I want this inn cleared and all outside duties done." Once satisfied that the soldiers had left, he followed out after them.

Saura smiled to herself. This was her chance to deliver the letter of essay, she decided. She headed toward the long bar to seek out the proprietor but at that very moment the door banged open and the doctor entered. He was an elderly man with a balding gray pate and nose spectacles. Not much taller than herself, he was portly and carried a large black bag made of carpet. He neared the owner.

"What's so blasted important that my tea was interrupted, Stackpole?"

"The British captain was kicked in the leg by a mule, I gather."

"He deserved it, no doubt. All right. Where is he?"

"Upstairs in his room, or rather in my business suite. This lad can show you up." Stackpole looked at Saura and she sighed.

The doctor nodded and she led the way to the room, turning to leave when he stopped her. "I'll be needing a bucket of water. I forgot. Bring one up right away."

He knocked at the door and she hurried down the stairs and out to the pump. She worked furiously until the bucket was full and then carried it in. She struggled up the stairs with the water, sloshing some of it on the steps despite the scowl from Stackpole. She hurried down the hall to the door and rapped on it. Bade to enter, she did so, heaving the bucket inside.

The captain sat in a chair, his leg stretched out before him. His breeches had been removed and a towel cast carelessly across his body. Saura was shocked at this indecency before she realized that to him she was no more than a boy.

"Where do you want this?" she asked gruffly, indicating the bucket.

The doctor nodded to a nearby stool. She heaved it up and then turned again to leave. "Wait," he said. "I might need some help since my hands are full."

She squirmed uncomfortably but the captain nodded to a nearby chair. "Sit there, lad."

She could not help but notice the bruised and cut thigh that stretched out strong and bare before her. A half-moon cut streaked across the masculine leg, the muscle taut. She looked away, horribly embarrassed by this intimate view of Captain Adams.

"Wash your hands," the doctor ordered. "No use in getting the bandages all filthy with those dirty hands. Pour some water from that bucket into the bowl and lather up."

She did so, relieved at the distraction. She was careful to leave some dirt beneath the nails lest she have hands too feminine. She watched as the doctor rinsed out a cloth in the bucket, tingeing the water with blood. He cleaned out all the dirt from the wound, an action that must have been painful, Saura thought. But the captain did not make a sound; he just sat there solemnly watching the process. The bleeding finally stopped and the doctor studied the injury.

"Must have been some ornery mule to have cut in like that," he mused.

Captain Adams smiled grimly. "I'd have shot the

brainless beast if I'd had my revolver. But he ran off right after slamming me with his hind leg."

A perverse humor struck Saura and she stifled a smile. "You find that funny, Willy?" the captain asked sternly.

Her smile faded quickly and she said nothing. The doctor had her hand him the bandages, winding them around the propped-up leg. "You'll have a scar, you know. There's nothing much else I can do. It will be sore for a week or more so take a spot of rum for the pain. I'll be back in a couple of days to check it," he said, tying the ends tightly as Saura held the knot in place with her finger. "And stay off of it as much as you can. Have the lad do your fetching for you."

Captain Adams had noticed that the boy had kept his eyes averted from his leg as though it were difficult for him to look. He had even appeared pale under all that dirt. No doubt the youth was more tender than he appeared. As the doctor left, he turned to the lad. "Willy, help me to the bed, will you?"

Reluctantly she neared, letting him lean on her as he held the towel with one hand and limped to the bed, where he lay down. "Now, would you get that quilt for me?"

She unfolded the quilt covering the foot of the bedstead and helped him to pull it up. He handed her the towel, which she immediately dropped on a nearby chair. He instructed her to shut the drapes and the door into the sitting room, the same room that held the desk at which he had interviewed her. She drew the drapes, the room darkening, and then stepped to the sitting-room door. One of the drawers of the desk was open halfway. She could see a mess of dusty letters with Stackpole's name, or the inn's, on the envelopes. A sudden thought struck her and she glanced back to make certain that the captain's eyes were shut. If she were to slip the letter of essay in the drawer, Stackpole could gain excuse to receive it. All she would need do was to tell him where it was. Quickly she pulled the envelope from her vest, slipping it beneath the pile of old letters. Then she slid the drawer closed and pulled the door shut. It was as though a heavy burden had been lifted; her mission was half done!

"Anything else?" she asked, nearing the captain. He opened his eyes.

"I hadn't planned on napping but maybe I'll rest for a while. Don't you think it would be better if you met your grandmother with a clean face?" he asked with a yawn.

Saura stared at him hostilely for a moment. "She loves me the way I is," she said curtly.

The captain said nothing more but closed his eyes again, and she left. She went downstairs to find that Sergeant Gorely had returned and was finding new chores for her to do.

By the time of the evening meal, the main hall was full of soldiers, red jackets cast here and there along with rifles, swords and knapsacks. Saura still had not been able to get word to Stackpole and this fact alone began to wear on her nerves. If ever she could just once catch the busy man by himself!

Major Putnam arrived with the British army chaplain, a rather laconic-appearing man, the severity of his vestment bespeaking his calling. They sat down at a table to be served up pheasant with wine sauce and glazed carrots. Captain Adams limped down the stairs to join them at their table. He recounted the events of the past two days, including his experience with the supply mule. This brought out a smile from Major Putnam and a nod of sympathy from the chaplain, Major Berkely. Although somewhat better for his rest, the wound still hurt and he ordered up a large mug of rum.

"I am not normally a heavy imbiber," he said, offering a sort of apology to the chaplain, "but the local doctor recommended it for the wound."

Major Berkely nodded sagely. "Yes, indeed. Rum is the best cure for it. It is most medicinal and I use it often myself for headaches."

The troops, however, did not drink their ales for health reasons although they spoke of whiskey as a cure-all for any ailment. While their food was paid for by the king's gold, they paid for their own drink. This fact did not still the liquor from flowing freely. By the time the meal had ended, each soldier had drunk in at least two glasses of spirits, some even more than that. The outcome was lighter hearts and looser tongues.

Saura studied Captain Adams as he sat in his chair, his bad leg stretched out before him, his shiny black boots those that she had polished earlier in the day. They came up to the knee; his tight breeches were white and his red vest displayed silver buttons down the front. His white neckcloth and linen shirtsleeves were immaculate and his heavily buttoned red jacket was casually cast across the back of a nearby chair. His tricorn was black with a thin white edging of braid, and this too was set aside.

He ate and talked with a lazy and appealing ease. His dark brown eyes looked about the room, glancing off the scruffy lad who ate his meal with surprisingly good manners. The captain's hair was pulled away from his brow and caught back with a ribbon as was the hair of his brother soldiers. On him it was quite handsome, Saura thought, with his strong nose, well placed, and his expressive mouth. He certainly was every inch the soldier, she concluded. She was seated not far from him and she listened as best she could to the conversation among the officers.

"We'll be marching down to Boston then," the captain was saying and Major Putnam nodded.

"Yes. We'll leave the first of next week."

"After the Sabbath," the chaplain said. "Much better that the men march after a sermon. It bolsters their spiritual valor."

Saura's heart sank and the break stuck in her throat; she forced herself to swallow as she looked down into the crude plate filled with beans and bread. The first of next week! That was three days away. There would be no excuse for her mythical grandmother's absence and she did not know how much longer she would be able to hold out in this charade. She must take action tonight! The soldiers were imbibing a great deal of spirits and no doubt they would retire early. Then she would tell Stackpole where to find the cursed message and be

79

on her way. She had no desire to spend the night in the same room with the captain; it would be highly improper. Then she laughed at herself. Improper? Since when during the last twenty-four hours had she done one thing that was proper?

Despite the chaplain's strict-seeming nature, he appeared to be drinking a good deal of the spirits, Captain Adams thought. He himself was putting away his third serving of rum and ordering another. The pain was ebbing as a feeling of warmth and well-being spread over him. He knew, despite the fact that he still carried on a conversation well, that the rum was quite affecting him. Relaxed now, he watched as many of the men sauntered out the door to take the crisp evening air and a pipeful. Sergeant Gorely was looking about for service but the service was not very good at this understaffed country inn and the sergeant appeared to be growing a bit anxious. Adams noticed Gorely's gaze rest on the little orphaned youth and he ordered the lad to fetch him another mug of beer. The boy seemed to balk at this but then thought better of it and went off to do as told. The captain observed the lad as he carried the heavy mug, slopping foam, down the narrow aisle. Saura did not see the captain's outstretched leg until it was too late. She tripped over it and sent the beer flying. As Captain Adams gritted his teeth against the pain, gold-colored drink arced through the air and came in full contact with the face and front of Sergeant Gorely. Total silence prevailed as the lad scrambled to his feet, looking in horror between the captain's wounded leg and the sergeant's soaked face. A wave of snickering laughter swept across the hall, catching up everyone's humor except the sergeant's as it grew into boisterous laughter, finally dying down as the crowd looked on with interest. Captain Adams said nothing, the initial pain dulled again by the rum. But Gorely rose in a tower of anger.

"What kind of worthless baggage are you that you do not even watch your big feet?" he bellowed.

Saura's humiliation ignited into anger. "It was an accident," she ground out, not the least apologetic.

Captain Adams leaned forward. "That's right, sergeant. Take it easy on the child."

With further anger, she turned on him. "I ain't no babe. I can fend for myself."

He held up his hands as though in surrender and this brought new laughter. Gorely, on the other hand, still felt no humor in the situation. "You can just launder my uniform for me since you are the one what dirtied it."

"I ain't your slave, lobsterback," she retorted. "You can do your own laundry."

"You'll do it or I'll box your ears so smart you won't hear proper for a week!" As they stood glaring nose to nose in their anger, Captain Adams imagined that there was something familiar about the waif. "Now I have to go take a bath, thanks to the likes of a child barely off mother's milk!"

When the laughter died down, she backed away, wrinkling up her nose. "Smells to me like I done this camp a favor."

The regiment roared at this and a new flush of embarrassment spread up the back of Sergeant Gorely's neck. "Ain't you the kettle calling the pot black? If anyone in this room ever needed a bath, it was you! The grime's so thick, it looks like it'll need to be scraped off with a boot-scrape. And I know just the place to soak it off, if it don't poison the horses!"

As Gorely hoisted the lad into his arms, the merriment was infectious and half the troop led the way. Captain Adams smiled to himself as the lad gave the sergeant the fight of his life, bellowing in a shrill cry of fury and pulling the disgruntled Gorely's hair. He hadn't seen spirited argument and spunk like that since...

Major Putnam watched in surprise as the captain bolted out of his chair despite his injured leg and hurried toward the door, shoving interested spectators aside.

Gorely stood over the large watering trough that was beneath the huge, spreading oak. His goal, that of drenching the large-mouthed lad in the water, was not immediately apparent for his foe would not release the hold on hair and collar. But with a sudden rending sound, the handhold gave way, plummeting the boy into the trough, yet not before the overhanging branches of the tree had snatched off the large woolen cap. Coffee-colored hair tumbled down the lad's back only a second before he splashed into the water. And it became immediately apparent to all concerned that the youth, soaked through, with soot running off of a small face, was not a boy at all. The jovial merriment of a minute ago vanished. Captain Adams limped nearer, coming to stand arms akimbo before the trough, watching a girl rise spluttering out of the water. He swore under his breath, helping her out.

"What is the meaning of all this?" Major Berkely called from the doorway and the soldiers parted to let him through.

"I'm afraid that this lad, who has been waiting here for his grandmother, is no boy after all," the captain told him.

As the two majors, the captain and a crowd of soldiers stood around Saura and stared at her, she looked down at her clothes, water streaming into a puddle at her feet. Her situation, difficult before, was now impossible.

The small storage room was filled with kitchen supplies as well as extra bedding and linens. Shelves reached to the high ceiling. A barrel of whiskey, casks of salt and spices and the wet wool blanket wrapped around Saura combined to make a musty smell. There was one small window, high placed and with bars over it. And only one door. The window gave a tiny glimpse of orange sky as the sunset flamed to death but Saura paid it no notice. She sat atop a barrel, her chin in her hands, uncomfortable in her wet clothes. There was little comfort to be had and she was miserable. As she sat in the dim little storage room, her fate was being decided without. And whatever it might be, it would not be pleasant.

She had been brought before the Majors Berkely and Putnam, her hands clasped tightly together as water plopped from her clothes onto the wooden floor. Except for the captain and Sergeant Gorely, the soldiers waited without while the chaplain searched for an explanation to the unusual circumstances. The interview had not gone well and she cringed as she remembered it.

"Let me see if I understand this," the chaplain had said in a severe voice. "This boy is not a boy at all but a young woman. Quite shocking, I must say. Explain your actions, young lady."

Saura stood there silently, staring down at the floor, until Major Putnam spoke. "Maybe you can shed some light on this, Captain Adams."

"Sergeant Gorely found him...excuse me, her, hiding in a supply wagon. He brought the lad to me and I will admit he lied quite profusely. I believed him to be an orphan waiting for his grandmother to come fetch him. That was her story, and quite convincing."

Major Berkely stared at her. "And is this true? Are you an orphan waiting for your grandmother?"

When again she did not answer, fearing to speak one of the lies that formed wild plots of excuse in her brain, the captain spoke up again. "If I may, sir. I know of this girl. While in Greenhollow, I happened to see her. Her father is the local blacksmith there. Miss Ainsley, does your father know you are here?"

She looked up at him, piercing him with eyes dark with anger, knowing that it had been foolish to assume that he might not betray her and her father. "No," she said.

He sat down, resting his leg and taking a deep draught of a new tankard of rum. "I thought not. Her father is quite a respectable man, widowed, and has the difficult task of raising a headstrong daughter by himself."

She stared daggers at him, then looked away, a haughty tilt to her chin. Despite the fact that her hair fell in wet ribbons down her back and her clothes were wet, she was still very pretty. Captain Adams marveled that he had been so blind to her disguise. No doubt it was the soot.

"This still does not explain what she is doing here among our soldiers and dressed like a boy," the chaplain said, leveling his eyes on her. "And unless you tell us otherwise, I will have to assume that you were spying, which is an act of treason."

She looked up in alarm. "I was not spying! What could I learn? I tried not to stay here but the captain would not let me go as I desired. He is the one who forced me to remain in your midst."

Captain Adams nodded. "That is true. But it doesn't explain why you are dressed like a boy. You weren't trying to run away by any chance?"

She looked at him in stunned surprise. He had given her the perfect out without even knowing it! "And what if I was?"

"Ha! I thought so. When you are returned to your father, who is no doubt sick with worry, I hope he disciplines you properly," the captain said.

"A wayward child is a sorry sight!" Major Berkely asserted. "Honor thy mother and thy father that thy days may be long upon the land which the Lord thy God giveth thee. That is one of the Ten Commandments, young lady, and you are grievously wrong to betray your father so. Likely he spared the rod too often in raising you."

"He did fine," she ground out angrily. "He didn't raise me, anyway. I was raised in Bristol!" she added haughtily and then worried that she should not have revealed this bit of her past.

"Indeed?" Major Berkely asked. "A British girl? I do not understand."

"Well...when my mother died, I was entrusted to the care of my godparents. They raised me in Bristol. I even have a brother serving there in His Majesty's service," she confided, hoping to win over the chaplain.

"Godparents. Very good. I have a godson of my own. A lovely custom," the chaplain nodded.

"But that still does not explain your strange clothes, you dressing like a boy," Major Putnam spoke up. "Why have you done this foolish thing, run away from home and all?"

What could she say? She had no excuse to give without betraying her true intent. Suddenly she had a flash of inspiration. "I ran away to join the army," she said coolly.

"What?" several voices asked in unison.

"It's true! I don't like being treated like a lady, with Sunday suitors and prissy knitting circles. Why can a woman not ride and shoot like a man?" Did Captain Adams smile into his cup?

"Well!" the chaplain exclaimed, leaning back in his chair. "This is most extraordinary. And yet I am quite touched that you would want to fight for the king. But you must understand, my dear, that a woman can help just as much at home, sewing uniforms, gathering supplies and offering help and support from the sidelines of the trouble, where it is safe. You go home and be a good girl and pray for our forces. That is the best thing you can do."

She nodded at this, suppressing a smile. She began to feel relief, believing herself to have talked her way out of her difficulties.

"Begging your pardon, sir," the sergeant said, removing his tricorn. "I think the army that this lass wanted to join was that of the colonial rebels. When I found her in the supply wagon, I was most suspicious. Just last week two barrels of powder were watered down—and there she was! And she spoke in anger, calling us lobsterbacks, redcoats and other unkind names. It has been obvious to me where her sympathies lie. She may have come from Bristol. Whether she lied about that or not, I don't know. But it is obvious that she is a colonist through and through. I've encountered enough of them to know a rebel spirit when I see one, sir."

Saura's heart sank like a stone as the chaplain's countenance visibly hardened. "Is what the sergeant says true?"

She clamped her lips together tight, fearing further denial since Captain Adams had witnessed her attitudes before. When would she learn that lying was folly?

The chaplain stared at her sternly, finally reaching into the folds of his jacket and producing a small Bible. He set it on the table, ordering her to place her right hand on it and raise her left hand. "Swear that you are not a colonist nor in sympathy with them. But before you do, let me caution you that you are accountable before God to tell the truth. Swear it!"

With trembling fingers she reached out, placing her hand on the worn black cover. If she were a true revolutionist, a brave spy, she would swear it with ease. But her strict upbringing and many hours spent in church would not let her take a vow lightly. Finally she removed her hand, staring down at the table.

"I cannot."

So it was that she was locked into the storeroom, her sopping-wet jacket, vest and the troublesome cap cast aside, the smelly wool blanket wrapped around her. On the other side of the heavy door, they were trying her case and would certainly pass down judgment.

"It is a shameful display of a lack of discipline," the chaplain stated. "And yet you say that her father is a good man?"

"What I saw of him," the captain said. "A God-fearing man, a good working man, but a colonist."

"Shameful!" the chaplain cried. "No doubt that is where she has learned such fanciful ideas. Still, I do not think she is a bad girl, just misled. After all, she would not take a wrong oath on the Bible and that speaks of good teaching and breeding. But it is our responsibility to see that she is set on a proper course, one on which she is supervised by a man of loyalty to the king. She spoke of a brother but, sadly, he is still in England. Therefore it is up to us."

"How do you plan to put her on that proper course?" Captain Adams asked with interest.

"H-m-m. I do not know exactly. Major Putnam, you have a daughter of about the same age, do you not? A fine girl if I recollect aright, and very correct. What would you recommend?"

Major Putnam coughed, finishing the last of his drink. "Well, I do not know exactly. Her care is quite out of my hands now, you see. She was wed last year and hence is taken care of by her husband, a lieutenant serving in London. Last I heard, she was at home, sewing baby clothes."

"I see," the chaplain said as he finished his draught of rum, taken solely for his headache, just gained. He sat quietly in thought for a minute and then looked up, thumbing through his Bible. "Ah, here it is, right in Ephesians," and he began reading aloud. "'Wives, submit yourself unto your husbands, as unto the Lord. For the husband is the head of the wife, even as Christ is the head of the church.... Therefore as the church is subject unto Christ, so let the wives be to their own husbands in everything.' There, that says it all. Let her become a dutiful wife and she will no longer cleave unto her father and his colonist views. Once wed to a king's man, she will have no choice but to receive the proper guidance. With a British soldier for husband, having say over her every action and thought she will truly become a ward of the king's army. And she will lose those fanciful, foolish ideas and settle down."

Captain Adams put down his empty tankard, fearing that the rum had dulled his wit. "Do you mean to say that you will wed her to one of our soldiers?"

The chaplain brought his hands together in a prayerful pose. "Truly inspiration from above. That is exactly what I propose to do."

"But you have seen the strong will of the maid. She will not bend easily."

"She will under the heat of right."

"Would it not be best to just return her to her father?"

"So that she may run off again to join the rebel cause, perhaps falling into harm? If she does indeed come from Bristol and have a brother serving in the army there, we have a responsibility to the mother country. And I swear that I shall see it through! Let us get this matter over with."

"But what shall you do for her husband?" asked Major Putnam. "I mean, how will you pick a soldier willing to wed her? Will you call for volunteers?"

"No! Most men find themselves frightened of the altar, even under the best of circumstances. This is a call of duty. Any man should be honored to take this responsibility for his brother soldier in Bristol. And since a married man's wages are increased, they should— any one of them—be happy to wed the wench."

"Well," Major Putnam said, "she is a comely lass, whether in lads' breeches or no. Perhaps it will work, even if she isn't in a skirt."

"Exactly!"

"The girl will not agree," the captain said.

"Whether she does or not," the chaplain replied sternly, "is of no matter. But to make it more agreeable, we shall let her choose. Now let's hurry on with this so that we may retire. It is nearly dark outside. Major, if you and the sergeant will order all single men forward and explain the situation to them, we can be done with it." As the two men stepped out to speak to the soldiers, the chaplain turned to the captain. "Bring in the girl."

Saura had cast off her soggy shoes and was sitting atop the barrel, her feet tucked beneath her. She glanced up as the door opened, letting in a beam of yellow lamp-light. The captain stepped in.

"You can come out now," he said and she cast off the blanket, walking into the main room with as much pride as she could muster. She fully expected to be imprisoned as a traitor. She stood before the long table, her hands clasped together carefully.

"We have given your offenses careful consideration, Miss Ainsley," the chaplain said, having obtained her name from the captain. "And we have been deciding what to do with you." He paused here for a moment for effect. "Since your father's sympathies have led you in a wayward direction despite your earlier upbringing, we think it best that you be given guidance. It is time that a young woman of your age...how old are you?"

"Nearly eighteen."

"Yes, well, it is time that a young woman of your age settle down and domesticate herself. Once you are busy caring for a husband and children, you will have little time for such fanciful ideas as running off to join the army. Even though you will reside in your father's house for the time being, you will at least receive better guidance. Cleave unto your husband and leave your father's house, if you understand what I mean."

"Do you mean," she asked in surpirse, "that you will turn me over to my father with the stipulation that I wed?"

"No, indeed! For no doubt the husband your father would choose for you would be no better guardian than himself. For this purpose you will wed one of our splendid British soldiers and thereby be led back onto a proper course of upbringing."

She stared at him in shocked silence, finally regaining her voice. "A redcoat?"

"A British soldier of the king's army."

"A lobsterback?"

"That is the exact attitude that has led you into such harmful straits! A firm hand and a will stronger than your own are just what is needed. The unmarried men of my troop are being gathered and you will be allowed to pick one."

"And if I do not?"

He leveled a brimstone stare at her, speaking out each word clearly. "Then you will be hanged for treason, as a spy."

Saura's knees felt weak as her resolve melted. There was no hope left. Any kindness she might have seen in Major Berkely had hardened like a drop of candle wax in cold water.

The regiment of twenty-three unmarried soldiers filed glumly into the large room of the inn. Dimly lit by a few low-placed lamps and a small fire in the stone hearth, the room flickered with shadows. The other soldiers, flooded with relief at their exclusion from this mission, milled about the walls, eager to watch. Major Putnam, a firm believer in wedded bliss, had explained the full situation to the men. His words had not been taken happily. Some, who had drunk more than they should, found it difficult to understand that the harmless lad who had provided a little merriment in the trough—and who was after all no lad—had turned out to be such a serious threat to their well-being. Despite the large number who now filled the room, it was unusually quiet, the only sound being an occasional cough or the shuffle of feet. The men glanced around to find the center of this disturbance, their eyes coming to rest, one by one, on the small figure standing rigidly by the chaplain's table. A sudden light of interest flickered into the steadfast gazes.

The girl stood staring into the charred fireplace, paying them no attention, her back as straight as a rod. The jacket and vest discarded, she wore a white linen shirt, too large, the sleeves rolled up. This was tucked into tight-fitting dark breeches, shameful apparel for a young lady, yet in itself presenting a whole new view of her. The lithe curves were quite out of place in the masculine attire, the feet stockinged and small. The shirt was open at the neck, revealing a white throat; the face was now free from dirt. The chin was held high; hair, tangled in a silken mass of brown, cascaded down her back. The soft curve of mouth, never before noticed on the lad, was held primly in check. The eyes, as dark as chocolate, stared into the distance, giving no notice of their shuffling presence. The only sign of agitation was in the small white hands, tightly clenched.

Major Berkely stood up, walking before the men. "No doubt Major Putnam has explained the situation. This is a serious responsibility and I expect the best behavior, no matter the outcome. This young woman will choose one of you as a husband and she will then be placed in your charge. Your income will be increased and you will be expected to support her, although during maneuvers she will reside at her father's house in Greenhollow, not far from here. Once a ward of the British army, she will be led down the straight and narrow and I would caution whomever she chooses to guide her with a firm but gentle hand. Very well, let us proceed. Come, miss. Look them over and decide which one appeals to you as a fitting husband."

During the chaplain's discourse, all eyes had kept flitting to the fair young woman who was the center of unprecedented effort. Now all eyes remained fixed on her. "Come now! I told you it was either this course or death as a traitor. Make up your mind."

"One fate is not better than the other," Saura called out dispassionately. "Have them turn and face the wall."

"What?" asked the chaplain in surprise.

"Have them turn and face the wall so that I might set about the ugly task of choosing!"

The stunned officers looked at each other for a moment. Then Major Berkely nodded at Captain Adams, who had been watching the whole procedure with even more interest than the others. "About, face!" he called and the long line of soldiers snapped about quickly as one. He himself stood at the far end to make certain that they were aligned in straight formation.

Saura finally turned toward them and came forward, nearing the men but not looking at them. She answered the chaplain's questioning stare. "It matters not to me which redcoat I am forced to wed. One is not better than the next." Slowly she walked down the line, past their straight backs and tied-back hair. Few were still in their uniform jackets and they all looked the same to her. They were men, strangers, taller than herself, standing shoulder to shoulder. The magnitude of her despicable situation hit her full blow, shattering her reserve of strength. Halfway down the line her knees threatened to buckle, her courage seeming to drain from her very fingertips, hanging limply by her sides. She stopped, able to go no farther.

Chaplain Berkely approached. "Have you made the decision?"

She nodded down the line, not able to see the end of it in the dim light. "Just call out the one on the last. He'll do as well as any other."

The heads in the line whipped to the right to catch a view of the soldier thrown such recent fortune. A muffled murmur arose as Captain Adams lolled forward, a look of questioning surprise on his face.

Ne're take a wife till thou hast a house
(and a fire) to put her in.

—POOR RICHARD

# Chapter V

"I BELIEVE THAT Captain Adams was merely checking
the line," Major Putnam said as Saura stared at the
young officer in amazement.

Major Berkely looked at the tall captain, well-built
with an alert face despite his recent intake of drink.
Well-bred, intelligent, the officer commanded the troops
with ease, leadership worn comfortably by him. The
girl too was smart for a woman and much stronger
willed than he had earlier believed. No ordinary man
would have the strength to tame this young lady. And
her strong character would be an asset when rightly
directed. Everyone waited a surprisingly long time for
the chaplain to speak.

"The decision has been called out and I am not one
for changing a command. What do you say, Captain
Adams? Does the decision stand?"

All eyes, including Saura's, turned to the captain. He glanced up, his brown eyes meeting the brown in another's and holding for a moment. He lifted his empty tankard as though in a mock toast. "Why not?"

Saura groaned inwardly. The buffoon was drunk. A cheer of sorts, composed more of catcalls and hoots than actual hurrahs, went up. This was silenced right away by the chaplain's stern glare; the formal line was dismissed, the men gathering about the walls in a circle. Major Berkely then motioned the couple together, his back to the hearth. Major Putnam stood on the other side of the captain, removing the drink from his hand. The chaplain placed Saura's and Seth Adams's hands together and she felt her own small, cold fingers encircled in the bold warmth of the captain's.

The ceremony was brief. There were admonitions to honor and obey, to live under the guidance of God and to multiply and replenish in this new land. When the time came for her to give assent, her teeth were too tightly clenched to answer and so the chaplain did it for her. Captain Adams was not as difficult, although he had to be reminded to answer. When it was over, Major Berkely nodded.

"You may kiss your wife now, Captain."

Before she could take in a breath to protest, she was swept up into the captain's tight embrace. As he bent her head back, his mouth came down over hers in the ritual's acclaim. His lips pressed into hers, the warm taste of rum flooding through her. A long and lingering kiss, it spread heat to her very marrow, strong as a swallow of hot whiskey. She felt the strength go out of her limbs, already weak with the day's trauma. When he finally released her, it took all her willpower to stand and he had to steady her for a moment before she pulled away. Now a real cheer went up from the men and in a movement of sudden swiftness, Captain Adams swept her into his arms and surged up the stairs, two steps at a time. For a man who was half-drunk, he was surprisingly able. The chaplain watched in surprise, then lowered his eyebrows and turned away in approval. His efforts were complete.

When he had made it to the door of his room, Captain Adams stopped in puzzlement and considered kicking it in with his foot. But despite the numbing effects of the liquor, his leg still throbbed and he thought better of it. Instead he struggled with his hand at the knob until the door pushed open; then he staggered back two steps before stumbling through the door and shutting it with his back. The room was dark. Its only light came from the dying embers in the hearth, which glowed red; there was no light through the window since clouds hid the moon; a night wind had arisen, whining at the window latchings.

Saura could hear the man's steady breathing, its warmth brushing her cheek. She had felt exhausted, too drained to struggle, but now as renewed adrenaline shot into her veins, she felt strength return to her limbs. Above her head he spoke, his tongue a bit thick.

"Your breeches are still damp."

She struggled out of his arms, sliding her feet to the floor. But he did not release her from his hold and his arms were still around her as she tossed back angrily, "What did you expect, after nearly being drowned in a blasted trough?"

He chuckled softly into the darkness, his arms tightening a bit in a manner of careless friendship. She placed her palms against him, feeling his lean ribs beneath the light chambray fabric of his shirt, pushing until the bindings of his arms were broken and she was free. She shivered; the second-story room was much cooler than the main hall and her damp clothing added to the chill. The captain was reluctant to have her free of his grasp for there had been a pleasantness in holding her small form. The sweet smell of woman that lodged in her hair, that tangled mass so close beneath his face, still lingered in his nostrils. There was a sudden intimacy between them as the darkness removed the last of her masculine disguise. He was fully aware that she was not a lad but a woman, well-made.

"Do we stand in the darkness till the cock crows?" she asked angrily and he reached for the candle, carrying it to the embers until the wick caught, the flame wavering into life. It was not much light but as the yellow taper sent the shadows into the corners, he knelt and tossed kindling onto the low blaze. Flames licked their way into the wood and the room gained more light still. Then he stood, turning to see her eyeing him with a mingling of dislike and distrust—and something else that he could not fathom.

One of the sleeves of Saura's shirt had come unrolled and the cuff hung past her fingertips, the whole blouse looking humorously large. But the breeches, fitting even tighter than before because they were wet, were irritatingly distracting. Her hair tumbled about her shoulders in unruly disarray, curling tangles of brown in dire need of a combing. But it was a manner in which a gentleman seldom saw a young woman and there was something about it that stirred a mild aching in him. He became irritated at this disturbance of feeling and suddenly he glared at her. "This is a fine mess you've made for us, Miss Ainsley."

She looked at him in surprise, disappointed that there was no hint of sympathy. She felt a kindling of anger and arched her brows, bringing her hands to her hips. "I? Might I remind you, sir, that it was your foolhardy actions that kept me here at the inn against my desires? Had you not meddled, Captain, I should have long been gone."

"To join the colonial conspiracy. H-m-m, I remember that!"

"To have returned to my father, having tasted once of freedom. And that is exactly what I intend to do. If you will give me a moment's aid and let me out of this inn, I shall return home and we shall both be free of this bargain for which neither of us bartered."

"Major Berkely would like that!"

"Major Berkely is a meddling fanatic. Is your army full of nothing but meddlers who impede others?" She turned away from him in anger.

"You should be grateful to the goodly chaplain," he retorted. "A harder man would have seen you tried and hanged as a spy—which I'm not so sure you aren't. Your actions have been most suspicious and I was gullible at first but now I shall watch you most closely; should I see any cause for thinking you a traitor, I shall be forced to take action."

"Tory!" she ground out as though it were the vilest curse she could find. She was about to say more when she stopped, caught for the moment by a succession of sneezes.

"There!" He nodded sagely. "Wet breeches and that is what happens to you. I cannot return you to your father's house ill. You'd best be out of them," he said, nodding again as if in agreement to his own thought.

She glared at him in disbelief. "That drink must still befuddle your brain, redcoat!"

He stepped forward, suddenly angry, taking her arms in a firm grasp. He stared down into eyes so brown they looked black in the night, catching the golden gleam of candle flame. "That is enough of your sharp tongue, Saura. You forget that this redcoat is your husband." She stared up at him as he continued. "You have fared better than you might for I am a gentleman where some of the other men are of rougher nature. They are soldiers first. You would do well to court with kindness the man who holds your fate." He loosened his grip, his thumbs rubbing gently along her arms. "You are wet and cold and it is for this reason I ask you to take off your things. Go there, behind the screen, and I will seek out something else for you to wear."

Saura suddenly felt bone-weary, the discomfort of the wet clothes growing as the wind increased its howl without. Shivering, she pulled away from him and stepped behind the large dressing screen. She stripped off her shirt and breeches and then her wet stockings, the cold air wrapping about her as she stood in the darkness. She felt very vulnerable, the shadow of night not enough of a cover. Presently a white garment was tossed over the screen, falling into her grasp. Of soft, silky fabric, she examined it, discovering it to be a silk nightshirt.

"Is this the best you can do?" she bit out as she pulled it over her head and slid her arms into the long sleeves.

"That is all I could find," he answered lazily from

the other side as she fastened the small buttons in a
line from her naval to her throat. "It's my best nightshirt, although hardly appropriate for a wedding night,
I suppose." At this she ceased for a moment in rolling
up the sleeves, then continued the chore. The shirt hung
off her shoulders and the hem reached her feet, whereas
the captain would wear it at calf length. But still, it
was modest and Saura had to admit that it felt good to
be out of the soggy clothes. She peeked around the corner of the screen. "The robe, sir?"

He looked at the small oval of face that peered at
him and shrugged with a smile. "I said it was the best
I have to offer. I'm afraid that I have no dressing robe."

"A silk nightshirt and no dressing robe?"

"This is an army, not a cotillion. And actually that's
the only nightshirt I can boast of. I prefer to wear no
such foppery when I sleep."

Even in the darkness of the room she could not emerge
in such a thin garment. She snatched up the comfortable folded at the foot of the nearby bed, wrapping it
about her. Then she stepped out, bringing with her the
wet clothes and spreading them before the crackling
fire. They would soon be dry and she could don them
again. This done, she turned around to find the captain
standing close behind her. He held two glasses of amber
liquid, extending one to her. "I do not drink spirits, sir."

"Not even for medicinal purposes? My father often
prescribed brandy to ward off a chill. There was always
a decanter on his desk for just such a purpose." He
swayed a bit and steadied himself against a chair. She
took the glass, sipping from the warming liquid, thinking that if the captain drank in more spirits, he might
soon fall into a drunken stupor that would allow her to
slip away. He smiled and raised his glass to her, then
tossed the liquid down and poured himself some more.

"You know," he said slowly, "I cannot believe that I
stared right at you when you were dressed like a boy
and didn't notice the deception. How did such a soft
mouth miss my notice?"

He sat down, struggling to remove his boots, a disconcerting effort with the impediments of drink and an

injured leg. She watched as he applied the bootjack, the muscles of his back pulling against his shirt as he bent to the task. This done, he stretched out before the fire, leaning back into the chair.

As she stood in the center of the room watching him, she felt small and alone. Frightfully alone with this large stranger whose name had been forged into her own a short while ago downstairs. The truth, also frightening, was that this man was her lawful husband. By every law in England and America, she was now his property. And he had every right to lay claim to that property. A gentleman, yes. But a man also. She pulled the quilt tighter about her throat with one hand and brushed her hair from her face with the other. Her fingers caught in the snarled tangles.

Seth had been studying her actions, his eyes dark coals in the tan of his face; he nodded at the dressing table. "You are welcome to my comb and brush."

She went to the table, seating herself before the narrow mirror. Laid out were his toilette articles and she picked up his comb; Seth watched her as she ran it through the dark tresses, freeing them of snarls. The comb turned the locks about her face into silk but the back was more difficult, falling in disarray past her shoulders. She struggled with the comb until a reflection, tall and dark behind her, drew her eyes to the mirror. His hand moved past her to the table and caught up the brush and he silently stroked it down the length of her hair. Saura's hands fell to rest as she stared at the man standing behind her who steadily moved the brush through her hair. He was careful, gently coaxing out the tangles she herself had dealt with more harshly. His stroke smoothed out the static, his fingers brushing against her back before he took his hand away. The task done, he still stood behind her, his shirt, gleaming whitely in the mirror, open down the front, revealing a chest well-tanned and lightly furred with dark hair. Their gaze met in the glass and she looked at him with a question in her eyes.

"When I called you out of the line in error, why did

you agree?" She asked so softly that she feared he had not heard until he answered.

"My reasons were more than one."

"I was the one forced to it. 'Twas not you threatened with the hangman's noose."

"The chaplain is my major also."

She nodded, seeming to understand this. "I see. I am one to understand a soldier doing his duty."

His hands came to rest upon her shoulders, a smile coming slow to his lips. "'Twas more than duty made me forge the bonds." The heat of his touch spread through her and she was no longer cold. She struggled with her thoughts.

"Captain Adams, as you can see, my situation is dire. It must be obvious to you that I did not agree to this marriage—it was forced by the times. The threat of hanging made me weaken and I stood as the vows were made. Thus I ask you," and at this point she rose to face him, her expression earnest with appeal, "to act as a gentleman."

He quirked an eyebrow at her as though in question. "And?"

She took in a deep breath. "Release me from my obligation as wife. Let me slip away now and return to the home of my father. And I shall give my word to you that I shall nevermore stray away from his guidance or be a disobedient daughter! Should not such a promise prove that I shall not be a threat to your army again?"

He stared at her for a long while and she began to grow warm under his look. Then he said, "You desire to return to your father and abandon all plots?"

"Indeed! It is the truth," she said eagerly. "Then you shall be free of any responsibility toward me and all shall be solved."

"If I release you from your wifely obligation, it shall be the same as though released from the vows themselves, our marriage being neither consecrated nor consummated," he said thoughtfully.

"True! And then you shall be free and I shall have no hold on you or you on me. You shall be able to follow

*100*

the course of your life as you desire and never even see me again."

He pondered her words and then neared her. She looked up anxiously for his agreement and he bent down, his mouth coming in full and sudden contact with hers. Shock at his action was washed away with the heat of the touch and she started back. She stumbled away from his grasp, dragging the heavy comfortable with her. She moved hastily but the drink had not slowed his skill and he caught her again, turning her around to face him.

"As to your question, I shall be a gentleman," he said softly. "A gentleman keeps his word and observes his half of all agreements."

The impact of his words stung her as would a slap and she tried to jump away, to escape, to run blindly out the door. But the quilt had twisted itself around her and as she tried to pull free, it became entangled around Seth's ankles also, jerking his feet from the floor and sending them tumbling onto the bed. Saura kicked at the traitorous quilt, squirming away from it and her husband's reach. But his hand shot out and caught her ankle, causing her to let out a scream. The sound brought him surging forward, trying to subdue her outcry. He pulled her down beneath him, the flimsy silk of the nightshirt little protection as their bodies came together. She was softness beneath the steel of his weight and his mouth pressed hard over hers, silencing her sound, the wash of weakness that fanned through her causing a moment's surrender. Slowly he pulled his mouth away and looked down at her face.

"Do not cry out!" he ordered in a fierce whisper. "Do you wish the entire inn to think that I take my wife by force?"

"Do you?" she questioned in a half sob. That one sob caused more to follow and then she could not stop them. Her fingers brushed away a trickle of tear and others that verged on spilling over. She coughed them back, an aching lump in her throat.

"Did I hurt you?" he asked in concern, his breath hot

against her cheek as he loomed above her, his manliness urging her compliance.

She shook her head, blinking the wetness from her lashes. "It is just that this has been a terrible day and I fear its outcome. If only you would listen to my reasoning and see that this union can never be!"

He looked at her in dismay. "There is another man?"

"No," she said slowly, "but there will be. And he shall not be a Tory."

He chuckled softly, his mouth nearing hers, and he spoke against her lips. "'Tis the uniform then and not the man you protest. Think of it as a marriage of two politics. To a Tory or a Patriot, it matters little which uniform lies unused, tossed across the back of a chair."

Desire flamed in his eyes and his mouth came down then, molding soft lips against her own, and an uncontrollable shudder ran through her. She had no artillery for combatting this siege. Slowly he pulled back, his mouth releasing its tender prisoner, and he penetrated her with his gaze. She felt smothered in the heat of his searing embrace, the steel strength of manliness a foreigner to her. His fingers brushed across her cheek, one fingertip tracing the outline of her lips.

What is happening to me? she wondered frantically as the merciless sweeping of heat left her weak. His lips traveled to her throat, seeking out the delicate pulse there, and her whole body shuddered. Saura fought against the deliciousness that excited her at the feel of his hand slipping beneath the nape of her neck. But he is a Tory! she thought, as he drew her mouth to his again. Then, as the sensation of his lips on hers flooded her senses: Ah, but he is a man.

As a person drowning, she clutched at reason. He was a soldier, fighting against the cause to which she was dedicated. Yet, as the womanhood was awakened in her and an avalanche of new longings threatened to engulf her, a voice countered: But he is my husband, legally wed.

She, bright daughter of the revolution, was overcome with the intense desire to surrender to this captain for the king, as that dark soldier loomed above her, his hoarse voice breathing warm into her ear.

"Be my wife," he pleaded.

As without a will of their own, her arms lifted, and slipped about his neck. She could think of no rational argument against the sweeping want she felt for him. There was, finally, no entreaty against this surrender to desire. She looked into the handsome face etched with passion and in one last attempt at petition, she cried, "Did you not promise to be a gentleman?"

"Yes," he said against her lips. "I am a man, Saura. And I will be gentle."

The autumn wind had caught up rain clouds as though they were mere playthings, clapping them together for a streak of lightning and the ensuing rumble. The rain was not heavy but its falling quieted the land, trickling tears down the windowpanes of the Musket Inn. Neither was it a steady rain, but started and stopped at random throughout the night.

The slumber that had fallen so heavily on Saura was slow to depart. But when another flash of lightning sheathed the room in white, her eyes opened. The slow drumroll of thunder reached her ears. The bed she slept in was warm, a comfort so pleasant that it took her a moment before she remembered.

Awareness shot into her veins, stirring her blood. She lay next to a man, the weight of his long frame pinning her to him. The touch of his skin against hers sent a flush through her. In the dim light from the embers she watched him. This man, this Tory captain, was now her husband in more than name.

She bit her lip to check the emotions that threatened to spill forth. Pleasure and sorrow certainly had never yielded a more bittersweet dreg! This man was everything that a woman could desire. This man was also a captain in His Majesty's army, a leader of all that she had come to work against.

Her mission, taken on the moment's spur, was vastly important. Not only had she spoiled its purpose, she had betrayed its cause. The delivery of the message was not a child's light play, some mischief of spying, but a mission upon which the very fate of the Sons of Liberty rested. During all those nights when she had listened at the meetings—unnoticed in the shadows, learning of her new country—and during all those times when she had listened to her father's dreams of the land that he had never seen, she too had dreamed. She had wanted more than anything else to help fulfill the birth of the new government, one of freedom for the people. And that simple letter of essay, so carelessly given into her hands, had been her chance. Yet she had been waylaid and she had tarried too long when she should have had her mind lit to her purpose. She derided men who were fools of passion, yet now she saw the name-caller as the greatest blunderer of all. There would be no help for her failure, and her betrayal.

She studied Seth Adams now—deep in slumber and the cause of her difficulties from the very beginning. What had she allowed to happen? Even at this moment his hand rested comfortably about her waist, the familiarity of his embrace signature to their physical contract.

Another slice of lightning split the blackness, leaving the room darker than before. Her soul felt equally black.

Carefully she slid from under his grasp, fearful that she might awaken him but he did not stir. She moved out from under the quilt, coming to stand on the cold floor. She shivered, glancing back at the bed where Seth slumbered deeply under the influence of the rum. She steeled her resolve and crept to the fire. There was little warmth there and slowly she undid the buttons of the nightshirt until it fell from her shoulders. She folded it neatly, laying it on the dressing table and fingering the thin fabric for a second before its release.

Then she struggled into her stockings, cloyingly cold, as well as the breeches, not quite free of dampness, and her shirt. She could not dispel the memory of the bed's warmth and hurried into the adjoining sitting room. She opened the drawer as slowly as she could, searching in the blackness for the special letter. How she wished for a candle, or even a match, but she dared do no more than fumble through the drawer. There were so many dusty letters there; she pulled out several, peering at them in the dark, but was unable to identify any one of them. She simply could not make out the letter or even be sure it was there. The flashes of lightning were too quick to be of any help. She began to grow frantic and stopped in her movements as Seth moaned in his sleep, reaching out for her. She shut the drawer. She could not risk his waking. She would have to assume the letter was still there.

She crept to the door, turning the knob and praying that it would not creak. She slipped out, closing the door carefully behind her on the memories of the night. She hurried down the hall and stairs, noiseless in her stockinged feet. She stopped at the foot of the stairs. The guard on duty was sitting before the fireplace, his feet propped up, his eyes closed; his grunting snore assured her of safety. Cautiously she moved to the storage room where she had been locked up, finding her vest, coat and boots right where she had left them. Hurriedly she donned them; they were cold, the boots still wet. She snatched up Willy's woolen cap, tucking in her tresses and pulling the hat down tight.

There was no one else in the hall except the sleeping guard and she stopped at Stackpole's desk, grabbing up paper and quill. She scribbled: "In your upstairs desk is a letter of essay." Then she folded the paper and put it in the proprietor's letter box. It was inconspicuous enough, she hoped, and in any event, it was the best she could do. Silently she slipped outside, glancing around before heading for the livery.

Rain still fell sparsely, slapping into the muddied courtyard. The air smelled fresh and the wind had stopped its earlier howling. To the east the hills dawned gray, speaking of early morning. But there would be no vivid sunrise today.

Captain Seth Adams lay still in the warmth of his bed listening to the dull roll of thunder. He watched from beneath his nearly closed lids as his bride of less than a day searched through the desk drawer. He stirred and gave a pretended murmur, his eyes following her as she hurried from the room and shut the door between them. He listened for a moment but her stockinged feet gave no sound of retreat and he tossed the covers off. Chill air struck his skin as he sat up, his thigh throbbing in rhythm with his head. Last night's medicinal drink had worn off, leaving a bitter taste on his tongue. He grabbed at his pants and struggled into them. Then he made his way to the dressing table and lit the candle. It was barely a stub, having burned low in the night. He carried the candle to the sitting room, placing it on the desk. Then he opened the very drawer that Saura had searched through. In light it did not take long for him to find what he looked for: a letter different from the others, and newer. He caught it up, shutting the drawer and breaking the wax seal on the envelope. He pulled out the single sheet and read it twice. His face was expressionless as he strode into the bedroom, standing before the fire and staring into the few embers. Suddenly, with a motion that was almost angry, he tossed the envelope and letter into the hearth. The parchment lay there for a few seconds before its edges began to curl and brown, then burst into consuming flame.

He watched it for a moment before going to the window and staring out at the gray landscape through the drizzle of rain on the glass pane. He felt anger— uncertain, strange in its cause and self-directed. He recalled the events of the past night, those that he could remember clearly through the fogging of drink. And there was one remembrance that stood out clearly. It was that of a brown-haired girl, warm in his embrace, with a sweet response that spoke of extreme pleasure. He could not shake the memory; it lingered like the fragrance of a sweet, musky perfume.

What had he done? He thought of his wife, lithe in his arms, the mingling of protest and pleasure within her voice. Had he been so drunken, such a sotted fool, that he had forged the final bond of marriage with no thought? Had he chosen, he could have let her slip away as she had pleaded, to return to the safety of her father's home. But he had not allowed himself to grant that request, so taken was he by his desire for her, a desire that was not quenched. Even now as he let her slip away, he longed for a return to the pleasure she had given him. Saura Ainsley was, by all the laws he had ever read, his wife. He had laid claim to her in a fool-hardy moment of desire, entwining their lives forever. He shook his head, thinking that his life was becoming truly complicated. He glanced back at the warmth of the bed, refusing its invitation for it seemed so empty with her absence. He stared out the window, trying to sort out his feelings.

Saura forced the bit into the mouth of her reluctant stallion and then she saddled him. She climbed onto his back, clinging, and rode out of the livery. She bent down in the saddle to shut the door behind her and as she straightened, she looked at the windows of the inn, staring back blankly at her. But one, on the second floor, had the faintest gleam of candlelight. She strained her eyes, noticing the outline of a form, still and mas-culine. Her heart began a wild race and she dug her boots into the horse's sides, sending him galloping off down the muddy road that twisted out of Braintree.

The captain stared at the small boylike figure on horseback that paused for a moment, gazing up at him. The lithe form, the oval of face, were familiar and he watched with mixed feelings as horse and rider dis-appeared in the distance.

Saura spurred her horse on as though the very devil were at her back. The destry's hoofs churned up chunks of mud, flinging them behind. She raced on, steeled by the determination to escape the village and Captain Adams. She felt no easing of spirit, no freedom from the ache in her breast, despite the miles she put be-tween herself and her wedded husband. The day shaded into a light gray, the world still appearing as a charcoal sketch in an artist's hand. The rain came down in thin veils and her sorry disguise became wet again, dark-ening to different color as it was soaked. Still she gritted her teeth, urging the churning hoofs beneath her to quicken their pace even more.

Erastus Clay traveled the same wet road but in an easterly direction, riding into the graying light of morning. He had been traveling for several hours and was wet. His coat collar was turned up, his tricorn pulled low, the rain glistening on his ebony face and hands. He and Peter had finally figured out what had become of Saura after having traced down clues with Willy and his father. Erastus had returned from Concord to find Peter still ailing and in a worried snit. And reason for worry he had, they saw, as they figured out her actions. Erastus almost had to use force to keep his friend down, insisting that he himself should go after her. That mission in mind, he hurried down the road.

Now, in the dim distance, he saw a rider coming in his direction at a gallop. He guided his steed to the side of the road but did not slacken its pace. He would have passed the rider without a thought but the other halted his horse and called out, "Erastus!" He reined in, spinning about and coming to face the boy on horseback. He studied the face for a moment.

"Miss Saura?" he questioned incredulously.

She nodded, sliding from her horse and fleeing to him, seeking the comfort of his familiarity. He was off his horse too as she came into his arms, burying her face in the rough wool of his coat collar. All his inquiries and angry words were dispelled from his tongue as she sobbed against his chest, his arms holding her close to him. Finally he managed, "What is wrong, miss? Are you hurt?"

She shook her head, drawing back. "No. I'm all right but we must hurry! There is a captain in the king's army who will be looking for me." He nodded, helping her back into the saddle, and they spurred their horses on, riding side by side down the narrow road.

Saura had not been able to check her tears upon seeing Erastus. Now a feeling of security came over her, greater than any she had known for the past two days. Erastus would take her home, she knew, and there would be safety within those familiar walls. Like a child frightened by lightning, hiding under the bed, she thought there was not any real safety to be had in any place. But her desire to return home overwhelmed her and she drove her horse ever faster down the thread of lane that split the forest of huge trees.

Tears mingled with the rain on her cheeks as she blinked to clear her vision, guiding her mount away from Captain Adams, the Musket Inn and the fateful township of Braintree.

The early morning sky was gray still, the crack of its thunder echoing through the tall pine trees.

Wedlock, as old men note, hath likened been,
Unto a publick crowd or common rout;
Where those that are without would fain get in,
And those that are within would fain get out.

—BENJAMIN FRANKLIN

# Chapter VI

THE MAPLE TREES that covered the hills around Green-hollow were red, just recently turned from yellow. They had clothed the hills in green during the summer, brightening to gold in early fall and now, in late October, they were scarlet. Their cycle would end in russet brown just before the white of snow sheathed them over, but for the present their beauty was brilliant against the blue sky. No doubt had the founder of the nestled township dedicated the ground in fall, the place should then have been named Crimsonhollow, or some such. The sight of the changing over and shading from lightest yellow to darkest red left the passing traveler breathless. And even the occupants of the Hollow commented on their village's special beauty.

The autumn colors, combined with the last clear days of cloudless blue skies and crisp air, generated an exciting feeling in the town. More than harvest or the upcoming Hallow'd Eve's party, each person sensed an eagerness brought on by this lively time of year.

Bathsheba Brightwater was one of these, babbling on about many things as she and Saura made soap. Not an easy endeavor, yet quite worthwhile, she reminded the girl. She had asked Peter's daughter to come help her with the heavier work in return for half the product.

Saura wrinkled her nose at the fumes, turning her head away and coughing. The smell of the lye, so carefully gleaned from the ashes and now combined with other chemicals, assaulted her senses. She stirred in the melted fat, recently added to the large enameled pan, and swirled it with a long-handled wooden spoon. Despite the cool October air, the sun was warm on her back. Slowly the substance began to thicken to the consistency of buff-colored honey as she stirred rhythmically, gazing into the depths of the cauldron.

A fortnight had passed since her stay at the Musket Inn. And now, as time had lapsed deeper into fall, it seemed a distant episode, fading in memory. Yet its effect on her was greater than she would admit.

When she returned home with Erastus, she had found Peter in a profound state of anxiety. But upon seeing her soaked and shivering, teeth chattering, he softened a bit. He worried that her chill would lead into sickness and had Erastus fill the tub in the bathing closet with hot water. Once shut away in the steamy warmth of the small room, she stripped off the wet disguise and sank gratefully into the warmth of the tub. She had lathered her hair and rinsed it clean, washing away feelings of shame and sorrow. Then she had dressed in her warmest flannel gown and her heavy robe, brushing her hair dry as best she could. Thus fortified she had tread softly into Peter's library, where he and Erastus sat, coming to stand before the heat of the crackling fire.

She had explained to her father her reasons for wanting to deliver the letter herself and for going in his stead. She described the inn, crowded with redcoats, and her capture. She spared no detail—except that of her marriage to Captain Adams and all that had followed. She circumvented this with a few twisting of facts, ending with the hidden letter of essay, the note to Stackpole, and her escape. She had neither the courage nor the desire to tell her father of her betrayal by accepting a Tory captain as her husband. She could only hope that Adams would march to Boston as planned and stay there. Perhaps in his drunken state the night would be a blur to him; perhaps he had arisen the next morning regretting his marriage and wishing to avoid her.

Saura had seemed so sad to Peter, so remorseful, that he scolded her only a little, seeing the tears she held back and her face as still as stone. He felt that there was something more to her story, some deeper worry, but press as he might, he could draw no more from her. Finally he accepted the fact that her failure for the cause—and her difficulties—proved her a bit weaker than she pretended. He sighed, gave her a quick embrace and a glass of brandy to ward off a chill and then sent her to her room, where she fell into an exhausted sleep for most of the day.

Her melancholy attitude did not dissipate, however. She moped about the house, cooking or straightening the rooms as usual although her mind seemed far away. Several times she had been prone to tears, so unlike their feisty Saura that it was a great puzzlement. Peter concluded that her melancholy had something to do with her experience in Braintree but he could figure nothing out as to what. As the days passed, she became less apt to cry but her unusual quietness remained.

The truth was that she was plagued by her marriage, sealed with more than a justice's stamp. Perhaps Seth Adams had been drunk but she had not. Indeed, she remembered it all too clearly. Whenever that handsome face or those strong hands came to mind, she shoved the memory back. Unbidden, those thoughts would yet come, bearing memory of silken embrace and heated kiss. What she had done, that single night's experience, was a firebrand in her mind. She could neither forget nor forgive Seth Adams. By what right did he crash in upon her senses and claim unjustly, despite his tenderness, her womanhood? She fought to rid herself of the memory of this betraying redcoat and their passionate tryst. But the task was neither easy nor quickly done. He came unsought and unwelcome into her dreams, stirring up coals better left to die on the hearth. She clamped her lips in a grimace of determination. "Blast you, Captain Adams, you'll not trespass so easily upon my mind. I'll not forgive the betrayal of my plans, Sir Redcoat!"

Uriah's boy, Harley, strolled along the lane that led to the Brightwater house. He was delivering some items: tea, just in from Boston harbor's black market, a packet of needles, two vials of ink and a pot of honey. He resented delivering a basket of such puny items, preferring to stay in the store and count the coins. But his father took a concern for Miss Brightwater since she had no one to help her with the heavy work, her brother being an invalid. Harley's dislike of such minor chores turned to pleasure as he rounded a corner in the tidy lane and viewed the yard that was his destination. There, right in front, stood the charming Miss Ainsley.

Despite the fact that she was stirring the soap kettle and clothed in an old muslin dress and a blue apron, she was quite breathtaking. Her hair was caught back with a length of ribbon, a few tendrils escaping around her lovely face. Her large brown eyes stared down into the kettle's depths, her mind a hundred miles away. Strange, he had always thought her very pretty, yet now on this crisp autumn afternoon, her profile edged by golden light, she was beautiful. His heart began to race as he strode up to the gate.

"Good day, Saura," he greeted her.

She glanced up. "Oh, hello, Harley."

"You look as though you were daydreaming," he said with a smile. "Now what thoughts were bothering a pretty head like yours?"

She sighed, taking the spoon out and setting it aside. "I was just wondering who would help me with this. It needs to be dumped into the soap trough."

"I'd be honored to help," he offered, setting down his basket. The youth on one side and she on the other, they carried the kettle to the wooden trough and carefully poured it into the flat soap pan. Bathsheba came out at just that moment.

"Why, hello, Harley. Oh, dear, we forgot the scent!" She scurried back into the house and returned shortly with a small vial. "Lavender this time, I think." They watched as she poured from the bottle, stirring in the sweet scent with the wooden spoon.

"Now you watch," she said. "When it dries, it will be as sweetly scented as anything your father sells at his store for a penny a bar! Perhaps not as prettily shaped since I don't use molds but it does just as good a job. Now you come by in two weeks, Saura, and I'll give you your share. Oh, before you go, this is for helping, dear. No, no, don't protest." She handed Saura a little cloth packet.

Delicate rose petals, sun-dried, had changed their pink to scarlet and red to crimson like crinkled silk. They were neatly tied in a cheesecloth sack. "Now you put that in your wardrobe and your clothes will smell as nice as can be. Thank you for your help. And, Harley, here's your basket. I'll just take all these things in the house and you can walk our Saura home."

That was exactly what Harley had in mind, so he accepted the task readily. As Saura saw no out, they walked along the lane toward the blacksmith's. Harley talked on about all sorts of things, trying to show her how well-educated he was for a home-grown man. He recalled his father's admonition not to court a maid whose tongue was so sharp and wit so wise lest she rule the household in marriage. He had advised his son rather to seek out the company of Mary Sillman or Mercy Carver. And despite the fact that they were of mild disposition, the one was too plump and the other too plain. Saura, despite her tongue, was bright with beauty and she inspired him to poetry. Unfortunately, it was the same with most of the young men in the Hollow. Yet now as they walked along, she seemed so subdued, so surprisingly quiet, that he was encouraged by this new countenance. Perhaps his father had been mistaken. Surprisingly, there was something about her that had changed. She was more mature in his eyes, al-

though he could not explain why. It was hard to believe
that just last year she had been a little girl in boys'
breeches, wanting to race the men. Yet here she stood,
magically changed into a woman and the change was
mysterious.

The change was also apparent to Saura. She had
previously regarded Harley Chase as one of the more
important young men in the community; now, compared to another man she had known, Harley's attentions seemed like those of a boy. Her mind wandered
often from their conversation despite his persistent efforts. And at the door he asked if he might call again
that evening.

"Perhaps some other time, Harley," she said quietly.
"I am really very tired." It was the truth and she turned,
going into the house and up the stairs to her room. She
did not bother with dinner that night, being unusually
fatigued, but fell to sleep.

During the night the sound of voices invaded her
dreams and she awoke once, uncertain whether the
voices were real or fancied. She was unable to rouse
herself to investigate and fell back into deep sleep, not
waking until morning. The tin-scraping sound of a
rooster's crow, repeated like the off-key strains of a
fiddle, brought her around. Cloudy sunlight, the sky
pale and pearly, met her glance through the window.
She arose and stretched, her mind already full of the
day's activities. Her agenda was full of small chores
and errands; she anticipated the busy schedule.

She washed sleep from her face and eyes, then sat
at her dressing table, brushing her hair away from her
face, twisting it into a soft mass at the nape of her neck.
Her face was still flushed from sleep, her eyes dark
pools of chocolate, her lips softly pink. She smiled at
the pretty reflection in the glass, tossing off her gown
and pulling on her chemise and slip, tying the strings
at her waist. She pulled on her hosiery and buckled on
her slippers, then slipped into her dress of red dimity.
She fastened the row of buttons that ran up the bodice
to the white lace edging along the square-cut neckline.
The soft cloth fell gracefully in the gathered skirt and

sleeves and red was a color that she wore well. A day of shopping might prove diverting indeed, she thought, catching up her reticule and descending the stairs to breakfast.

As she walked down the stairwell, her ear caught the sound of conversation and she surmised that Peter had company, which was not unusual. The aroma of hot ham and sliced melon reached her as she rounded the corner into the dining room. The thought of a pleasant breakfast fled as she stood in shocked silence. There, stretched out before the chair nearest her, were black boots, well-shined. Her eyes followed them up to white trousers, a red jacket and a Tory face, tanned and handsome. A slow smile dawned upon the visitor's lips as he nodded to her. She stared back at Captain Seth Adams with a mingling of emotions, dismay the foremost.

"Good morn, Miss Ainsley," he greeted as he continued his meal.

Slowly she turned to Peter, her old animosity rising. "Father, what is this redcoat captain doing at our table?"

"Now, Saura," Peter admonished. "'Tis no way to talk to a guest in our home."

"A guest!"

Captain Adams took up some papers, tossing them open on the table. They were a writ from the quartermaster, issuing him housing here under the Quartering Act. Saura continued to stare at the intruder. He was as handsome—and as Tory—as ever. Peter continued, "The captain will be staying with us for three days, up in the attic room. We will do our best to make him comfortable, daughter." The warning in his voice was obvious. He needed no run-in with the king's army and would gladly suffer this inconvenience to their personal lives.

Despite her dismay at the captain's presence, she knew from Peter's words that Seth Adams had said nothing of their marriage or what had followed. She felt a flood of relief and forced herself to keep from glancing at the British soldier with gratitude. Perhaps there was reasoning with him after all, although his presence here left her with a multitude of mixed and worried feelings. Why had he come back here and into her life again? She knew for the first time why she truly hated the meddlings of the British. Could they never leave the concerns of the colonists alone, either in public or in private?

She went to the sideboard, taking up a plate of ham, melon and a muffin with butter. Then she flounced down at the point farthest from the captain, little realizing that this afforded him a perfect view of her.

Dressed in a soft gown of red dimity, cut low enough to reveal a column of slender throat, she was beautiful in the extreme. She reminded him of the bright hills around Greenhollow. That perfect face and soft mouth appealed to his senses in a way that they never had before and he could not blame his desires on drink this time. She kept her eyes down, avoiding him and denying a glimpse into those dark recesses shaded by smoky lash. Inwardly he cursed the mission that had brought him here, squarely into the presence of his secret wife.

Conversation at the breakfast table did not exist. Each person paid close and silent attention to his plate. Peter finished his breakfast and pushed back from the table. Rising, he kissed his daughter's brow.

"You look lovely, miss. Do you have plans?"

"I've errands in town. Do you want anything?"

He shook his head. "Only that you check on the captain's room to see it well-provided before you leave. Have a pleasant day, daughter. Captain." He left to join Erastus in the livery.

The silence thickened until at last Seth spoke, addressing her as casually as though he asked whether she desired lemon in her tea. "Why did you run away?"

She did not look up, absorbing herself in taking a spoonful of melon. "Why did you say nothing to my father of our . . . encounter?"

"Because you had said nothing to him." She looked up at this, her eyes meeting his, and he explained, "He met me with such an affable nature that I knew him to be unaware of the past happenings. Why did you not tell him?"

"And destroy his Patriot hopes for his daughter? 'Tis best I keep the deceit to myself...unless you plan to tell him." She looked at him inquiringly.

He shrugged, tossing off the last of the apple juice in his mug. "If you prefer to keep our marriage secret, I will agree for the time being. Just say the word."

"I have more than just a word to say! It was a mistake, sir. Against my will and agreed to by you in a drunken stupor, is that not so? Then let us agree to end this mockery. I ask you to annul the bonds of this wedded state."

He leaned back in his chair, studying her for such a length of time that she grew warm under his watch. "I would agree were not those bonds sealed by a greater act than mere ceremony.".

Her eyes widened, her cheeks flushing at his words. For some foolish reason she had hoped that he would not remember the night clearly but now she saw that drink had not blurred his memory.

Seth smiled slowly as he took in her blushing cheeks. "And one more reason you've not thought of, I'll wager. Before you cast aside those vows we made too hastily, had you not better assure that our actions of that late night bear no fruit?"

She puzzled over his words; then her eyes flew open in startled realization of his meaning. Her lashes dropped down, only to lift up in embarrassment, for the possibility that a child might have been conceived in that brief moment had never occurred to her mind. She stifled a groan.

Seth, watching the various emotions generated by this new thought, could not refrain from laughing and he sat there right before her—grand and Tory—amused at her plight!

She leveled a stare that burned through his red coat and he stilled his mirth. "I am sorry, mistress," he apologized. "I meant no indelicacy. It is just that you are such an innocent."

She rose from the table, nearly knocking over the

straight-backed chair behind her. "An innocent," she repeated icily. "You did not think me such an innocent on our wedding night."

He leaned forward on his elbows, taking in her slender form. "That is true."

"Then tell me, Sir Redcoat, what ill wind brings you to Greenhollow?"

"One reason is a mission of no great deed, a message easily delivered to troops on their way here, due three days hence. But then perhaps I should not entrust you with even this small news, remembering that you were suspect as a spy and are certainly no Loyalist. I have wondered since if Major Berkely was wise to entrust you to one whose information might be easily gleaned. I shall have to be careful."

"I see. And this mission is so important that they use you as messenger boy. My, my, the king's army must be in dire need of good men to run its errands."

"Major Berkely had a greater task for which to send me, this light message being but a decoy. It seems that I am to take charge of my Patriot ward already, for the good chaplain is determined that no small matters of war shall deter me from this ordination."

"So you barge into my home, bearing your papers?"

He glanced at the quartermaster's letter and then at the wrathful beauty. "I have other papers, still." He reached into his coat pocket, drawing out a fine piece of parchment, well-signed and stamped. "Did you forget about this?"

He tossed the paper across the table and Saura picked it up, staring down at the legal certificate of marriage. She gasped, glancing up at him and dropping it onto the table as though it seared her fingers. Seth caught it up and returned it to his pocket in case she should try to destroy it. And knowing her fiery temper, she might well make the attempt!

"Those bonds are quite legal. Regardless of our wishes and despite your anger, you are my wife. If you desire, I will keep the secret from your father until you gain the courage to tell him. I think highly of the man and I will only be quiet on one promise."

"And what is that?"

"That you subject yourself as my wife," he said slowly.

She stared at him, for a moment speechless, then spat out, "Most certainly, sir. When Sunday comes in the middle of the week! How dare you ask for that which is mine to give for love, not barter, whether you are my husband or not?"

Seth threw his head back, laughing boisterously, his hands clasped behind his head. When he had stilled his merriment, he gazed at her. "Why, Mistress Saura, do you so readily assume that the wifely duties for which I ask are those dark and splendid pleasures? You did not let me end my sentence to explain that a wife provides more than that. A button sewn on a shirt, a laundered vest and bed linens. Only that, and one other thing, although it might prove more difficult for you. A tongue less sharp would be an added delight."

At that moment she fervently prayed that his chair legs might collapse but as nothing happened, she turned and strode up the stairs. He bolted after, following her up the stairs as she wrenched open the linen closet, throwing clean towels and sheets into his arms. She went up the short flight into the attic room. She flipped the latch on its high, narrow window, pushing it open to admit the fresh fall air that would dispel the stuffiness. Then she proceeded to make the bed and he hurried to help her as she smoothed the sheets into place and tucked in the edges. After that she cast on a heavy eiderdown quilt. She fluffed the pillow, encased it and folded the towels and face cloth on the washstand. He watched her scurry about, dusting the furniture and filling the pitcher with fresh water. As she passed by him, he caught a hint of the scent unique to her and stiffened at its effect on his senses. Her presence, so near, stirred the memories he was determined to let rest.

Her chores done, she surveyed the room and nodded. "'Tis the best I can do, having little practice in the wifely arts. Though I am poor with a needle and thread, I'll risk pricking my finger for any buttons you need sewn on. And though the laundress does our washing,

I can try my hand at sudsing your vest. I did make soap yesterday," she added, standing primly straight before him, hands clasped together.

He grinned at her chiding mockery, folding his arms. "It appears that you are gaining skills at this time of matrimony."

"If I can hence but curb my vile tongue, so despised by my husband, I shall indeed prove sainted."

"Indeed, Mistress Adams. Indeed."

"Now if you will excuse me, I have errands at the market." Saura turned on her heel. Seth followed her down the stairs.

"I've nothing better to do and there are some things I need from the common store, shaving supplies and such, so I'll accompany you."

She looked at him in surprise. "If seen in your company, what might the townfolk think?"

"Their speculation could be no worse than the truth, could it? And if you are to be my wife, then should you not try to grow accustomed to my company, no matter how distasteful it may be to you?"

This brought a smile to her lips and she shrugged, catching up her reticule and basket, striding out the door. He walked along by her side, tall next to her, his tricorn cocked over his lean features, his chin strong. The cut of his red jacket did not disguise the muscular strength of shoulder and chest and she thought that despite his British nature, he was most handsome.

The maple leaves were hued in scarlet, edged in gold, and the boughs of the tall pines furnished the only green remaining; as they walked along, the autumn beauty touched them. The smells of crisp apples in the vendor's cart, ripe pumpkins huge and orange, and the last of pungent grapes, filled the air. Seth stopped and purchased some apples, putting them in her basket— which he took from her arm to carry—and shining one on his coat sleeve. When it fairly gleamed, he bit into it. No apples were quite so crisp as these American apples, he thought.

Saura was more than just a little conscious of the tall soldier by her side, casual in his attitude and demeanor. He acted as though there were nothing more on his mind than an autumn stroll. He stood here beside her, so carefree of the past while she was full aware that he knew her intimately, in a way no other had.

They reached the common store and entered, the tinkling bells on the door declaring their presence. She selected the things she wished to purchase, the captain watching her. The straightness of her stance, the jaunty course of her movements that shook the dark curls down her back, appealed to Seth's manly senses. Now out of boys' breeches and into feminine attire, her appearance bespoke the womanhood known only to himself. And known only once. The memories of a lightning-streaked night seemed to swarm about him and with an effort he pulled himself away from them. What was there about this mere girl that threatened his very senses?

In the tight quarters of the goods-crowded store, her skirt brushed against him as she moved by to pick up a buttonhook and shoe polish. The narrowness of the aisle brought them closer together than Saura would have otherwise permitted and Seth seemed to loom above her. Despite the fact that the place was public and the security of daylight surrounded them, the moment began to seem strangely intimate. Sunlight filtered in through the streaked panes, the amber darkness of the room lending itself to their mood. Their eyes caught and held and she felt breathless as he leaned near. When it seemed as though his mouth might sweep down and claim hers, she nearly cried out—but the fragile moment was broken by the jangling sound of the door opening and they quickly moved apart.

Saura busied herself with some jars of tonic water, trying to still the racing beat of her heart. "Black-eyed devil," she thought. "What evil does this Tory work that I am thrown under his sorcery? He is a disturbing presence, just as are all of his kind here in America. Three more days of this and I'll be rid of him! Let him go off to battle and meet his fate, but let him leave me be." She fought to control herself, turning to see that it was Harley who had come in. He was accompanied by Molly.

"Why, Captain Adams!" Molly called out. "It is you, is it not? What brings you back to Greenhollow?"

He nodded at her. "Good day, Miss Yates. I am just passing through for a few days."

"Oh. I didn't see your name on the register."

"Actually I'm not housed at the inn. I am quartered with the Blake household."

Molly's eyes narrowed as she took in Saura's pert appearance and studied observance of tonic water. "How very strange. There are plenty of rooms at the Crooked Horne."

Captain Adams shrugged noncommittally. "Who knows the thinking of the king's quartermaster?"

Saura pretended disinterest in the conversation, wandering off to look at wig powders. Harley followed her. He doffed his hat, standing awkwardly behind her until he caught her attention. "How are you today?" he asked cordially.

"Quite fine," she answered, nodding a bit as she took in the other woman's proximity to Seth and her open neckline. Molly was smiling, the better to show her dimples, and looking up at the captain as her hand rested on his arm. Saura felt a sudden outrage at this inappropriate behavior although she had previously felt none at the girl's indecencies. "What did you say, Harley?" she asked, totally having missed his words.

He cleared his throat to start again. "Well, I was asking if I might call this evening, after evening meal of course." He had prepared himself for the usual refusal but she suddenly slipped her arm through his.

"Why, Harley, that would be just lovely," she said softly, smiling up at him in a way that made him feel as though he might melt right down into his boots. "And I would be very happy if you would come to evening meal. Of course we are having only pheasant with sweet potatoes and pumpkin bread, if you don't mind such a small fare."

"Oh, no! I mean yes! It all sounds very nice and I would be honored. What time?"

"Half-past six?"

"I will be there!" Harley was in heaven as she re-

124

moved her arm from his and he helped her gather up the items she needed.

As Seth extracted himself from Molly's grasp, he overheard Saura's invitation to the gangling youth. He frowned a bit, wondering what game she played. As they paid for their purchases and he put his shaving items in her basket, he looked at her sternly—but she only smiled at him with an air of gay innocence.

They left the store, Molly accompanying them and chattering merrily. She fought for the captain's attention, which Saura won by keeping still. They stopped at the tinker's and dropped off Saura's shears and then at the glass-blower's and the silversmith's shop. Seth picked up a button to match the others on his jacket.

The young proprietor nodded at the match, charging him the correct amount of coin. "Did you wish that sewn on here?"

The captain shook his head, smiling lazily at Saura. "Thank you, no. Miss Ainsley has volunteered to do my mending." Saura compressed her lips, pushing back the words that threatened to put the captain in his proper place.

As they left, Molly volunteered her services. "I would not mind sewing on that button, Captain. Saura is quite a disaster with needle and thread." As they were silent, she hurried on. "Not that there's anything wrong with preferring to hunt and ride like a man, even if the people of the community do frown on it! Heaven knows that some do better with needle and thread than others and just because Peter has to hire out the mending, it does not mean that she's not good at some things. Would you rather I sew on his button for him?" she finished breathlessly.

"Thank you, Molly, but I can manage," Saura said coolly. "Unless, of course, the captain would prefer your services."

Seth felt that he was treading on tender ground as the two women looked up at him. He smiled and shrugged. "I do not mind if Miss Ainsley practices her skill upon my jacket. After all, mending is one thing a young lady must learn to do before looking to be married."

Molly laughed softly. "I do not think that marriage is something Saura much thinks about."

Saura felt a slight sting of insult, as though the tone suggested an immaturity staying her from wedlock. By this point they had reached the inn and Molly was ready to go in. She smiled her farewell but Saura stayed her. "I'll be making rum cake for dessert, Molly, so you need not bring anything over." The fact that Saura saw through Molly's oft-used ruse of bringing over gifts of food in order to gain entrance when a male guest was around sent a flush of embarrassment across the older girl's cheeks.

Seth and Saura strolled back to the house in silence. Inside, he removed his jacket, the firm strength of his muscles showing well beneath the light linen of his shirt. He handed her the coat and button and then sat down to watch as she made a dozen attempts to thread a needle. This done, she set about sewing on the silver button. She handled the chore quite well until the sharp point of the needle found her finger and drew a tiny crimson drop. She dropped the jacket and Seth pulled out his handkerchief, handing it to her with a smile. "The goal is not to do battle with the needle," he said.

She glared at him and he stilled his mirth. She cut the thread with her teeth and tossed him his jacket. "Now if you will excuse me, I will change so that I can make my rum cake. We're having a guest tonight, besides yourself."

"That stick of a lad who works in the common store?"

"That well-educated young man," she corrected. "His name is Harley Chase and he is a frequent caller here."

"Ah! A family friend."

"Aye, and more."

"H-m-m," he scoffed. "There are more impressive boot-cleaners in my army."

"You should know," she said. "You married one."

"Indeed I did. And since you are my wife, could you not at least present a proper appearance instead of continuing to receive suitors?"

"As you noted, Harley is a dear friend of the family's. And as to this marriage, it is a mockery! I wish to see it annulled and were you a decent man, you would release me from these legal ties."

"But how can I?" he asked, leaning close to pierce her with his dark eyes, "when indeed such ties are legal? And these matters have been consummated?"

She sighed and turned away, tossing the thread into its box. "Must you humiliate me with such a coarse reminder?" she cried.

"Perhaps you flinch at the memory but the facts stand. And talk of breaking those bonds is futile. Major Berkely is a legal clergy."

"He is a king's clergy and when the colony breaks its bonds from your England, I shall break my bonds from you." Having had the last word, Saura hurried up the stairs and into her room. She shut the door and leaned against it lest he intrude into her quarters as he had intruded into her life.

She changed into a light work dress, tied back her tresses with a bright piece of wool and went downstairs to bake the rum cake. She was relieved to find the captain gone. Her spirits lifted as she set about the tasks in the kitchen, humming to herself as she cracked eggs into a bowl. In three days, she told herself, she would be free of the pesky redcoat and his influence over her.

Seth sat atop the low garden wall, curling pumpkin vines at his feet, as he thoughtfully stared into the distance. Why did he let that slender maid prick his pride so? The distant strains of a voice, slow-humming, caught his attention and he glanced through the open door and caught sight of her. She was busy cooking, a white apron tied around her slender waist. Why did this girl, and she was but a girl, always catch his eye as few had? That pert quickness, those dark and perceptive eyes, the slender shape that spoke more of womanliness than any other's, formed a maid so very pleasing.

He shoved off from the wall and went to lean on the

closed portion of the Dutch door. As Saura looked up, he caught her eye with a smile and she returned it primly, her ire gone. Despite Molly's comments, Saura looked quite proper in the neat, homey little kitchen with its breadbaskets, rolling pins, tongs and towel rollers hanging from the high overhead beam. She poured the cake into a pan and placed it in the oven. Then she handed him the smaller butter churn. "You might as well earn your lodging."

"What do I do with this?"

"Make butter," she replied with patience. "Pull up and down, like this."

"Whatever you order. Even if it is woman's work."

"He that cannot obey cannot command," she chided. "'Tis best you remember that, Captain, should you wish to advance."

"Yes, sir, General."

She smiled at this but turned away, not wishing to be charmed by a Tory. She began to knead dough in a long, wooden trough; when it attained the right texture, she turned it into a bowl and covered it. Then she stepped over to Seth, checking the thickness of the butter as he leaned near to inhale the sweet scent of her hair. She turned the butter into a bowl, mashing out the remaining water, and then pressed it into butter molds having varied designs. These chores done, she sat down to rest and Seth joined her.

"I think it is best that we talk, Miss Ainsley," he said, his deep voice resounding throughout the kitchen.

"It seems that when we do, there is always anger to contend with," she replied.

"That is true. And for this reason I think we both need to strive to ward off that emotion. Fate has brought our lives together and it is important that we try to make the best of a difficult situation. Whether or not either of us wanted what happened that night to happen, the past does not change."

"That is true, Captain," she said, her meekness surprising him.

"Then let us make a treaty of peace. You cannot help it that you are my wife and I cannot help it that my major commands me to a duty about which neither of us is happy. Had you been forced to marry some other soldier, you might find yourself in an even more difficult situation. As it is, I am willing to respect your wishes that neither your father nor the townfolk know of our marriage contract. Do you still want it to be so?"

"I do indeed! I do not know how to explain this to my father and until the time that I do, I would appreciate your silence."

"Very well. I will comply. But you must know that Major Berkely will expect a report from me as to my visits and your actions. To ease this burden, you might try not to crusade too boldly for your cause."

She nodded. "I agree and I will do my best. Only...it seems as though it would be so much easier just to end this marriage and let us go each our own way."

"To attain an annulment, we would need the major's signature. And even if I could convince him that you had changed your ways, he would ask if the marriage had been consummated. Could you lie to a clergyman?"

She shook her head. "If only you had been a gentleman and not demanded that...."

"Which you gave to me? Hold, Saura. Let us not quarrel again over that which cannot be undone. You have agreed to accept my help, what more can I offer?"

She looked at him suspiciously. "Why do you play the gentleman now, offering to protect me from embarrassment?"

"I do it for your father," he replied. "He is a good man and I wish no ill feelings to come to him. Perhaps I will be shipped back home and be out of your life."

"Indeed?"

"You need not appear so pleased."

"'Tis only that I look for an end to all this confusion." Saura rose, wiping off the wooden sink and drainboard that stood against the wall on spindle legs. She straightened the nutmeg grater, the knife-and-fork cleaner, the muffin irons and teapot, as though her hands felt suddenly idle. Why did his stare bother her? Someday the confusion would end—but hardly soon, of that she was certain.

* * *

That night Harley arrived promptly on time for dinner, much to Peter's surprise. The smithy could not fathom why Saura had invited the young man or why she was so cordial to him. She treated Harley with overwhelming kindness and appeared enraptured by his mediocre tales.

Seth squirmed in his seat, finishing a piece of rum cake as he listened to Harley's droning discussion of the mathematical rule of three, his newly learned short cut to calculation. What did she see in this foppish lad?

Saura covertly watched Captain Adams grow more surly with each passing moment. Was he a little jealous, or just as bored as she was? Why had she invited Harley when she had known all along what he was like and how he prided himself on his scholarship? She regretted the hasty action, spurred on by Molly's irksome fawning over the captain. Yet what did she care if Molly flaunted herself in his direction? She herself had stated that she wanted no claim from this marriage.

The meal finally over, Harley lingered in the parlor until tact prompted him to leave; yet still he spent a quarter-hour on the doorstep in the act of departing, trying to win her favor. When finally he left, he deemed the night a grand success despite the dark presence of the British captain.

Erastus helped to clear away the dishes and said, "A learned blockhead is a greater blockhead than an ignorant one."

Saura laughed softly. "True. But he means well."

They joined Peter and Seth in the library, where they sat talking. "Well, that was a most interesting evening, daughter. I had forgotten just what a huffinpuff that young lad is."

"Indeed," Seth said a bit dourly. "Who would have thought that one so young could know so much?"

Peter laughed. "I hope you do not invite him to sup for some while, or at least until my ears cool off."

"Do you discourage my suitors, Father?" she asked in surprise.

"Ha! Not likely. What is that sage advice? Marry

your son when you will, but your daughter when you can."

The three men chuckled at this although Saura found nothing amusing. As the talk waned, the two older men excused themselves, believing in "early to bed and early to rise." Seth and Saura found themselves alone and the silence was awkward, only the fire crackling softly to break the quiet. Saura sat before the flames, holding out her hands, and Seth rubbed his sore leg to dispel the evening chill that sometimes made the bone ache. She noted the action and turned to him.

"Does that wound still pain you?"

"Not too often."

It was quiet again until he spoke. "I am not surprised that that youth...what is his name?"

"Harley."

"Yes, that Harley tries to win you over. He is quite smitten with you."

"He is just a friend of the family's, really. His father and mine are friends, you see. And Harley is a bit of a blow-hard, but very nice. He has always treated me with the highest respect."

"You mean he has never tried for a kiss?"

"Captain Adams!"

"You can confide the truth to me, Saura. After all, I am the only one you know who holds the title of husband." He leaned back idly in his chair, swirling the liquor in his glass. He could not help but notice how really lovely she was, the fire highlighting the red glints in her hair. "No doubt he has wished to but lacks the courage."

"'Tis unfair to ridicule Harley when he is not here to defend himself."

"And if I confronted him with the fact that he wants to kiss that sweet mouth of yours, no doubt he would blush like a schoolboy and stammer that such a statement was most inappropriate."

"As it is! My lips are no concern of yours, sir!"

"Indeed?" he asked, putting down his glass and leaning forward. "Who else has tasted of such tender fare?" He stood up, coming to her and pulling her from her chair. Before she could utter a single word of protest, he pulled her to him, bringing his mouth down to hers. His arms were as steel bands about her, encircling, forcing her tight against him despite the fury of her hands that tried frantically to push him away. The warmth of his mouth on hers sent a wash of weakness through her until further protest was futile. How long they kissed, she did not know—only that when he did release her, she staggered back, flame rising to her cheeks, her lips bright from his assault.

She fought back the urge to flee, determined that he would not see his effect upon her. Instead she turned her back on him, clasping her hands tightly. And Seth did not move. He stood near, looming above her. He leaned close then and whispered in her ear, his voice husky, his breath candied with rum.

"You have a choice before you, Saura. The fawning of a school lad or the embrace of a man."

She whirled about, shoving him back into his chair with such force that he looked up at her in surprise. "I am no mere schoolmaid to be so teased, lobsterback! You have the affront to come into my home, under what pretense I hardly understand, and then you ridicule my suitors and trifle with my affections. Lest you think to press your lips to mine again, knave redcoat, remember that I shall fight with soldiers' tactics if need be. Unless you desire to find a bayonet in your ribs, then keep your hands and your lips in control!"

She turned and nearly ran from the room and up the stairs. She feared that he might follow, having seen through her bravado, but once in her room, her worries were stilled. She tried to catch her breath, blinking back tears of frustration. Never must he see what he did to her, how his touch melted her reserve as though it were mere tallow tossed to flame. The reason she had surrendered to him on that stormy wedding night was clearly brought back to memory and she only hoped that he did not understand. Her pride would never allow it. She threw herself on the bed, choking back sobs and stifling the noise lest that handsome redcoat pass her room on the way to his.

* * *

The next two days passed with little incident. Seth took the warning seriously and kept at arms' length despite the difficulty. She was as appealing as a wild rose—a rose he had a free license to pick—yet her thorny dislike of him was obvious and he knew he must tread with care if he desired to win her.

When he left, there was no farewell; he was determined to go away from the source, and the easement, of his pain.

The hillsides were dappled in scattered autumn color, distant hills blue-gray while those nearer were crimson with the dying leaves. Their beauty was obscured by the gray sky and the slow drizzle of rain. Saura sat gloomily at her writing desk. Frequently she dipped quill in ink but her thoughts ran out before the indigo did. She was writing to her mother, yet her words seemed stilted. What was there to speak of? Any trivia she could think of was centered around Captain Adams...and she had no desire to write to her mother of him!

Since he had left in haste, leaving a note of quick thanks at his vacant place at the breakfast table, things had fallen back into their smooth routine. She picked up the soap she had made with Bathsheba and dropped off the material for her new riding habit. She wrote letters, waxed the furniture and baked her first plum pudding. Yet she felt strangely restless and attributed it to being confined to the house during the heavy rains.

Piper, her gray tom, leaped to the desk and poked his nose into a pile of papers there. He perched for a moment before jumping down again, letting the papers slide away beneath his paws to scatter on the floor. Guiltless, he walked off to explore another site. She watched him and smiled, leaning back in her chair.

What had happened to the carefree days of youth when her greatest worries were about what to cook or how to sneak away for a race? Why had such simple thoughts been replaced by the darker ones of an unbidden stranger? What was this yearning she could not identify? She sighed, pushing aside the curious Piper, who had returned to investigate her quill. Saura retrieved her papers from the floor, finished the letter and folded it, readying it for post with the stage.

She studied the drizzling gray day outside, watching the raindrops trace a teary path down the cheeks of leaded-glass windowpanes. So would pass the weeks of dark autumn rain.

So then he that giveth her
in marriage doeth well;
but he that giveth her not
in marriage doeth better.

I CORINTHIANS 7:38

## Chapter VII

WINTER WAS in the wind. The last golden boughs were
bitten by frost, the striplings grown bare as their leaves
formed a papery carpet in the forest. The woods had a
filtering of early snow; black tree trunks were stark
against the white as Saura's mare picked its way along
the powdered ground. November had come cruelly to
Massachusetts, she thought. This was the first week in
which there had been no rain and she was thankful for
the crisp air. The sunlight was weak but she reveled
in the freedom from damp as her horse crossed a shallow
stream that flowed over rocks and roots.

Her face was bright from the cold but her hands were
warm in their leather gloves and her new riding habit
was lined with flannel. She thought that Bathsheba
had outdone herself for the outfit was most attractive.
Of heavy brown fabric the color of chocolate, it fit well
and was trimmed with soft rabbit's fur. She spurred the
horse on out of the forest to where the meadow began,
feeling as though she rode the crisp wind itself.

*   *   *

The sky was streaked in gray and smoke-blue, the river gone dark and choppy as Seth Adams's horse picked its way along until they came to the meadow's edge. Despite his heavy clothing, he was tired and chilled and his bones ached from traveling. He had spent the night at a tavern on the water's edge where the ferry crossed back and forth. He had left the Posthaste Road to cut across the countryside; it was a shorter but rougher route.

Seth rubbed the growth at his chin, sorry that he could not arrive at the smithy's house in better attire but his travels had been long and the trek to and from New York exhausting. He longed for a soak in a hot tub and tried to hurry his tired horse along the edge of the fields. Suddenly a movement caught his eye and he squinted to catch sight of the distant form that was heading in his direction. It was a rider. As he studied the figure that finally neared enough that he could make it out, a smile touched his lips. Saura Ainsley was riding her horse to beat the wind! She was dressed in brown, leaning forward, her long tresses blowing behind her in the crisp breeze. He could not help but appreciate the slender lines of face and form, the energy that spurred her on. She neared him and he could see the flush that cold had brought to her face and her eyes wild with excitement; she stirred something equally wild in his veins. Had he remembered that she was so breathtaking?

Her horse slowed its gait as she and the mare caught their breaths. She felt renewed by the vigorous activity, feeling free for the first time in weeks of the restrictions of being confined at home. Her horse took its own direction and she let it wander until it snorted and hurried forward. Then she pulled her mind quickly from her random thoughts and stared at the man whom she was fast approaching. With a start she identified him but by then it was too late to turn away her headstrong horse.

Captain Adams looked roguishly handsome despite his travel-worn appearance. There was something so

136

startling in his rugged face and the dark-colored eyes that she was glad her face was flushed from the ride so as to hide the blush that further crept into her cheeks. She felt a sudden surge of excitement at the captain's return. Why should it matter to her whether he came to the Hollow or not? He nodded a greeting as casually as though he had been gone for only a few days rather than weeks.

"Saura," he said. The appreciative tone in that single word sent a chill through her. "You were meant for this autumn setting. It becomes you. Is that a new riding habit?"

When she nodded, he grinned. "It is much more becoming than boys' pants."

"You notice a difference?" she asked, raising her eyebrows in mock surprise. She would never admit to him that she did not have the heart to don boys' pants again. "What brings you back to Greenhollow this time, Captain?"

Ever the sharp tongue, he thought. "I am just passing through and am on my way to Boston."

"Ah," she said. "Just passing through! No doubt you can stay for only a day then."

"Actually, since my expected return is not until December the first, I am in no demand for two weeks. And of course I will be quartered at your house again, with this permanent order of stay from the quartermaster," he said, touching his breast pocket.

"Two weeks!"

He smiled at her. "I do so anticipate the kindness of the hospitality that only you can give me, Saura."

She rolled her eyes heavenward. "Well, Captain Adams, if there is one thing I know, having lived as a colonist, it is how to make the best of a difficult situation. If one must have a lobsterback in one's home for a fortnight, one must make do." Since she could not keep from smiling when she spoke, he was not too offended.

They guided their horses in a homeward direction, the silence somewhat stiff between them. "Did you see battle, sir?"

"No. All appears quiet on the rebel front."

"H-m-m. And does your wound still pain you?"

"My wound?"

"The one inflicted by that brave army mule."

He snorted in disgust. "No glorious wound, that! Need you recall it?"

"You forget that I was there when it was inflicted."

"And no doubt laughed at my misfortune!"

She chuckled softly. "It is humorous. If not at the time, certainly it must be so in retrospect."

They were riding close together and he leaned near. "Not so much the wound as its healing. I recall an uncomfortable lad who helped to nurse me. Had I known his true identity, no doubt I would have been less careless of appearing without breeches."

Embarrassment spread through her at the memory. She rode on, speechless, ignoring his laughter that echoed on the crisp morning air. "You need not be shy with me about it," he said. "Only you and I know of it."

"And the entire king's army! Had I known of the dire straits into which I would fall, I would never have left home."

"A lesson learned too late, I would say."

"Deign not to make yourself my teacher, sir."

"Can you forget so easily that I was your teacher in one special matter? Passion has its mentor."

She spurred her horse ahead of his, anger her whip, until she outdistanced him. The scoundrel! Must he refer to that most secret moment with so little caution? She could not survive two weeks of his presence were he to flaunt that strange and painful memory.

She brought her horse into the livery at a gallop, reined it to a halt before a startled Peter. She jumped off, landing breathless and wind-blown only moments before the captain arrived.

"Saura! What are you doing, girl?" Peter exclaimed.

Seth arrived in time to hear her say, "I've come to warn you that the British are coming!"

"Good day, Mister Blake. I am on my way back to Boston and I have another writ of stay from the quartermaster. I hope that a two-week stay will not inconvenience you overly much."

Saura looked expectantly at her father and did not hide her amazement as he answered, "No inconvenience at all, Captain Adams."

"Father!"

"You have something to say, daughter?"

"Half of the rooms at Wilfred's inn are empty. Why can he not be quartered there?"

"Please excuse my bold daughter. She appears to have completely forgotten her manners." He turned to her sternly. "The captain has quartering papers for our house, Saura, and this is where the army wishes him to stay, although I cannot guess why. But military workings are often strange, is that not so, Captain?"

"Indeed."

"Please come in and make yourself at home, sir. No doubt a bath would feel pleasant after your ride. You are free to use our bath closet off the kitchen. Saura will see to your linens."

"Thank you, sir," the captain said, nodding at the smithy. He turned to unsaddle his horse and find the animal feed and water. Then he carried his bag into the house and Saura watched him go.

"I just do not understand it, Father. How can you welcome him with open arms? Does he not represent everything that our colonies fight against?"

"Yes and no, girl. His uniform does represent that which we oppose but his demeanor is that of a gentleman. Despite his wearing of the red, he is a well-educated man with good manners. Would you have us turn him away and let suspicion fall on this household?"

"Yes."

Peter sighed and tried to be patient. "If we fight openly for the cause, we will be of little use. But if we stay low with our ears open, who knows what knowledge we might happen across? Just think of the captain as a library of military knowledge ready to be studied."

"But two weeks!"

"Try to show a little kindness to the man and the time will go fast. Were you to get to know him, I am sure that you would not find him such a bad fellow. In truth, you might grow to like him. He is most personable."

I know him better than you think, she thought to herself but dared not utter the words.

"You might be surprised and find in him a friend. He is certainly more prepossessing than the foppish suitors about whom you complain."

"You would consider the captain as a suitor?" she asked in amazement.

"I did not say that, girl. Only that you might find him to be a gentleman, worthy of kindness. And should your pretty face win his heart and charm him over to our side of the cause, I have no doubt that Samuel Adams would not mind," he said with a teasing smile.

"He has no heart to win over," she muttered to herself as Peter slipped his arm around his daughter and guided her toward the house.

She did as her father admonished, supplying the captain with linens and serving up a lunch of pork chops with apple rings and baked acorn squash. The meal was unusually quiet and Peter assumed that Saura's idea of politeness was simply not to talk. He sighed. What was he to do with this girl whom he loved so much?

The captain discussed the weather and his travels and gave no word of his military activities. Saura watched him as she ate. He talked seriously, his dark eyes alert, his face a study of interest in all things of which her father or Erastus spoke. And if some common jest was shared, he laughed, amber flashes lighting his dark eyes. And now and then, more frequently than not, his gaze would come to rest on her and then her heart would quicken. And should her glance meet his, she would look away. She sat there so demurely, he thought, her demeanor so falsely meek, that she could deceive the angels. When not biting out a tart reply or putting him in his place with a look of disdain, she seemed like an angel herself. That gentle curve of cheek with its pink tinge, the lips so softly inviting and the eyes as deep as a shadowed well were all deceptive. He knew well the light that could flicker in those eyes and the mocking that could touch those lips.

The dinner finished, Saura started to clear away the dishes and Seth rose to help her. At her questioning glance, he shrugged. "I only seek to earn my keep." She said nothing as he helped her put away the silver sugar box, porringer and chafing dish. Peter watched in amusement as the king's soldier carried dishes and removed a bowl of table bones.

Saura stood at the wooden sink and drainboard, grating soap into flakes and pouring a kettle of boiling water in the tub. Seth watched her add more water to reach the right temperature and then soap the dishes with a cloth. As she dipped the plates into a pot of clear hot water to rinse them, she nodded toward a towel. "You said you wished to help." He caught up the towel and began to dry the water off before the dishes grew cold. The task was strange to him and he did his best under her scrutiny.

That familiar feeling of wordless intimacy returned, as it often did when they were alone. When she handed him a dish, he leaned over her, catching a whiff of her tresses; then the memory of a heated night and a haunting fragrance invaded his senses. Suddenly he bent down, kissing her hair in a movement so light that Saura looked up unsure whether he had touched her. Their faces were only inches apart. She did not pull away but stared instead into his deep-burning eyes. She had no power to stay him; neither did she move but stood instead breathless as he gazed at her. His mouth came closer to her own and his warm lips touched hers.

Suddenly he dropped the towel to the floor and as though his arms had a will of their own, they encircled the slender girl and pulled her to him. Deaf to any protest, he knew only the aching desire to hold her. His kiss spoke of unuttered longing, of passion too long withheld. The moistness of her velvety lips so appealed to his manly senses that quick-leaping heat bolted through the very marrow of his bones.

* * *

Peter and Erastus were aware that a platter hit the floor as the tinny sound of clattering metal reached the library. There was a commotion of some kind and low, strained voices could be heard. Curiosity drew them to the kitchen's threshold and they looked in at the couple standing before the wooden sink.

At Saura's feet lay the large silver platter. The girl's cheeks were flushed, her lips unusually bright as her eyes widened in feigned innocence. The captain bent down to retrieve the platter, slipping it into the sink. "She dropped it," he explained casually enough.

Peter nodded. "I see. When you are finished here, Captain, you might wish to join us in the library for a taste of brandy."

"Thank you. I would like that."

As they turned to leave, Erastus held back a smile. He had not missed the dishtowel on the floor.

Saura angrily sloshed soapy water over the platter and dipped it in the rinse kettle. Then she thrust it at the captain, who caught it as he might a bayonet's thrust. She hurriedly finished the dishes, ignoring him as she wiped her hands on her apron. Then she hastily tugged at the ties of her apron, inadvertently pulling them into a knot. The more she struggled, the less the ties co-operated. Seth pushed her hands aside and she stood there in the throes of humiliation as his fingers deftly freed the knot. She whipped the apron off, tossing it onto a hook.

"No need to thank me. Freeing you from apron strings was a pleasure."

She turned on him, pointing an accusing finger. "You have gone too far, Tory! I will not be accosted in my own home."

He held up his hands in jesting treaty. "Let me apologize, miss. It was most improper of me."

"Do you mock me, sir?"

He shook his head. "No. I am in earnest. I should not have kissed you, despite the desires that urged me on."

"You had best agree to make no further advances in my home for I cannot hide the truth from my father for long. I will not cover your actions and play the inno-cent!"

"You are right. I think it is best if we go to your father and explain the situation."

"What?" Her eyes were blazing.

"How can you expect me to play the fool? And is that not what happens? Here I am, thrust into your presence where you are so near to me and yet I am forbidden to touch you in even the slightest way."

"What makes you think you have any right?" she demanded sharply.

His eyes narrowed and he leaned near her. When he spoke his voice chilled her. "Right? I have every legal right, Mistress Adams."

She took in a breath and stepped back, her eyes wid-ening as she stared at him. She was speechless as he continued, "Do you expect me to dwell in this house with you and never be allowed the slightest touch when I have memories of you that fire my very blood?"

"Then go to the inn and be out of these difficult circumstances."

"That is what I will do. But it will bring up questions and I will lie no more! When your father asks why I depart, I shall tell him the truth."

He started to leave the kitchen and she caught ahold of his arm and spun him around. He stared down into eyes wide with panic. "Captain Adams! I beg you not to take such folly!" she whispered fiercely. "You prom-ised to keep the secret. Are you not a man of your word?"

"I am. And that is exactly why I cannot go on in this pretended lie."

"Will you at least reconsider?"

He paused for a minute. "Perhaps. Maybe there is a way."

"Yes?" she urged, anxious for any solution at this point.

A hint of a smile touched his lips as he looked down at her. "Be my wife." She stared at him in stunned silence, unable to answer. "Do not be so horrified. I do not ask that you come to my room or bear my children. But I do desire the tender companionship that you do not allow. Would it break your icy heart to grant me a smile or to speak with kindness? Would you be so repulsed were you to accept a loving kiss once in a while from me, such as was given just now?"

An ache welled up inside Saura. He thought her heart icy! Did he not sense the response she fought to control? She stood there, stilling the trembling of her lips until he spoke once more, a hard note creeping into his voice. "I thought not."

He moved past her and through the door into the hall. She watched him stride toward the library—and then something like a floodgate broke within her. She turned and ran after him, scurrying around to stand before him as his hand rested on the library doorknob. Seth took in her countenance, the dark tendrils of hair escaping about her face, her lips breathlessly catching at words.

"Very well! I strike the bargain, redcoat."

"That is not my name," he said casually.

She stared at him for a moment. "All right. I strike the bargain, Captain Adams."

"My name is Seth."

She rolled her eyes and he reached for the knob. "Seth!" she cried out, placing her palms against him as though to ward off his entry despite the fact that she stood between him and the door.

He drew back, nodding. "For my silence you will treat me with kindness and courtesy?"

She nodded.

"And you will try to affect a wife's demeanor?"

After a pause she nodded again and he smiled down at her, knowing the sweet taste of victory. "Then let us seal the bargain."

She sighed and extended her hand; he grasped it in the warmth of his own before sweeping her into his arms and kissing her hungrily. Saura caught back an outcry of protest as his mouth lingered on her own until its heat spread throughout her veins. Finally he released her, stepping back. She restrained any words she might have spoken. Instead she stood before him meekly although within, her emotions were seething.

Seth smiled and nodded his approval. "Now that is the way a wife should behave," he said before stepping past her into the library.

Every redcoat taunt or insulting British name that she could think of came to mind. She had been bested by this Tory and he knew it! She fled up to her room and bolted the door shut.

Morning crept into Seth Adams's room, gray and chill and preaching of November. He had spent a peaceful night even though interrupted by dreams of Saura. The young woman who was now his wife in name only had disturbed his sleep. He stretched and cast off the warmth of the quilt, going to the washstand and breaking the ice in the pitcher. He washed as briefly as possible, pulling on his breeches, boots and shirt. He ran a comb through his hair and tied it back neatly with a black band of ribbon. Then he went downstairs, where the sounds of the kitchen caught his attention.

Morning found Saura already in the throes of making marrow dumplings. Seth stood in the door's frame watching her scoop up the marrow with a dipper made from a hollowed gourd. She cracked in four brown eggs, stirred in bread crumbs, parsley, nutmeg and then seasoned the mixture with salt and pepper.

Saura felt his eyes on her and glanced toward the threshold, her heart jumping a beat.

"Good morn, Captain Adams. You are up unusually early." She sounded so cordial, he mused, that she must be taking their bargain seriously.

"Good morn. I might say the same about you. You do appear to be every inch the domestic wife."

"These wifely chores I did long before I was provided a husband," she said as she formed the dumplings and dropped them into hot chicken soup. "Would you like some bread and honey?"

He accepted the offer, spooning the honey thoughtfully. She appeared so sweet in manner this morning that he thought he had best test the security of his bargain. "It appears that you have accepted my bargain, so kind are you at this early hour."

She glanced up at him. "It takes more than one night's rest to break my promise, Captain."

"Will you please address me on less formal terms? I've a first name, you know. And since you say the bargain still holds, then let me ask a favor."

"What might that be?"

"A proper morning greeting."

Her smile faded. Did this knave wish to taste her lips before the cock had hardly crowed? "Captain... Seth, you cannot wish more than words when it is scarcely light outside."

"What better time to ward off the chill of the night?" he smiled.

"Do you test me, and the bargain?"

He laughed. "You are coming to know me well." He held out his hand to her and she sighed, wiping her hands on her apron and stepping near. He caught her and pulled her to him, lifting her chin with his fingers. "So modest and prim a bride, even the preacher could not complain. I would have my wife more willing."

"You test the limit of my abilities," she said but lifted her face so that he could bring his mouth to hers. The familiar warmth engulfed her. She was swept away from the kitchen chores and into the heated darkness of his embrace. Her hands rested against his muscular chest and she fought to control their desire to slip about his neck. When he at last released her mouth, his arms were still holding her close and she glanced up at him.

"I would have another," he said.

She shook her head and lowered it lest his mouth sweep down again to claim hers. "I will be unable to keep my end of the bargain should you press your advantage too frequently, sir. 'Tis at a disadvantage you place me and I desire that you should not take use of me too freely."

He nodded and let his arms slip away from her waist. "You have passed my testing and I shall hold to my part of our bargain. I think I'll go see how my horse fares and whether he needs feed." He went out the kitchen door and into the cold morning air.

It was bracing, and he needed that! As she requested,

he would not seek a kiss too frequently—not because the restraint would please her but rather to stay the effect that the touch of her lips had upon him.

In the kitchen Saura leaned against the sink. This was the second day in the anticipated two-week period and already her defenses were weakening. If only that fateful night had never happened, she would have easily found the strength to hold strong against his attacks. But there was always that dark memory to undermine her resistance. How could she ease the mounting of her inner conflict?

The following two days passed with less emotional turmoil and Saura was relieved. Captain Adams seemed to keep his distance, rarely demanding that she partake of her "wifely duty." Yet this left her nerves on end, never knowing when his approach might catch her unaware.

The Sabbath arrived and the Blakes went to church. Since Greenhollow was small, there was only one church. The minister, Reverend Fretwell, was a kindly man and well-learned. This Sunday his sermon was on patience and he stated that patience and a meek countenance were virtues to be prized. Saura, seated between the captain and her father, received swift glances from both. Did she really appear as such a prickly rose? Afterward she was met by a smiling Harley, and Molly came forward quickly to engage Seth in conversation. Mistress Finchley and Mistress Cronwiller were all a-twitter at this new and dashing stranger. And even the Cummin sisters, despite their prim attitudes, accepted an introduction. But the captain had eyes only for Saura, who seemed to catch the attention of nearly every youth in the church.

The next day brought a bit of warmth to the Hollow and Seth made arrangements with Peter to have his horse shod. He would trade labor for the shoeing. Much to Saura's relief, he spent the day in the blacksmith's, coming to the house only for the noon meal. When by afternoon her curiosity got the best of her, she slipped out the back door to go around to the smithy's. As she entered, the fluid conversation between the men ceased. Were these two forming bonds of friendship, she to become the outsider? Nonsense. Peter was only showing the redcoat courtesy.

She took in the familiar rectangular brick fireplace with its chimney jutting out from one side. The waist-high well held a charcoal fire, the heat spreading through the enclosure. The counter at the far end of the hearth had been straightened and cleaned of debris, a place made for every tool. Behind the chimney and connected to the firewell was the bellows that pumped air in and made a great heat. There was a pole-and-chain contraption connected to the bellows and this Seth now operated while Peter did the drawing to lengthen the piece of hot metal. Erastus was putting together the wood pit. By burning hard woods in a conelike pile, without air, charcoal would be created. Smokeless, it burned hotter than wood and suited the men's needs.

Yet of the three men at their chores, it was Seth who caught Saura's attention. Having donned a set of Peter's leather breeches, his chest naked in the heat and gleaming with sweat, he appeared every inch the virile man. His muscles were taut as he worked, the dark hair on his chest curling in the dampness. She watched as he cradled his horse's hoof in his lap and pulled out eight nails. Then he pared the hoof with a knife, cutting away the unwanted growth, giving the hoof a proper slope and a good flat surface. His hands were strong as he worked, yet gentle. She knew those hands, and their touch. She tore her gaze away from him, watching Peter forge the shoes, shaping them around the anvil's horn, bending up the ends and welding a clip to the front topside. He finished off the sharp ends, bending the edges downward. Then he proceeded with a gentle filing to make the shoe and hoof even.

Seth's horse shod, they went on to other things, for Peter was a jack-of-all-trades who forged the red-hot iron into manufactures from tools and plowshares to weather vanes. Saura left the men to their work, returning to the house as a light drift of snow began to fall. It appeared that Seth Adams was a man of varied experience for he had handled the shoeing as though he had been born to it. The man was ever a puzzlement to her.

Thoughtfully she went into the kitchen and donned her apron. Into the large soup pot she put butter, onion, milk and chicken stock. Then she added salt and grated nutmeg. Lastly she added a beaten egg yolk. This mixture would be poured over toasted slices of her homemade bread. It was called the king's soup, although she would never know why for it was more likely a common folk dish. This and a cabbage salad she had already prepared would make up their fare. She had managed simply so that she could finish reading the book of Shakespeare's sonnets. Yet as she read, her mind kept wandering back to the half-naked, muscular man at the fire bellows. She finally threw the book aside, thinking that such praise of love was not what she wished to read.

The following day Seth again spent his time with Peter and Saura wondered why friendship was fast forming between these two who should be foe. Besides preparing the meals, she spent her time in reading, or walking in the forest despite the smattering of snow. She was restless, wanting something, yet not knowing what it was.

She wrapped a shawl around her shoulders and took to one of the paths behind the house. She had felt strangely trapped inside. She never knew when she might turn to find Seth watching her or hear his approaching footsteps. And more nerve-wracking than these surprise moments were the times when she turned, expecting to see him and finding him not there. Although his demands on her as a wife had not become too frequent, still they shook her.

She breathed deeply of the solitude as she passed a white birch that cast a shadow across the untouched snow. She walked along a path beside a small stream and rounded its bend to come face to face with a shadowed form. She let out a cry and nearly fell but a hand shot out, grasping her arm and steadying her.

"Seth," she gasped. "You startled me out of my wits!"

He stepped out of the trees' shadows. Suddenly she felt very small as the menacing form loomed above her. "So, we meet in the woods."

"I had no idea that you were out here. This is always the path I take when I want some solitude."

"H-m-m. Then chance has brought us together for I just spied this walk from the other side of the wall and wondered where it led."

"It reaches a small clearing not far on. 'Tis a fine and secluded place for meditation."

"Then show it to me, will you?"

She led the way to a spot where the trees were tall and arched. Its beauty always left Saura in awe as she lifted her eyes to the tops of the towering spruces. Even in the onset of winter she loved this special place. Seth whipped off his cloak, spreading it on the ground with a flourish. Bowing, he offered her a seat and she could do nothing but smile and accept. She sat down on the comfort of the cloak and he lowered himself beside her.

"This is a secluded place indeed, a place where—" He paused.

"Yes?"

"I was going to say a place where lovers might come."

"And you thought I would be offended should you refer to lovers?"

He shrugged and smiled. "You can be prickly prim, lass."

Her lips broke into a smile. "If I so afflict you, it is only because you try me so."

He was sitting close to her, his arm behind her, and he leaned over. "I may try your patience but you try my self-control." He lightly brushed her hair with his lips. "Have you never wished to bring a lover here?"

She said nothing for she could not deny it. Indeed she had and if ever a man fit that lover's description, it was Seth Adams.

As the clouds moved, sunlight cast a golden ribbon among the trees to lie across the forest snow. Seth's fingers reached her chin, turning her face to his and she was helpless in the grasp of sudden emotion.

"Why do you do this to me?" she murmured just before his eager lips pressed warm into her own. She knew the rushing sweep of surrender and he felt her body tremble as she lay back in his arms. The passion of his lips and his tight embrace carried her away. She was helpless against the surging assault on her senses and her arms slipped readily around his neck. Again he kissed her, and again. And she could do nothing but give in to the tides that swept over her. Was he not her husband? Did he not have legal and moral claim to her? Was it sinful to surrender to his husbandly affection?

The softness of her body was pressed into his steel-like frame, the fabric too thin between them, and too thick. Seth's head reeled as she lay in his embrace and returned his kisses, her arms urgently entwined about his neck. Desire was a hot brand, scorching him. If only she could lie in his clasp as a newly wedded bride should! He had never experienced such intense desire for her as now. She was an unrelenting thirst that must be quenched! Would the quiet of the meadowy knoll serve as a marriage bed, he wondered as a yearning not to be denied wiped away all sense of propriety.

Their deep absorption was broken by the sound of distant footsteps. Startled, Saura was jolted back to her senses and she pulled away despite Seth's reluctant release. They were surprised to hear a feminine voice call out Seth's name and they stared down the curving path as Molly Yates stumbled into the grove.

Her white blouse was tightly tucked into a full skirt, her shawl falling away to show the deep cut of her neckline. The smile on her face quickly disappeared as she took in Seth's proximity to Saura and the disheveled state of Saura's clothes. The three were caught in awkward silence until Saura came to her feet. "Molly."

"Well, Saura! Imagine finding you here with the captain."

No doubt that was the last thing Molly had expected to find, Saura thought. "I was just going back. If you will excuse me now."

Seth stood up and retrieved his cloak as she strode away, anger apparent in her stride. Did she think that he and Molly...? Never! He turned on the serving maid. "How did you know to find me here?" he asked coolly.

"I saw you head up the path while on my way to drop off a meal to old Mister Waverly. I never would have thought you'd be meeting Saura," she said slyly.

"Our meeting was by accident."

"I thought so!" she said too eagerly. "I know that a man like yourself would not bother with a mere girl. It seems to me that a man's real affection should be given to a real woman." She neared him, linking her arm in his and leaning against him seductively. It was apparent that the maid was begging for a kiss. He looked down at the pretty upturned face but a fairer vision came to mind. With the memory of her taste still on his lips, it was like exchanging the sweet smell of spring for a cloying perfume. He disengaged Molly's arm, walking down the path to leave her gaping after him.

Saura's anger brought her storming into the house. She shook the snow from her shawl and cast the wrap on the hook in the closet. Peter took in her appearance—the bits of grass caught in her tumbled mass of hair, her flushed face and bright lips.

He leaned back in his chair. "Is something wrong, girl?"

"Everything!" she cried, pacing up and down in agitation. "Will you tell that lobsterback to get out of our house?"

Peter and Erastus looked at her in surprise. "You want us to eject him from the house? But he has orders from the quartermaster."

"Then let him use them at the inn!"

"Why are you so angry with the captain?" Peter asked, studying her closely. "He hasn't done anything improper?"

"Well, of course he has!" she blurted out in exasperation. "Can you be so blind to what the man is?"

Peter stood up just as Seth entered, shutting the door behind him and looking into the three faces before him. Trouble, he thought to himself.

"Captain Adams," Peter said sternly, "it appears that

152

something has been going on under my roof that I should know about. Will you explain?"

"No!" The three men looked at her in surprise. Her anger was replaced with obvious fear.

Peter looked again at the captain. "Is what has happened such that my daughter fears to speak of it?"

"Pardon my anger, Father," Saura pleaded. "Ask him not for explanation."

Peter felt his ire rise. "First you disdain this man with vehemence. Then you show him kindness these past few days and now you return with a demand that he be quartered at the inn."

"It appears to me that he would be happier there!" Seth smiled when she said this. Was she jealous? "See? He smiles at the very thought!" Saura groaned and turned away in indignation.

"Captain Adams, I demand an explanation of what has been going on," Peter said, his face grim. "Speak the truth, man."

Saura whirled about, her eyes wide with appeal, but Seth ignored her. "If you want the truth, so be it!" he said angrily. He grabbed Saura and pulled her to him, blatantly kissing her before the two men. She struggled away, flushed and angry, the air filled with stunned silence. "This is what has been going on," Seth stated coolly.

Peter regarded the captain, his fists clenched. "You, whom I have taken in, would take advantage of my daughter?"

"No, sir. I have not taken advantage of your daughter. I have taken the mildest of liberties with...my wife."

Saura moaned and sank into a chair. No one moved or said a word until finally Peter turned to her with an expression she could not even begin to fathom. "Is what the captain says true? You need not answer. I can see it in your countenance. How, I do not understand. I cannot even guess it." He turned to Seth for an explanation.

The captain sighed. "Do you remember the time that

153

she ran away from home? She went to Braintree and we were wed there."

"How did you ever get her permission?" Erastus asked in amazement.

"There was no permission!" Saura cried out. "I was forced to it through the cruel actions of the bloody redcoats!"

Seth explained briefly the happenings since his account was more truthful and less colorful than Saura's would be. He concluded with, "And so we were wed; my Major Berkely was certain that this step would give her the guidance she needed."

Peter sank back into his chair, nodding his head. "So this is the course your headstrong will has brought you through!" he said to his daughter, whose tears gleamed brightly unshed. This explained her moping unhappiness after her return. "But why have you kept the marriage a secret if the whole king's army knows of it?"

There was silence for a minute and Seth answered for her. "She did not wish to bear the news to you that your only daughter was wed to an enemy of the colonists. Or at least that is her feeling."

"Is this true?"

She nodded. "I have shamed you, Father," she whispered. "All that we fight for and believe in, he opposes!"

"You could have come to me," Peter said, holding out his hand. She flew to him and burst into tears in his arms. The release of her burden was a great easement to her heart. "I do not make a very good soldier," she sobbed against his chest. He comforted her until she pulled away, drying her tears.

"I am disappointed, most of all because you did not come to me with the truth of your plight. But it was not of your choosing—I can see that well enough." He sighed and patted her shoulder. "I find no anger with you, daughter. It was not of your planning but rather that of the king's army."

She sniffed, thinking that she should have confided in her father long ago. He would set everything right now. "And he," she cried, pointing an accusing finger at the captain, "refused to be a gentleman and annul this folly!"

Seth appeared helpless for a moment but Peter did not look at him with accusation. Instead he asked, "This Major Berkely who married you, he is a clergy?"

The captain nodded. "Ordained of the cloth and a righteous man, despite his interference in your daughter's life."

"I see."

"Well?" Saura asked, staring up at Peter with tear-brimmed eyes. "What are you going to do, Father?"

He was thoughtful for a moment, stroking her hair. "What am I going to do? Why, nothing."

"What?" she cried, pulling away as though he had slapped her.

"There is nothing I can do. A man of the cloth, whether British or American, still has the power to bind God's law. And you are subject to it." He shook his head in dismay. "Perhaps this will teach you what folly your willful ways can bring. I cannot say that I am happy about this. A British soldier for your husband? No, not in a thousand years would I have guessed it. And how shall we explain it to our neighbors, who believe in the cause? This shall stir up a hornets' nest."

"Then you are against the marriage," she stated hopefully.

"Whether or not I am is unimportant. As Captain Adams has stated, the marriage was bound by a servant of God. And perhaps this is His punishment to teach you. You will have to learn from this to make the best of a miserable happening."

It was then that Peter caught sight of the captain and softened a bit. "As for you, I am sorry to say that a king's soldier is not what I had in mind for my daughter's husband. Though I think you to be an honest man and as a person, I like you well, still our political views are far apart and I dread to think of such conflict under the same roof. But it is true that there are people in the Hollow who hold fast to their loyalty for King George and yet I consider them friends. However, should we come to war with England, sides must be chosen up. And it is apparent as to which way each of us shall go."

With a sigh he rested his large hands on his knees. "I shall accept you as a family member as best I can, although it seems to me that this cannot but become a household of unrest."

"You mean that you will not fight for an annulment?" Saura cried incredulously, finally finding her voice.

"No, I will not."

"But you have not heard the worst! When he came here, housed under this very roof, he took advantage of my helplessness. He promised only to keep his silence as long as I would..." She faltered, embarrassment spreading a pink tinge along her cheek. She took a deep breath, "...as long as I would treat him kindly and let him kiss me."

This latest revelation would surely bring some reaction, she thought. Suddenly the silence was broken by a deep, mellow sound from Erastus. Laughter! It rang through the house and caught her unaware. "Now, that," he managed between guffaws, "is what I call enterprise!"

Even her angry stare could not silence the laughing Erastus. In plea she turned to her father. "How can he laugh at my plight? Do none of you see how wrongly I have been abused? Do you plan to let this rogue get away with such scandalous actions?"

"You agreed to the bargain," Seth said calmly, his words bringing a new gust of merriment from Erastus.

"He's right," Peter said, his New England common sense coming to the surface. "Captain Adams has every right to ask of you what a wife should give. The deed is done and we cannot return spilled cider to the pitcher. You had best come to make a difficult situation acceptable, for our home must always be hospitable to the captain."

Her dearest allies had turned traitor and her eyes showed exactly what she thought. Her own father was punishing her for that which she had been helpless to stop. Had he been the true patriot she had always believed, he would have cast out this detestable soldier! She turned to flee up the stairs but then whirled about, coming face to face with the captain. She shook her finger at him.

"The bargain is off, redcoat! Wife in name only, do you understand? This is no marriage in my view and I shall deny it so do not spread the rumor about Green-hollow. I shall brand it a lie. You have no claim to me and if you dare to lay one finger on me ever again, it shall come back to you a bloodied stump!"

She turned and fairly flew up the stairs, slamming the door shut. She threw herself across the bed, sobbing loudly into her pillow. Piper jumped up beside her, meowing mournfully as though to share her misery. But his mistress would not be comforted.

Outside the window the sky was a dark gray and snow filtered down to hush the frozen land.

All day the hoary meteor fell;
And when the second morning shone,
We looked upon a world unknown.

—JOHN GREENLEAF WHITTIER

# Chapter VIII

AS THOUGH Massachusetts had received too little snow in the past few months, the heavens made up for the negligence. The gray cotton masses overhead released snow for two days without let-up. The river moved dark, indigo among the white crystalline edges of its banks. The trees were gowned in the pristine featherings of winter, the lane to town packed hard and slick. A cord of maple was cut and now stood stacked in comfort against the threat of the snow, fires burning continually in the hearths.

The world appeared lonely without, yet within the Blake household it was even more dreary. Saura refused to come down to meals or to have anything to do with the three treacherous men below. She did not cook their meals, leaving the chore to Erastus. They did not eat as well as they had for she had learned a skill at cooking. While the house itself showed neglect, it was the lack of her bright appearance that most pained the three. She had seldom unlocked her door, ignoring their knocks. Whether she supped, sneaking portions from the kitchen at night, or whether she chose to starve herself, they did not know.

They sat about the table eating an overseasoned porridge and hard biscuits. Peter leaned back, pushing away his half-eaten gruel. "Erastus, I'd forgotten just how really awful your cooking is!"

"Necessity never made a good bargain," he retorted. "You could try your hand at it if you think you'd do better."

"Ha! I'd poison us all."

"Well," Seth said, taking a heavy draught of tea to wash away the taste of the porridge, "she cannot stay locked away in her room forever."

The older men stared at him. Finally Erastus said, "You do not know our Saura."

He nodded, accepting this. Saura, on the other hand, was just as miserable as they. She had no liking for being so alone. Even Piper was deserting her as the days turned colder, escaping downstairs to the warmth of the main hearth. She had tried to read but nothing long held her attention. Looking out through the frosted window now, she saw that the snow had finally stopped. Perhaps the chill would ease and a little sunlight come in. Her hopes were dashed as the air grew frigid during the night, the river freezing over into a ribbon of slick blue-white ice. The snow froze and the air in her room could be seen as she breathed. She gained the courage to leave her bed and dress hastily, donning a frock of red wool over layers of extra petticoats. She put on her heaviest slippers, lined with fur, but still she was cold through. She had used up the last of her supply of wood during the night and now the embers were dead. As she rubbed her hands, she went to the pitcher of water to wash. When she looked in it, she saw that the water was frozen solid. With that her pride snapped. She could cloister herself in her room no longer! Even nature had turned against her. She managed to grab her hairbrush before the cold drove her from the room.

* * *

Seth sat back in his chair, having poured himself a mug of hot drink and two for his friends, who had just stumbled in after seeing to the horses. Peter held his hands out before the fire while Erastus beat his arms together, exclaiming, "It is colder than hell's cavern!"

"I always thought that hell was hot," Seth mused.

"Then send me there! Winter's not begun, yet I am ready for spring."

Seth growled noncommittally and slammed the cup down, some of the hot liquid spilling on his hand. He swore and brushed it off.

"You are in poor spirits today," Peter said.

"Why shouldn't I be?" he snapped.

"She'll come down sometime. She's just being ornery. When the cold gets to her, she'll bend her pride a bit."

"Peter's right. She'll soon run out of wood. I've been keeping an eye on the firewood and she hasn't taken any."

"We all know how stubborn she is," Seth said. "How can she hold on to her pride like this?"

"It's her feelings that have been hurt," Erastus replied. "I should not have laughed at your bargain."

"Damn the bargain! That is the cause of all her anger."

"Bargaining has neither friends nor relations," Peter said. "And you have both learned that too late."

They were thinking this over then they heard a light tread on the stair and glanced up expectantly. Saura paused for a moment before entering and taking a seat by the fire. She had not anticipated a receiving party. She held her fingers out to the heat, letting them thaw.

Peter brought his daughter a steaming mug as casually as though she had never been away. She wrapped her fingers around it gratefully and sipped at the warmth. Erastus brought her a plate of ham and fried-potato slices.

She nodded her thanks and ate heartily, her stolen fare of old bread and cheese having left her wanting. Once through with the food and drink, she felt in better humor and glanced at Seth, who was gazing intently at her. She expected some mocking word but there was none and he smiled at her in greeting. She could not refrain from returning a slight smile. Then she took up her hairbrush and busied herself with the locks she had been too cold to brush properly.

The captain leaned back in his chair, stretching his legs out to catch the heat. He felt comfortable for the first time in two days. He watched the lovely maid brush her brown tresses until they gleamed. Then she parted the hair and brought it to the side, her fingers deftly plaiting it. When she had braided the silken length, she brought it into a loop, tying it with a strand of red velvet. Then she turned her head to the other side and began the plaiting again.

Saura was aware of the captain's study of her and more than once her fingers faltered. Had she known his thoughts, she could not have done so deft a job. He was concentrating on the nape of her neck, where the hair was gracefully swept upward, thinking of what a tender delight it would be to kiss that special hollow.

As the two older men busied themselves, he leaned near her, speaking softly for her ears only. "I have missed you."

She could not help but smile as she tied the second braid. "Strange as it seems to me," she responded, "I have missed you too."

He was so surprised that he half laughed. "You have?"

She nodded. "I have always liked a fight and you are a good foe."

When the smithy and his assistant heard the laughter from the other room, they smiled to themselves. Saura's gay spirits had been sorely missed.

It had been cold before but now it turned frigid. An icy wind sweeping down from northern regions whipped and whistled about the house and moaned with freezing breath. The windows and doors, although tightened against the cold, could not keep out the icy drafts.

"We're running low on firewood, not having expected this cold spell so soon," Peter declared. "Good thing I stacked up an extra load for Bathsheba and put in more hay for the horses."

"Do you want me to go cut some wood?" Seth volunteered.

"No, no! It is far too cold. You would never get the axe through the logs and no doubt you'd come back frozen like a block of ice."

"Then what shall we do?" Saura asked, not having seen a winter like this one since her move to America.

"We've enough for two more fires should we conserve our energies. That will last us until tomorrow when, hopefully, this freeze will have fled. Erastus is more familiar with cold weather. What's best to do?"

"Let's close off the main hearth. It sucks up too much heat. Then we can go upstairs. The wood will last longer if we use the bedroom fireplaces."

"All right. And let's take out more quilts and pile them on the beds. We can spend the day there until the weather abates."

"Indeed?" Erastus asked. "What about my room? It's backed only on your fireplace and there isn't enough warmth that way."

"Bunk with me," Peter said. "We can have a discourse on Jefferson's new freedom letter."

"Just let me first grab some bread and cheese and a basket of apples from the cellar." In passing Seth, he paused for a moment, his face bemused. "We forgot the captain."

"What? Oh. If the fire has gone out down here, he'll freeze. Isn't this where you spent last night? That attic room must have ice in it by now. You'll have to bundle with Saura."

She looked up at her father as though he had lost his mind. "Father! Do you know what you suggest?"

"Well, you can leave your clothes on. That's the idea, girl. You're safe enough under all those petticoats."

She blushed with embarrassment and Seth dared not laugh. It hurt her feelings that her father surrendered so easily. Did he still seek to punish her? She could see the determination in him to accept Seth Adams as a family member. "I thought you were supposed to protect me," she said to Peter. "Instead you room me with a redcoat?"

"Heavens, girl! Look at who I have to bunk with and

163

you don't see me complaining. Besides, he is your husband."

"That is all the more reason for me to trust him less. I stated once that to me this is no marriage. Only to him."

"I'll be right next door."

"I shall stay here, where a lady is safe."

Peter's angry reply was cut short by Erastus returning from the cellar with a small basket of apples and a long, dusty board. The latter he wiped off with a rag.

"What is that?" Peter questioned. It was a foot wide and an oval the size of a face had been cut in it.

"Don't you know?" Erastus laughed. "This is a bundling board. The people out here use them all the time. 'Cept there hasn't been a cold enough winter to use one since we've been here. Much to the misery of courting youth. I'll be willing to bet that these are being brought out of attics and cellars all over the state. You just put this between the two and they can talk."

Peter thought it a great jest. "There! You can have no complaint of using this device, suited to proper young misses, and you are wed besides. A great invention, I think. Tell me again, what is this thing called?"

"A bundling board," Erastus said.

Peter laughed again, although Saura found no humor in it. Yet as the flue was closed off, the cold drove them upstairs, where the men stoked up the fires until the flames roared in the two hearths. Peter watched as Seth bowed gallantly to allow Saura to climb into bed, the heavy feather comfortables wrapped around her. The bundling board in place, the captain did likewise and she lay upon her pillow looking at her husband through the oval. Erastus dumped out half of the apples on their bed and then hurried to the room on the other side of the wall. As Seth lay looking at Saura through the board, the talk from the other room drifting in, he smiled and shrugged, handing her an apple through the hole. She could not help but burst into laughter and he joined her.

"I will admit," he said, "that it has been my most

recent desire to come to this room and gain admittance. However, this is hardly how I imagined it."

This renewed her laughter and finally she said, "Ever since you have come into my life, everything has turned upside down and now I do not understand what my life is coming to."

"Perhaps you have despised my entrance into your life but at least you cannot be plagued with boredom."

"True! When you are here, nothing is staid. Do you know that after all we have been through, I know almost nothing of you? Who are you, Seth Adams?"

"There is nothing too exciting to tell. I lost my mother at an early age and was raised by a kind father. He is a good man, God-fearing and a man of principles."

"What does he do for support?"

"He is a blacksmith."

She looked at him in surprise. "He is? What a peculiar coincidence. That must explain your skill in the livery and with the anvil. I wondered about that."

"He is not unlike your father."

"And what did he think of your joining the army?"

"It was his idea. He is most approving. He helped me get my commission and not long after enrollment in the ranks, I advanced. Sooner than I planned, I found myself a captain. Then, a few months ago, I was sent here. Not a very interesting tale, I suppose."

"Interesting enough. Yet I think there must be more to you than that. You are a complex man, Captain. And a puzzlement."

"I've thought the same of you, lass. You are an enigma to me. And yet I fear that should I solve the puzzle, I might still receive no answer. Why I should be so plagued by thoughts of you, I do not know. I think it is that dark memory of you in my arms that haunts me," he said softly.

Their faces were close and she could feel his breath on her cheek. "That was an error and should not be brought up. Can you not let those embers die on the hearth?"

He smiled sadly. "Would that I could. Your lips are so near to mine and yet there is no temptation so long as this damned board lies between us. Do you see the sad level to which you have brought me?"

"I suppose that it is foolish when once we..." Her voice faltered. "Should you wish to remove it, I will not protest if you promise to keep your distance."

"Thank you, no! If I am not allowed to hold my wife in my arms, even with her father's approval, the board can stay in place."

Why was he angry? She tried only to show him a little kindness. She changed the subject and they talked about many things—their upbringing and their families, friends, enjoyed activities. Politics were carefully avoided.

After several hours the winds abated and the cloud cover began to thin. When it was warm enough for Peter to leave the bed, he went to his daughter's room to find the bundling board on the floor and Saura asleep in Seth's arms. She had not slept well in the cold during the past two nights and now, in the warmth of his embrace, she slept soundly, damp tendrils curling around her face. Peter went back to his room.

When the cold relented, the sun sent out weak rays by late afternoon. The household gathered down in the kitchen as Saura stirred up the last of the berries preserved in the cooler. She topped the mashed fruit with biscuit dough and then steamed them. They were called "grunts" because of the noise they made as they cooked. When they were ready, they were served with brandy sauce and were quite filling. Later, in the library, Seth borrowed Peter's copy of "The Tempest."

"This is my favorite of the Shakespeares," he said, sitting down and starting to read. Saura cleaned up the kitchen and by dark she retired to her bedroom. After stoking the fire, she fell to sleep immediately.

At a late hour she awakened, staring into the blackness of the room. Why she had awakened she did not know but she assumed that the earlier nap in Seth's arms had kept her from a full night's rest. Finally she arose, finding her silk wrapper and pulling it on over her gown. Then she went to the slipper box at the foot of the bed, taking out her slippers and sliding her feet into them. She lit a small candle and by its wavering light she crept down the stairs. She stopped at the kitchen for a glass of milk and a piece of bread and then went into the library. A dying fire was golden in the hearth and she shut the door behind her, coming to stand by the heat of the embers. Even cloaked in shadows, the room was familiar. It was her favorite room in Peter's house. A large scroll-top desk dominated and there were turned easy chairs, a Flemish-style couch of cane, and a Dutch chamber-clock on the mantel. The shelves on one wall held leather-bound volumes, and an oak ship's chest beneath stored important articles. Peter loved his books. As she stood there before the fire, the comfort of the room reached her, calming her nerves as her gown grew warm against her legs.

Seth's eyes slowly opened and he realized that he had fallen asleep in the comfortable chair in the shadow's corner, "The Tempest" in his lap. The candle had flickered out, the flames in the hearth burned low. Now, standing before the same fire, there was a form so fair he thought it a dream. The thin fabric of gown and robe showed sheer as the firelight silhouetted the womanly shape. Her features were edged in golden light, the tumbled mass of dark hair fading into the blackness of the room. For a moment it was as though he looked at an old master's still life. Then she moved, taking a draught from a glass and setting it down on the mantel. The spell was broken and he knew her for what she was. Despite her denials, she was fully a woman. He stood and approached her.

Saura cried out as the form of a man neared until she realized that it was Seth. She sighed and looked at him in exasperation. "Must you always spring at me from hidden shadows? My heart will not bear such shocks well."

"Pardon. I was not waiting to entrap you, you know. I fell asleep while I was reading. It was "The Tempest," a favorite of mine."

"I am familiar with the work."

"And my favorite character is Miranda. It is amazing

to me that such a woman could harbor so much passionate concern for others. Shakespeare gave her a tender heart."

"I have read it. So you think highly of a woman whose countenance is gentle and kind and caring?"

"I do."

"And no doubt you think that I have none of those qualities."

"I did not say that."

"Then would you compare me to Miranda and do so favorably?"

"I would compare you to another in one of his tales," Seth said, his hands slipping around her waist. "You bring to mind Katherine."

She looked thoughtful for a moment and he studied her. "I cannot recall which heroine she is," she mused as his hands tightened about her waist and she looked up at his rugged features etched in firelight. She went through the plays she knew so well, naming off the heroines. "No, I do not remember," she said at last.

"That is because your father does not have it in his library. I know because I looked to read it."

"But the only work my father does not have yet is 'The Taming of the Shrew,'" she said, looking up at him in innocence until she noted his rueful grin and his hands tightened about her. "Get your hands off me!" she cried, pushing him away despite his iron hold on her. She tore free, turning her back on him to leave, but he caught her arm.

"And so you prove my point further still! You choose any slight word to let you turn away in vexation, damning my cruel heart. Can you never laugh at any jest?"

"Do I really appear so ugly to you that you think me heartless, without passion or kindness?"

"Your passion I know. I had testimony of it once and I long for further proof." With this he caught her to him, his mouth capturing hers in tender entrapment. He would not release her but instead slipped his arms full about her so that her womanly softness was pressed close against him. Any words of quick retort that had been on her lips melted away and her mind was swept to regions where she feared to soar. At last he released his hold on her, staring into the depths of those dark eyes. His hands slipped up her back to entangle themselves in the silken masses of her hair. The heat of his desire for her left her awash with weakness. The fiery fight within her had frozen, useless against this man who could defeat her with his merest touch.

Suddenly the memory of their wedding night assailed her senses, a deep inner ache longing once again for that passionate entwining. All the words she used for holding him in check, all the reasoning she summoned to convince herself of what was right, seemed to evaporate like morning mist in the heat of sunlight. She placed her hands against him, running her fingers up the shirt that covered the manliness of his chest until they slipped about his neck. At this moment the aggressor slackened his grip and spoke, his voice hoarse against her ear.

"If you step from behind your barricade, Saura, I've not the strength to hold back."

It was then she knew that she wanted to be the victor in this, no matter the morrow's regrets. The sudden power she felt over this man who was superior in all things made her lightheaded. She lusted for the chance to conquer the victor. Slowly she let her fingers caress the back of his neck, bending his head down so that his lips might meet hers. She claimed his mouth in a manner similar to that in which he had claimed hers only moments before and she was exhilarated at the weakening she felt in this titan of a soldier. But this was cut short as he caused her robe to slip away, the thin gown no shield from his manly strength. Fear began to erase her earlier thrill of triumph as she realized too late the course of her actions. But there was no stopping; the road she traveled had but one destination.

He swept her up in his arms, carrying her to the long, reclining couch before the flickering fire. She lay back in his embrace, helpless to ward off the onslaught against her senses, never allowing herself a plea for release. She wanted him, this Tory who melted her with his touch.

It was as though she were made of snow, formed like the frost ladies that the Hollow's children made on wintery days. And he was the radiant sun, heat from its furnace searing her until even that heart of ice of which he complained melted beneath him.

Their bodies came together as Seth claimed her, his fingers a brush of fire wherever they stroked her skin. His lips sought her mouth and throat, to leave a shudder running through her veins. What was this ecstasy that consumed her, causing her to moan as he took her? Had she forgotten that time not so long ago when they had become one as man and woman? Once again the bond was forged in the molten ore as successive waves of heat thundered through her limbs. She who had sought to be the victor found herself now in willing surrender, eager for his conquering to come. The fight was gone from her, changed to a fierce wanting as she welcomed the embrace of her foe. She had needed him desperately. Yet even while his touch swept her away to heights that left her shaken and trembling, something deep and quiet ached within her. She wanted more from this man than just the physical taking; belonging to him in body was not enough—she wanted him to claim her very soul. But that could never be and the only harmony found between them was this. Then she had no more room for thought as she lay back in his arms, stolen away to the secret place where only he could take her.

The coals in the fireplace glowed red, mesmerizing the eyes. Saura stared at them and they edged her features in fire. Seth studied the emotions—the conflict—in that beautiful face. He cursed himself. The time had not been ripe, although it had been so deceptively close! What wicked, teasing fate had brought them together tonight in the seclusion of the library with its dark invitation? He could not help but want her, to desire her soft flesh that was like nothing else he had ever known. The passion that she was helpless to check when they were in each other's arms was further enticement to him for he had known it once and had since held the memory close. She was a woman in every beautiful sense of the name and now he breathed in her sweet fragrance as though he could never get enough of it. How he desperately longed to truly tell her of himself— not the trivia of which they spoke this morning through the bundling board but rather the deeper part of his life and his thoughts.

He cursed the war that kept them apart while bringing them together. He looked down at her face, her warring emotions apparent even in the shallow light from the fireplace.

"Saura," he said softly.

"Don't," she whispered harshly. "Say nothing, Seth." She sat up, trying to ignore his hand gently stroking the small of her back.

"Do you hate me more?"

She was still for a moment and then shook her head. Her feelings, the intensity within her, stunned her. She wanted to speak to him of many things—of dreams and of hopes. Most of all, she wanted to speak of the tenderness she felt. For there was no victory for her in this; her enemy still proved to be the champion. She was weaker for her surrender and she was appalled by her willing acceptance of it.

"Can we talk?" Seth asked.

She shook her head again. "Talking, between us, ends only in conflict."

Seth lay numbly watching her. It was as though her emotions were ripping her apart. Yet he could only guess at those emotions. He assumed that the foremost was unhappiness at her surrender to him. If only he could comfort her, offer her words of tenderness and love. But this fair maid, who had given herself in lovemaking to him for the second time, left him quaking with fear. She was the only woman he had ever met who had rebuked and rejected him and now, after this sweetest of all surrenders, he feared again that discarding of his emotions. There were things he wanted to say to her, to talk about, and secret things to tell her of. But she was right. Words between them ended in anger—and he could not face that now. He sat up, slipping his arms about her and tenderly kissing her hair. Then he stood, gathering his belongings and slipping away into the darkness.

Saura sat motionless. Deep sobs formed in her throat as she felt that his actions were the gentlest and the harshest that she had ever witnessed. She felt very alone when he left, yet she knew his departure was his gift of dignity to her. She wanted to call him back, to run after him, but something halted her. She was so confused. Did she love Seth? Her passions, her heart, said yes! Her mind, although working like a mathematician's rule, tried to convince her of a different logic.

The morning dawned with a brilliant sky, streaked with orange and yellow and blushed with pink. The bitter cold receded with the coming of the day and the town stirred from its two days of hibernation. Seth and Saura slept late and she was hurrying downstairs to see to the breakfast when he came from his room. His eyes caught hers and they held for a moment before she glanced away, going to the kitchen. Peter and Erastus were already eating when she arrived and she sat down at the table. The conversation between the captain and Saura was stilted, mild in its discussion. She seemed surprisingly subdued and her father studied her with interest.

So did Captain Adams. She was even more beautiful this morning although her face was pale and her eyes shadowed from lack of sleep. Yet there was something in her countenance that touched him deeply. But she did not look at him, avoiding him as though he had leprosy! If only he could catch her glance, perhaps lighten her mood with a smile. He needed to talk to her, to tell her of the many things he felt. But whether she would give him that chance, he did not know.

Saura kept her eyes on the small fare on her plate. She felt that if she were to look at Seth, she would turn helpless. One smile from him, one look of pleading, and she would melt as she had last night. It was all she could do to keep from bolting from her chair, running to him and kneeling down to look up into that rugged face and tell him that she loved him. Whether he was a redcoat or not, whether even a despised Tory, he was a man and her husband—and she loved him. Her heart thudded heavily in her breast and a hollow aching welled up within her. Could she, who had spoken only of pride and right, and denied their marriage, go to this man called her husband and speak words of desire and love? Would he think it another of her cruel jests? He had spoken wistfully of Miranda, a woman kind and good, yet compared his wife instead to the shrew, Katherine! Why had she not been of a kinder nature so that she could not go to him without fear of rebuke? She set down her fork. She had no appetite for this food that nearly choked her. She stood and went to a closet, taking out her heavy winter cape, pulling it on and fastening the frogs at the throat and raising up the hood. Then she slipped her hands into her white rabbit's-fur muff and went out the door with no words of explanation.

Seth watched her go and then he too rose from the table and turned up the stairs. A few moments later he came down, handing his book to Peter; his bag was in his other hand. "Thank you for letting me read this. I'd forgotten how much I enjoyed the tale."

"You know that you are welcome to anything from my library. What was the book you were looking for the other day? Ah, yes. 'The Taming of the Shrew.' I'd forgotten. It is the only one of Shakespeare's that I don't have."

He did not seem to notice Seth's paling at the words and Erastus said, "It appears that that is the book the captain needs the most."

The two older men chuckled at this, surprised that Seth found no humor in it. "I want to thank you for your kind hospitality. I have to be going now."

"I thought that you did not need to be to Boston for several days yet," Peter said in surprise. "Is this a change of plan?"

"Yes," the captain replied. "I have decided to go to Boston early." He offered his hand to Peter and then tossed on his riding cloak. Nodding to Erastus, he went out the door, heading for the livery to find his horse.

Peter looked at Erastus, shrugging. "I think you'll find," the latter said, "that your daughter will soon be coming to a conclusion about all this. Despite her protestation, it appears to me that she is feeling something other than just animosity for that young man. I'll be interested to see the outcome of this play."

Peter nodded, sipping at the hot brew in his cup and staring blankly at the closed door. "There is but well-wishing in me. With politics put aside, I can only want the best for these two young people," he mused.

Saura strode along rapidly, taking in deep breaths of the cold air that stung her nose and mouth. She would not cry, she determined, hastening her steps as she walked down the snow-slick road to town. What was happening to her? If this was love, why was she so miserable? The sound of hoofbeats echoing behind her made her turn and study the approaching rider. His black riding cloak whipping in the icy wind, his eyes burning like two embers from the depths of hell, he leaned over his beast, urging it on. The horse's hoofs cut into the ground, flinging clumps of mud onto the white snow. She looked up expectantly, wondering if this rider from hell would sweep her up in his arms and take her away with him.

Seth saw the oval face turned up to him and he could not fathom the emotions there. If he were to stop, to say one word to that fair woman standing in the snow, he would dissolve, weakening into a lovesick fool like the simpering sots she so despised. If he were to ever win her over, he must be strong. Strength was what she most admired. He urged his horse on to a faster pace, the hoofs of the destry churning beneath him.

Saura stood watching as the horseman spurred his mount past her, leaving her in his wake. She watched the galloping steed thunder through the little town and down the ribbon of road that led out of the Hollow. As the man and horse disappeared from view, she continued her slow walk to town, tears tracing an icy path down her cheeks.

> He that can have patience
> can have what he will.
>
> —RICHARD SAUNDERS

# Chapter IX

THE SKY WAS as drab as matted gray wool, casting a dreary light. There was little wind but what there was was cool. The day's dark cast made one wish to stay in the house, curled up with a good book or baking pies that would fill the rooms with tangy smells. No recent glint of sunlight had come to strike the edges of snowbanks and transform the dull wintery mass into a sparkling carpet. The only spot of warmth to be found was near the hearths, where flames licked at the massive logs and crackled their heat into the chilly air. When the river that passed through Greenhollow thawed, it was frosted with mist.

The somber winter seemed to mirror Saura's countenance. If her mood had been sorrowful before Seth left, it was set in misery after his departure. She thought of him with a mixture of love and anger. Why had the cocky soldier come into her life to stir up her feelings in such a manner? And now, despite his absence, he was ever with her, haunting her thoughts as though he were a ghost in the house. If she worked in the kitchen, she could not help but remember his playful kiss and if she lay in her bed, she could think only of the bundling board. But the library, the room that had always been her favorite room in the house, was the most painful of all. She seldom entered it.

She busied herself in every way that she could, almost as though she were driven to be occupied from dawn until dusk. She forced herself to sit through sewing lessons from Bathsheba, doggedly working needle through thread despite her clumsiness. Still, she was improving, or so Miss Brightwater would say with encouragement. Saura detested the sessions.

She went out riding whenever the weather was warm enough or dry enough. She baked many new foods; the house abounded with the aromas of delicious dishes in which Peter and Erastus took delight, although Saura herself had little appetite for her culinary creations. All the closets were rearranged as well as the many wardrobes, trunks and cupboards. The silver was always polished now, and the linens pressed.

The two men hardly knew what to make of it for as their house became more homelike, the girl became more difficult. What had once been a bright and sunny nature was now become dour and churlish. And every time that Saura spoke harshly to her father or his friend, she felt guilty and embarrassed.

After a week of such irritability, her countenance brightened a bit as the active routine released her anxiety. Certainly some quick mind had penned that time is a healer and she found this to be so. She forced herself to think less frequently of the captain and when she did, the memory was bittersweet. The little things he had said sharpened in her mind, growing tender in her thoughts. Daily she tried valiantly to sort out her feelings, succeeding bit by bit as the days slipped past.

One afternoon late, she stood in the kitchen, opening the door to the brick oven and basting the golden-brown turkey that had been long cooking. She had stuffed it with chestnuts and now eagerly awaited the taste of the bird. She closed the door, checking on the red cabbage in wine sauce, and the baked onions. Then she went to the dining room, setting the table for three; soon the smithy and his helper would be in and ready for dinner. Outside the windows, the sky was becoming streaked with orange, signaling the day's end.

She was startled to hear a quick rapping of the front-door knocker and as usual in the past weeks, her first thoughts were of a captain in the king's army. Instinctively she ran her fingers through her tangled mass of hair. Then she chided herself. No doubt the person calling was the button salesman, traveling through Green-hollow and calling on ladies and gents to show them his wares.

She hurried to the door, pulling it open. Before her stood a British soldier—but not the one she expected. The sight of a red coat made her catch her breath before she realized that the man who wore it was not Seth Adams. Dressed also in officers' apparel and wigged, she did not recognize him for a moment. Then she stared at him in astonishment.

"Lawrence!"

Suddenly she was swept up in strong arms and embraced, then quickly released. She took a step back, embarrassment sending a tinge of coral to her cheeks.

"I can hardly believe it," he said, looking her up and down. "Who would have thought that such a skinny little girl would grow up into such a fine young woman?"

She looked at Lawrence, finding him older and heavier than she had remembered. "I am quite surprised," she managed. "From where have you traveled?"

"I arrived in Boston two weeks ago and at the very first chance I slipped away on leave to come see you. Are you going to invite me in or will you greet your brother on the doorstep all day?"

"Oh! Yes, of course. Come in, Lawrence." She showed him into the library, offering him a chair and then some brandy, thinking to ward off the effects of a chilling ride. "How is Mama?" she asked.

"Quite well," he answered after downing the drink. "She took Father's death hard but she recovered well. That's what happens when you are of good stock. She plans on arriving here in a few months."

"That is wonderful! I can hardly wait for her to come."

"I think it is foolhardy. She sold our half of Ainsley and Comstock, not that I had any time for bookkeeping or that I wanted it. She could live quite comfortably in Bristol on the money she will receive but there was no persuading her of that. Especially when I was shipped over here—through no will of my own, hell knows. She said that unless she came to America, there would be nothing left in her life, not with you staying on here. I thought you would be coming back for Christmastime; it was quite a shock to me that you have remained for so long."

"Things happened here," she said slowly, wondering if she should tell him of her true parentage.

"Oh, I know. Your real father has claimed you. I suppose I can't blame you for that!"

She sighed. "I didn't know that you knew."

"I've known for years. I think I even remember when you came to live with us. I think I resented you a little at first. But that is all past," he said, taking her hand in his. "Mother explained about your father's being widowed and your need for a family and how we took you in. Unusual, in a way. But then I know several people from the best families in England who have been raised by godparents."

"Well, I am glad to see you again and it is thoughtful of you to make this trip to Greenhollow. How was your sea voyage?"

"Not too bad. We hit surprisingly good weather for this time of year. I traveled over in the company of our cousin Nancy."

Saura asked about the Comstocks and caught up on as much gossip as she cared to hear. Then she asked, "How long can you stay in the Hollow?"

"Only two days and then I must be back to Boston. I met your father outside and he kindly offered me his hospitality. He told me to tell you to fix the extra room."

She nodded, climbing the stairs and gathering the necessary items. Then she went to the attic room and fixed the bedding, Lawrence leaning in the doorframe, arms folded, watching her. Everything in order, she turned to go but he stopped her.

"Do you know, I just cannot believe how pretty you have turned out to be. You are quite a comely lass, sister, I must admit."

She smiled. "I think it is called growing up." Slipping past him, she went down to the kitchen, serving the dinner onto platters and taking them to the sideboard in the dining room.

Peter soon came in, and then Erastus. When they sat down at the table, Saura noted Lawrence's expression of horror that a black servant should join them at the table. She smiled and thought to herself that America might be ready for Lawrence but he would never be ready for the colonies. He ate with his usual impeccable manners, wishing to compliment the cook. When Saura explained that she herself had cooked the fare, she could not tell whether he was impressed or shocked. During the meal he told them of his duties in the army, his life in England, his travels and accomplishments. Saura noticed that Erastus stifled several yawns. She herself was also bored despite her close attention to his talk. After dinner she cleaned up in the kitchen while he and Peter went to the library. Just as she was finishing her chores, she heard somone enter and turned to see Lawrence.

"Good heavens! Are you cleaning up the dinner dishes?"

"Someone must."

"What of the black servant who joined us at the family dinner table?"

"Erastus has enough to do around here and at the livery. Did you have a nice talk with Father?"

"Well, interesting at the least. His views appear to be quite liberal, I must say. Was I mistaken in assuming that you had been sent to live in a Loyalist household?" he asked in deadly earnest.

She burst out laughing, wiping off a platter and slipping it away. "Oh, Lawrence! This household is not what you are used to. Colonists differ from the folk with whom you are familiar. The concerns of my people dwell on what is best for America."

"Here we agree after all, then. King George feels nothing but concern for the colonists."

She looked at him in stunned silence, as though he were an idiot. "You cannot believe that?"

"Of course I do."

She shook her head, biting back a thousand-word discourse. She must remember from past experience that arguing with him was useless. She did not wish ill words to arise between them. "Let us not argue. Things are different here than in England. We live very simple lives, through necessity."

"So I have seen. A blackamoor at the table. Really, Saura. That is most unconventional."

"This is not a house of convention and if you wish to accept our hospitality, you'd best conform to our habits."

Her tone surprised him and he shrugged.

Everyone retired early that night, Saura relieved to go to the solitude of her room. Once asleep, she had a dream in which Seth was in the library, standing at the hearth and staring down into the flames. He turned to her slowly, holding out one of those strong masculine hands she knew so well. She lifted her hand to his, letting him take it in his warm grasp. Then he took her into his embrace, his lips claiming hers. It was a long, lingeringly sweet kiss before he pulled away. As she looked up into his eyes, she saw that they were different—rounder and more heavily lidded. When she drew back and stared at the man in horror, she saw that it was Lawrence. Somehow, through a wicked trick, Seth had changed into her brother. She was powerless to flee, standing there in fear as a slow, strangely cruel smile split his face.

Saura awoke from her dream with a jolt, staring up into the blackness of the room, her senses alert. The slightest movement and sound caught her attention, her eyes flicking to the door. Was it her imagination or did it close silently? She chided herself for the sense of dread she felt; why had she been frightened of Lawrence? He was her brother. Finally she sighed, turning over and willing sleep to come. Dreams could not be explained.

The next morning had a parting of the cloud cover and watery sunlight wavered down. Saura spent a rather tedious day. Lawrence had little to do, following her about and spurring her into conversations that she did not enjoy. While debating politics with Captain Adams had been a challenge to her, it was a different experience with Lawrence. He was quicker to anger and more forceful in his point of view. Lolling about as he did all day, she understood why she had always found his company less than enjoyable.

About noontime Molly Yates came by with a message for Peter from Wilfred. She was pleasantly surprised to meet the Blake's houseguest for things had been slow at the inn. She caught Lawrence's fancy right away, engaging him in animated conversation. He found her charming and most obliging since she had no real opinion of her own and agreed with him in everything he said. Saura thought that the girl would claim the moon was blue if her brother so stated. Lawrence offered to escort her back to the inn and Molly was elated, having snatched a prize away from her rival. She did not know how relieved Saura was that Lawrence was gone for a while.

He spent the afternoon at the inn, returning in time for the evening meal. Afterward he drew Saura into idle conversation in the library and even after Peter and Erastus retired, she could not escape his small talk. Tired from her day's labors, she sat down in the large chair, stretching her small feet out to the fire. As she watched the flickering flames, she could not help but let her mind wander to times past, particularly one spent in the warmth of this very room. Finally Lawrence interrupted her thoughts.

"Have you heard anything I've said in the past quarter-hour?"

"I'm sorry," she sighed. "I just started thinking about other things. You know how it is. What were you saying?"

"I was discussing your future."

"You were?" She looked at him in surprise. "What about my future?"

"Isn't it about time you start planning for yourself? Did you know that two years ago Nancy was introduced into London society, and she is younger than you are?"

"Not by very much."

"That isn't the point. The facts are that you are of marriageable age and stuck in this forsaken little shire. Certainly there is no one here to pay you court other than green schoolboys or country farmers."

She gave him that steady look that always disconcerted him. Finally she asked, "Why are you so concerned about my welfare?"

"I have always taken a personal interest in you. And for this reason I have decided to make a magnanimous offer—even though it might seem rash to you." He took a deep breath. "Your needs have touched me, Saura. And out of concern for you, I am offering you a marriage contract." She looked at him in shock, speechless at the suggestion. Finally she spoke.

"Did I hear you right?"

"Yes," he said, nodding.

"But what on earth for?"

"I've been trying to explain that," he said testily. "If I don't do my best to help you get out of this little township, what will happen to you? Who will ever marry you if I don't?"

She looked at him with piercing dark eyes. "Who? You might be surprised, sir."

"I did not mean that as it sounded. I meant who of any worthy reputation could find you here in this barbaric place. After all, you are nearly of legal age and still have had no marriage offers, am I right?"

"No, you are not," she said slowly. "I have had many offers and many suitors, although it may not be apparent to you. I did not realize that I appear so uncomely that my own brother would think that no one should want me."

He stood up, coming to stand over her. "You twist my words, Saura. I find you most fair to look upon and I will admit that that is why I am spurred on to such an offer." He took her hand, pulling her to her feet and before she could protest, he had his arms around her, his mouth clamping moistly down upon her own. No struggle or word of denial could make him release her and she grew rapidly flustered. His kiss did not leave her trembling as that other's had; instead she experienced an embarrassing repulsion. This was nothing like Seth's embrace!

Finally she wrenched herself free of his clammy touch, stepping back and gasping for breath. "Lawrence! You should be ashamed of yourself!"

He laughed, standing arms akimbo. "What an innocent you are. But I shall teach you special things when we are wed and you will be a little girl no more."

Her cheeks flushed with anger. She nearly blurted out the facts of her marriage but then thought better of it, biting back the words. She had no desire to explain to this oaf her darkest secrets. Instead she glared at him. "Do not ever touch me again like that, Lawrence. I'll not stand for being pawed. Perhaps your offer of marriage is a gracious one but I have no interest in it."

"You need not give me your answer right away. Take some time to think it over; I know it is very sudden."

"I need no time! I cannot marry you."

He scoffed at her words. "There is nothing better for you here, Saura. As an officer's wife, you could live quite well on a lieutenant's income. You could stay in Boston and I would come home between maneuvers."

"Lawrence, listen to me. I could never think of you as anything other than family. To me you will always be my brother."

He stared at her for a while, a hard glint coming into his eyes. "But I am not your brother, am I?"

"If you will excuse me, I think it is time I retire." Without waiting for another word from him, she turned and hurried up the stairs. Once in her room, she shut the door, locking it as an afterthought.

The next morning she was up early, fixing a simple breakfast of eggs and beef. Lawrence came down with his saddlebag packed, his jacket on. After downing the meal, he thanked Peter for his hospitality and took Saura aside. He kissed her on the cheek, a lingering touch on her skin that made her pull away.

"Now you think over my offer and when I can get away in a month or so, I will come back. Then we can make our plans and I will talk to your father."

She tried to protest but he would hear nothing of it. He went out the door, heading for the livery, and she stared after him. She sighed, coming in the house and shutting the door. She would not think on him further.

By mid-December all of Greenhollow was caught up in anticipation of Christmas. A winter fair was held each year in which many hand-crafted items could be bought, from quilts and afghans to sets of carved wooden soldiers and dolls with china faces. Erastus sold several weather vanes he had made and Saura purchased a number of items for Christmas gifts.

The weather held good, with the snow thinning on the ground and no fresh fall in sight as the holy days neared. Two days before Christmas, Saura sat at the dining-room table reading a book. As Peter entered the house past sunset, she glanced up at him.

"Do you want something for dinner?" she asked.

"Why should I want to sup now when there is all that holiday fare to be served at the Christmas dance? I think it has already started; the sounds of fiddle and fife drifted on down to the livery. Why aren't you ready?"

She shrugged, closing the book. "I've decided to stay home."

He looked at her in surprise. "Every young lass in Greenhollow and for twenty miles around will be there tonight, and every young man too. I don't think there's a person in the Hollow who won't attend unless it's Bathsheba's brother. You're not feeling ill, are you?"

*184*

She shook her head. "I am fine. I just have no desire to go, that's all."

He sat down at the table, across from her. "I recall seeing a pretty new dress hanging on your door that Bathsheba said she worked on for three days in a row. Will you be disappointing her and all the young men in the town?"

"Those young men hold no interest for me. There is no one there I care about, Father. I suppose that is one of my reasons for not wanting to go."

"There will be a great many unhappy lads at that dance who will spend the evening watching for you. Will you disappoint their interests?"

"Their interests are in a married woman then, and need disappointing."

He smiled at her. "I thought that you swore to ignore the bonds of marriage." Then he looked at her softly. "You're not fooling me, girl. I know quite well who has won your heart. If you knew that the redcoat you so loudly disclaim were to be at the Christmas dance, you'd be putting on your satin dance slippers."

She scowled at her father. "That is not true!"

"Then why do you mope about for the man you want, yet are loath to claim?"

"Do you defend the enemy?"

"No," he said slowly. "I defend the man. And you, despite all your harsh words to him, cannot help but admire him as would any maid! And for this reason you stay away from all other sources of enjoyment, ridiculing those who seek what you already have."

Saura stood up, slid the chair back beneath the table, turned and fled up the stairs. She threw off her wool frock and underdress, then pulled on her finest slip. She sat down before the dressing mirror, brushing her hair. This was swirled into a soft knot atop her head and pinned into place with tortoise combs. A few wisps escaped about her face and neck, curling softly. Satisfied, she pulled on her hosiery and then put on the dainty slippers that were of white satin with a semi-pointed toe. Next she went to the dress that hung on her wardrobe door. It was lovely, rivaling the dresses that were imported from faraway places like France or Holland. The Cummin sisters had made a special trip to Boston with their mother to pick out their gowns for the biggest dance of the year. But Bathsheba's work was exceptionally beautiful and Saura felt a rush of anticipation at putting on the frock. She took down the quilted petticoat of topaz color, stepping into it and tying the strings at her small waist. Then she pulled on the overdress. It was a gown of yellow silk damask, looped with ribbons of dark gold and narrow braid. The bodice and edges were finished with ruchings of pinked material the color of the underskirt. The neckline dipped lower than Saura would have chosen, Bathsheba being very daring with her shears. But the dress fit perfectly and she knew that her elderly friend had put extra effort into the making of it.

She searched through her jewelry box until she found the gold chain with the topaz teardrop, fastening it about her neck. Then she stood back to stare at her reflection in the looking glass. Where was the little girl who had existed only last summer? There was no awkwardness here for she was no longer too slim, carrying instead the softer curves of womanhood, yet not the heaviness of Molly or some of the other girls. This woman in the mirror was beautiful—but she did not appear happy. Her mouth did not smile that smile that had once lit her eyes. She knew the cause, and she cursed it.

Saura caught up her cloak, hurrying downstairs. Peter was waiting for her, dressed in his finery. He let out a slow whistle of appreciation. "It's hard for me to believe what a woman you've become. Let's be off; the dance began an hour ago."

At the door to the inn they were handed silk masks since the festivity was a masquerade, and they put them on. Once inside they noted the change in the main room. Large before, it seemed even more so now with the tables removed and the chairs lined against one wall. A bright fire crackled in the hearth, which was hung over with boughs of pine and holly. This and a few lanterns lit the room with flickering shadows of light.

The gay strains of fiddles, fife and flute mingled in the room. Young and old stepped to the lively tunes and the floor was filled with dancers in swirling dresses of every hue. Molly wore a dress of bright green silk that offset her red curls and she moved about the floor on the arm of one of Greenhollow's most eligible.

The aroma of food and drink, pine and sawdust, filled the air. Peter led Saura to the table, where they filled their plates with braised pork roast in port wine sauce, chicken, oysters and candied sweet potatoes. There were platters of sliced breads made from bran, whole wheat and rye. The fare was tempting and they ate heartily, standing about talking with friends. Saura had barely finished when Jacob Trenn spied her beneath her mask, whisking her away. He danced her beneath the nose of Harley Chase, who, mouth agape, watched her having searched for her all evening long. The two youths, along with other suitors, fought over her hand and she was stolen from one or snatched away by another. The hour grew late and she anticipated an end to such foolish play when the masks would be removed and the desserts brought out.

The musicians slowed the pace of the music, picking out a melody that was sweetly muted in rhythm. Suddenly Saura felt herself whisked away from one suitor into the arms of another. She stared up into a face that she could tell, despite the black silk mask, was handsome. He was dressed in a jacket of plain black velvet worn over a white silk shirt that was carelessly open at the throat. She stared up into a set of dark eyes that looked down at her steadily.

Breathlessly she asked, "Do I know you?"

He smiled slowly, his arm slipping tighter about her waist. "You'd better."

She gasped, her eyes widening. Where had he come from? How had he slipped into the room without her knowing and stolen her away? She had no idea. Looking at him gravely as he swept her across the floor, she said, "I did not recognize you without your red coat."

"You must learn to look beyond the color of a man's

jacket," Seth said softly and she could not help but laugh.

He looked so devilishly handsome in black, the firelight glinting golden-red in the dark of his hair, that she could not help but admire his appearance. He made a very handsome civilian indeed. "This is an unexpected surprise," she said.

"All was calm in Boston so my major sent me to Greenhollow for the holidays. I know what a burden that will be for you but I shall try to remain out of the way."

She said nothing as they glided across the floor, her hand in his. There was little she could think of to say for her heart was thudding wildly in her breast, a flush of excitement tingeing her cheeks with color.

"You look breathtaking," he said as casually as though he commented on the weather. "I had thought you beautiful before but when I came into this room and saw you dancing from across the floor, dressed in gold, I saw that all others faded before your beauty. I should not have thought that the girl in boys' breeches whom I wed would blossom into such a woman. You have quite won my admiration, Saura." She could see no hint of mockery in his countenance and was taken aback by his flattery. "Thank you, sir. I fear you are too kind."

He shook his head and smiled at her. "Shall I admit to you that your vision has haunted me these past weeks? I returned to see whether my memory of you was true or I had embellished it. Then I find you here, a flame in the midst of mirrors. A foolish man I must be to leave a wife with such fairness in the midst of so many drooling suitors. I trust that you have turned away any proposals?"

She smiled, studying him. "I have tried. But some are ardent and continue their pursuit." She shrugged. "Perhaps war will come at last and take them away."

"Then I shall shoot at them! Better yet, if you would but admit the fact of our marriage, they would go away heartbroken and leave you to my care."

She did not reply for, glancing around, she saw that

the music had stopped and the floor had nearly emptied as she and Seth stood conversing. They walked toward the sideline as Wilfred came forward, telling everyone to take off their masks. This was quite exciting and there was much talk and shrieking. The Cummin sisters and several other young women had been studying Saura's dance companion with interest, coming over to her for renewed introductions. The homemade desserts were brought out to fill the long table and everyone lined up to heap their plates, choosing from pumpkin pudding, brandied apple cake, orange marmalade tipple cake, bread pudding and apple pie. She and Seth selected some cake and then went to stand by the hearth. Peter joined them, greeting the captain with kindness. They talked for a while and Saura looked at the man who spoke with such seriousness to her father. Why was the rake so handsome? How easily she could reject his attentions and tender words did he look like Harley or some of her other suitors. But the subtle manliness that he wore as casually as though it were a cravat plagued her.

They danced late into the night and every time some youth would try to steal her away from his embrace, Seth would thwart the attempt with a stare or a curt word. Finally the two were left alone, the swains murmuring that such monopolizing of her time was most inappropriate. Where before Saura had been bored, her feet tired, now she felt vibrantly alive, enjoying every moment of the dance in his arms.

Finally people began to gather their dishes, slipping away in twos and threes. Peter had departed some time ago. Seth fetched her cloak, wrapping it about her, and led her home. They came inside and she went to the kitchen, where she made a pitcher of eggnog and passed around brimming cups. They talked for a while and then she slipped upstairs, readying Seth's room. She was just finishing and turned to find him in the doorway, studying her.

"Your room should be comfortable now," she said. "If you need anything, let me know." She started to leave but he stopped her.

"Thank you, I'll remember that."

She did not understand why his words, so casually spoken, sent a chill up her spine.

The next morning she was up early, poaching eggs in the kitchen. She hummed softly, stopping to check her appearance in a shiny silver platter before filling it with slices of ham. Her spirits were lighter than they had been for days and she did not let herself dwell on the cause.

She set the table with plates of cooked potatoes and garnishes, filling the mugs with hot cider against the chill of morning. Peter came downstairs and they sat down to breakfast, not waiting for the captain since it appeared that he slept in. Saura's eyes kept glancing to the stairway and at last Seth made an appearance. He looked roguishly handsome in a brown shirt with dark breeches tucked into his high boots. He sat down, helping himself to the breakfast.

"It looks cold outdoors," he commented.

"Started snowing sometime during the early morning," Peter said. "But that means we'll have snow on the ground tomorrow for Christmas."

"There is holy mass tonight at the church," Saura said to him. "If you would like to come for services, we would be pleased."

"Thank you, that would be nice. Do you have plans for today?" he asked casually.

"I promised to help decorate the church for mass but after that there awaits nothing special."

He nodded, taking a bit of poached egg. "I saw a sled in the livery. If we have enough new snow, I'd like to go for a ride and thought you might like to come along. That is, if your father does not mind the use of his sled."

Peter nodded and Saura thought it over. "I haven't been on a sled since last year. After I am finished at the church, I'd like that."

Breakfast over with, she donned a heavy white shawl over her red wool dress. She went out into the soft drift of falling snow and down the lane a short distance to the church. Once inside she found the Cummin sisters already there along with the Mistresses Shoburry and

Blackwell and Doctor Barton's wife. Willy brought in boughs of fir and yew and they strung them around the walls and pews. Rosemary and prickly holly were tied onto the boughs with streamers of red cloth and fresh candles were set into the sconces. The laughing and chattering voices were out of place in the usually solemn little chapel but the gaiety was infectious and Saura found herself picking up the excitement of Christmas Eve.

Her work finished at the church, she caught up her shawl and went out the door and back up the lane toward home. She stopped at the livery, seeing the sleigh readied and the horses hitched to it, prancing with excitement and snorting puffs of cold air.

She hurried into the house and found Seth waiting for her. He handed her the heavy cloak she would wear, slipping it over her shoulders. She fastened the frogs and pulled up the hood, its soft fur lining brushing against her face. She took her muff as Seth fastened on his heavy riding cape. Then they slipped outside and went through the still-filtering snow to the livery. Peter nodded at them as they climbed into the sleigh and Seth tucked the heavy fur rug around their knees. Snapping the reins, they were off, the bells on the sleigh jingling merrily. The horses trotted along briskly, the runners slipping easily over the snow and leaving tracks in the fresh fall of white. The air was sharp against their faces and Saura snuggled her hands into the warmth of her muff. The vehicle was narrow and she sat in close proximity to Seth. They passed people she knew and she waved, enjoying the shouts of "Merry Christmas!" echoing after the sleigh. Seth led the horses out of town and along the curving road that joined the Posthaste Road. Then they turned westward, the route an untouched thread of pure white satin stretching before them.

A peaceful solitude enveloped the pair as they traveled along in the quiet of the surrounding forest, the trees layered in snow, and Saura began to feel at ease.

Seth looked over at her, that familiar smile on his

lips that she could never quite decipher. "At last I have you alone, Miss Ainsley."

"Is that a goal of yours, sir?" she questioned in surprise.

"It is. It was my understanding that when a man married, he took his wife away to a secluded cottage or house where they could learn to know each other better without interruption. But here I find my wife in a town where I must fight off simpering fops for her hand and in a house under the protecting eye of her father."

"I find my father's protection of little comfort, Captain. He has all but embraced you as kin, taking your side in this ordeal."

"Your father loves you very much, Saura."

"I know."

"I think highly of the man. I also think highly of his daughter."

She looked at him for a moment, catching the flicker in those rust-brown eyes. "Thank you, Captain Adams."

"Do you know," he said as he snapped the reigns, "that sometimes I think that you hardly know my given name. So few times has it been upon your lips that it seems a foreigner to me. I long to hear you say it even though I know that many still use the formal address to their husbands."

She laughed, the cold wind stinging her face. "I suppose that I could call you by your Christian name although I am so accustomed to thinking of you as the enemy captain."

"Enemy still? I had hoped that a truce might be in sight."

His words were interrupted by the sudden flight of a huge owl, black-winged and tufted in white. "Look!" Saura called, pointing at the creature, her arm in front of his face. The sudden distraction made him lose an instant's control on the horses; the animals raced across the icy surface and veered, the sled plowing into a bank of snow.

They were blinded by a cloud of white before the vehicle came to a standstill. Neither spoke for a minute, Saura wiping the icy snow from her face and lap. The horses stood looking back guiltily, snorting and neigh-ing at the distress. Seth looked down at her in anger.

"Thank you, madam!"

He threw off the lap rug, jumping down from the sleigh to survey the damage. As he did so, he sank into snow deeper than he expected, causing him to swear in annoyance. The whole situation struck Saura as hu-morous and she tried to stifle the giggles that threat-ened to erupt. One stern glance from Seth and she could not help herself, laughter bubbling over every time she surveyed their plight. As he struggled with the tangled lines, he was forced to doff his gloves, his fingers thereby growing cold. "You will not find the situation so funny should you have to get out and push this sled."

Finally sobering, she asked if he thought he could free them from the snowdrift and he shrugged. "I hope so. I would not enjoy a night spent out in this cold, or even half a day." He straightened the lines, handing them to her, and taking the horses by their harnesses, he made them struggle to pull free. After two attempts it was accomplished and he climbed back in the sled, turning it around. But before he headed home, he made the horses halt. He turned to her. "Before we start back, I think I shall take advantage of having you alone."

"Indeed?" she asked as his hands slipped around her shoulders, pulling her near.

He did not answer. Instead he lowered his mouth to her own. There was such tenderness in his touch of lips, such passion barely held in check, that Saura felt her-self weaken. A shudder ran through her and she was no longer cold. Why did his merest touch have this power over her? When she felt herself at the brink of surrender, she was gently released and she looked at the man who was above her. "Thank you, Mistress Ad-ams."

She forced herself to pull away, sitting up primly, her back as straight as a rod. "Please do not call me that," she said, looking off down the wintery lane.

"But it is your rightful title."

She turned to him with a sigh. "Captain Adams—"

He stopped her. "Then we are agreed on wrong titles?"

She caught his meaning and paused. "Yes...Seth. We are agreed and you have won your cause in this."

He smiled, leaning back in the sleigh then and snapping the reins so that the horses took on a quick trot. Faster he spurred them on, and faster, until—after one accident on the icy road—she feared going over a steep embankment. She tried to tell him to slow the speed but the chill wind swept away her words and she could do nothing but cling to him lest she be thrown from the sled. The horses' spirits up, they raced along, whizzing across the narrow bridge and through the town. Finally Seth slowed the pace, coming to a stop at the livery. Once inside, she threw off the fur rug and jumped down, not waiting for his assistance.

Peter came in from the blacksmith shop and smiled at them. "Have a nice ride?"

"Until the man drove like a madman! We are lucky not to be swimming now in that half-thawed river. Before that we went off into a snowbank."

"Might I remind you that that was your fault? You are the one who shot your arm in front of my face when you caught sight of an owl."

"True," she admitted, brushing the snow from her skirt. "But there was no excuse for that wild ride home. Your pants are soaked. You'd best come into the house and change."

Peter offered to unhitch the horses and they went inside. Seth filled the tub with hot water. The bath closet was off the kitchen and she could hear him as he plunged into the water, splashing about. As she heated the cider, he began to sing in a deeply resonant voice. It sounded quite pleasant and eventually he emerged from the room, wrapped only in a towel.

"Captain!" she gasped, turning around.

"I forgot my dry clothing," he said casually.

"Then you'd best hurry upstairs before you catch a chill," she said over her shoulder, not looking at him.

He chuckled softly, coming up behind her. "You've seen me in a state of undress before, Mistress Adams."

She groaned softly, turning in anger to confront his words only to take in a naked chest that tapered down to a flat stomach. Further view was hidden by the towel but she had already seen enough of this lean Tory. She sighed and turned around. "Clothe yourself, sir!"

She heard him chuckle behind her as he stepped near. She could sense the closeness of his presence, the warmth of his breath on her neck sending a chill up her spine. Suddenly his lips brushed her neck and she shuddered, helpless to step away. The prickly situation of being in the kitchen in the bright light of day with a man who was half-naked, or more so, and kissing her neck, left her nerves on edge. A sudden rap at the front door made her start away and he smiled after her as she went to answer it; then he bolted up the stairs. Still flustered, she pulled the door open and looked into the thick features of Sergeant Gorely.

He began to speak and then halted, narrowing his eyes to stare at the fair maid clothed in red wool who stood so meekly before him. As recognition dawned, his face grew ruddy and he snatched his hat from his head, politely holding it before him. "Good day, ma'am. I was told that I could find Captain Adams here."

She stepped aside, showing him in and saying, "I'll go tell him you are here, Sergeant Gorely."

She went up the stairs and Gorely watched her, squirming uncomfortably as his worries were affirmed. The young woman did indeed remember him! She returned momentarily and ushered him into the library. "Please sit down. Captain Adams is dressing and will be down in a moment. Can I offer you some applejack?"

He nodded at this courtesy, accepting the glass she handed him. But he only sipped at it and the silence became a burden. Finally he put the glass down and looked at her. "I have something I'd like to say, ma'am."

She regarded him with interest. "Yes?"

He gripped his tricorn. "I'd like to offer my apology," he mumbled.

"You would? What for, Sergeant?"

"For the incident what happened in Braintree. I was mighty rough on you, not knowing you was a lady. I've given it a lot of thought, about what happened and you being forced to marry Captain Adams."

"I hold no grudge against you," she assured him.

He sighed with relief. "Then you and the captain must be getting along half well. Mayhaps the chaplain was right that you should marry him."

A feisty glint came into her eyes and he thought that maybe he had spoken too soon. "Hardly," she said.

There was no time for her to expound further since Seth entered the room and Gorely stood up, saying he had brought a message in and was quartering at the inn. Saura left them alone, going to the kitchen. She was preparing a goose for dinner and she invited the sergeant to join them and to also attend Christmas dinner on the morrow. He was most pleased at her gracious hospitality.

That afternoon Erastus arrived home. He had been away for several days in Concord and his knapsack was bulging with intriguing packages.

While the goose was cooking, Erastus and Seth brought in boughs of spruce and holly and other greenery. Garlands were festooned across the mantels and the windowsills and tied into place with red ribbons. Saura draped ivy across the candle sconces and Erastus stood on a chair to hang mistletoe from a chandelier. She admonished herself to avoid that spot. Even Gorely stayed close to help and Peter brought in the fat yule log with the help of the others. They tossed the heavy stump into the dining-room hearth. Then they lit it, promising that it remain lit for twelve hours for the avoidance of ill luck.

Soon after that they sat down to a delicious dinner of baked goose with brown-sugar apples and sweet potatoes, eggnog and walnut honey-bread. The talk was cheerful and everyone reminisced over past Christmases.

Afterward they went to mass at the church; there was a fine sermon by Reverend Fretwell and a reciting from Matthew of the birth of the Chirst child. Later they gathered about, singing hymns of Christmas. Saura told Seth that a century earlier, the celebration of

Christmas had been a penal offense in Massachusetts. The Puritans had deemed the tradition pagan and the law had been in effect for several years; people had had to celebrate the season in secret. Soon following there was a pageant protraying the birth, children filling many of the roles. Willy was a shepherd and Harley a king. When it was over, yuletide foods were served— plum puddings, mince pies and nut-brown ale for the grown-ups, cider for the young.

When they left the church, Seth and Saura joined a group of young carolers who sang at the houses where candles were lit in the windows. Arriving at her house, she and Seth slipped inside. She put her cloak on its hook and went to the yule log to warm her hands. Peter and Erastus came in, setting their chairs before the peaceful heat of a Christmas fire. Saura went into the kitchen, taking out a large pot and hanging it in the fire over the yule log. She poured water into it and let it heat; then she brought out the spice chest. She added two cloves of nutmeg and a pennyweight of powdered ginger. After that she tossed in a tiny blade of mace, five allspice berries and a cinnamon stick.

"Is that not the recipe, Father?"

"Yes, indeed. Now let it boil once or twice."

As they awaited the boiling, they listened to the caroling and bell-ringing fade into the distance. After the wassail pot came to a boil, Peter poured in wine and sugar. Saura beat twelve egg yolks until they were light and frothy; then she folded them into the egg whites, which she had had Seth whip. This done, she poured them into the wine mixture and while it still foamed, she brought in apples that had been baking in the brick oven and added them. Then they passed around the mugs and each dipped into the mixture, tasting it with murmurs of pleasure. Its tangy flavors sent a spread of warmth through Saura and they sat about telling ghost stories as the light grew dim with the candles flickering out and the yule log's blaze lowering. Even Gorley added a tale or two of his own before finally taking his leave to return to the inn. Peter and Erastus noted the late hour and retired with yawns as Saura dipped one last time into the wassail. She felt a bit lightheaded as she gazed into the fire. Seth leaned back in his chair, studying her.

"The hour grows late, lady. And Christmas is tomorrow."

"I know," she said, putting down her cup and standing. "Good night, Seth." She walked away but had barely gone a few feet when he called out to her and she turned around.

"Wait! Look what you have done." He stood up, sauntering over to her as she stared at him in puzzlement, not understanding. He came to stand next to her and pointed a finger upward. Slowly she lifted her eyes to see the chandelier and its sprig of green with white berries.

"Oh! You cannot mean—"

"It is tradition."

"Not one I know of!"

"Then let me educate you to it. Mistletoe is a symbol of hope and peace. It is said that enemies lay down their arms beneath the mistletoe and forget their enmities. Do you not think that to be the best custom of all?"

She thought it over. "It does seem like a tradition to fit the thoughts of Christmastime."

"Then you will accept a truce, a peace offering?"

She thought for another minute. "Yes," she said slowly. "Anger has been at this hearth too long."

He laughed softly, sweeping her into his arms and bringing his mouth down upon hers. It was not the coolness of peace he offered but rather the onslaught of desire. Heat raced through her body, the softness of his mouth the kindling. The intensity of his passion overwhelmed her senses and she pulled away but he did not release his hold on her. Instead his lips traveled down her neck, leaving a burning of heat upon her skin. With one last effort she wrenched herself away from him, gasping for breath. She stared at him with wild eyes, remembering that look of hunger on his face all too well from another time! How close she was to the tender surrender that had parted them enemies once

*198*

before when they had come together. Anger flooded her at the treachery of this pretended ally.

"Tory!" she cried before turning and fleeing up the stairs. She reached her bedroom door only to find him close behind her, grasping her wrist before she could hurry inside.

"One word, Saura," he said, his voice so harsh that she hardly recognized it. "Twice before I have tasted of that sweet passion from you and twice I have lost you. But soon you shall be mine—even though I must cross through hell to win you!" He released her, opening the door for her. "Good night," he said before turning and striding away to his room, anger in his step.

> I am as peremptory as she proud-minded;
> And where two raging fires meet together,
> They do consume the thing that feeds
>   their fury....

> —WILLIAM SHAKESPEARE
> *The Taming of the Shrew*

## Chapter X

SAURA, rubbing the frost from the pane, peered out at the snow-covered world. Every bough was heavily sheathed in snow from a new fall during the night. No tracks marred the lane in the early gray light of the yule morning. Anticipation tingled through her as she hastily buttoned the bodice of her white and brown wool dress. She could not help but feel excitement even though she chastised herself for such childishness. Every Christmas was the same, the eagerness in part coming because it was also her birthday. Today she was eighteen.

Hurriedly she brushed her dark tresses and then caught them back with a brown velvet ribbon. After that she went downstairs, lighting the white candles and setting them in the windows to dispel the early gray light. She checked the yule log to make certain it still burned and tossed on extra wood until it became a heated blaze. Then she hung the wassail pot back over the fire, letting it simmer before taking a cupful.

She peered into the crackling flames, her mind wandering for a bit before the sound of footsteps behind her made her turn. She looked at Seth in surprise as he neared her. Dressed in the same dark brown as before, with no hint of the red, he looked as handsome as always.

"You are up early, Seth."

He shrugged, taking the wassail she offered him. "It is Christmas."

"And I've things to be about," she said, going into the kitchen. He followed her, watching her take out three baskets. These she filled with hot cross buns, a mince pie in each, a loaf of squash-rum bread, and plum pudding. Then she took some apples, handing him a few. "Will you shine these?"

He did so and she added them to the baskets. In one basket she placed some bayberry candles and in another several skeins of new sewing floss. In the third she put some toy soldiers and a whittled pine horse with bright-painted faces. After this she covered the baskets with linen napkins to hide their bulging contents.

"What is all this?" he asked as she went for her cloak. "Do you play Saint Nicholas?"

"I do."

"May I come?" He did not wait for an answer, but caught up his cloak and tied it on. He took two of the baskets and she was relieved for they were large and she did not know how she would carry all three. They went out the door and to the lane, where they left the first tracks of the day in the snow. A soft filtering of powder drifted down and they trudged through it. The first house they came to was the Brightwaters' and Saura picked out the basket with the floss in it, setting it on the high porch before the front door. Then they headed into a different direction.

"You have a generous nature where others are concerned," he mused.

"Does that mean I do not, for you?"

"You are quick to catch a meaning."

"It is only that I know how hard you think me."

"I think more highly of you than you could imagine. And this act of charity is proof of my suspicions."

"Do not be fooled, Sir Redcoat! I do this only because it is Christmastime and I wish to believe in Saint Nicholas."

"Ah, yes. I know the tale. When he learned that three young women had no dowries, he threw three bags filled with gold into their windows. That started the tradition."

"Would that he were so kind as to provide me such," she murmured.

"Why should he when he has seen fit to give you a husband instead?"

She chuckled at this and they stopped at another door. She selected the basket with the toy soldiers in it and left it on the doorstep of a small house along the river's bank. "This is the Webster household. They have a nice little son whom I helped with his primer in Sunday school. Mister Webster broke his foot a few weeks ago and has been laid up."

"I did not know that you were fond of children," he said, taking the last basket from her hand. "They say that children around a hearth soften the heart."

She glanced up at the rogue. What did he suggest? The final basket they left at the widow Shoburry's house and then they headed home. He guided her along the snow-slick path with his hand at her elbow. When they reached home, they brushed the snow off their cloaks before entering. Taking their wraps off, they went to stand before the warmth of the fire, toasting their cold fingers. Then Saura went into the kitchen and started breakfast. Seth joined her, seating himself in a chair and studying her. He stared at her so intently that she felt a flush spread across her cheeks. His heated look caused her to hasten the preparations.

"By the way," he said lazily, "happy birthday, Saura."

She looked at him in surprise. "Why, thank you, Seth. How did you know that today was my birthday?" she asked a bit suspiciously.

He shrugged and leaned back. It was obvious that he would not tell. "You are now of accountable age," he said. "But then, legally you became so when you took your marriage vows."

"Marriage vows forced upon me," she scoffed.

"That raises your ire still?"

She shrugged and sighed, handing him a glass of the nog and sitting down next to him. She took a draught before answering. "I think it is the fact that I was offered so little choice. Less and less have I come to mind the groom in the marriage, yet still I resent its nature. That piece of paper called a certificate of marriage hangs over my head like a sword. And that I cannot help but resent."

The sound of voices in the house drew their attention and they went out to the hearth to greet Peter and Erastus. Seth carried out the eggnog and she a tray of blueberry muffins. Peter greeted his daughter with a kiss.

"Happy birthday, daughter. I have thought fondly of these eighteen Christmases past because of your birth."

"Thank you, Father. And Merry Christmas to you, and to you, Erastus."

The latter nodded. "You are up early, Captain."

"I accompanied Saura on her gift-giving this morning." He handed the men brimming cups of eggnog.

"Speaking of gift-giving," Peter said with a twinkle in his eyes, "where are the presents, Erastus?"

Erastus nodded and arose, disappearing to the cellar and returning with a satchel well-stocked.

"Did you steal this from Saint Nicholas?" Saura teased.

With a touch of ceremony he reached in, pulling out a box and handing it to her. With excited fingers she lifted the lid, peering inside. There was a pair of finely tooled skates, the blades having been honed by Erastus himself. She laughed with pleasure, for her old skates had become too small and she had not been able to use them. She thanked him with a hug. Then she handed him a gift that she had kept hidden behind the wood box. It was the newest edition of the almanac and he was truly pleased. She handed Peter his package and he was quite in praise of the new riding gloves and scarf. Then Erastus brought out a large box wrapped in cloth and she eagerly untied it. Inside she found a bonnet of dark brown velvet in the latest of fashion, lined with silk ruching. Saura knew that Peter had brought it back with him from Boston; it had obviously come straight from France to the city's docks.

"Thank you!" she cried with pleasure. "It is exactly what I wanted!" Then she caught sight of Seth, who was returning from upstairs with packages of his own. She tried on the bonnet.

"Very fetching," he commented. He handed wrapped presents to Erastus and Peter. Inside they discovered books, both of very good reading, and Peter especially was pleased.

"Will you look at that! It is the entire collection of John Osborn!"

Saura looked at Seth in wonderment. "Father has been looking for that set for years. How did you know?"

He did not answer, instead handing her a large, square tin. It was from Holland, beautifully engraved and hand-painted. On its lid was the picture of two lovers sitting on the bank of a lake, a lovely and delicate scene.

"Oh, how beautiful!" she exclaimed.

"Open it."

Saura pried off the lid and looked inside. She saw two objects there—and one made her gasp. Lining the bottom was a sheet of parchment, finely written upon and stamped with a seal, bearing both of their names. It was their wedding certificate. She glanced up at him, touched by this tender thoughtfulness. Then another box, smaller, caught her attention and she took it out, opening it. There inside was the golden orb of a ring. It was a simple band, set with three diamonds.

She stared at him, not knowing what to say. He took it out, slipping it on her left-hand ring finger. "I hope you like it, Saura," he said softly.

Erastus leaned near, letting out a low whistle. "That must have cost you a pretty coin," he mused.

"'Tis fine workmanship," Peter confirmed.

"Looks like a wedding band," Erastus said.

Saura was well aware of that! It was a wedding band, fitting so comfortably on her finger that she had not the heart to remove it. Did this sign and seal her fate as the captain's wife? She looked up at Seth in embarrassment. She had nothing to give him. Unwittingly Peter came to the rescue handing the captain a package.

Seth nodded his head in appreciation, opening the box. It was a beautiful leather-bound volume, illustrated and with handsome print. He laughed softly. "My thanks!"

"What book is it?" Saura asked, leaning closer to read the title. Suddenly she looked at Peter. "'The Taming of the Shrew'?" she asked.

"He said it was a play that he wanted to read, and it was not in my collection," Peter said defensively.

She walked away and stared down thoughtfully at the beautiful ring. Seth came to join her and she looked up at him. "It is lovely. I thank you for it; I am embarrassed to say that I have no gift for you."

He stood before her, leaning near so that she alone caught his words. "There is only one gift that I want, Saura. And only you can give it to me."

Her eyes flew open at his meaning. He could not ask for...oh, but he did! He smiled down knowingly at her in affirmation of it.

Peter cleared his throat. "Well?"

The young people looked at him in question. "Do you not see that you are standing plum under the mistletoe?"

Saura glanced up and groaned. "Who hung that piece of green? Why is that annoyance up there?" she asked, remembering all too well last night's incident.

"Well, we didn't hang it for Erastus and me to be caught under it," Peter chuckled. "The least you can do is to give your husband a Christmas kiss to thank him for his gift. You would like that, wouldn't you, Seth?"

The captain smiled and shrugged helplessly before Saura's piercing gaze. She turned to her father. "Do you match-make me with a Tory?"

"Heavens, daughter! Is your heart so hard that you cannot thank your legal husband?"

"It is not! Since you side against me, I shall acquiesce!" Besides, she thought, she was safe enough in this crowded midst. She turned to Seth, looking up at him. "Merry Christmas, Seth," she said, letting her hands slip up the soft fabric of his shirt and around his neck. She pulled his head down to her own, reaching his mouth with hers. She kissed him long and ardently. Finally she released his mouth, pulling back and letting her eyes sweep open. Her arms slid down, his hands yet clasped behind her waist. She had been wrong! She was no safer here from the onslaught of emotion than when they were alone.

Slowly he smiled down at her. "Merry Christmas, Saura," he returned.

Erastus and Peter had by this time expelled the breaths they had been holding and they smiled at each other.

Saura busied herself in the kitchen, preparing the ham for its baking. She arranged apples and potatoes around it and slid it into the oven. This done, she went to the library, seeking out her father. Seth was there, sitting in the large chair with his feet propped up. He was reading "The Taming of the Shrew" and chuckling softly. For reasons she could not say, this irritated her and she turned to Peter.

"It has stopped snowing and I am going down to the pond; I can hardly wait to try my new skates."

"Have fun then," he said.

She gave a glance at Seth, who was completely absorbed, and went to get her skates. Since it had stopped snowing and the sun was shining weakly through a clouded sky, the ice should be just right for skating and she smiled in anticipation. She put on her short cape and tied on the new bonnet. It framed her face prettily. Catching up her skates and muff, she hurried out the door and to the large pond in back of the Clarks' farm where there were already a number of skaters, young and old. She sat down on a stump and put on the skates; they were an excellent fit and the blades honed sharp. She stepped onto the ice, trying them out. She glided about, taking little time to gain her balance. Jacob Trenn came up to her, skidding to a stop and then skating by her side.

"Merry Christmas," he said, pacing himself to stay by her.

"Merry Christmas to you, Jacob."

"It is now," he said. "I am really glad to see you! Heaven knows I have seen little of you these past months. You hardly ever come to the dances, except the one at Christmas. Who is the man who monopolized your time so rudely there?" he asked, skating backward to impress her.

"Do you mean Captain Adams?"

"Oh...the redcoat that has been quartered so often at your house. You would think that the king's army would be more careful of a lady's reputation. He has been quartered with you so often that people are beginning to speak. You must grow tired of his presence."

She stifled a sharp retort about who she found tiresome and increased her speed, but still he stayed by her side. "Tonight we are getting together—several of us, that is—for a sleigh-ride. Would you like to ride with me in our sled?"

"Thank you, Jacob, but I've other plans for tonight," she said coolly.

"Well, if you are doing other things then..." he said a bit testily. He took the opportunity to wave at Molly, who had just come on the ice and looked very fetching in a blue wool outfit. He glanced over to see the effect this might have on the miss next to him. Irritated, he saw that there was none. "There is Molly," he said as the barmaid skated over to them. They nodded a greeting to each other and a merry yule.

"I heard that Captain Adams is quartered at your house again," Molly said. "That is quite unusual, I think. There are vacant rooms at the inn. You would think that the army would be less slanderous of a girl's reputation."

"That is what I just said," Jacob stated. "Do you not get tired of having him around your house?"

"No, not at all," Saura replied, skating along

smoothly. "I find the Tory captain charming and most well-behaved."

They stared at her as she glided along innocently. "And as if to speak of him, there he is!" Molly exclaimed. Without another word she veered off, coming to a halt before the stump where the captain sat tying on Erastus's skates.

"Why did he have to show up?" Jacob muttered, half to himself.

Saura did not answer, instead watching the captain glide along with the ease that he showed in so many things he did. He skated by Molly's side and she chattered cheerfully to him. Once she pretended a fall and he caught her, steadying her, and she linked her arm through his for support. She smiled up at him in such a suggestive manner that Saura nearly choked. But her ire was cut short as the toe of Molly's skate caught a bump in the ice and she tripped, taking Seth down with her. There was a flurry of skirts and petticoats and scrambling efforts to get up but two times the effort failed and Molly, in a fit of laughter, managed to keep the captain by her side.

Jacob looked after Saura, who skated off in the middle of his dialogue to see to the fallen couple. She skidded to a halt before them, spraying them with ice particles. Molly looked up, her laughter dying as Seth finally managed to bring them to their feet. He brushed the snow off his coat and pants, absorbing himself with the task. Molly smiled at him.

"You are not a very good crutch, Seth. You will have to hold on to me tighter than that if I'm to keep from falling."

"Maybe you had better learn to skate before you take to a crowded pond," Saura said.

"I do just fine," Molly retorted, narrowing her eyes, "if I have the help of someone strong, like Seth. Saura wouldn't know about that since she's no doubt never leaned on a man in her life. Why don't you run along now, Saura? You would not know what to do with a real man. Why not go back to Jacob or one of the other boys?" Her voice rang in a sweetly false tone.

"Because," Saura said slowly, and Seth recognized the hard glint in her eyes, "my place is here, on Seth's arm."

Molly looked at her in feigned surprise. "Because he boards at your house? Little claim, I think! He has roomed at my inn too."

"Along with half the soldiers in Massachusetts. Do you lay claim to them also?"

Molly's face flushed and she felt betrayed by the guilty blush. "You prudish snit! Virgin still, despite all efforts, I've no doubt. You will find that the captain turns from such priggish pride to seek the comforts only a real woman knows to give." She smiled up at Seth. "You know that you are welcome at the inn when you grow tired of her abusive tongue." She was about to skate away when Saura's voice stopped her.

"Your offer is generous, as always, Molly. But I doubt that he'll be seeking out the amenities at the Crooked Horne when he has a wife at my home."

Molly whirled about, nearly losing her balance. "Is this another of your highbrowed jests?" She looked at Seth for denial but his face was blank. She turned to Saura. "Huh! I thought so. You will not play me for the fool, girl. I would not believe that you are wed." Her tone, however, belied her words.

"Believe it or not, it is the truth."

"You cannot prove it," Molly countered, wavering a bit.

Saura stared at her for a moment before slowly taking her left hand from her mitt. Molly looked down at the ring, gaping in disbelief at the evidence. Then she looked up at Seth and the expression on his face put the signature to the proof.

Saura linked her arm through his. "Skate with me for a while, Seth, before we go home."

They circled the pond several times, Saura close beneath the protection of his arm. Seth felt an exhilaration not solely from the brisk skate. His wife had taken the first step in accepting their marriage with her open affirmation to another.

Saura, on the other hand, was angry at herself. Thus it was vented to Seth: "Why did you let me do that?"

He laughed. "Have I ever had control over your actions? Certainly it was not so difficult to admit that I am your husband? I thought you actually enjoyed spurring poor Molly."

"She pawed and pranced over you as though she'd gained some win over me. Since when did she and I become enemies?"

"Women who court in the same area are always enemies. But you need not worry about that. Soon it will be all through town that you are wed to the notorious redcoat."

Saura thought this over but had little for response. Perhaps it was best this way for the news would have leaked out eventually since half the king's army knew of the marriage.

Afterward they went home and she prepared the Christmas dinner, to which Sergeant Gorely came. Seth spent most of the time reading the book that Peter had given him. Then later they went to see a play staged by minstrels and dancers portraying yuletide cheer. They returned home late from the merry festivities. When they arrived, they found a caller waiting for Peter. Saura recognized him immediately; it was Lewis, the man who had brought the fateful message that had sent her to Braintree. He paled a bit upon seeing the captain but Peter led him into the library with ease. Shortly thereafter he left.

Saura went to her room, doffing her dress and putting on her nightgown. She was ready to climb into bed when there was a knock at her door and she heard Peter's voice. She opened the door, peering at her father through the darkness.

"I came to tell you," he said softly, "that I'll be leaving in the early morning, long before daybreak."

She nodded, knowing the cause. "Where will you be going?" she asked.

"I'd best not say. If anyone asks, tell them I have a job to do in Braintree and that I took Erastus with me to help. If there's any emergency with a horse's shoe, Seth will tend to it, I'm sure."

"How long will you be gone?"

"About three days, I reckon. Don't look for us before then."

"Three days!"

"Shhh! No need to wake the household. You'll be fine here. Seth will watch over you."

"The watching-over is what I fear!"

Peter chuckled quietly, shaking his head and walking back to his room. She quietly shut the door, climbing into the warmth of the eiderdown quilt. But sleep was slow in coming as she lay staring into the darkness. She felt as though she were being deserted and left defenseless. There would be no sudden appearance of Erastus, no security of Peter's sleeping presence on the other side of her wall to protect her from the dark intimacies that she both longed for and feared.

The following morning Saura was up early, finding that her father and his helper had indeed left before dawn. She made a simple breakfast of bread and milk, listening for Seth's tread on the stairs but she did not hear it. It appeared that the captain slept in. Finally she put on her cloak and went out the door, heading to Bathsheba's. She had paid Miss Brightwater to make her some new gowns and underslips, most of her old ones too short or too tight, and at the play the seamstress had told Saura that they were ready and she could pick them up. Saura spent an hour at the Brightwater house, having tea and scones and talking with her elderly friend. Then, gathering up the bundle of new things, she returned home through the cold.

Once inside she doffed her cloak and came into the main hearth to find Seth sitting at the table, his legs propped up, eating a slice of bread with honey. "Good morning, Seth," she said.

"Where have you been?" he asked curtly.

She looked at him in surprise for he was usually so good-natured. "I was at Bathsheba's, picking up some things she had sewn for me."

"Where is everyone this morning? Is your father already out at the livery?"

She looked at him a bit nervously, setting her bundle on the table. "Father and Erastus had to go into Braintree to do some work for a friend."

He thought this over for a minute. "When will they be back?"

"Oh, in a day or two," she said vaguely.

He leaned back and smiled satanically. "Do not tell me that you and I are left to one another's care?"

"The only thing you need to think on, redcoat, is that you keep your hands to yourself!" she said angrily, confronting the source of her worries.

"I assure you, my wife, that I shall act properly."

"Thank you, sir."

"As any husband should." He picked up the bundle from the table, untying the yarn that was wrapped around the cloth. He took off the outer material before she could protest, dumping the contents onto the table. She blushed with embarrassment as he sorted through two nightgowns, a slip and several silky chemises and other undergarments. "What are all these?"

Angrily she snatched them up, trying to stuff them back into the bundle. "Have you never seen a woman's undergarments before?" she snapped.

"I have, and many a time. But these are hand-sewn by some local lady, I assume."

"They are."

"And how did you gain coin to pay for them?"

"Father paid Bathsheba," she said, wondering at the direction his words took. "She sews all my clothes."

"Ha! My point exactly! A few months ago you became my wife. Do you recall it?"

"I do indeed, sir! It is forever burned into my memory as a bad fright."

"At that time you became my legal ward. I shall not have your father pay for clothing that I should be buying ."

She looked at him, amazed at the change in his personality. "If you feel so strongly about the matter, then

*213*

take it up with my father and you can give him back the coin he paid."

"I shall do that!"

She picked up the bundle and was ready to leave when he snatched it from her hands. "What are you doing?" she cried.

"No clothing from some local seamstress will do for my wife. You must wear only the finest garments, imported from England or France. That is my will, Saura," he said with eyes as hard as glinting iron. "Will you obey it?"

She could not fathom the perverse change that had overtaken him. She sighed. "If you wish to purchase me things from the Old World, I will not object."

"Good," he said, sweeping up the bundle, striding through the kitchen and opening the back door. She followed in his wake, crying out in horror as he tossed the garments out in the snow, shutting the door. He turned around, walking past her, and she ran to the door, pulling it open and retrieving the bundle of fine new clothing that was already beginning to soak up moisture. Furiously she brought it into the kitchen, setting it on the counter and going to seek out the insane man! She went into the dining room but he was not there and she could hear him clomping about upstairs. As reason dawned on her, she bolted up the stairs, flying into her room. Seth was in her wardrobe, pulling out dresses and petticoats, pantalettes and chemises, throwing them into a mound on the rug. She cried out as he tossed her yellow silk damask onto the heap.

"Are you mad? What rabid dog has infected you? Cease this nonsense, Captain!"

He stopped for a moment to look at her in surprise. "Did you not say that you would deign to wear the clothes I buy? Why, these mere rags are not as good as I would have my fair bride wear!" He strode to the window, flipping the latch and shoving it open. Then he came and collected a handful of the garments. When she saw his intent, a scream pierced the air. Saura threw herself in front of the window, barring his actions.

"I beg you to stop such insane play! I know no reason for you to have turned from your kind nature, sir. Can marriage have blighted your senses?"

He struggled to remove her. "You will thank me when you are clothed in the finest velvets from France. These rags do not befit your position in life, Mistress Adams."

"I asked you not to call me that!"

"Is it not your rightful title?" He bellowed so loudly that she could only stare at him dumfounded.

In the lull of their quarrel they heard the sound of the knocker at the front door. "We have callers," Seth stated calmly. "I shall see to it." He turned on his heel, striding out the door, and she could only stare after him in total bewilderment.

She started to collect her things, shoving them into the wardrobe. Then she flew to her dressing table, searching through her jewelry box until she found the key she looked for. She ran back to the wardrobe, locking it lest he return and try his foolish stunt again. She calmed a bit, listening to the voices downstairs. She could tell from Seth's loud tone that not all was well and she hurried down the steps.

Harley Chase and Jacob Trenn had stood on the doorstep of the Blake household, knocking at the door. There appeared to be a good deal of yelling and commotion coming from the second story but they could not make out the cause. It had ended for the moment before the door was wrenched open and they stared into the blazing eyes of a wild British soldier. They were so taken aback that they stood there dumfounded.

"Well?" he barked.

Finally Jacob managed to doff his hat. "We have come to call on Miss Ainsley. Is she at home?" he concluded bravely.

"Miss Ainsley?" the captain shouted at them. "There is no Miss Ainsley in this house."

At that point Miss Ainsley herself had come down the stairs, her hair falling in a tumbled disarray that only enhanced her feminine appearance. Both young men forgot the soldier for the moment as they took in her flushed face and the buttons of her bodice that had come somewhat undone in her struggle. She stepped forward, nodding in a calm greeting that defied her inner turmoil.

"Saura," Harley said to her, "we came by to see ...because we heard that, well, ah..." He glanced, unsure of himself, at the captain.

"There is a rumor about that you are wed to this lobsterback"—Jacob said boldly—"a vicious piece of gossip that we trust you can dispel."

Both young men glanced uncertainly at the captain as Saura stood there mute. Finally Harley turned to her with a plea. "Can you not deny it, Miss Ainsley?"

Seth stepped forward, standing arms akimbo before them. "I said that no Miss Ainsley resides here. You are addressing Mistress Adams. Mistress Seth Adams, my wife. Could you remember that?"

Harley paled visibly but Jacob stepped forward. "Deny it, Saura! Say that you are not wed to this redcoat."

"He speaks the truth, gentlemen. This is my husband."

Harley looked at her from eyes filled with woe. "Then tell me that it was of your choosing, that you desired to marry this man. I must hear it from your own lips."

Seth faced her. "Tell them of the circumstances, Saura. You will not?" He turned to the youths again. "She was forced by the British army to wed me or face a traitor's trial."

The words took them aback and they stared at her in shock. "Then it was not of her own choosing!" Harley managed and in a brave moment he added, "If you wish to escape him, I will help you."

Seth turned and glared at the young man until he withered. "Would you turn aside what God has bonded together, young fools? Be out of here before I toss you out!"

"We'll not leave until Saura tells us to," Jacob declared. Suddenly he found himself hoisted upward by collar scruff and seat of pants. He flew through the air to land in the snow and Harley turned away quickly lest he follow. "I'll tell you young coots once and once only. Stay away from Saura. She is my wife—and mine alone. And you can tell any other suitors in Greenhollow that the first simpering fop I find trying to court my wife shall feel the sharp end of my bayonet!" So saying, Seth slammed the door and Jacob scrambled to his feet, Harley aiding him.

They ran from the place, quickly spreading word of the terrible fate that had befallen their beloved Saura. That a maid so fair should be wed to such a beast was to be highly mourned by youth from twenty to thirty-five. But the women in the town, although finding the news highly flavored, would see no sorrow in what had befallen her. Especially those who had taken in the English captain's appearance.

After the incident Saura looked at Seth in total bewilderment. "What has o'ercome you?" she cried as he slammed the door. "Would you treat those young men so unkindly?"

"I would have them leave my wife to me!" he shouted. "Must I endure the sight of every drooling embrace or longing glance that such fools wish to give my wife? Is loyalty such a hard thing to find?"

"Would you say that I have been disloyal to you?" she gasped.

"Nay, not disloyal. But neither loyal. For a loyal wife would willingly come into my arms instead of playing the prickly rose that will not be plucked. And a good wife would fix her husband a morning meal lest he grow faint with hunger."

"Then I shall be about it!" she cried, running into the kitchen. "The man has truly turned insane. I know not how to please him. What perverse hold has been gained on his nature?" she said to herself, hurrying to heat left-over turkey and frying a batch of eggs. She threw the food onto a plate and hurried into the dining room to set it before him.

Seth stared down into the eggs, then leaned back. "The yoke on these eggs is too runny." He shoved the dish away.

Saura felt her ire rising. "Will you tell me what has happened to pervert your nature? Are you ill, that you have turned to such madness?"

"Now that is a good wife," he said, nodding his head with pleasure. "To think of my health, as always. Come feel my brow and tell me if I am fevered."

She came near, resting her hand on his forehead. "There is no fever."

He looked at her in amazement. "Can you not feel it? My brow burns."

"No, Seth, it feels only warm to my touch."

"I say it burns! Can you deny that I am fevered?"

"I cannot deny that you are ill. But what malady plagues you, I have no idea."

"Then we agree. I am ill. And I alone know the cause."

"Then will you tell me?" she questioned with concern.

"No," he said slowly. "But I will tell the cure."

"What is it?" she asked eagerly.

"I am in need of kindness to nurse my wounds. Care from your tender hands is what I need. Are we in agreement?"

She thought this over for a minute. "Yes, we are in agreement."

"And will you agree so easily with me on other things?"

She paused again. "If that is what you wish, I will."

"If I say the moon shines now and not the sun, will you agree?"

"What buffoonery is this?" she asked. "Are you playing me for the fool?"

"You do not agree?" he bellowed, bolting from his chair to circle the table and come stand looming in front of her. By this time she was on her feet also, alarmed by his wild-eyed look.

"I did not say that, sir!" she hastily amended.

"Then say it is the moon that shines outside the window," he shouted.

"Very well!" she cried, thinking him raving mad at this point. "It is the moon."

"The moon? No, Saura, you are wrong. I say it is the

sun." He looked at her so seriously that she could do nothing but stare at him in amazement. "Do you agree? Is it the sun?" he cried.

"It is the sun!" she replied hastily seeking only to appease him. "If you say it is the sun, then I will say so also."

Then he did the thing she least expected. He threw back his head and laughed, the sound echoing to the rafters. "It works!" he cried. "I am so fortunate as to finally find the source!"

Suddenly he swept her up in his arms, kissing her with such tender ardor that she was totally at a loss. But since it was his first sane action in the past hour, she could do nothing but let him hold her and sweetly smother her mouth. There was such a shuddering within her being that she thought were he insane, she would wish to be also. Her hands slipped about his neck, her mouth responding to his, and she was pressed full against this man of iron. Slowly he released her from his kiss, looking down into her face.

"Now that I have you agreeing with me, I want to discuss more than the light or dark outside but rather the color of our marriage. Until now it has been faintly etched, waiting for the hues. There have been too few bright spots in this union. Do you agree?"

"Yes," she said slowly. "But what can we do about it?"

"There is only one cure for it that I can see. I want to live with you as a husband lives with a wife."

She looked at him in amazement, denial on her lips. "You cannot mean that!"

"Do you not understand my statement? Let me clarify. I wish to hold you in my arms and love you as a husband does his bride."

Saura pulled away, staggering back a few steps and shaking her head. She was helpless to answer but she stood before him, staring down at the patterned carpet. "Do not ask that of me," she whispered.

Did this man know what he did to her? Inside, she was sobbing; outside, she fought to control the tears that came too easily. She turned to leave, seeking retreat in her room, but he stopped her, his voice strangely low.

"Saura," he said softly, "I love you." His voice was hoarse and she turned to see such appeal in his face that she was overwhelmed. The source of his madness was laid bare before her. And her choice of the cure lay in two forms. She could turn and flee up the stairs; she could leave the redcoat to his sorrow, to retreat to his own place to heal his heart. Or she could give him the kinder cure, the same salve for which her own heart begged.

Saura Ainsley Adams stood at the brink of her decision before turning and running into the arms of her husband. Her mouth sought his in the fervored passion of acceptance and release from bonds. The cause she believed in and had fought for lay cast aside; whether it would tarnish from her neglect or shine without her, she did not know. Nor did she any longer care. All the hurtful ache that she had suffered in these past months healed beneath the caring touch of this man. She wanted him and she loved him. And the simple words that he had spoken had forged the sword that cut her bonds and championed for her freedom.

Seth kissed his wife with such intense demand, receiving again a mirroring of his passion, that his head reeled. In this final battle to win the war in which he had engaged her, he had become the victor. It was a surprising triumph, one he had not expected to gain, and he felt overwhelmed. This slender maid in his arms, this beautiful vision of womanhood, returned his love's passion. And this victory feast bore sweeter morsel than tasted ever before.

He caught her up in his arms, carrying her away and up the stairs with total ease. This time there was no liquor to dull his senses, no animosity between them as there had been on their wedding night. Her arms encircled his neck, her eyes looking into his with a knowing seriousness that bespoke her knowledge and acceptance of what was to come. He kicked open the door to his room, carrying her inside before it swung back and slammed shut. As carefully as though she were the most delicate crystal, he set her down on the bed, seating himself next to her.

Her hands reached the fabric of his shirt, slowly unbuttoning the front of it until his chest was bared before her. She let her fingers brush the dark curl of hair and then slipped her arms around his neck for the passionate kiss that she demanded. Soon after, clothing dropped away to lie in unused heaps on the wooden floor. This room, small and with but one window that caught the pale northern light, was half dark, enticingly so. The heavy eiderdown welcomed to its warm comfort the entwining of silken limbs as Seth Adams came to know his wife.

The day came and went in winter's fashion, the snow blanketing the ground, the air chilly as the setting sun slanted low, orange rays across the land. It made the snow appear to glow as though it melted, belieing the iciness it held. The river, sluggishly dark through the day, now snaked as though it were a golden rope, molten in its course.

Saura stirred from sleep with the sweet drowsiness that is the after-drink of love. Her head rested on Seth's naked chest and she could hear the gentle rhythm of his breathing, the thudding of his heart beneath her ear. His arms held her in a comfortable embrace, his skin warm against her own. She remembered another such time when she had awakened in a similar position. Then she had experienced horror at her deeds. But this time she knew only the lingering aftertaste of pleasure. Her decision had been the right one. And she loved this man, Tory or no! For through this day, icy cold outside, she had known the comfort of warmth more than once. Carefully she pulled away lest she awake him and snuggled further down into the heavy quilt. Before she lay back, a book resting on his night table caught her glance. She picked it up, recognizing the Shakespeare play her father had given him. She opened its cover, turning on her side to read. She began to immediately enjoy the humor in the book that she had once resented. She laughed softly, careful not to disturb her husband.

Through several pages she enjoyed the interplay of words, not even minding any longer the shrewish countenance of Katherine. For after this day, no one—most of all, her Tory—could call her the unwilling shrew. But as she read, less and less witful it appeared to her. There was too marked a resemblance to Petruchio's disdain of the tailor's clothing provided for the shrew and the incident over her own dresses. Then on she read, faster and with more interest, skipping to parts that pertained only to Katherine. But it was not until she reached Scene Five in Act Four that her ire began to rise.

Seth pulled out of his drowsy slumber, awakened by the voice of his wife next to him. She appeared to be reading to him, strange as it seemed. And her words rang out clear:

"'But sun it is not, when you say it is not; and the moon changes even as your mind. What you will have it nam'd, even that it is. And so, it shall be so for Katherine.' Where have I heard similar conversation?" Saura asked bitingly and Seth sat bolt upright. He stared at the vision of his beautiful young wife, dark brown curls wild and unruly falling down the nakedness of her back, a sheet held about her in clenched fists, her eyes wild and angry.

"Saura," he said calmly, "do not jump to hasty conclusions. I did not do it to ridicule you but rather to win you over." He smiled ruefully. "Is it not forgiven if it succeeded?"

She bolted from the bed, heedless of her lack of clothing. He was so struck by this vision that he barely ducked in time to keep the leather-bound volume from glancing off his head. "Saura!" he shouted, jumping out of the warmth of the bed and racing after her as she ran down the hallway. He reached her door as it slammed shut in his face.

Saura's chest was heaving as she tried to catch her breath, gasping as though strangled by anger. She fumbled with the key to her wardrobe as her husband banged on her door until she thought he would split the wood. She took out a chemise, pulling it on.

"Saura!" Seth bellowed, pounding on the door. "Open this or I will break it down!"

Saura ignored him, searching for a slip. Then as there was a large thump and crash, the wood around the lock splintered, the door flying open. Seth charged in, a splendid naked animal, wild with fury.

Saura's eyes widened as she took in the splintered door and the angry man confronting her. "Knave!" she cried. "Wicked scoundrel!" She glanced around for something to throw at him but could see nothing she wished to break. Instead she brandished him with her tongue. "Lobsterback! You take my love so lightly and play me for the fool. You decried that you had lost me for these past months but now you'll not have me again!"

Seth charged forward, grabbing her harshly and pressing his mouth down upon hers until he silenced her angry cries. With only the thin silk of the chemise between them, there was no protection against this onslaught and finally she stopped flailing him with her fists. But still he did not release her from his heated embrace and she could do nothing but surrender to the sensations that assaulted her. Finally, when she had given back his kisses, forgetting for the moment her anger, he loosened his grasp on her.

"Wicked Tory," she murmured, seeking again his mouth. Then she pulled back, looking up into the handsome face of the man. "You treat me cruelly, sir, to ridicule me so."

"I did not ridicule you, love. Can you not see that I was a desperate man? I sought to win you over in any way that I could. If Shakespeare was good enough to give me the idea, I felt I should use it. And can you blame me, knowing what gains it has brought about for us both?" He let his lips travel down to her throat, seeking out the pulse that hastened its beat.

"'Twas not your trickery that won me over, Tory," she said.

He pulled back, looking at her in surprise. "It was not? Then what?"

"It was your confession of love. I have yearned to hear those words for a long time now."

"Had I known, I should have spoken them far sooner, my love. And yet those lines with which I tricked you led me to speak the words and so you cannot be too angered at me for it. You did not read the discourse that Katherine gives the other wives, did you? It is at the end of the book."

"I did not get that far before I felt it necessary to break your crown with its cover."

"Then let us seek it out," he said, guiding her down the hall to his room. He picked up the book, showing her the shrew's kind counsel. "Do you see? Wise words, I think."

She sat down on the bed, pulling the quilt about her. "Do I really appear to be so sharp of tongue that you and other men despise me for my outspoken manner?"

"I cannot speak for other men," Seth said, looking her over with renewing passion. "But could they see you here, with tumbled locks over skin of silk, they would not care if you had a viper's tongue. Your beauty bears witness first of your goodness. And as for me, it is the wit behind those dark eyes of yours that gives them the light that glints forth. What I find so appealing beneath your beauty is the sharpness of mind that hones your handsomeness. I will take you as you are, Mistress Adams. No mealy-mouthed, prim girl for me," he said, grabbing her and pulling her down into the depths of the bed.

She handed him the play. "What of this, sir?"

"Let us follow out its end," he suggested.

"I do not know it for I have not read that far."

"See here," he said, pointing to the verse. "It is in print, but rather let me tell you of it." He closed the book, tossing it to the foot of the bed. "I believe the quote is, 'Why, there's a wench! Come on, and kiss me, Kate.' And then, 'We'll to bed.'"

Saura's eyes widened a bit and she laughed softly. "Good advice, sir," she said, slipping her arms around her husband's neck and bringing his mouth down to her own. Outside, the sun sank orange and glowing behind the frosted hills, although they were oblivious to it.

* * *

Peter and Erastus led their tired horses into the livery, pulling off the saddles and rubbing down the steeds. They gave them oats and watered them, eager to turn into the house and stand before a fire to heat their cold hands. There had been much riding in the three days and they were weary, glad to be home. They were nearly ready to start to the house when they caught sight of Uriah's boy, Harley, hurrying toward them. He stepped quickly but cautiously, careful of his new, shiny-buckled shoes on the slick ground lest he fall.

He came up to Peter, breathless and panting, pulling his scarf tighter about his neck and stepping close. "Mister Blake, I have to speak to you on the utmost important happening!" he managed.

"What is it, boy?" Peter asked, placing a calming hand on the lad's shoulder.

"Saura!" he gasped.

Peter and Erastus glanced at each other. "What of Saura?" the first said.

Harley, having caught his breath after running the full distance from town to their place, spoke a little more coherently. "In your absence you cannot guess what has happened! It is concerning that redcoat who has been quartered at your house."

"Do you mean Captain Adams?" Erastus supplied.

"That's the villain!"

"What of him and Saura?" Peter asked.

"Well, Jacob Trenn and I caught a terrible rumor that she was wed to that Britisher. So we came to ask Miss Saura herself about it and when we got here, we heard screaming and yelling and finally the door is flung open by that madman. When we ask him if she is home, he says that there isn't any Miss Ainsley living here and then she comes down looking all pale and upset and we tell her of the rumor that she and he are married. Are you aware of such, sir?"

"I am," Peter said. "Go on."

"Well, he up and says that they are and when I ask her to say if it is of her own choosing, she won't say so and he tells us that she was forced to marry him by the

225

king's army—and she doesn't deny it! Then he yells at us to not come around again, or any other suitors, or he will run us through with his bayonet. And I believe it! Then when Jacob tries to stand his ground, the villain picks him up by his collar and breeches and tosses him in the snow. I, of course, stood watching, not daring to wrestle with such a madman. Jacob was frosted all over! Then the man slams the door in our faces. After I came home that night, I told Father, who said it was none of our affair. But I snuck back later and heard more shouting and banging like you could not believe! I just thought you would want to know," he concluded.

Peter was silent and Harley pulled off his hat, wringing it. "I know that something dreadful has happened to her. That villain has probably killed her or heaven knows what! She hasn't been seen since. She hasn't even come to town once and I know that several ladies have called on her to see how she fared while you were gone. Especially since I told what happened."

"And?" Erastus urged.

"Not one time was the door even answered."

The two older men looked at each other before turning and heading toward the house, heedless of Harley's following in their wake. They hurried inside to find everything was in its place just as when they left but there was no sign of either occupant. They went up the stairs while Harley waited below, wringing his hat into a mess of felt. They could hear faint voices as they went down the hall, stopping at Saura's bedroom door. There was no one inside but they could not miss the door's lock, splintered and broken as though it had been kicked in. They glanced at each other again, walking on down the hall and stopping before Seth's bedroom door.

The captain, dressed only in a robe that was open in the front to reveal a naked chest, was sitting on his bed, eating cold turkey. Saura, with a heavy dressing robe of gray velvet worn over a nightgown, sat next to him doing likewise. Her hair fell in a silky tangle down her back and she brushed it aside self-consciously as they looked at her. Strange attire when the sun was barely in the act of setting.

"Hello, Father," Saura said.

"Daughter."

"Did you have a nice trip?"

He nodded. "We did. Harley Chase is downstairs. He had quite a long tale to tell us. In a walnut shell, he says that a certain redcoat made threats to run your suitors through with a bayonet and it appears that he has been keeping you prisoner."

Erastus concurred. "He's down there now, trembling like a rabbit."

"Oh," Saura said, coming to her feet. "Well...you know how Harley can get carried away and blow things up all out of proportion. I had best go talk to him."

They watched her leave and Peter looked at his son-in-law. "We saw her door latch," he said calmly. "Did you have to break the door down to win her over?"

Seth shook his head and reached for the volume Peter had given him for Christmas. "I followed your discourse."

Erastus chuckled softly, heading for his room. Seth looked at Peter. "You charged her to my care while you were gone. Are you angry, sir?"

Peter looked at him thoughtfully for a while and then grabbed Seth's hand. "You'll not have my ire, son, but rather my congratulations."


Saura descended the stairs to find Harley waiting at the bottom. He took in her unusual attire and mussed hair. Her face, as pretty as always, was flushed, her lips tinted a darker hue of pink. He forgot his momentary upset, seeing her so. She was the type of woman who inspired poetry and he should know, being one who had an ear for a phrase. "Saura," he said, stepping up to her. Instinctively he grabbed her hand, glancing up the stairs to make certain that he was not seen by the redcoat.

"I have been sick with worry over you! The minute I saw your father come home, I ran to inform him of the terrible incident. Tell me from your own lips, without that villain leaning over us, that you are wed to him."

"Yes, Harley. We were married by a British clergy a few months ago."

He seemed to pale at this. "And as the redcoat said, were you forced to it?"

"I was."

"Then your father can see that it is annulled! They cannot get away with doing this to you and if you bear testimony that it is not what you want, surely you can have it erased. I would forget that it ever happened."

"Harley," she said kindly, "you are a dear, sweet friend. And for this reason I will confide the truth in you."

"Yes?" he invited, leaning near.

"I do not wish the marriage annulled."

"But why?" he cried.

"Because I love Captain Adams. And he loves me."

"He is a lobsterback!"

"He is my husband and I shall be faithful to him. Now go home and have some hot tea; things will look better to you in the morning."

She leaned near, kissing him on the cheek and turning to go up the stairs.

"And to think Father said you were too sharp-tongued and unkind," he said, a sob in his voice, before turning and fleeing from the Blake household.

She sat down on the steps, resting her chin in her hands. The new year, which symbolized a fresh start in life, would be here in a few days. She smiled to herself. Seventeen seventy-five would surely be a good year for her—for hadn't she already begun on an exciting new adventure?

Love and tooth-ache have many cures,
but none infallible,
Except Possession and Dispossession.

—BENJAMIN FRANKLIN

# Chapter XI

THE BOUGHS of trees dripped wet in spring's silent arousal; the pink buds of early flowers held the beaded moisture upon their bright heads. The snow was gone from the ground but the earth was often wet, glistening from spring rains. The large carriage that traveled the road to Boston veered around the ruts, careening to one side and the other as it sped along.

The beautiful countryside, coming out of its starkness as winter faded, whipped past the window from which Saura looked out. She had not driven this road since coming to Greenhollow and now she traveled away from the pretty little township nestled in the hillocks. Anxiously she anticipated her arrival in Boston as the miles sped away beneath the spinning wheels of the carriage. Her mother was due to disembark in Boston, if she had not already done so, and Saura eagerly awaited the meeting with Elizabeth. There were so many, many things to catch up on! She felt as though she had grown years in just the few weeks recently past.

In the two months following Christmas and her acceptance of Seth Adams as her husband, she had seen the captain only twice. He was away on active duty and came to her when he was able. These times were like stolen treasures, moments snatched from the harsh realities of everyday living. And between his visits the days stretched away gray and dull, her hours occupied with the ordinary duties and chores. But still, she was content; the misery of unfulfilled want no longer plagued her. Instead she bided her time until she could be with Seth again. Her countenance grew kinder for she was not now haunted by the warring of her emotions.

Yet one thing still gnawed at her, worrying away at her courage. The menace of war was ever-present. The colonies were a simmering stew from which the steam began to signal the threat of boiling over. No lid clamped on was able to contain the heat of anger and each day that passed left Saura grateful that no further mishap neared the sides to battle. Once she had longed for a fight for freedom but now that was changed. Every step the colonies took approaching revolution threatened her love. She knew that war was inevitable and she dreaded from the depths of her heart the rending that would separate her from her Tory. She prayed each night that the force would not come that would turn her lover into her enemy.

The coach veered around a bend, jolting down the hill that led to the outskirts of Boston. The road followed the Charles river, which caught the sparkling glint of sunlight as the carriage raced along. Then they turned off, meandering down streets faced on each side by tidy buildings of brick and stone. In time they passed the old North Church that stood tall and grand and eventually they reached the coach stop, where the vehicle shuddered to a halt.

Saura alighted with the help of the coachman; she was glad to stand on firm ground again. She glanced about the city that was bustling with people on foot and on horseback. Well-dressed men passed along the muddy streets with large blocks of wood beneath their shoes to keep from getting soiled. There were those who appeared to wear fine dress if one did not notice a ragged lace on the cuff or worn heels. Women with powdered hair and fine clothing drove by in landaus while workmen loaded wagons with crates and barrels. She had quite forgotten just how exciting the bustle of an active city was! She had been cloistered in the quiet of her sleeping township too long, she realized, for here everything seemed active and bright and alive with energy. She suddenly understood why Molly Yates had grown tired of Greenhollow and had run off without a word. It had been soon after the beginning of the new year that Molly had left the Hollow, leaving not even a farewell note or a clue to her whereabouts. Willy said he thought that she had run off with one of the young lords who had passed through Greenhollow the night before and had stayed at the inn. Her sudden disappearance was quite a mystery.

Saura looked around at the busy platform and all the commotion until she heard her name called. She glanced about until she spied Timothy, who waved at her and hurried through the milling crowd. He caught her up in his arms, hugging her.

"Oh, pretty miss, it is good to see you! It has been nearly a year since I ventured down to Greenhollow; I have been such a neglectful cousin."

"Nonsense! I know how busy you've been, practically running the furrier business by yourself. Tell me, has Mama arrived yet?"

"Yesterday. And I knew you were coming so I've been checking every hour for your arrival. She's waiting for you at home, and most anxiously too. She has inquired about you a hundred times. I could not tell her that you are more beautiful than ever since I have not seen you for so long."

"Tim, you flatter me!"

"As well someone should," he said, picking up her bags and carrying them with him to his carriage. He hoisted them into the back and then helped her up, taking the seat next to her and snapping the reins. They went along a narrow street that wound its way out of the heavy congestion of people and vehicles.

"How is your family?" she asked.

"Mother and Father are still over in England although they plan to sail here later this month. But Beatrice came over with your mother and brought her friend, Margaret, quite a nice girl and from a good family. And then, of course, Nancy sailed earlier and was accompanied by your brother. Have you seen him? He said that he was going to visit you in Greenhollow."

"Yes, I've seen him," she replied, thinking dourly of his last visit. It had been fairly brief for his regiment was in town, passing through on its way to Cambridge, and he had stopped in for one day soon after the new year had begun. His stay had not been pleasant. He had been even more ardent in his persistence and she had locked herself away, speaking to him only at dinner or when she was with Erastus or Peter. She had avoided being alone with him for it had been bad enough that he slept in the room that Seth occupied on his stays. Lawrence had left disgruntled and she glad to have him gone. Her stepbrother was a thorn in her side. She hoped that her rudeness had made him aware of her feelings toward him.

"What made Beatrice and Nancy come back here?" she asked. "I thought they wished to stay in London."

"They thought so too," he said with a smile, "until their first and second seasons out. I think they did not do as well at court as they had hoped. Though I love my sisters dearly, I am honest and must admit that they are not great lookers. Not that they are ugly, like William Beacon's sisters, or anything like that. But they are not like you either, Saura. You are as blithe as a spring day and could easily win the heart of some lord or viscount. But Beatrice is not, despite her winning smile and talkative nature; and that Nancy—she is the sweetest girl a brother could want but as plain as homespun. And although plainness does not keep girls from winning at court, they must do it with a title. And despite all our money, we've not enough of a family name. So my darlings have come to America, where wealthy men—even though of common stock—abound and search for wives to help them spend their finances."

"I think that common stock is best," she said.

"Has some man of American stock caught your heart?" he asked in a teasing friendliness.

"No," she replied honestly—for the man who had her heart was not a colonist.

He turned the carriage down a pretty lane lined with well-kept brownstone houses, stopping at a three-storied house with a fine front and massive doors. It was surrounded by a sloping lawn and a stone wall topped with iron spikes. "Welcome to Comstock House," Tim said.

"It is most grand!" Saura exclaimed. "I'd no idea that the furrier business is doing so well."

"We could not go on staying at the Boston Grande," he said, helping her out and turning the carriage over to a groom. He led her inside and they had scarcely entered the door when Elizabeth hurried into the hall from the parlor. She stopped for a moment to gaze at her daughter and then they flew into each other's arms. There were exclamations and cries of happiness all mingled together. Saura greeted her cousins, who led the way into the parlor so that mother and daughter could enjoy their reunion. There were so many things, little and large, that Saura wished to tell her mother...and now she could think of none of them!

They spent two days in talking, sharing a room so they might be together. There was a great deal of catching up to do and Saura told Elizabeth everything about Peter and Greenhollow, insisting that her mother travel there with her. Elizabeth told Saura everything of Thomas's death and of her stay in Bristol longer than planned; this interim was vague and Saura did not quite understand it. But nothing mattered except that she was with her mother.

Saura also spent time with her girl cousins, getting to know them once more. They were older of course, yet still much the same. Beatrice was as outgoing as ever and Nancy remained shyly reserved. Their friend, Margaret, was a very nice girl with large blue eyes and soft brown hair. And those eyes, she noted, were for Timothy only. It did not take her long to see that the girl was in love with her cousin. Yet Tim went blindly along, oblivious to this tender love.

After a day spent in buying new gloves and some new shoes from the old cobbler that Tim favored, Saura and Elizabeth returned home in late afternoon. The girls had been invited to tea at the Beacons' home and Tim was at the furriers' and so Saura and her mother took refreshments alone in the parlor. Saura poured and Elizabeth watched her.

"I've been meaning to ask you," she said, "where you got your ring. It is quite a fine piece of jewelry."

Saura paused for a moment, then continued to pour the tea, handing her mother a cup. Until now she had said nothing to Elizabeth about Seth. His name had come to her lips many times but she had not uttered it. It was not as though she kept her marriage a secret but neither did she boast of it. The circumstances of it were hard to explain but that was not the reason for her reluctance. There was something about their union, forbidden yet wonderful, that she had been unwilling to speak of. She thought of a play in her father's library that she had read before leaving—"Romeo and Juliet." Certainly she and Seth were not star-crossed by coming together from opposing families; she and her love were joined from opposing causes. Which was the greater and more painful obstacle, she did not know.

"Mama, there is something I must tell you of. A hundred times I lifted the pen to write you of it but I could not find the words. This ring is a wedding band."

Elizabeth looked at her in surprise, setting down her teacup. "You are married, Saura?"

She nodded. "Yes, I am. And it is an intricate tale. You cannot believe how strangely fate has twisted the path of my life. The marriage was not of my doing, not at first. I will tell you in a minute how it came to pass. But what you need to know is that the man is a Tory, a redcoat! Perhaps that doesn't sound so bad to you since Lawrence is a British officer and until now you have lived in England. But over these past years I have come to love America, the America that Papa spoke of before he died. And I feel as though I have betrayed my cause."

"But if it was not of your doing," Elizabeth cried, "do you still blame yourself?"

"I do," Saura said.

"Tell me about it," Elizabeth urged. "Why was the marriage not of your doing and how did you come to marry a British soldier?"

Saura sighed, leaning back into the comfort of the Chippendale sofa. She told her mother of the happenings as best she could until the whole peculiar tale was ended. "And that is what has happened. The captain is now my husband."

"You call him the captain," Elizabeth said. "Does he have a name?"

"Yes," Saura replied, coming to stand at the window and watch her cousins alight from the carriage. "His name is Seth Adams." She stood at the window for a moment before turning to look at her mother. Elizabeth had a peculiar expression of concern on her face that Saura could not fathom.

"And do you love him, this Seth?" she asked softly.

Saura came and sat down beside her mother. "Yes, I love him. Who could not? You should see him, Mama. He is as handsome as any man I've ever seen, and smart and strong, and he has other things about him that I cannot describe but that make me love him whether or not he is a redcoat."

Elizabeth smiled and pulled her daughter to her. "Oh, Saura! That is what I wanted to hear! As long as you are happy in the marriage, what else matters?"

"But every day war threatens and we grow closer to it. And I fear that the conflict will rip our love apart as nothing has before."

"If you love him and if he loves you, what else can matter? Love has survived worse things than war," Elizabeth said, pulling back to look at her daughter.

"I needed to hear that," Saura whispered. "Thank you, Mama."

"Your cousins are coming in."

"I know," she said, brushing off a tear that had escaped her lashes. "I haven't told them of my marriage. It is just that it is something that is special, something I cannot speak of with easy freedom. Until the threat of war is past, I think that I will not tell them about it."

"That is wise," Elizabeth said. "When the time comes, you can introduce your captain to them. You will stand stronger with him by your side. I think things will be fine. I am so glad that you have had this time with your father; I can see Peter's touch on you and it has been a good influence."

"And I am so glad that he entrusted me to your care," Saura said and gave her mother a hug. "I love you, Mama. And I hope that you will love Seth too."

Elizabeth smiled at her daughter before Beatrice rushed into the room, all excited about a bit of gossip she had heard.

The next day Saura went shopping with Beatrice and Margaret. Nancy was at home with a cold and slight fever and they promised to bring back some fabric samples to show her. The Quinceys were throwing a ball and the Comstock girls were excited about planning for it. Saura looked through the bolts of fine fabrics newly in from France and Holland, fewer things coming in from England with the growing unrest of the times. But her mind was not on the silks and laces, her thoughts turning instead to Seth. It seemed as though it were ages since she had seen him last and with all the troops pouring into Boston, she wondered whether he might be here and she did not know it. She found herself glancing at every redcoat in case she might catch a glimpse of the handsome Tory she sought.

Once done at the dressmaker's shop, the three girls headed down the street, dry now that the rains had ceased for the past few days. It was a nice spring day with a pale blue sky and a cool touch still in the air; Saura felt lighthearted as she walked with her friends toward the small apothecary shop on the corner where they planned to buy a powder for Nancy. Then Saura caught a glimpse of the office across the street. It was a British dispatch office where records were kept of the soldiers coming in and out of the city.

"Bea, get what you need from the apothecary and I'll be back in a minute. I'm just going over to the British dispatch across the road."

"To see about Lawrence? That's fine. We want to look about for a little anyway since the fragrances are in from France."

Saura nodded, picking her way across the street. Lawrence was not the one she looked for but if that was what Beatrice thought, there was no harm in it. As she stepped around the potholes in the road, careful not to soil her hem, she caught the eyes of several men standing outside the office. Dressed in blue poplin, with her hair swept up and a white shawl about her shoulders, she was a very attractive young woman. Several in the group doffed their hats as she stepped up to the board sidewalk, entering the office.

There was a mild debate going on between the dispatch clerk and a lieutenant but it ended as she approached the desk. The clerk looked into eyes as dark as mahogany and feigned a polite smile, pushing his spectacles higher on his long nose. "Good day, miss. May I help you?"

"I'm not sure," she said. "I wish to leave a message for one of your soldiers and was wondering if you could tell me whether or not he has come into Boston."

"I am afraid it is quite out of the question. We cannot give information to citizens on the whereabouts of our soldiers."

This set her back for a moment but before she could reply, a lieutenant standing next to her spoke up. "Come now, Fergus. You cannot be suspect of such a pretty young lady."

"I did not say that I was," Fergus retorted, growing a bit warm under the steady gaze of the girl. "But we have our rules. Citizens may not request military information."

"Only military personnel can?" the lieutenant asked.

"Yes," the clerk replied.

Then the lieutenant turned to Saura and smiled. "If

you give me the name you're looking for, I'll make the request."

She returned his smile. "Thank you, Lieutenant. Captain Seth Adams."

The lieutenant turned to the clerk and repeated the name. Fergus scowled but riffled through his records. "Here his name is. No, he has not been in Boston for several weeks."

"Then may I leave a message?"

"That you can," Fergus replied. He handed her a quill and paper and she wrote a brief note to Seth, telling him where she resided and how long she planned to stay. Folding the paper in half, she handed it to the clerk, who filed it in the proper place.

"Thank you," she said. "And thank you for your help, Lieutenant."

He smiled, walking her to the door. "James Waite is the name behind the rank and I am glad to be of assistance to such a pretty girl."

"I am Saura Ainsley," she said.

"Ah. Then the name you asked for is not a brother's."

"No," she said softly as they stepped outside.

He shook his head and smiled. "I am sorry of that. I cannot place it but your name is familiar."

She was wondering if the tale of her marriage had spread far in the king's army when he said, "Are you familiar with Lawrence Ainsley? He is a lieutenant in the army. Why, speak of Satan, here he comes!"

Saura looked in the direction he indicated and saw Lawrence stride toward her in the company of Beatrice and Margaret. He looked a bit stormy as he stepped up onto the walk. "Hello, Saura. Lieutenant Waite." He greeted her with a kiss on her cheek.

"We were just speaking of you," James Waite said. "I was asking her if she knew you since you share a name. So you are her brother! And a very lucky brother to have such a fair sister. Would you mind, Lieutenant, if I were to call on your sister sometime?"

"Indeed I would," Lawrence growled, his eyes growing hooded.

Lieutenant Waite and the young ladies were set back at his tone, looking at him in surprise.

"Lawrence!" Saura exclaimed.

"Perhaps there is some reason that you do not wish me to call on your sister. You could give it to me so I might make amends," the lieutenant said.

"Not my sister," Lawrence snapped. "She is my step-sister."

James Waite nodded his head slightly and folded his arms. "I see."

Saura stepped up to Lawrence. "Do you have business to attend to in here?"

"Yes, I do."

"Then see to it," she said calmly. "We will wait for you."

He supposed that she would be safe enough in Beatrice's and Margaret's company. After a sharp glance at Lieutenant Waite, he strode inside.

"Isn't he a bit protective for just a stepbrother?" James asked Saura as the two other girls became engaged in conversation with several boys from home.

"He is," she said. "But I've not seen him for two months and that eases the burden."

He laughed softly. "I've heard talk in the ranks that your brother has a hard hand with his men. It appears that he might try the same with you, I might add if you would not think me too forward."

"I can handle my brother, or stepbrother as the case may be."

"He stated the latter clearly and I am smart enough to see that he has eyes for you whether he is a brother or not. But he and I are of the same rank and so that does not bother me. I would like to ask permission to call on you sometime," he said.

He reminded her a little of Seth, although not as handsome or dark, and she smiled at him. "Thank you, sir. I would be honored were my heart not already promised to someone else."

"Ah! The lucky captain, I forgot. Then good luck to you, Miss Ainsley." He doffed his hat just as Lawrence came out of the office. Her brother took ahold of her arm, leading her away with no word to his fellow soldier, as the girls caught up with them.

There was a time when she would have looked with disdain on the proposals of a British soldier but she had mellowed since her truce with Seth. She pulled her arm from Lawrence's grasp, walking on her own.

"I can see that you are in need of my guidance. What on earth were you doing at the dispatch office?"

"She was asking about you, silly." Beatrice said. "She wanted to check on your return."

Lawrence looked at her in surprise. "You were? Why, I am touched by that." He slipped his arm about her waist and she inwardly groaned. "I will be quartering at your house," he said. "I hope you don't mind, Bea."

"Of course not. And Nancy will be happy to see you too."

They reached their carriage and Lawrence tossed his bags up before helping the ladies in. Then the groom snapped his whip and they were heading back to Comstock House, everyone but Saura chatting happily.

She stared out the window, thinking that were Lawrence in the house, she would return to Greenhollow as soon as she could persuade Elizabeth.

The weather turned cold in Boston, and rainy. Saura had been right. Lawrence's presence in the house was as depressing as the rain without.

Since he constantly sought out her presence when she was alone, she tried to stay in the company of her cousins or her mother. Elizabeth was her salvation since Lawrence was highly pleased to see his mother again. But when they were alone, he confided to Saura that he still wanted to wed her.

When he brought the subject up, she again told him that she could never think of him as anything but a brother. Unfortunately this seemed to have no effect on his enthusiasm and she came close to telling him of her marriage to Seth but thought better of it and retired.

Several days passed; they attended the theater and played billiards. There were also four-handed games of lanterloo and other card games but Saura felt her interest wane. She decided that if she did not hear from Seth in a few days, she would persuade her mother to travel with her to Greenhollow.

The weather cleared and the skies were bluer than they had been in many months. Saura took the opportunity to go for long walks as she was beginning to feel the confines of the crowded city dwellings; she longed for the country freedom of her home. One of the walks took place at dusk, the time she thought Boston was at its prettiest. It was that twilight time, neither day nor evening as the sun set smokily behind the steep rooftops that layered into the distance, chimneys behind chimneys. The sunset was diffused in the city soot, coloring the smoke pink before the night's inky onset.

She was just about to return home when the sound of echoing footsteps caught her ear and she turned to find Lawrence walking after her in haste. She tugged her short cape tighter about her shoulders, stifling a groan. He was the very reason she sought the solitude of her walks!

Lawrence caught up with her, glancing down at the pretty face that was shielded from full view by the brown ruchings of her bonnet. "It is highly improper for a young lady to walk out all by herself. You should have someone accompany you for safety. There are many rough colonists here who might fancy a young girl," he advised solemnly.

"I walk for the solitude," she said, stopping and turning around. "And I was just heading back."

"I shall accompany you."

They walked along in silence for a while. Then, as they approached the house, he said, "Have you given further thought to my proposal? I said I would give you time to think it over."

She looked at him in amazement. Could his skull really be so dense? "Lawrence, I thought I made it clear that I cannot marry you. I have bordered on bluntness and yet you turn a deaf ear. I do not love you."

"Oh, love!" he laughed. "What could a girl such as yourself know of love? It is not the fancy you read of

241

in novels. It is an art to be taught and I would gladly be your teacher." His voice was softly chilling.

"I know more of love than you would think. There is another man whom I love and for this reason I cannot even discuss this with you. You must desist in your pestering of me!" she snapped. She had not intended to be so harsh with him but her patience was exhausted.

"Pestering?" he cried, stopping for a moment and then hurrying to catch up with her. At this point she had turned into the walkway that led into the house. "You call some small infatuation love and hold it up to me? You foolish little wren!"

She turned angry eyes on him, thinking that at this moment she truly detested him even if he were her stepbrother. "Call it what you will but I have known love and I have known the man I love."

They passed between two high bushes and he grabbed her arm, spinning her around to face him. "What do you say, Saura? You cannot mean that literally."

She leveled grave eyes at him, her voice speaking with truth. "Indeed I do, brother."

His grip on her arm tightened, his face growing dark with a rage so violent that the veins in his neck stood out and she felt fear. Suddenly his hands were upon her, biting into the soft flesh of her arm and back as he pulled her to him. Like a kitten caught in the forceful brutality of a cruel child, she felt helpless and terrified. She tried to cry out as his mouth viciously clamped down over hers.

Lawrence felt an exhilaration run through him at the strength he used upon his sister. He was not aware of a shadowed form standing on the front doorstep of Comstock House until that person leaped from the darkness and he felt himself wrenched away from Saura. A fist smashed full force into his face and he slid down into unconsciousness.

Saura felt her brother jerked away as she gasped for breath. She saw him struck before he fell inert to the ground and she turned to look at the man who had saved her. A redcoat captain dearly familiar to her, she gasped his name and ran into his arms.

The comfort of their strength encircled her as the front door was pulled open and Elizabeth appeared. "Saura...Lawrence!" she cried, looking at her son who lay moaning on the ground.

Saura pulled herself away from Seth, glancing in concern at her mother. "Mama, this is Seth whom I told you about. Seth, this is my mother."

He smiled ruefully, bowing slightly. "I am sorry to meet you under such ill circumstances."

"What has happened to Lawrence?" she asked in alarm.

"I found him kissing my wife."

She stared dumfounded at them and Saura spoke up. "I am sorry, Mama. But since Lawrence claims that I am not truly his sister, he is bent on some wild notion that I should marry him. I have tried to dissuade him but you know his determination. I said nothing of it to worry you. Then just now I angered him and he kissed me despite my protests and that is when Seth interceded."

"I see," Elizabeth said. "Then you had best help me get him onto the sofa in the parlor, Captain Adams."

He nodded and they carried Lawrence in the house and into the parlor, where Nancy sat embroidering. She gasped and stood up, dropping her needlework. "What has happened, Aunt Elizabeth?"

"Lawrence met with a fall. Will you get me some cold vinegar-water and a cloth?"

Nancy hurried from the room and the others watched as Lawrence struggled to regain consciousness. Elizabeth looked at the young pair. "You had best take your wife out for the evening, Captain. Go, Saura; you know your brother's temper. When he calms down a bit, I will have a talk with him. After that you can pick a better time to join our family, sir."

"That is wise," Saura said, kissing her mother's cheek. They went out of the house and to the carriage in which Seth had arrived. Once they were off and down the road under the driver's whip, Saura fell into his arms.

His mouth sought hers in a kiss so sweetly tender that it was the exact opposite of the assault she had experienced a short while earlier. His arms held her to him, his handsome face shadowed in the darkness of the coach. "I could eat you up," he murmured between kisses.

"It has been a hundred years, Tory, since I saw you last!"

"I got your message at the dispatch office and headed to your house straightaway. That is when I saw your brother force himself upon you," he said, pulling back, and even in the darkness she could see his scowl.

She leaned into the comfort of his arms. "Lawrence is a strange one. He has these grand ideas and is highly stubborn. I should have told him that we are married but he has such a foul temper that I thought to ease it by simply refusing him."

"I saw how easily he was refused!"

"When we return, I shall tell him that I am married. I was about to when he grabbed me."

"No, my wife. I think it best if I tell him. He will heed my words more readily than yours. Promise me that you will let me handle this situation."

She sighed. "Perhaps you know best. Very well." She looked up at him and his mouth claimed hers with passionate warmth. Her hands slipped to the back of his neck and she murmured, "I have missed you, my Tory."

The carriage halted in front of a large inn and Seth helped her out. "This is where I am staying for two days. Then I must go back to duty." He led her into the entry, through a well-furnished front hall and to the stairs. The desk clerk looked at them and Seth smiled. "This is my wife, Mistress Adams."

The man nodded, covertly studying the young lady. She appeared proper enough but the captain was unusually handsome and no doubt traveled in higher circles. He glanced away, busying himself with the books.

"I do not think he believed us," Saura said.

"I do not think it matters what some shilling-scraper believes." He opened the door and they entered a simply furnished room. "And I do not mind stealing my beautiful wife away for an evening."

His fingers untied the ribbons of her bonnet and

pulled it off to allow her hair to tumble onto her shoulders. He lifted her chin and brought his mouth down slowly. He caught her hair in his hands, rubbing the silkiness in his fingers.

The room was dark as they shed their clothing. Moonlight filtered through the high windows, illuminating Saura's satiny flesh. She came into his arms and his senses reeled.

"Is this how you conquer the enemy?" he asked hoarsely, his lips against her throat.

"Do not speak of enemies," she moaned as he swept her into his arms, carrying her away into unexplored realms of pleasure. Saura lay in her captor's embrace, savoring the waves of ecstasy that swept over her as they entwined to become one, forging bonds that would unite them forever.

The moon had sunk low onto the horizon, its white rays slanting across the windowsill to lie in silver streaks along the bedcovers. Saura nestled in her husband's arms as sleep threatened to carry her away. "Seth," she murmured.

"Yes," he said softly, pulling the cover around her shoulders.

"The war is coming soon."

"I know that, my love."

"I am afraid of what it will do to us," she said quietly. "I do not want it to tear at our bonds of love. But you know on which side of the rending my allegiance lies."

He stroked her hair. "I know. And I know that you love me."

She sighed, closing her eyes. "I have come to love the enemy. And that love, given once, will never be given again. I pray that God will watch over you when the battle starts."

She drifted off to sleep but Seth stared into the darkness for a while before sleep brought him equal peace. There were things he should tell his wife, this woman whom he entrusted with his love. He cursed the intrigues of war that bade him hold his tongue a hundred times when he would speak.

Beatrice and Nancy were a-chatter with excitement as they tied on their crinolines and perfumed themselves. Margaret's eyes glowed with eagerness as Saura helped her pull on her new mauve-colored dress; she and Bea had talked her into buying it. Of a somewhat mature line and deep cut, it added years to her usually childlike appearance. Saura thought that if this dress did not catch Tim's eye, nothing would short of a brick tossed at his head!

She tied on her own quilted petticoat of pale green and then pulled on the overdress of ivory edged with green ribbons. Elizabeth was already dressed and was helping the girls with their preparations; she smiled affectionately at her daughter.

Saura had come home from the inn the next morning to find Lawrence gone, having had to report for duty. She was much relieved. The moments stolen with her husband still lingered about her. More and more was she coming to love her redcoat.

Finally ready, they entered the carriage and in chattering excitement they rode to the Quinceys' house. Saura would not have gone at all had her husband not promised to try to attend.

When they arrived, the house was already alive with people and bright with lantern lights. As Tim removed Margaret's cloak, he was surprised at the dramatic change in her appearance. Saura smiled as she witnessed the awakening in her male cousin. The ballroom was very grand. Candlelight was reflected in huge mirrors, and garlands of fruit blossoms decorated the tables that were heavily laden with food.

Saura stayed with Elizabeth until a young man introduced himself as Blair Quincey and asked her to dance. She did so reluctantly, glancing about to see if she could catch a glimpse of Seth. She had many partners that evening but not the one she most desired. She noticed that the house must be Loyalist since several British officers were present.

Lawrence arrived a little late and took her away from Elizabeth's side to dance. She could not help but note the bruise along his jaw. Tactfully she said nothing.

"Mother talked to me about last night," he said casually.

"She did?"

"Yes. It was in motherly concern for your welfare and mine. She tried to explain why I must not press you about marriage even though we are not brother and sister in blood."

"And what did you say?"

"I humored her of course. But I think that from now on it would be wise to keep our private happenings to ourselves. And as to your friend who thought it best to interfere, you can tell him that next time he will not be so lucky as to catch me unaware."

She had no chance to respond as the music ended and Tim came to sweep her away. "I am quite glad I came," he said.

"It certainly is a grand ball even though it is held in a Loyalist house."

"The Quinceys are a solid family in Boston and well-respected. Did you meet Blair? He is quite taken with you and commented that I was lucky to have such a pretty cousin."

"Yes, I met him. Isn't that him dancing with Margaret?"

"H-m-m. Yes, it is. I think this is his second dance with her already. I had hardly realized how much Nancy's and Beatrice's little friend had grown up. It must be that new dress."

"I helped her pick it out. It goes well with her coloring. And she has such luminous eyes." He did not answer and she smiled as he stared across the ballroom at Margaret, whose dimpled smile was directed at Blair Quincey. More people had arrived—women in beautiful dresses and gentlemen in elegant finery. One such lady in a gown of lavender silk moire danced on the arm of a handsome soldier. Her hair was built up high and powdered white in ringlets and curls. Though overdone, she was beautiful and Saura strained for a further glimpse of her.

"Who is that, Tim? She looks familiar," she asked and then she gasped. "It's Molly! Look, Tim, that is Molly Yates," she whispered. "I hardly recognized her under all that hair-powder and face-coloring.

"Yes, I know," he said a bit coolly. "I forgot to tell you that she made quite a showing in Boston last month and since that time has not missed a single social event."

"But how? The last thing we heard in Greenhollow was that she disappeared from the inn at the first of the year."

"She came to Boston with some young man who persuaded her that she would show well on his arm. But once they got here, she was abandoned by him and that is when she came to see me."

"You?"

"Yes. She came to the office of Ainsley and Comstock to ask for my assistance. She said she remembered my kindness at the inn and briefly explained her predicament. It was quite unusual but I did feel sorry for her. Before our discussion was through, a Robert Widdle turned up for his buying appointment and I showed him in. He was quite taken by Molly—she is a beautiful woman—and she let fall a hint of her distress. Before I could say anything, she had him believing that her father had died and the machinations of a greedy uncle had left her penniless."

"She didn't!"

"I was quite as surprised as you, believe me, Saura. But what could I say? He was immediately sympathetic and offered his assistance; I feared to say anything lest I look the fool. I had always thought her to be such a nice girl, even if not from the best family. One week later they were married and now she calls herself Madeline Widdle; only you and I know the truth of her past."

"Well, I shall say nothing of it. I know that she was unhappy in Greenhollow and now that she is out, I wish her well. Is that handsome young man she dances with Mister Widdle?"

"Heavens no! That is he over there, talking to the elder Mister Quincey by the punch bowl."

"The short man with the fringe of gray hair, wearing a yellow waistcoat? But he is older than Peter."

"Yes, and I think that he is learning that his fickle bride is not such a bargain."

As Saura glanced about the room, she suddenly caught sight of a man entering and her heart leaped. Seth, tall and roguishly handsome in gray pants and a black cutaway jacket, was looking around. "Tim, will you excuse me?"

She broke away, weaving her way through the dancers until she reached him. He bowed slightly, taking her hand to lead her to the dance floor. She did not see the fallen countenances of many young women who had been eagerly eyeing the handsome new arrival.

"May I say that you look very beautiful tonight?"

"You may," she answered. "And you are more than handsome, sir." She was delighted to be once more in his arms. They hardly spoke, words seeming unnecessary as they danced. "I have glanced at the door a hundred times, hoping for your coming."

"I was delayed a bit by business," he said, leading her off the floor as the music ended. Suddenly a voice called out to them.

"Isn't it Captain Adams?"

They turned to see Molly Yates approaching. Seth stared at her until recognition dawned. "Molly?" he asked in wonder.

"Madeline, if you please. Hello, Saura. What a surprise to see you in Boston."

"I came to be with my husband," she stated coolly. "I heard that you have recently married. May I congratulate you?"

"You may, and thank you. It was quite sudden; we were both swept off our feet. Boston is such an exciting place in which to fall in love! Not at all like dowdy old Greenhollow! And the shops in Boston! Why, there are so many fine things to buy. Mister Widdle just loves to buy me all kinds of beautiful things."

"You look very lovely," Saura told her.

"The music is starting again," Seth said. "If you'll excuse us..." He led Saura back onto the floor, gliding her about with ease as Molly looked after them, her icy blue eyes narrowing.

Tim wondered who the man was that monopolized Saura's time and at whom she stared with softly loving eyes. He danced with Molly, as did his cousin Lawrence and numerous other young men. But he spent much of his time in keeping track of Margaret and engaging her in a dance when she had a free moment.

A partner-changing dance came up and Saura was swept off into the arms of Blair Quincey despite her reluctance. As the changes took place, she found herself in Lawrence's arms. "Hello again, my dear. Who is that man who so rudely monopolizes your time?"

"That is Captain Adams."

"A British officer? I am glad at least of that! But you must watch protocol, Saura."

"Oh, Lawrence!" she said with exasperation, watching Molly move into Seth's arms and then disappear in the crowd; she felt a burst of irritation at her brother's interruption and hoped she could soon escape him.

Seth also had his problems for before he knew it, he and Molly were on the patio that led into the rose garden. "It seems that we have lost our way. The music is fading out here," he said.

"Oh, let us stay!" she gasped. "It is so crowded on the dance floor. A bit of fresh air will do us a world of good."

He said nothing but stood looking over the railing and out into the garden where the lilacs attempted to bloom and the rose bushes had the first tight buds ready to open. He took in a deep breath, as did Molly.

"It smells so good out here! I think the Quincey house is beautiful. Their gardens are made for a lovers' meeting, don't you think?" He looked down at her in surprise as she leaned her body suggestively against his. Seth put his hands on her shoulders and carefully extricated himself.

"Molly—"

"Please don't call me that, Seth. Everyone here knows me as Madeline."

"Madeline, do you forget that we are both married?"

"Oh, pah! Robert is kind, if a bit eccentric, but he cannot expect me not to seek pleasure where I would, although I think he is considerably blind. It is quite the popular thing for women of wealth to take lovers. And to be honest with you, Seth, I have always admired you. You are a fine form of a man." She slipped her arms about his neck as though to kiss him but he stopped her.

"You may not honor your marriage vows but I do mine."

"What?" she cried. "To that chit? She could not give you what you want. Certainly your marriage was a mistake. I have heard that it was not the choice of either of you. You and I could make each other happy."

He stepped back. "If you care to open your eyes, Molly, you will see that Saura is not only a woman but a very beautiful woman. And more than that, she gives me everything that I could want out of marriage."

Molly sucked in her breath as though she had been slapped. The sting of rejection brought a spot of color to her cheeks beneath the powder and her features became hard.

"I do not need you!" she cried out passionately. "There are fifty to take your place! One tonight whom I have known before will come crawling after me. Go back to your insipid little wife!" Her anger grew as she saw that he did not even listen to her but instead stared intently out into the garden.

Caught in the pale moonlight was the outline of a couple that might at first seem to be lovers. But on closer examination it appeared that there was a struggle. Suddenly Seth vaulted the patio rail to land in the garden and Molly gaped after him as he ran through the shrubbery.

Saura wrenched herself free of Lawrence's grasp. "Lay one finger on me and I shall scream! You shall not kiss me again," she cried in anger.

"Why are you so difficult?" he hissed, grabbing ahold of her arm.

"You drag me to this garden and with what intent? What do you plan for me, Lawrence? Will you paw me as you would some common strumpet?"

"Lower your voice!" he ordered harshly. "I am losing my temper, Saura."

"Get your hands off my wife," a voice said coldly.

Lawrence looked up at Captain Adams and then glanced about to see to whom he spoke. "Did you hear me?" the stern voice demanded.

Lawrence's mouth gaped open and he let his hand slip away from Saura's arm. "Are you addressing me, sir?"

"Do you see anyone else out here?"

"But you spoke of your wife!"

"Exactly."

Lawrence stared at Saura, his features going hard. "Is this your husband, Saura?"

"Yes. I tried to tell you."

"You led me on, playing me for the fool, while all the time you were married to him?" His fists clenched as fury ran through him, yet he dared do nothing violent.

"I did not lead you on, Lawrence. I tried at every turn to dissuade you. I told you that I loved another," she said softly.

"He is the one who struck me?" He turned glaring eyes on Seth. "My honor is at stake, sir. I demand a duel."

Saura looked at him in amazement. "Lawrence, do not be so foolish."

"I plan to fight for you and to have you," he said icily.

"You lay one hand on my wife, Lieutenant, and I shall see you drawn and quartered. Saura is mine, lawfully married by a British chaplain. You are to forget about her except in light of being a sister. That is an order. Do you understand?"

"Yes, sir! I'll obey your order until we duel."

"I shall not fight you, Lieutenant."

Lawrence looked at him in amazement. "You refuse to honor my challenge?"

"If you were up on your regulations, you would know that it is against the law for the ranks of the king's army to duel. And besides," he said, his voice softening a bit, "I do not wish to kill my wife's brother. I hope that we can get off on a better footing." He extended his hand but Lawrence turned away. Seth took Saura's hand then, leading her away. Once they were inside the house again, he smiled reassuringly at her. "He'll cool down in a bit and then things will be amicable enough."

"I am not so sure, Seth. His temper does not go away easily." They were interrupted in their conversation by Tim's appearance. It was apparent that he was intent on rescuing her from the monopolizing attentions of the stranger.

"May I have this dance, Saura?"

"Thank you, Tim, but I am quite content. Seth, this is my cousin Tim. And this is Seth Adams, my husband."

Tim stared at her. "Did I hear you correctly?"

"I know that it sounds sudden but we have been wed for nearly half a year. I wanted Seth to be here to meet you when I told you of our marriage."

"Well!" Timothy said, extending his hand and fervently shaking Seth's. "This is quite extraordinary— but things about Saura often are." Then, "Elizabeth knows?" he asked in sudden concern.

"Oh, yes," she said with a smile.

"Well, come then! Let us go tell Nancy and Beatrice! Poor Blair will be quite disappointed," he said over his shoulder.

Molly Widdle stood in the solitude of the library where a fire crackled in the hearth, the room otherwise dark. It was a beautifully furnished room, as were all the rooms in Quincey House. The fine Chippendale furniture, the wainscoted walls and the thick carpet soothed her frayed nerves. Wealth appeased her senses as nothing else could. She took in a deep breath, smoothing the lavender silk of her expensive dress. She softly cursed Seth Adams. She had offered herself as any street tart

might and he had looked away with embarrassed disinterest. She would show him and all like him who had
scorned her because she had been a serving wench. She
was no barmaid now! She could take lovers from Boston's finest and then discard them as she wished. She
swore never to feel the slap of rejection again.

Daintily she patted her powdered coiffure. Soon she
would have a tryst right here in the solitude of the
library; she savored the thrill of danger. This one had
been easily won over, not like Seth Adams. This one
had also rejected her once, bringing her to this huge
city only to desert her and leave her in desperate straits.
But it had all worked out for the best. She had dear old
Robert and his money and now she would be the one
who rejected. She would use this man and then cast
him aside!

The dancers whirled about to the music as the large
clock chimed. Just as the last resonant tone died away,
the air was rent by a scream. The music ceased abruptly
and a murmur of anxiety ran through the crowd. Several of the men hurried in the direction of the sound,
Seth among them. Two gentlemen were behind him as
he opened the library door, peering into the darkness.
Their eyes took in the macabre sight, trying to understand what they saw. Molly Widdle supported herself
against the back of a tall chair. Her eyes were filled
with bewilderment, her face a ghastly white; she moved
her lips to speak but no sound came forth. Crimson
stained the lavender silk like wine on snow and from
the center of the splotch there glinted the dull hilt of
a knife. It was a mere letter-opener, common in librar-
ies, seemingly harmless.

Seth rushed forward, his face grim as he caught her.
Slowly she sank down, her head lolling against his arm,
her fingers going limp. He lowered her as shouts and
a woman's scream filled the house that had only minutes before known nothing but gaiety.

I would be true for there are those who trust me.

—H. A. WALTER

## Chapter XII

SETH STEPPED out from the inn where he had been staying, his bags in hand. He secured them to his horse and then cinched up the saddle. He was reluctant to leave the charming old inn where his wife had spent two nights deep in his embrace; after the hellish happening at Quincey House, he had taken her home with him. He shook his head to wipe away the memory of Molly dying in his arms. He had disdained her attempts to win him but she had not deserved to fall victim to the freakish accident that had taken her life.

Everyone had stood about dumfounded, poor Mister Widdle nearly fainting from shock. And then the constable had arrived, determined to make short work of the foul deed. After much discussion and debate, it was decided that Molly had tripped over an out-of-place footstool for the library had been quite dark. And the fateful fall had sent her sprawling onto the desk, where the wicked letter-knife had lain point out.

He pulled on his tricorn and mounted the horse, reins in hand. He guided the steed along the narrow road that led in a single direction to the outskirts of Boston. He was to report to his commander within the half hour. His mind wandered to his young wife. Memories of her passionate ways and willing embraces made his ride less boring. By keeping her with him in his mind, he dispelled any thought of gloom. Like her, he was aware that war came closer every day, but the fact did not haunt him. Instead he saw the impending confrontation as an end to deception and he anticipated the time when differences of politics could be bridged. The only threat to him from war was that of a physical nature. But that was not a thing he feared; he felt no nagging worry that harm might befall him in battle.

A Brown Bess rifle was steadied against the limb of a tree from where it had been sighting travelers for most of the morning. Perhaps less than a mile from the dispatch office, it pointed once again at an approaching rider. This time a finger sought the cold metal of trigger, squeezing it at the precise moment.

Seth's thoughts were shattered as a heavy ball of iron lodged into his body, knocking him from his horse, and the sound of gunshot rang in his ears. Slowly he sank to the ground, the dust of the road powdering about him. In amazement he lifted his head to stare at the dark stain of crimson that spread on the red of his jacket. He felt nothing, thinking only of another bloodied stain that he had seen before. Shock spread through him and he descended into darkness.

Major Berkely stood in the parlor of the Comstock home, pacing the floor in agitation. The ten-minute wait already seemed an hour long and he looked repeatedly out the window, relieved at last to see a carriage pull up. He watched as Saura Adams and several young ladies alighted; he hardly recognized her, so lovely she looked in a dress of pink dimity. It appeared that he had been right about the marriage since she was the picture of refinement. She entered the house and he heard the maid tell her that there was a caller in the parlor.

Saura untied her green velvet bonnet and pulled it off, pushing back stray wisps of hair. Then she stepped into the room to see standing there the last person she expected. "Why, Major Berkely! This is quite a surprise. Do not tell me that you have come to see if I hold to my part of the bargain?"

Her pretty smile made his heart ache. "They told me I could find you here when I checked at the dispatch office; I've come about Captain Adams."

Her smile faded, the sun slipping behind a cloud as the room darkened. A terrible sense of foreboding swept over her. "What about Seth?"

"I am afraid that I have bad news, my dear. He was on his way to the dispatcher when he was shot down by a rebel bullet, fired no doubt by some angry Patriot who decided to shoot at one of our officers. We have not found the villain although a search is being conducted in the area."

"Seth," she managed. "He is dead?"

"No, no! But he is severely wounded. The doctors are not optimistic, I am afraid. Here, you'd best sit down. I'll call for some wine."

She shook her head. "No! I must go to him. Will you see me there?"

"Yes, of course." He helped her out of the house and into his carriage. "I was at the dispatch office when it happened and so I came to tell you of it, although I told his mother first."

She leaned back against the cushions in the carriage, her face ashen as she went over in her mind a hundred times the thought of Seth injured and dying.

"Do you see? You should have had some wine before we left. You look ill. Fortunately I carry a flask of spirits for medicinal reasons. It is stronger than wine but you must have some. No, no, don't protest. I insist."

He handed her the flask and she took a sip, the hot liquid sending a bracing heat through her. "Can we not go faster?"

"If we do, I fear we will meet with disaster. Be patient. We will be there soon enough." He tried to give her comfort. It appeared that his plan for her marriage had worked remarkably well; the concern she showed for her husband could only be wrought of love. He prayed that all his goodly effort might not now be in vain.

The coach lurched to a halt in front of the large hospital used by the British army. She did not wait for assistance but jumped from the carriage and ran into the hospital, the major in her wake. He directed her to Seth's room and she hurried inside, letting her eyes adjust to the darkness. Kneeling by his side was Elizabeth, her face pale and streaked with tears. Saura flew to her side, sinking down beside her and reaching out to touch Seth. His face was as white as snow, even his lips without color, and his eyes were closed. He lay so still that she bent to catch a sound of the shallow breathing.

Then two men came in and lifted him onto a stretcher and Saura stared at the spot of red beneath the bandages on his shoulder. They took him out and she burst into tears, falling into her mother's arms. "Where are they taking him?"

"Doctor Winters is ready to operate," Major Berkely answered kindly. "He is our best surgeon. The ball is lodged in the captain's shoulder and unless the metal is removed, it will poison his blood. If there is anyone who can do the job, it is Israel Winters so don't worry yourselves too much. It is in God's hands and I will pray for him. I must be going now but I will be back."

"Thank you, sir," Elizabeth said, brushing away her tears. "You have been most kind to us."

"You take care," he said, patting her shoulder. "Your son will be just fine if God wills it. Saura, see to your husband's mother and get something to eat; the surgery will take some time."

He turned and left, Saura staring after him in puzzlement. Then she turned her tear-stained face to her mother, sitting down in the chair that was next to the

258

one Elizabeth had taken. She wiped away her tears and looked at her mother.

"Mama, what did he say?"

Elizabeth stared down at her hands, folded in her lap. "What can I tell you, Saura?" She took a deep breath, ragged from crying. "Seth Adams is my son."

Saura drew back in surprise. "Seth your son? But how can that be?"

"Circumstances came about that made it necessary for him to leave our home. At the time he was just a young lad, a boy of nine years."

"Seth . . . is an Ainsley?" she gasped.

"Yes. He is the son that Thomas and I waited so long for. We loved him beyond words, this little boy who was so good and happy-natured. But then circumstances came about—"

"Was that when you and Papa took me in? Father left me with you at that time, didn't he?"

Elizabeth nodded. "Seth came to the Americas with Peter."

"What?" she gasped. "With Father? How can that be?"

"It was such a dreadful mix-up at the time. Peter had been involved in the French-Indian War because he wanted to aid the colonists in breaking free." She kept her voice low lest a passerby might hear.

"But the French-Indian War had nothing to do with us, did it?"

"The Patriots felt it was imperative that the Americans be able to amass the troops that would later aid in the fight that will soon ensue. Peter greatly helped in this organizing and Thomas did what he could, although his illness held him back. Then one day it was important that Thomas send a message to Peter. But your Papa was ill and going was impossible so Seth said that he would go. Though he was still but a boy, he was quite grown up for his age and took the task seriously. None of us knew how fateful that cursed message was! Seth was to take the information from his father directly to Peter but when he got there, officers of the king were waiting to speak to Peter and they intercepted the message. Seth managed to escape but the entire king's guard was looking for a lad of his description and it was only a matter of time before he would be found. They sought Peter also, intending to try him for treason could they prove a case. So for this reason Peter and Seth were forced to sail for the colonies. Peter entrusted you to our care, bless that day, and he took our son with him. Seth became Peter's son and later called himself by the name of Adams, which is his middle name."

Saura leaned back in her chair. "That explains so much!" she whispered. "Peter accepted Seth so easily and with such kindness that I was often exasperated. And that is why. He has been son to Peter as I have been daughter to you. But I cannot understand how one raised as a colonist could turn into a redcoat."

"Seth is hardly that!" Elizabeth said.

Saura stared at her mother in surprise. "There is more to this tale?"

"Indeed there is. About the time that you arrived in Boston, he left on a ship for England. Not long after that he joined the king's army and rose quickly in the ranks of officers."

"But why should he do that?" she asked quietly.

"Because our Mister Franklin—and even Samuel Adams himself—commissioned him to do so. You cannot imagine the benefit to the colonies that he is; the cause will be won by such as he. But it is a secret so highly kept that there are but a handful who know and I tell you this now because I do not wish to have you think further that he is a redcoat, as you call them!" Tears welled up in Elizabeth's eyes as she thought about how close to death her beloved son lingered. "Then when he came to England and I could be with him after the space of more than a decade, I had not the heart to leave for the colonies. That is why I kept writing that I would come when I could. I just could not leave my son again."

"Why did Father say nothing to me of his true identity?" Saura wanted to know. "How many times would the way have been easier for me had I known the truth!"

"Would you have had them gamble with his life? How suspicious it would have seemed had you accepted with ease that which you oppose. I am sure that Peter feared to endanger your life—for these are perilous times. And did it not prove your love greater that he won you over despite your differences? And still this secret must be guarded with our lives until the war shall set us free."

Saura's heart soared. Her Tory had turned to Patriot before her eyes, and glorious were his deeds. Yes, she understood his vows of silence although no doubt he had wanted to tell her of himself a hundred times, knowing that the truth would win her heart. Tears stung her eyes. And now that bright soldier lay in the tight fist of death.

"What of Lawrence?" she questioned hopefully. "Is he too masquerading as a British soldier?"

Elizabeth shook her head. "No, his dress is real. He loves the king and his cause and I pray daily that when the war does come, God will watch over my headstrong boy."

"Does he know that Seth is his brother?"

"No, he knows nothing of it. But Seth knows, of course, and came to see me as soon as he got to Boston, although we had to be most discreet. I will admit that all this play-acting has been difficult. Before you told me of your marriage, I was anxious for Peter had written to me of it but his last letter left me knowing that you were giving poor Seth a difficult time indeed. I was so happy that you had come to love him, as you told me so from your own lips. I prayed daily that your union might succeed for I could not think of a match to give me more joy."

"Seth will be all right! He must be," Saura said, no longer able to stop herself from crying. "He has been through so much that certainly God will not let him die. What foolish rebel thought to help the revolution and does not know that he has tried to slay the brightest champion for our cause?"

Elizabeth held her daughter in her arms, receiving comfort as she gave it, the hours ticking past until the doctor entered the quiet of the room. The women arose, going to him expectantly as he dried his hands.

A tall gentleman with gray muttonchops, he smiled down at them. "I have succeeded in removing the ball; it was from a Brown Bess rifle, a gun common to our troops as well as to the revolutionaries. It was lodged and took some difficulty to retrieve; I had to break the bone to get it out. And now, if there is enough blood left in him, he shall mend."

"He will not die?" Saura asked.

"I cannot promise that," he said in a no-nonsense way for which Saura was grateful. "But his chance looks more hopeful than it did an hour ago. Now it is up to him. We can do nothing but watch over him and wait. Are you his wife, and this his mother?"

They nodded. "Good. You are welcome to stay and attend him as long as you like. But you look pale. Are you ill?"

"Until now I have felt fine," Saura said. "But I think that I am with child."

Elizabeth gasped and took her daughter's hand and the doctor stepped near, taking her pulse and looking into her lower eyelids. "Have you felt any nausea or dizziness?"

"No, and that is why I have wondered about it. I have heard many women speak of the awful illness and lightheadedness, while I have never felt in better health."

He chuckled softly. "That is perfectly normal, young lady. Have you missed the time of women?"

"For two months."

"Then you should have your child in early fall but you can check this with your own doctor or midwife. Until then you must take care of yourself while your husband tries to get well. And, Mother, you take her to eat something. I'll stay with the young man until you return."

Saura was reluctant to go but Elizabeth dragged her away. "Such good news to follow such ill! How I anticipate having a grandchild. Oh, Saura, what a blessing that will be when fall comes."

"September twenty-sixth if the nine months are true to their dates," she said. They went to a nearby inn, taking a quick repast before returning to the hospital.

When they arrived, Seth was back in his bed, lying still and breathing shallowly. Saura took his hand, warming it in her own. If only he would get well, this Patriot that she loved! Yet to her he would ever be her Tory.

She sought the courage that she had always been so proud of, that she had held up like a banner before her. But it failed her as she saw this threat to the existence of the man whom she loved so very much. All the sharp words that she had used too cruelly, all the difficulties she had given him when he had tried to win her over, came to mind. She took in a ragged breath. If only she had known how precious each moment was to be. The hours slipped by slowly until the day had gone. Elizabeth tried to urge her to come home but she would not and even Doctor Winters could not persuade her. Saura spent her time in praying for her husband's recovery and talking to him, softly urging him to come back to her. Concerned for her daughter's health, Elizabeth went to the nearby inn to purchase food that she could bring back to her.

Saura sat in the quiet room, a lamp lit in one of the corners to dispel the darkness. She took her husband's hand in her own, feeling for the shallow beat of life. "Seth," she said softly. "Seth. How many times your name has been on my lips even when I disdained to say it. You could not know how often I turned to that first book in the Bible to see it in print. How I longed for you to win over my ill-tempered nature and how my heart rejoiced when you did. Forever I will remember our wedding and the night that followed it. How I pretended to despise it when in truth it awoke something in me for which I had longed.

"And forever will I remember that time when we were alone after Christmas, when you forced me to show that I loved you. You forced me to be your wife in more than name only, never really guessing how I craved it to come about. Oh, Seth, you could not know—foolishly

I waited to tell you—that during those days we spent together, your child was conceived. During one of those wondrous moments we came together to make this baby that nestles so quietly and secretly within me."

She paused here, her tears falling onto the sheet that covered him. "You have always been so strong. Please be strong for me now. Come back to me, my darling."

She studied his face, shadowed in such quiet repose that it seemed as though all the former light and laughter had never been there. Where was even hint of the mocking smile that had once plagued her and the lift of brows in pretended surprise? And the depth of his eyes was shut off to her as his dark lashes cast feathered shadows on his pale cheeks. As she looked at him, there was the slightest fluttering of those lashes and she held her breath lest it was merely a trick of the lamplight. But there it was again and she clasped his hand tighter in hers as the lids moved once more, his eyes opening slowly.

Seth fought against the fogginess that slowed his mind and his eyes focused feebly on the wavering lamplight. He felt an urgent panic, a distress that could not be explained. And then above him he saw a face, white and streaked with tears. It was the one thing he knew, his beloved Saura, and it was all that he cared about. He tried to speak but the words did not come; she stilled his lips with a finger, smiling at him with words of reassurance. It was all he needed. At peace, he let his eyes slip closed.

Two days passed and since Saura would not leave, under Doctor Winters's orders the hospital put a bed for her in Seth's room. During that time she and Elizabeth were always near. His mother returned home only to give news to the Comstock family and to pass the night. Tim paid visits daily and his sisters too, although less frequently. They did not see Lawrence for he had been sent to New York. Saura was inwardly relieved but she said nothing of it to Elizabeth.

Seth regained his strength, speaking to his wife in a manner that was unusually restrained. It was apparent to her just how close he had come to dying for even as he spoke to her or braved a smile, he was still very weak. Doctor Winters was surprised that he had recovered and confessed that he had given Captain Adams little hope. Major Berkely stated that he was not surprised for it was a miracle from God—probably brought about by Saura's change in attitudes, he added without a qualm. Saura also classed her husband's recovery as a miracle although not for the same reasons as the chaplain's. She simply could not envision in her young heart that God would let such a splendid man die.

She spent the hours in reading aloud or talking quietly to him. But most of the time he slept and she was content to sit beside him. As the days passed and his safety was assured, Saura was determined not to be far from him and was elated to find a small cottage nearby for rent, set back off a narrow road that led behind the hospital. The furnishings were simple but they would at least fill the needs of Elizabeth and herself.

Days went by and Seth regained his strength. Weak still, he talked with greater ease and attained some movement. His shoulder throbbed often and the doctor prescribed liquor for the pain. But Seth did not want to depend on strong drink and so he tried to endure the discomfort.

One morning Saura appeared at the hospital in a hurried state. She had overslept and now she arrived in time to find Seth sitting up to breakfast. He looked surprisingly well and greeted her with a smile as he took a bite of toast topped with poached egg.

"Seth, you look so well this morning," she smiled.

"I slept better last night than before. My arm is beginning to heal, I think." He touched his shoulder, even moving it a bit, forcing himself not to grimace.

"That is wonderful!" she cried, flouncing down into the chair next to him. "You do not know how I have prayed for this."

He raised his brows in the old way of teasing mockery. "You wasted a prayer on a British redcoat?"

She said nothing but only smiled and stole a piece

of toast from his plate. "Mother went to buy some supplies. She'll be by in a while."

"I hope she is all right. This has been such a strain on her."

"She has borne up well, as always. But it did worry her terribly when she thought that her son might die," she said softly.

Seth choked on his milk, spilling some of it down the front of his nightshirt. He set the glass down, boring through her with the dark stare she knew so well. She smiled slowly. "We had some very long talks while you lay in that bed, threatening to leave us."

"You know everything?"

She nodded. "It explains a great deal about you and Father and...well, all of it."

He looked at her, a bit embarrassed. "You are not angry, are you?"

She lowered her voice. "Angry that my redcoat is in truth a Patriot?" She leaned near to him. "I thought once that I could not love you more and now I have been proven wrong."

He blinked and looked away. "You do not know how many times I wanted to tell you, to talk to you about my true feelings." He reached up with his good arm, slipping it to the back of her neck where his fingers caught in the soft mass of silky hair. He pulled her mouth down to his with yearning. They kissed long and deeply, drinking of the passion on the surface of the well. His hand slipped away to release her but she lingered a moment longer before pulling back. She sat down in the chair again with a sigh.

"I have missed your touch," she said simply.

He grinned and slipped his hand about hers. "Such words will urge me on to quick recovery, miss."

"Would that I could give greater balm," she smiled.

Several more days went by and with each Seth was stronger and finally he began to walk about in the hospital. He decried the confines of the bed and longed for the time that he could be free. His wife and doctor asked him to be patient.

Saura arrived one afternoon to find him sitting on the bed, the doctor examining his shoulder. The wound was still red but at least untouched by infection. The doctor gave a satisfied nod. "I think you can rest at ease now. It appears that you are mending with good speed, Captain."

"How soon can I leave the hospital?"

"H-m-m. Another day or two."

"I was hoping for today. I do feel good, sir."

"Well, if you promise to take things easy. Your body has been through a serious ordeal. It will long need rest and good nourishment in order to heal."

Saura stepped forward. "You know that I've let the little cottage down the road, don't you? He could stay there and I could watch over him. We would be close to the hospital in case of any problem."

The doctor smiled. "It seems that your wife is as eager as you. And it is harder for me to disappoint her than you. All right, he can go. I'll have one of the orderlies drive you. But mind me, Captain, I am promoting this little lady to be your major. What she says goes. She can nurse you back to health if you listen to her."

Seth smiled and saluted his wife with his good arm. "I've taken her orders before."

Doctor Winters chuckled. "Where is home to you two?"

"Greenhollow," Seth replied. "A little town not far from here—about two days' travel."

"I've heard of it. Well, after you've healed for a month, or two weeks at least, you can go home to Greenhollow. Major Berkely says that you can take off as many months as you need in order to recuperate since your injury has no doubt impaired your shooting arm. As soon as he is well enough to travel, young lady, you can take him home."

"I would like that," she said. "And you can be sure that I will take good care of him, Doctor Winters."

"Just make certain that you do not overdo. You'd best take care of yourself in your condition." As Seth turned to look at her, the doctor said, "Oh, no! It appears that I have let the cat from the sack!"

267

"I did not want to worry him," she murmured.

Seth stared at her, his glance dropping to her abdomen and then lifting to her face again. She nodded. "Yes. But Elizabeth assures me I'll not be showing for another month or so."

He stood up, coming over to her and encircling her in his arms. He held her carefully. "I am very pleased with this," he said softly against her hair. "I hope we have a daughter with eyes like her mother's."

"If you want a daughter, then girl it shall be," she said demurely, pulling back and busying herself with buttoning his shirt for him.

"A son would be nice though. Peter would like that."

"Then we shall have a son," she said.

The doctor put his instruments back in his bag. "You are a lucky man, Captain Adams, to have a wife who considers your wishes first. I have known many men who have married beautiful women but they have turned out to be sharp of tongue and heedless." He left the room, calling for an orderly to drive the couple home.

"Who can name the price of a virtuous woman?" Seth jested with a smile. "The doctor sings your praises, as do most who have met you."

"It is because they see that marriage has tempered my sharp tongue."

He laughed and bent his head to kiss her again as though he could never get enough of her.

That night Elizabeth moved back to Comstock House since the cottage was small, with only one bed. She was grateful for Seth's progress and his release from the hospital.

Saura lit soft candles while they supped on stew and rolls. There was an intimacy in the small cottage with its steeply slanting roof and stone chimney. Moonlight came in through the windows to sheathe the room in a silvery light. As they sat across the small wooden table, conversing lightly, a sense of desire grew between them.

"Will you unpin your hair for me?" Seth asked of a sudden and without a word, she pulled the pins that held it up so that it might tumble in a silken mass about her shoulders. He sighed. "You are so beautiful," he breathed.

Although the yearning between them drew like a magnetic force, each was restrained. "I love you," she said, "and I want you."

He groaned softly, leaning back. "Do not tempt me, Saura. I will do nothing to harm you or our baby."

"You cannot harm us," she said in surprise. "Your child is steadfast within me."

"You have always been brave, Saura. I would not hasten to this."

"It is fine," she said. "I asked Mother and she should know since she has borne children. Nothing that is natural can harm me or the baby."

He thought this over, accepting the reasoning, and stood up. He came to her, taking her hand and helping her to her feet. He took her into an embrace, his mouth coming down to claim hers. Then he led her to the comfort of the old bed.

"What I do worry about is your arm. I would not wish to hurt you."

"You cannot hurt me," he said, his fingers clumsy with her buttons.

"But the doctor said that you must rest easy. I should prove to be a poor nurse should I bring you to harm."

He bent and kissed her neck as her clothing, and his, slipped away. "I shall rest easy with your love as healing for my wounds."

As passion swept over them, each surrendered to the other's touch. She was careful of his shoulder, her fingers gently brushing his arm, while he examined the slight curve of abdomen, barely discernible. Before long they were oblivious to all else, caught in the onrushing sweep of desire. The thick down quilt and the plume pillows and the dark intimacy of the cottage provided the nesting for their delight in each other's embrace as the shining orb without crossed the black sky.

The sting of a reproach
is the truth of it.

—Thomas Fuller, M.D.
*Gnomologia* (1732)

# Chapter XIII

ON APRIL NINETEENTH in the year seventeen hundred
and seventy-five, the British troops overwhelmed Lex-
ington and marched north to Concord. But the colonists
were not as green as expected when their militias came
to arms. Late in the day the redcoats were defeated and
sent reeling back to Boston.

That fine town was in an uproar, with British troops
wherever one looked. The news spread like a fire and
the talk grew heated. Until this time Seth and Saura
had lived in blessed solitude, oblivious to outer events.
Their cottage was set back on an obscure lane, shaded
under a huge oak whose boughs brushed the low, slanted
roof. Narrow windows opened out onto a tangled mass
of flower and shrub that had once been a garden, and
wild rose bushes climbed the walls and nodded over the
picket fence.

Elizabeth was their most frequent visitor and they
enjoyed her company. That and an occasional call from
Doctor Winters or Major Berkely were all the visitors

they had. Although Seth improved daily, he still had difficulty in moving his arm. But he was not so stiff that he could not embrace his wife or slip his arms about her. Another week and they would be ready to return to Greenhollow, taking Elizabeth with them. Tim stopped by to invite them to a dinner party that he and his sisters were having. He informed them that Lawrence had returned from duty and was again staying with them at Comstock House.

On the night of the dinner Seth helped his wife fasten her dress of dark green velvet edged in white lace. He bent and kissed the nape of her neck where the hair was swept away. She leaned her head against his chest for a moment. The cut of her dress successfully hid her condition and she smiled as she viewed herself in the small looking glass. Then she turned and buttoned his shirt for him, helping him with the lace cravat as he pulled on his brown jacket. Always the figure of manliness, she thought. She pulled a lace shawl about her shoulders and they went to Comstock House.

Once inside she greeted her cousins and their friend Margaret, who looked lovely and had matured a great deal since Saura had last seen her. They talked to Elizabeth for a while and then were surprised to meet the elder Comstocks, who had only recently arrived from England. Saura introduced Seth to her Uncle Edward and Aunt Jane.

Lawrence came downstairs dressed in formal attire that included a brocade vest and a jacket trimmed in gold braid. He was polite to her and Seth, yet a bit curt. But Saura was relieved that she was not the target of his attentions. They went in to dinner and had a sumptuous meal. The conversation was active and Saura could not help but notice that Lawrence spent his attentions on Margaret while Timothy looked on a bit dourly. Had her brother just now come to notice what a fair young girl his cousins' friend was, she wondered. Dinner over, the men went to the library for rum and brandy while the women went to the parlor for persimmon beer and wine. Saura chatted with her cousins and their friend about the latest fashions from France, about which they were excited, while her Aunt Jane and her mother talked quietly on the sofa.

After an hour the groups broke up, each going its different way, and when Seth had sought out Saura, they went for a stroll in the pleasant garden that was so well-kept. The sweet smell of flowers enticed them and she slipped her arms about her husband's waist. He bent for a kiss but before his lips reached hers, he pulled away with a gasp. Her eyes flew to where he stared and she caught a shadowed form on the balcony high above. It arced over the railing with a scream, grabbing frantically to catch the lower edge of the balustrade.

"Margaret!" Saura cried. Seth flew toward the stairs at the side of the house as Margaret's screams brought others. The girl's fingers appeared to be slipping and Saura stared at her in horror for the balcony was so high up that should she lose her grip, she would surely be crippled, if not killed, in a fall. A moment before Seth reached her, other hands caught Margaret's, pulling her up and into safety.

Tim stood holding her as she trembled in his arms; he stroked her hair and soothed her with gentle words. Then he lifted her in his arms and carried her to her room. The family gathered around as he placed her on the couch. Aunt Jane nearly fainted and her daughters hurried her to her room while Tim sought out some cool vinegar-water for Margaret's brow. Saura and Seth stayed to watch over the sobbing girl as the others went to their hurried tasks. Saura soothed her as best she could.

"That was a terrible mishap, Margaret. But you're all right now... Tim reached you in time. There, there, don't cry. Try to calm a bit."

The hysteria passed and Saura dried the girl's tears. "I thought I would die... I could not... hold on."

"It won't happen again, dear. I know it was an awful scare but Tim will fix the railing and put it higher."

"It's not that. I felt someone... push me!" She turned her head, crying afresh into the pillow. Saura and Seth stared at each other. Tim came in with the water, giving her comfort, and Elizabeth gave her a sleeping draught and stayed within hearing of her until she slept.

Outside in the hall, Tim was quite distraught. "I do not know what I should have done had she fallen!"

"It is not your fault, Tim. She'll be all right. Just make certain that someone is with her, either you or your mother or one of your sisters," Saura told him.

"I didn't really understand until now how much Margaret has come to mean to me. I love her and intend to ask her to marry me, once she has recovered of course."

Saura smiled. "That will be just the balm she needs, I am sure."

They joined the other family members in the parlor and Lawrence inquired as to how Margaret fared. Tim answered that she was all right but that she must be watched closely and he vowed to fix the balcony with a higher railing. Then he disclosed the fact that he intended to ask for Margaret's hand, cautioning them to say nothing of it to her until the time that he could ask her himself.

Beatrice leaned over to Saura and whispered, "Your brother will be quite disappointed. He has sought after her attentions ever since his return but she has had no thought for him. I tried to tell him that she has eyes for Tim only but he would not listen."

Saura studied her brother for a while, disquieting thoughts nagging at her. Then she asked for her wrap since it was time for them to leave. Nancy joined her and Bea as they sat talking.

"This is just so awful! I hope that Margaret will fare well after such an ill experience."

Bea nodded. "I trust that this is the last of the accidents. You know they come in threes, it is said, and perchance this is the end of them."

"Threes?" Saura asked.

"Oh, yes! Three of our friends have met with mishap. The first was Esther Bundy. Nancy remembers her. She was an acquaintance that she and Lawrence made on the ship coming over."

"That's right," Nancy said. "She was coming over to stay with her uncle and aunt."

"What happened to her?" Saura asked.

"It was horrible," Beatrice replied with a grimace. "Tim was there and he saw the whole awful thing. They had all departed ship and Tim was to pick up Nancy and Lawrence. It seems that Esther was standing on the platform where the coaches arrive and as one sped by, she lost her footing and was crushed beneath its wheels. Nancy hadn't the courage to look at her but Tim said it was quite bad. Well, as I see it, Esther was the first. Then there was poor Robert Widdle's wife. Not that she was a friend really, but at least another acquaintance. And you know the accident that she had with that ill-placed letter-knife. And now poor Margaret. Thank heavens she did not go the full way of the others!"

Nancy nodded her head. "Then she must be the last if mishap comes in threes."

Saura sighed. "Keep a close watch on her, will you?" Seth came then and slipped her shawl about her shoulders and they watched the couple leave.

Beatrice sighed. "Our cousin is a fortunate girl, Nancy."

The ride to the cottage was unusually quiet and Seth asked Saura of what she thought. She told him of all that had transpired in the parlor discussion. "Does it not sound strange? And then there is Margaret's account of being pushed."

"I think she was distraught. As for things happening in threes, I was never one to heed such suppositions."

"Well, I pray that it is true. I hope that nothing else so dire happens."

He took her hand in his, the warmth of his touch encircling her. Everything always seemed to be all right as long as Seth was with her.

Two days later Seth received orders to report to the dispatch office. He did so and when he returned, he told Saura that he must travel to Cambridge to meet with his major. She wanted to go with him but he said that the travel would be too rough for her. Since the lease on the cottage ran out and she did not wish to rent it for another month, she moved back to Comstock House to wait for Seth's return. They would then go to Greenhollow.

Lawrence had again gone back to duty so there was less tension for Saura in the house. She could not explain her lack of ease in his presence. Margaret had quite recovered and was looking forward with excitement to her wedding, which would take place at home in London. She seemed to have forgotten her bad experience and mentioned nothing of it to anyone.

Saura now confided that she was with child and her cousins and aunt were delighted for her. They went shopping for baby things that she would not be able to purchase in the Hollow, returning late in the day with packages full of tiny items—sacques and buntings, baby shawls, booties and bonnets. She happily showed these to her mother before tenderly folding them away in her trunk.

That night Tim took Margaret and his family to a new play at the theater. Saura declined the invitation since she was expecting Seth back either that evening or the next day, and Nancy stayed at home with a slight headache. They sat together in the parlor, Saura reading some of Joseph Green's poetry while Nancy busied herself with her embroidery. It was a quietly pleasant evening, interrupted when a knock came at the front door. Saura put down her book and hurried to the door, not waiting for the maid to answer. When she pulled it open, she was disappointed that it was not Seth. Instead she saw a small youth in dirty attire who quickly handed her an envelope and then disappeared. She turned it over and was amazed to find that it was addressed to herself. Hastily she broke the seal and read through the contents.

Mistress Adams:
I am sorry to inform you that your husband has met with an accident on his return to Boston. His horse took a fall and he has re-injured his arm. I have taken him to the Tankard and Barrel Inn

on the north side of town and am with him in Room 12 on the uppermost floor. He asks that you come to his aid.

Sincerely,
Captain Samuel Farthington

Saura cried out, leaning against the wall as Nancy hurried to her. "What is wrong?"

Saura handed her the letter and Nancy quickly scanned it. "Will you call for a coach?" Saura asked, worry muffling her voice.

Nancy nodded and sent the maid to inform the groom that they would need the second carriage and a driver. Then she took their shawls. "I had best go with you."

Saura nodded, seeming to regain her composure. She had come so close to losing him once that she felt again the wash of fear. She must go to him immediately and see that he was all right. The note that Nancy had returned to her slipped from her hand, lying crumpled on the floor. They hurried into the carriage, each silent with her own thoughts as the road sped away from beneath the wheels of the carriage.

Who was Captain Farthington? A soldier who had accompanied him on the journey home? She cursed the major for having sent for Seth before he was fully recovered. The coach wound through an older part of the city until finally it lurched to a halt in front of the Tankard and Barrel Inn.

"Stay here, will you, Nancy, in case you must fetch a doctor. If I do not send word in five minutes, you can know that they already have a doctor and you may come up to see if you can be of help."

Nancy nodded. "I will."

Saura hurried into the inn. It was dark and almost empty. She glanced about to find the stairwell, then practically ran up the flight of stairs. She had to stop several times to catch her breath, slowed by her condition. Finally she reached the top floor and moved down the dark hallway, glancing at the number that was painted on each door until she found 12. Hastily she rapped and a muffled voice called out for her to enter.

She pushed the door open and peered into the darkness. There was only one candle lit and she could discern the vague outline of furniture. The window, naked of drapery, showed a smattering of wet as rain began to fall outside. She could see a figure sitting in a chair, his dark head toward the window. She neared. "Seth?"

The man rose, touching the candle flame to the wick of a lamp, light filling the room as he came to her and shut the door. A chill swept across her like a sudden icy draft.

"Lawrence! Explain this," she said, making her words sound harder than her resolve truly was.

"Is that any way to greet your brother?"

"Where is Seth?"

"Seth, Seth!" he mimicked. "I am sick of your saying his name, just as I am sick of him!"

"Did you send the letter?" she asked quietly.

"Enterprising, do you not think? I had no desire to run into that barbarian who is your husband. He would never allow me to see you alone, you know, and you and I raised as brother and sister." He took a heavy draught of the liquor in his glass.

"I find no humor in such a cruel jest." She turned to leave but as her hand touched the knob, he spoke.

"You do not wish to know about Seth?"

She turned and looked at him, unable to hide a flicker of fear. It came upon her with heavy suddenness that she had always been frightened of Lawrence. "What about him?"

He laughed, the sound harsh as breaking glass. "I know a great deal about the captain's whereabouts—where he goes and how he travels. I have a friend at the dispatch office." He took a long draw on the liquor again, finishing it and tossing the glass off. "Do you really think that I could be so easily put off, dear sister? I have wanted you for a long time, did you know that? Even when I was a little boy and you came to intrude on our family, I was torn between hating you and loving you."

She wanted to leave, the sense of fear within her mounting steadily as she stood staring at him, helpless because he held knowledge of her husband. "I wanted you to love me as a brother and would have gladly sought that kinship had you allowed it," she said.

"Brother!" he spat. "I am not your brother. I should be your lover, did you know that? And I would have been had you not come to this hellishly barbaric land and stayed away for so long. But I can change the way things are—and you shall be mine after all."

"No," she managed. "I am married to Seth and I love him."

"And you will forget him when you are widowed, coming to me for comfort."

"What do you say? You have not harmed him?" she cried.

A flush of warmth spread through him at the fear he sensed in her. There was something helpless about her despite her bravado and it excited him. She was like the dove he had taken from its cage when he was a child, holding it in his hands and relishing the feel of its frightened heartbeat as he squeezed it too tight. He could heighten that fear and with it, his excitement.

"Not yet, dear Saura. But the time will come soon. I tried it once and failed. But the next time my rifle shall find its mark more sure."

"You cannot mean...that it was you? Oh, dear heavens, no!" She leaned against a nearby table. "Lawrence, he is your brother!"

"No!" he denied. "He may be Elizabeth's son but he is no brother of mine!"

"You know that he is an Ainsley?"

"I know. But what is that saying? A brother may not be a friend but a friend will always be a brother? Well, that uncivilized captain is neither for he has taken what is rightfully mine. And he has treated me vilely. No man can strike me and go free!"

Saura felt tears well up in her eyes and she stepped nearer, a note of pleading in her voice. "No, Lawrence, please. I beg you."

A cruel smile touched his mouth. "Yes, dear sister,

do beg." He grabbed her wrist, bending it back until she was brought to her knees, tears spilling down her cheeks from the pain. Still he did not release his hold on her. "Poor little sister, her pleas are all to no use! For I shall have her first, to flaunt it in that filthy captain's face before I kill him."

"And then will you kill me too, as you did the others? I know all about what you have done, how you destroyed those others who turned from you. Will you kill me too for similarly turning?" she sobbed.

He yanked her to her feet. "I do not know what you are talking of; it appears that you are tinged with madness. But insane or no, it matters little to me." He pulled her to him, his thick lips clamping down upon her mouth in a manner that filled her with horror. She struggled desperately but he held her tight against him, her long shawl slipping to the floor.

Suddenly he shoved her away, staring down at her softly rounded abdomen. She felt renewed fear as he clamped his teeth together, the veins in his neck bulging as he screamed at her with wild fury. He struck out, slapping her and knocking her down. Then his voice calmed to a more civilized tone as he wiped the blood from his hand, his words wavering in her ears. She put trembling fingers to her mouth to still the bleeding as he spoke.

"How dare you, you little whelp? How dare you let him touch you when you know that you are mine? When he is dead, I shall be rid of that filth now harbored within you, even if it kills you."

Saura gasped for breath, her fear brought to near panic. It was then that the door opened and a sob escaped her as she rose to her feet. Nancy stood outlined in the darkness of the hallway and Saura moved toward her. "Oh, Nancy," she cried, trying to hide the horror in her voice. They must get away, and quickly.

Nancy took a step into the room and Saura halted. Lamplight lit upon the features of her cousin but they were not features that Saura recognized. The girl was changed, her face dark and twisted with hatred. A snarl formed on her lips. "How dare you?"

"Nancy!" Lawrence said. "Get out of here! This is none of your concern."

"Isn't it?" Her eyes narrowed and Saura was astounded. Could her mild cousin feel such anger at his abuse of his sister? She stared at Nancy in amazement as the girl turned to face her. "Who would have thought that my cousin would be such a dirty little strumpet? Pretending all this time to be a married lady while it was just a ruse to get at Lawrence."

Saura was speechless. Did Nancy direct this fury at her? "I do not understand, Nancy. What of Lawrence? He is your cousin."

Nancy's lips drew back, her face livid. "He is my lover!"

Saura stared at her cousin and brother in disbelief. Lawrence stepped up to them. "So what of it, Nancy? You know nothing can come of it for we are blood cousins."

"You love me, Lawrence! You said so on the ship." Then, softening, "And you and I would be together still if these vile women did not tempt you away from me."

Lawrence looked at her blankly. "What are you talking of?"

"Those other women! They tempted you like common whores and I have ridded this town of them like all whores should be gotten rid of. You would have met with that strumpet, Esther Bundy. I overheard you on the ship."

"What are you saying? She met with an accident."

"She fell beneath the wheels of a carriage," Nancy said with a childlike simplicity that chilled Saura. "It was quite easy to shove her off the platform, you know. Just as it was easy to push a knife into that Widdle woman. She was the easiest of all! She stood in the library, waiting for you, and when I entered, she turned around expecting to see you—but it was too late. You did not think I overheard you? Oh, but I am very smart. I listen to the things people say and I know quite well what goes on. I know you brought that whore from Greenhollow and then left her. That leaving was wise but you should have also left her alone at the dance.

281

My poor Lawrence, you are so wayward. No other woman shall ever have you though."

"Like Margaret?" Saura asked quietly.

"Oh . . . yes, like Margaret. It was quite apparent that Lawrence tried to court her. I could not have her winning him over, could I? But then she came to love Tim and now they are to be married. I am quite glad of that for I should not like Margaret to have died."

Lawrence stared at her, appalled. "What have you done?"

Nancy took a step nearer and something in her hand shone dark. Saura studied it and horror welled up in her anew. The long and pointed shears that were used in her embroidery now glinted in Nancy's grip.

"I have only protected our love from others who would snare you!" She turned to Saura. "I am sorry but I cannot let you take him from me." She raised her hand and Saura moved back against the wall. But Nancy's action held for the moment; Lawrence threw back his head, laughing in amazement, and the distraught girl stared at him. He walked over to the window, still laughing, and looked through the rain-streaked panes that silhouetted his form.

"Why do you laugh?" Nancy asked in bewilderment.

"You follow in my wake like some deadly plague!"

"To protect you. I saw the note sent to our house. I recognized your writing and so I came with her. I know everything about you."

"You know nothing. Do you know that I despise you?"

Nancy grew ashen, her lips trembling. "You cannot mean that. You are only angry. On the ship you said that you love me."

"I said that only to have my way with you." She shook her head dazedly but he went on with his cruelty. "You were just a diversion on a long ocean voyage since I could not win over Miss Bundy. And there was not much pleasure in you for I became quite bored. Don't delude yourself with talk of love and for hell's sake, don't kill anyone else for my benefit."

"No . . . do not say this!"

"Get out of here now, you little fool, and leave me to the woman I love."

A scream, inhuman in sound, pierced the air. It did not die away but was renewed again as Nancy's eyes shone madly in the lamplight. Too late Lawrence saw the pointed instrument that was raised as she lunged for him, her poisonous love turned to hatred. She brought the scissors down, blood spurting onto his white shirt as she stabbed him, and he gasped and staggered backward, Nancy close upon him. The window glass, its webbing of lead thin, broke away under the pressure of the thrashing bodies and Saura screamed as they crashed through the opening and fell several stories to the road below.

The door to the room was flung open and Seth ran inside, the crumpled note clutched in his hand, Timothy in his wake. He and Tim looked about the room and Seth took his sobbing wife into his arms, holding her and shushing her fears as though she were a small child. He stroked her hair and rocked her soothingly, giving silent thanks that his wife had not been harmed.

Timothy went to the shattered window and looked out. Down on the cobbled street below, slick with rain, lay the twisted forms of Nancy and Lawrence in death's macabre embrace.

True as truth the lorn and lonely,
Tender, as the brave are only;
Men who tread where saints have trod,
Men for Country, Home—and God:
Give us men! I say again—again—
Give us men!

—E. H. Bickersteth

## Chapter XIV

THE COOL AUTUMN AIR wafted through the open kitchen
door to mingle with the smells of goose cooking in the
cast-iron oven and ripe apples that sat in a basket on
the floor. Over the open hearth Saura bent to stir the
navy beans and salt pork that simmered in the black
pot. She added brown sugar and sliced onions, then
stirred in mustard seeds and molasses. Putting her
hands to her back, which seemed to ache continually
now, she lowered herself into a chair and took a sip of
the camomile tea that she had grown fond of since reg-
ular tea was impossible to come by now. How large and
ungainly she felt! The time of having the child was soon
to come but she hoped to wait until Seth could return
home. At present he was at the center of battle.

She thought of him often, anxiously concerned for
his safety. On that fateful trip that had taken him from
her side, he had met with his major. He was told that
because of his shoulder injury, he would no longer be

able to lead his men; since he could not fire a musket, he was to be released from duty. The major had given him his payment and passage for himself and his wife on a packet returning to England. But the ship left without him, unbeknownst to the British army. Later Peter had openly introduced him to the townfolk of Greenhollow, the citizens gathered beneath the large oak known as the Liberty Tree. Nearly every town except Boston boasted a Liberty Tree. Now that war had actually begun, there were no more fence-sitters and the people of Greenhollow felt that there was no place in their midst for a Loyalist. So when Peter explained Seth's true identity and his work for the cause, the entire village took an oath as one to protect his past activities and accept him as a citizen.

Although the British had released him from duty because of his inability to fire a musket, there was much more that he could contribute to the war effort than his ability in the field. His knowledge of the British military gave the Patriots a valuable weapon. He was enlisted by the Continental Congress to aid General Washington in his military strategies.

On June seventeenth war began as British troops marched up Breed's Hill and a battle occurred that later gained its name from Bunker Hill, slightly to the north. The redcoat troops, in tight formation, were withered by the fire of the provincials; they were cut down like blades of grass. It was the worst defeat that the British army suffered, its planning and stratagem owed in part to Seth Adams. Only when the rebels ran out of ammunition did the redcoats finally occupy the hill.

Saura was proud of her husband, a major in the colonial army. But she missed him, longing hourly for his return. She was happy to be back in the Hollow, however, having also missed Peter. He was pleased to have her home once more and proud of the fact that he would soon gain a grandchild. He had been embarrassed a little when Saura had confronted him with the secret so well kept by himself and Erastus. But then she had laughed, admitting that it was best that way.

Elizabeth adapted serenely to Peter's home and the

community. She belonged at the house, it seemed, and before long her acquaintance with Peter returned to the deep friendship they had once known. As the months passed, it had become apparent to both Saura and Erastus that the smithy, a widower of many years, was once again feeling the light touch of growing love. At the end of August, Peter and Elizabeth were wed. Saura had been deeply pleased as her mother and her real father became husband and wife. She was glad that happiness lay in wait for Elizabeth after so many tragedies.

Soon Peter and Erastus would travel to New York, where they would assist Peter Townsend. The Continental Congress had engaged Townsend and an army of blacksmiths to forge a huge chain that would be stretched across the narrow neck of the Hudson River to prevent the British troops from sailing their ships into New York.

Saura sighed. At least her father would be safe from gunfire. Even though Seth did not shoot a musket in the front lines, he was often at the edge of the battle and she constantly worried about him. One close call with death was enough! He had returned to the fight after having brought Saura and Elizabeth to Greenhollow and remaining for several months. They had come home shortly after the funerals of Lawrence and Nancy.

She remembered that period of time with sadness, still feeling a chill of fear. She and Seth and Tim had decided not to tell their parents the whole story and her aunt and uncle never knew the truth of their daughter's sickness that had driven her to destroy innocent people. They thought the episode had simply been a tragic accident, and neither did Beatrice know the truth. Poor Tim carried the burden alone. And although Elizabeth knew that Nancy had been responsible for the deaths of Esther Bundy and Molly Widdle, Saura never told her of Lawrence's attempt on Seth's life.

Saura remembered how her mother had cried at her son's death. As she had comforted her, her mother had said, "He is still a son to me and I mourn his death as such even though I did not give birth to him."

Saura had looked at her in surprise. "Lawrence is not your real son?"

Elizabeth had shaken her head. "I have kept it secret these past years but now that he is gone, there is no use in protecting him. His mother was Thomas's sister, Clarice. She was a lovely girl, highly thought of at court despite her lack of title. A handsome young man wanted to marry her but she had eyes only for a nobleman, a viscount. It is an age-old story.

"When she found that she was with child, she was desperate for the viscount would have nothing more to do with her. We took her into our home and then when the baby was born, we kept him as ours. We had tried for such a long time to have a child and when we finally had Seth, we were elated. But since no more came for a long time, I was more than happy to raise Lawrence as ours. Three months later Clarice planned to wed the young man who was in love with her but she was killed in a fall from a horse. From that time on Lawrence really was ours, you see. Then we had our little Bess, who died, and after that you came to our home. It seems that I was destined to raise others' children," she sighed. "But to me it has been a blessing and although I knew that Lawrence's temper and difficult ways were not of our family ... still, I loved him."

"Did Lawrence know of his parentage?"

"I do not think so but I am not sure. The man who is his true father is prominent in English government and Lawrence said often how highly he did think of him." Saura had thought frequently of her conversation with Lawrence and would never know whether he knew the truth, although she suspected that he did.

But she could not think other than that things had ended best as they had, no matter how much it had hurt the families. When the time of mourning was over, they went on with their lives and Tim and Margaret were wed.

She got up from the table now and went into the library, where she found Elizabeth eagerly working on the embroidery of baby gowns. She had made her expected grandchild many lovely things since she did quite well with the needle. Between her mother and Bathsheba, Saura had accumulated a beautiful layette for the baby. Often she sorted through the tiny garments or rocked the small wooden cradle that yet seemed so empty.

Peter came into the library. "It seems that you have a visitor," he said with a twinkle in his eyes and she looked up to see Seth stepping over the threshold. She let out a cry and flew to his arms and he held her carefully.

He bent his head and kissed his wife, then stepped back to look at her. He smiled. "I was worried that I would not get back in time."

She put her hands on her hips, thinking how grand his appearance in the rough uniform of the colonist. "Do you suppose that I would let your baby come without your leave?" she jested.

He slipped his arm about her. "You look more beautiful than ever."

"I am as large as the fattest pumpkin in the garden and getting bigger every day!"

"To me you are always beautiful." He went over to his mother and kissed her. "Do you not agree?"

"I think all women are beautiful when they carry a child. It was my favorite time."

"Well, I shall be glad when it is all over," Saura smiled. She did not have much longer to wait.

That night as they sat around the dining-room table, Saura experienced the first tightening of childbirth. She soon lost her appetite and when her husband saw this, he stopped in his account of the recent military actions.

"Are you all right, my love?"

She smiled. "I am fine. Do go on. I think it is all so interesting. The only experience I have had with spying was in Braintree."

"And I have thanked the heavens time and again for that letter you carried! How else should you have been brought to me?"

"Seth...when did I tell you of the letter? I do not remember that we ever spoke of it."

"I have known of it from the time you delivered it. I found it in old Stackpole's desk and burned it after I read it."

"You did what?" she gasped. "That was an important message for the Sons of Liberty!"

"I know that."

"Then why did you destroy it?"

"It seems that you are misinformed, daughter," Peter spoke up. "You see, it was a letter for S.A.—Seth Adams."

Saura leaned back in her chair, her voice trailing off. "H-m-m. It was a fateful letter indeed that took me into the rogue Tory's arms then. Had I known, I could have handed it to him directly, without all the difficulties I went through."

"Those difficulties brought us together," Seth reminded her with a rueful smile.

She laughed softly at this but her laughter was cut short by a wave of tightening that brought with it pain.

"What is it?" Elizabeth asked. "Did you have a birth pang?"

Saura nodded, pushing herself away from the table. Seth bolted to his feet, helping her to rise. Then he swept her up in his arms and carried her up the stairs. Peter and Erastus looked on, feeling somewhat out of place as Elizabeth busied herself gathering towels and other necessary items.

"There is no need to get so excited, Seth," Saura admonished. "First births always take a long time. That is what every mother in Greenhollow has assured me."

Carefully he laid her on the bed, removing her slippers and sitting down beside her. "You can never be sure of anything when it comes to having a baby, I would think."

Seth was right. While he and his father-in-law waited downstairs, Elizabeth was busy with Saura upstairs and Erastus went to fetch Bathsheba, as had been previously arranged. When Miss Brightwater entered the house, she had scarcely a greeting for anyone but hurried breathlessly up the stairs. Erastus, attempting to divert the two men, told a number of antecdotes but Seth was unusually dour for he was reminded of the time that Saura had been cloistered upstairs for another reason. The young man was unfortunately beset with love and Erastus thought his eagerness at each sound from above to be humorous. Finally Seth poured himself a drink, downing it.

"What is taking so long?" he demanded.

"It has barely been two hours, son," Peter said calmly as he read a book. "I've heard tell that some first babies can take more than a day to arrive."

"You jest! A day?"

"Well, the way some women talk, the time gets longer with each telling of it."

"I can no longer sit down here idly waiting. I'm going up to see how she is." There was no dissuading him as he bolted up the steps and entered the room. He arrived in time to see his wife push the small black head of their child into the world. In seconds the lusty cry of the newborn filled the room and Elizabeth cut the cord, wrapping the baby in a blanket and handing it to Seth as she and Bathsheba tended to Saura.

He looked down at the little daughter whose black hair curled wetly about her head and whose eyes blinked at the first new brightness. He felt tears smart his eyes as he studied the tiny face that puckered up to cry, then stopped and started the process several times in a row.

Bathsheba came to take the baby and rub the white film into the little arms and legs and clean the head of its tinge of blood. "She is a lovely girl, healthy and already nice and pink."

Seth came over to his wife and knelt down beside her, taking her hand in his. "Oh, Saura! She is beautiful—like her mother." Then he kissed her tenderly. "Thank you," he murmured. "Thank you."

Saura smiled as Bathsheba handed her the baby before slipping downstairs to give the others the good news. "What shall we call her? I have thought only of names for sons."

"I have a name in mind," Seth replied, touching one

of the little fingers. "What do you think of Liberty Adams?"

Saura brushed her cheek against the soft head, the tiny bundle nestling quietly within her arms. "So, this is the end of all that we have sought. We are happy that you are here, our little American Liberty."

Elizabeth blinked back tears as she looked at the new little family. Suddenly she felt comforted, as though her loss of baby Bess and Thomas and Lawrence—and Seth's departure from her at such an early time—had all been worth the happening.

Liberty Adams sneezed and blinked and quieted down into the warm embrace of her mother's arms as her parents gazed at her with love. Her name was to be forever a banner for all they believed in and for that which had brought together two foes who had, all along, fought for the same cause.

## CAPTIVE of the HEART
**Kate Douglas**                     81125-1/$2.75

Set in the American Southwest in the mid-19th century, this big romantic novel is about a courageous white girl who has chosen to live with the Comanche, and the young chieftain who falls in love with her.

## DEFIANT DESTINY
**Nancy Moulton**                    81430-7/$2.95

While on a dangerous sea voyage to deliver secret information to the rebellious colonies, a young English beauty is captured by a notorious American privateer who soon captures her heart as well.

## LOVE'S CHOICE
**Rosie Thomas**          December 61713-7/$2.95

A lovely newspaper reporter finds herself caught in a passion for two rival wine-makers. As Bell tries to decide between them—a debonair, aristocratic Frenchman and a warm, vibrant Californian—a dangerous competition for her love arises.

# ADMIT DESIRE

**Catherine Lanigan**  **January 81810-8/$2.95**

The glamorous and wealthy milieu of Houston society
is the setting for the passionate romance between a
beautiful, talented artist and an exciting, worldly real
estate tycoon.

# DARK SOLDIER

**Katherine Myers**  **February 82214-8/$2.95**

A beautiful rebel, unwillingly married to a handsome
British captain in Revolutionary Massachusetts, finds
herself caught between fierce loyalty to the colonies
and growing passion for her charming husband.

# WHEN LOVE REMAINS

**Victoria Pade**  **March 82610-0/$2.95**

WHEN LOVE REMAINS is the novel of a willful young
beauty married in proxy to a rugged, wealthy Boston-
ian, who still loves her childhood sweetheart. Deadly
rivalries, uncontrolled passions, and physical danger
surround her as she struggles to discover which man is
her love.

THE AVON ROMANCE

**AVON Paperbacks**

# THE NEW NOVEL BY
# KATHLEEN E. WOODIWISS

## A ROSE IN WINTER

Erienne Fleming's debt-ridden father had given
her hand to the richest suitor. She was now
Lady Saxton, mistress of a great manor all but
ruined by fire, wife to a man whose mysteri-
ously shrouded form aroused fear and pity. Yet
even as she became devoted to her adoring
husband, Erienne despaired of freeing her
heart from the dashingly handsome Yankee,
Christopher Seton. The beautiful Erienne,
once filled with young dreams of romance,
was now a wife and woman...torn between the
two men she loved.

## Avon Trade Paperback                    81679-2/$6.95

Rose 12 82